## SISTERHOOD
## (CAN BE A PAIN IN THE NECK)

"I don't know why you're so worried." Greta Grimm sighed. "I've brought garlic, stakes, and we're wearing enough silver crosses to out-holy the Pope. I have taken every precaution for meeting one of the fiendish monsters."

"I only hope it impresses the vampires," her sibling retorted. "I beg you, let's leave at once."

"I'll protect you, Rae. I promise you that."

Rae shook her head. "You'd better, Greta. I attract men like flies. If there are vampires here, they are going to want to drink my blood first. Of course, after draining me, they'll probably be too full to attack you. So I guess I'm protecting you in a way."

With a modicum of civility, Greta managed not to berate her sister. The hour was late, her feet were freezing and she was tired of Rae's conceit. Enough was enough. "Perhaps they'll be female vampires and ignore you altogether. Or, mayhap, a male vampire might prefer me to you. Not everyone falls at your feet you know."

The shadows moved closer.

# MORE RAVES FOR MINDA WEBBER!

## *THE RELUCTANT MISS VAN HELSING*

"Webber delights readers with another laugh-out-loud tale of mayhem among the supernatural ton.... This wonderfully witty, wildly clever, gripping, sensual and exciting romp proves that Webber's reputation as an up-and-comer is well and truly deserved."

—*RT BOOKreviews* (Top Pick)

"This sensational screwy satirical sequel will have readers laughing at Jane's capers and Neil's reactions to her antics. The action-packed amusing story line also is loaded with literary references that are fun to follow as these witticisms augment a zany well-written tale that howls for more."

—The Best Reviews

"If you enjoy a funny, yet romantic, paranormal tale filled with monsters, vampires, werewolves and trouble-attracting heroines, then you will most certainly love this book."

—A Romance Review

## *THE REMARKABLE MISS FRANKENSTEIN*

"[A] clever, laugh-out-loud, madness-and-mayhem romp through vampire-, werewolf- and ghost-ridden London. Webber does for vampires what Sandra Hill did for Vikings!"

—*RT BOOKreviews*

"This wacky satirical paranormal romance will have readers howling in laughter....action-packed and amusing."

—*Midwest Book Review*

# Minda Webber

# *The Daughters Grimm*

LOVE SPELL  NEW YORK CITY

LOVE SPELL®

July 2008

Published by

Dorchester Publishing Co., Inc.
200 Madison Avenue
New York, NY 10016

ISBN 10: 0-505-52771-5
ISBN 13: 978-0-505-52771-4

10 9 8 7 6 5 4 3 2 1

Visit us on the web at www.dorchesterpub.com.

*To Will Watson, for sharing starry nights, moonlight, a Halloween night a monster would envy, and your stakes. Thanks for the amazing desk every writer should have, and for laughing at all the right parts in* Young Frankenstein.

# ACKNOWLEDGMENTS

To Margaret and David P. for all their help and kindness throughout the years to both myself and family; Karen Faltisek, for always lending a sometimes-needed shoulder; my family for their unending support; Kaye at the Red Rock for just being you and doing fabulous weddings; Kathleen Conner for not killing me when I broke the gingerbread Ferris wheel; Donna Jo Wagner for laughing at all the right places in my books and my vampire beanie; Judy York for bandaging my numerous accidents this year; Dave Lykins for giving me a chance to soar among eagles and giving me a lab to blow up; Laurel Romm for her help and smile—I forgive you the snakes, even the boa; Geoff Worssam for generously helping my classes with supplies; Jason Baldwin for surviving earth science madness; Marc Sterling for sharing his advice and chocolate—an absolute must for every teacher; Elaine Vail and Chris Violette for their help in the library and cheering me on, carrying my blow-up doll in the red mini across campus; Merrily Pychinka and K. Busche for helping me out on my strat. field trip; Greg Kirkham for stepping up to the plate, or rather the mountain, and helping me herd students. And last, but certainly not least…to my students, who have shared the learning, the laughter, the good, the bad and the beautiful. You have weathered a place in my heart that won't be forgotten (a little earth science humor there).

# The Daughters Grimm

# CHAPTER ONE

## Gentlemen Prefer Blonde Heiresses

The trouble with being a Grimm was that prospects were grim, Rae thought dejectedly. She was a remarkably lovely lady with no dowry. Alas, ladies with no dowries in 1786 were likely to remain spinsters unless they married beneath them. "A dowry—the stuff that dreams are made of," Rae sighed. She did not wish to marry out of her station in life; this she could not, would not do. So she would remain in Cornwall, an unmarried daughter in an impoverished family, with her father, Baron Grimm; her mother, her two younger brothers and her three sisters.

Shaking her head dolefully, Rae headed in the direction of the rose arbor. The third sister in the Grimm family line, she had just finished listening to her mother's latest complaints on the hideous embarrassment of having none of her daughters wedded. Since Razel (called Rae by her family) was the undisputed beauty of all the Grimm daughters, she often caught the brunt of their mother's harping. As the baroness often asked querulously of family, friends, the cook, the maid, the storekeeper in town, her breakfast kippers, the vicar and his wife and her fat pug dog, "If a lovely creature such as Rae can't capture a titled gentleman, what chance do my other daughters have for wedded bliss—or even wedded melancholy?"

It didn't seem fair that all their futures fell upon her fair and slender shoulders. "Bah! Spinsterhood is a humbug," Rae said, deciding that the best way to deal with misery was to share it with her loved ones. Thus, this afternoon found her traveling the well-worn garden path looking for her siblings.

Dark green foliage surrounded her, and sunlight sparkled off dew on the flowers in the English countryside. But for Rae, the pretty morning had evaporated into a most disappointing afternoon. First, she had been forced to listen to her mother's latest sermon about marriage. Next, she'd had to sit through a visit from Timothy Sterne, the vicar's youngest brother. "The man's a fool," Rae mused, even though she had to admit he had the good sense to be totally enraptured by her beauty. "But if I married a Sterne, what good would it do me? There's not much difference between being Grimm or Sterne. I need a name to match my wondrous countenance. I need . . . perhaps, to be married to the Earl of Blithe or Comte Debonair. Yes, to be French would be nice," Rae decided. After all, the French were often leaders in the world of fashion.

Hearing a shout in the distance, she headed toward it. Arriving on a crest near the bridge by the family garden, she spied her eldest sister and two younger brothers. All three were on bended knee, and were poking at something with a long stick beneath the deep shadows of the bridge.

As she took the slightly rocky path down the rise, Rae shook her head at the whole silly lot of them. The Grimms were the only family she knew who calmly sat around the dinner table discussing frog princes, trolls and werewolves—yes, wolves; even when the moon wasn't full—until their mother retired early with nerves. Rae rolled her eyes. Yes, Greta and her brothers loved to read fairy tales. The darker, the better. Rae much preferred tales of handsome princes rescuing their fair loves.

She sighed. "More fairy tales, no doubt." Once again, it

appeared that her rambunctious brothers had somehow managed to drag Greta into hunting for witches, werewolves, vampires and trolls—or had *Greta* enticed *them?* One could never tell. But she could tell one thing, from where they were poking: "It must be troll day."

Picking her way carefully toward the bridge and Greta, Rae wondered how her eldest sister felt about being an unmarried lady of almost twenty-five, certainly well past the first bloom of youth. Studying her, Rae could honestly say that her eldest sister was pretty, even if her hair was a dark blondish-brown and not Rae's own glorious color. Again Rae assessed her sister and could find no fault. It was true Greta's eyes were a grayish-blue, really neither color but both, yet they were still large and expressive. It wasn't Greta's fault that she hadn't been blessed with eyes the color of a bright summer sky like Rae had, or that her figure tended toward the slender side. Thousands of plainer ladies had married—but then, they had dowries or married men who smelled of the shop. Rae actually shuddered at the thought.

"I see it, I see it!" ten-year-old William cried out in jubilation.

As she caught sight of Rae, Greta's face lit with the thrill of discovery. "We've finally done it! We've cornered a troll!"

"Oh, look at its beady little eyes," Jakob exclaimed, hopping up and down and pointing to the deep shadows under the bridge.

"It's horrid!" William gleefully slapped his hands to his face.

"It's grotesque!" Greta's mouth opened wide.

"It's poppycock!" Rae complained.

"It's grunting," Jakob argued, his devious little mind plotting. "We shall capture it and—"

Before he could say more, the beastly little troll snuffled and charged out, covered in mud and with its porcine dignity affronted.

Rae quickly finished the sentence. "And serve it for Sunday dinner."

"It's a pig!" Greta's disappointment could not be clearer.

The pig in question, as it did not desire to be stuffed with an apple and baked for some Bohemian feast, swiftly galloped away.

"We were so close," Greta said. The boys both groaned.

"Casting trolls before swine. What will you think up next?" Rae asked. "But now it's a waddler under the bridge. Really, you three, use your heads. Do you really imagine any supernatural creature would be caught alive or dead in Cornwall?" Rae knew that if she had eternal youth or could cast spells, she certainly wouldn't be stuck in this small coastal hamlet, far from the maddening crowds of the world's big cities, like London and Paris.

Shaking his head in dismay, Jakob, the twelve-year-old, glanced over at her. His brown hair was streaked with dirt. "It could have been a troll. A big fat one," he peevishly pointed out.

"It was fat," Rae admitted with a grin. "But why did you think you'd find a troll today? You never have before."

Success, Greta had heard, could be a heady wine, while defeat was bitter vinegar. She herself had more than a few regrets poured over the salad of her life. For years she had been hunting for any truth behind fairy tales. There *were* monsters out there; the truth was out there somewhere, and someday she would find it.

"Hope springs eternal," she said, frowning slightly.

"Evidently, so do pigs," Rae replied. And fools, she thought, but politely kept that comment to herself.

"Never fear, someday we will find one," Greta said wistfully, encouraging both her brothers and herself. "We'll make a believer of Rae yet."

"In a pig's ear," Rae teased, looking her siblings up and down and shaking her finger at them. "But that's a truffling matter. Now, look how messy you all are! It looks as if you've been bathed in dirt."

Greta laughed, but Jakob narrowed his eyes and said, "You sound just like Mother."

Being the mature twenty-one-year-old that she was, Rae stuck her tongue out at him. She was *nothing* like their mawkish mother. "Brat-ling! I should give you a quick swat," she warned, and was pleased to note Jakob's sudden discomfiture. But the look passed quickly, and he laughed.

"Rae, you wouldn't hurt a fly," he retorted firmly.

She glared at him while her eldest sister brushed dirt off her gown, her expression discouraged. "It's almost time for tea, and you two have Latin lessons with the vicar's brother. I take it that's why you've come, Rae, judging by your smile. Mr. Sterne is here?"

William and Jakob headed grumbling to the house. Rae nodded. "Yes. Unfortunately he came early, wanting to thank Faye and me for reading to his great aunt, Mrs. Wentzelle, since her eyesight is failing."

"Well, it *is* nice that you and Faye are reading to her. Of course, she was your and Faye's art teacher for a number of years. And—"

Rae cut her sister off, knowing what she was about to say. "I read to her because she is a dear old woman and I like her, not so that Timothy will note and comment upon my wondrously sweet nature."

"As you say," Greta replied.

Ignoring her sister's teasing, Rae remarked, "Well, no good deed goes unpunished. Faye left after Timothy thanked her, which meant I, of course, was stuck listening to him—the foolish man."

Greta shook her head. "Aren't you ever going to forgive him? Mr. Sterne's apologized at least a dozen times for his faux pas."

Rae sniffed delicately. "He told me that gold makes me look pallid, when he should have been flattering me. How can I forgive that? The man is a nodcock."

Greta studied her sister as they walked. It was true that

Rae was the beauty of the family. Indeed, of all the countryside. She had a mass of thick, silvery-gold hair which hung down to her knees. Her figure was perfect, as was her complexion. Men were always making sheep eyes at her. But while Greta loved her sister dearly, she also knew Rae's beauty was exceeded by her vanity.

"Rae, shame on you to still be in a pelter over something so silly. Where is your Christian duty? It's been a good three months since Mr. Sterne made that silly comment."

"It appears my Christian charity went the way of Timothy Sterne's manners. Besides, I won't be married to a grave or somber name."

Greta laughed, the sound light and crystalline. It was a laugh that oft drew others to her side. "I rather think you marry the man, not his name," she suggested.

"But the man is *attached* to his name—or the name is attached to the man. I want a sunny last name to go with the duke or prince I marry. If only there were some cheerful princes or dukes about! Still, I shall not let location stop me. Once I figure out how to overcome this territorial problem, I know I shall find my prince."

Greta just shook her head. Her sister's hopes were foolish. Their father had no coin to send them to a season in Town where there were dukes, earls, mayhap even a prince—or at least a titled nobleman with a handsome last name.

"Why is it," Rae asked wistfully, "that there are so many wonderful unmarried women, and so few wonderful unmarried men? Or even mediocre unmarried men. With titles!"

Greta patted her sister on the shoulder. "That, my dear, is a question for the ages."

As they walked up the terraced steps of their family's small manor house, Rae gave Greta a long-suffering look.

"What?" Greta asked. "Is Mother kicking up another storm?"

"A veritable howler. Mother is in one of her *unmarried-*

*daughters-are-to-be-the-death-of-me* moods," Rae warned
solemnly. "She received a letter from Aunt Vivian in Prussia."

Greta's face became a perfect blank, and she tried to
hide her guilt. Something needed to be done about their
abysmal situation, and she had taken the reins in hand and
done just that. Aunt Vivian had written back at last. Greta
hadn't been sure that she would, and now her mother was
in one of her black moods. Did that bode well, or ill?

Unaware of her eldest sister's guilty thoughts, Rae sighed
philosophically. "We'll probably be subjected to the Shakespeare quote on ungrateful children and serpent teeth. I
never knew that snakes had sharp teeth, considering that
they don't do so much chewing. One doesn't often see a
snake smile, does one?"

Greta fought a grin and patted Rae on the back. "I believe that a serpent's teeth are fangs. You know, they're
*pointy* sharp." She did love her younger sister, even if Rae
was a bit silly. "Come, let's brave the dragon's lair and see
what's afoot."

Whatever her aunt had written, it couldn't be worse than
the situation the family now found themselves in. And perhaps, with a little good fortune, their circumstances might
soon improve.

# CHAPTER TWO

## Frog Princes Are Never Found in Cornwall

Once upon a time some minutes later, the four sisters Grimm sat down to tea while their mother officiated. As soon as all her daughters were arranged, Mrs. Grimm began her afternoon ritual: "I am cursed!" she cried. "Some gypsy must have cursed me."

The four sisters had heard it all before, and they sat quietly sipping from their cups, waiting for their father to enter and, with luck, end the unmarried-daughters lecture.

Rae leaned over to Faye and whispered, "Another thrilling tea at Grimm Manor."

Greta held her breath, hoping her aunt had not written and revealed her as the viper in the nest, and one with sharp teeth, too! Her mother would never forgive her for secretly writing to Vivian, much less hinting that she was incapable of finding suitable husbands for her four pretty daughters and in need of her sister's connections. Nonetheless, Greta had written, appealing to her aunt's vanity and the long-standing feud between the two.

"Since you are at your last prayers, Greta, you should have been here when Mr. Sterne arrived. Mr. Sterne would be perfect for you or Faye," Baroness Grimm scolded. "Neither of you can afford to be particular." She stopped and gave her second-eldest child the eye. "I never should have delivered you on a Wednesday, Faye. The brother of a vicar may be all we can hope for, in spite of your grand lineage. You are my little child of woe."

Faye, a typical Wednesday's child, was rather pale of face, with a long nose that was not unattractive. This same nose she used to best advantage when people displeased her; she used it now as she glared at her mother. She knew she was a twenty-three-year-old spinster and settled quite firmly upon the shelf. Another year or two, and she would be gathering dust.

Although not a beauty in the true sense of the word, she had lovely eyes and coppery, brownish hair. Her pale blue eyes, irises encircled by a rim of pure gray, were currently bright with anger and hurt. "I would rather wither away and die than marry Mr. Sterne. His interest lies with Rae. As do the interests of all."

Ignoring her second-eldest daughter's comment, the baroness snapped, "You'll marry whom I say, when I say, and I'll have no shilly-shallying over something so important. If Mr. Sterne concocts a fondness for you, all for the better. Beggars can't be choosers."

Greta snapped her gaze up and silently pursed her lips, angry that her mother had referred to Faye as a beggar. Just because Faye walked with a limp was no reason to make her feel less than attractive. Biting her lip to keep from speaking, Greta settled for a frown. Faye hated anyone to argue about her. Besides, even if one spoke up, doing so would only prolong the baroness's harangue. For it was well known at the manor and throughout Cornwall—probably through most of England, too—that any such opposition was like waving a red flag in front of a bull.

Not as astute as her eldest sister, Rae responded. "Faye has no need to court Mr. Sterne's attentions." Although a spoiled beauty, she was fierce while protecting her family. "When Faye decides she wants to marry, she will. But I really think a baron is the least she should aspire to, and certainly not a Sterne gentleman." She followed that thought with a shudder.

At last Baron Grimm entered the drawing room. He was relieved to see that his two rambunctious sons were missing. Unfortunately for his digestion, his wife was there, along with their pretty but slightly spoiled daughters. The fault of his wife, no doubt. At least his eldest, Greta, was present; she could be counted on to give a good report of her day.

Smiling at the room in general, he seated himself in his favorite chair and glanced over at his pinched-face wife, with her mop of gray-blonde curls and thin lips. He braced himself to do battle once again. Not yet did he know what they would fence about today, but with his usual good sense, he knew there would be something.

The baroness ignored her husband, pouring more fragrant tea into her pretty, rose-gilded cup. Her nerves were much overwrought. She knew in her heart of hearts that she and her daughters were penniless because of the baron's tightness with his coin—not because of the unfortunate circumstances he always claimed. Just because the estate was barely making ends meet, and the crops had failed the last two years due to some blasted blight . . . that was no excuse for him to deny his daughters their rightful due! They were spinsters one and all, desperately needing a season in London. How could a mother possibly make do on these yearly expectations, and with four lovely daughters to launch? She would be forced to rely on the kindness of an estranged sister, which had her gritting her teeth. And her husband would undoubtedly forbid the new gowns needed for the trip, which, verily, her daughters must make.

"My feet hurt," she announced.

"Perhaps we can afford a pair of new shoes for you, my dear. I take it the ones you bought last week are not to your satisfaction?" Baron Grimm asked politely.

She scowled at her obtuse spouse, the expression in her

eyes denouncing him as a fool. "Shoes? Who's speaking of shoes? My world is ending and you are talking of feet! I don't know how my nerves survive your constant foolishness. Why I ever married such a silly man who speaks of shoes when my sister has written from Prussia is beyond my comprehension."

Baron Grimm nodded. He now knew the battleground. His wife and her sister had been involved in a long-standing war of jealousy throughout their lives. What one had, the other coveted and vice versa.

"What did our dear Vivian have to say?" he asked, secretly wishing he could just go back inside his library and smoke his pipe. Whatever news from abroad—this broad, especially—they were undoubtedly bad tidings.

"Yes, what *did* she have to say?" Greta asked curiously, her heart pounding. Though she had not revealed the complete truth of their financial situation to her aunt, she had impressed upon Vivian the need for the daughters Grimm to marry and marry well. She had also begged her aunt for secrecy. Since her mother hadn't scolded her up one side and down the other when she entered, Greta prayed that she was safe.

The baroness pooh-poohed them both. "My sister has invited our daughters to join her through the winter months and into the spring. She made mention at least half-a-dozen times of their unmarried state. I literally had tears of shame in my eyes when I read the letter. A serpent's tooth is not sharper than a jealous sister."

Greta and Rae exchanged a knowing glance, and managed to bite their lips to keep from smiling. "How wonderful," Greta said, breathing a sigh of relief. Her aunt had come through!

Their mother, oblivious to all but her own consternation, continued. "Humph. I should have had six sons instead of two. Everyone of any wit knows that sons are much easier to marry off than daughters." The baroness sighed dramatically, continuing on with scarcely a breath between sentences. "I can't bear Vivian's boasting and sly criticisms—years and years of her bragging. When her son married, she wrote seven times. Seven, I tell you. Eight pages each, at least! Can you imagine the gall, to write me of weddings when there are no weddings on the horizon at Grimm Manor?" She eyed each of her daughters with disgust.

Rae squealed in delight. She had half-tuned out, daydreaming, but suddenly the impact of her mother's words registered. "Trip? What trip? To Prussia, to find husbands?" Finally, her dream was coming true. She would be washed ashore in a lovely foreign country and not buried alive in this backwater of England. She and her sisters would go to Prussia, and she would be the toast of the town. Men would worship at her feet, and a prince would find her slipper and offer his hand, his heart, his title and his castle. She would live in a palace with hundreds of servants, and wear dazzling jewels. She and her new husband would travel, and everywhere they went she would be admired. From near and afar.

"Prussia—doesn't it snow all the time there?" Faye asked, her nose wrinkling. "I don't like snow."

The youngest Grimm sister spoke up. "Miss Darby will be pea-green with envy that I am traveling to the Continent like young gentlemen do," Taylor bragged. "I shall tell her our aunt is married to a count or something. Maybe a duke!"

Baron Grimm shook his head. "I think you should stick to the truth, my dear." He would have said more but was interrupted by his wife, who looked appalled.

"You will do no such thing. I will not have the village think that my sister married above me." The baroness sat, glowering. "Bite your wicked tongue. Remember that pretty girls are seen and not heard . . . though beautiful ones may be both."

"Just think: I shall live in a palace. I shall have a crown made of diamonds and sapphires to match my eyes. Maybe rubies for my lips," Rae rhapsodized.

Greta smiled, secretly pleased for reasons other than husband-seeking. Her aunt lived in a village on the outskirts of the Black Forest—the land of legends.

Baroness Grimm called for quiet and then dramatically announced, "My sister boasts that she can get at least two of our daughters married if they have a nice long visit. Although it pains me to have to enlist her help, I have decided that they must go. We shall all need new gowns. In fact, we'll need whole new wardrobes for the trip." She momentarily halted her impassioned speech. Thinking about her words, she added, "I hate that I must accept this invitation, but I can't lift my head up in town anymore on account of our poor, unmarried daughters. People laugh behind my back!"

The baron merely nodded. His mind was busy going over his accounts.

The baroness's exclamation of ire caused him, a moment later, to turn his attention back to the conversation. "I never," she said, "approved of the match, but my sister did marry a baron of Prussia. Of course, I have never heard the end of it. Although an English baron is most assuredly higher in the instep than a Prussian baron, still Vivian insists she has better connections. We must prove her wrong. The girls must go and be outfitted as bespeaks their station in life."

The baron sighed audibly. He disliked having to argue with his wife. It was much easier to just nod and let her have her way, much like with a rebellious goat one was trying to herd. "I have heard nothing of this. Why is your sister inviting them now, when she never has before? In fact, my daughters last saw Vivian when they were quite small!"

Greta looked away, trying to appear nonchalant. Their family was in dire straits with no coin coming in. Her father would not accept charity, even if her aunt were willing to bestow it. Therefore, she had not told him of her letter to her aunt some four months past. Their only salvation lay in getting some of the daughters Grimm married to gentlemen with means. Rae was their hope, their saving grace. They would go to Prussia and marry—or at least some of them would—and save the family estate.

Feeling a bit guilty, Greta stared down at her teacup. She would also be able to continue her search for the truth behind the Gothic tales. There were supernatural creatures out there—they just weren't in Cornwall, England— and at the advanced age of twenty-four, she was tired of chasing shadows. She wanted to chase substance; and what better place than the Black Forest?

"I imagine," Baroness Grimm snapped imperiously, "that she has written because she enjoys lording my situation over my head, and is probably herself shamed by the fact that I have four grown, unwed daughters. Although, heaven knows, without a proper dowry, marriages are impossible to arrange. Even harder when one is stuck in nowhere and not in London. If all remains as it is now, our daughters will either remain spinsters or, in spite of their loveliness, they will have to marry men in trade!" She gave a horrified gasp. "I won't have it. I shall expire of shame." She clutched at her ample chest and moaned piteously. "Is it not enough that *I* married beneath my station?"

Greta shared a smile with Faye. Both knew that their father was the one who'd married down, wedding a vicar's daughter.

Ignoring his wife's attempt to rewrite history, the baron fidgeted nervously. He hoped the scene's melodrama would not progress further. In the past ten years, the baroness had put on some weight, and it was no mean feat to carry her to her bed when she was in a dead faint. Still, the truth, although not palatable, was preferable. He did not have the coin to spare, and he would not end up in debtor's prison. "We cannot afford a whole new wardrobe for the four of them."

"But of course we can! We must have ball gowns and walking dresses and hats and gloves and diamonds. And I must have some diamond earrings," Rae spoke up, her blue eyes bright with excitement.

"Rae, you know Papa can't afford new togs for all of us," Greta scolded. "You know the crops have failed for the past few years."

Baron Grimm fidgeted some more, feeling tremendously guilty about his lack of funds. His wife glared at him.

"Oh, do be still, husband. My daughters cannot go to my sister in Wolfach for their grand débuts with the rags they are wearing. I will not have them shame me. And my sister would just love to see how far in life I've fallen."

The baron carefully inspected his wife. "Fallen? I fail to see any bruises or mud upon you, my dear," he said, a twinkle in his eye.

"Oh, how can you tease at a time such as this? It's a matter of life and death. My sister will introduce them to the elite of Prussian Society. They will meet princes and barons, and might finally marry well—what with their fresh-faced prettiness and my training, of course. Just think how much you will have, dear husband, with two or more daughters married!"

Glancing at her father, Greta noted his resignation. She put down her plate and decided to change the subject. She hated to see her father in a gloomy mood. "Why, Mother, only yesterday you told me I wasn't attractive enough to catch a frog, let alone a prince."

The baroness glared at her eldest, the pretty girl who was, alas, a trial to her. Greta was the hoydenish planner of her brood of children, always curious, always getting into things better left alone. "You were covered in soot, and your face was smudged. If you aren't running around dirty and unkempt, you're off telling those silly tales. Where you developed a lurid fascination for such demoralizing subjects as ghastly villains, ghosts and werewolves is beyond me. I just know it comes from your father's side of the family. Certainly, my family members are too

delicate in constitution to dwell on monsters or depravity.
How your father can let you read that tripe is beyond me.
But then, he does read all that awful Latin nonsense."

Greta shared a smile with their father. He had taught her
to read that "awful Latin nonsense" as well. She could
quote Cicero with the best of them.

"Mama, you know Jakob and I were looking for trolls
under the bridge and the old fireplace in the kitchen," she
responded.

Rae, who was seated next to their mother, returned from
her private thoughts of fairy castles and princes, "Don't
forget the frog William brought home yesterday. And he
had the audacity to suggest I kiss it!"

Greta hid a smile. Having lived with Rae all her life, she
knew where this tale was headed. She would bet her last
ribbon that Rae would now attempt to sway their father in
favor of the gowns, with her pleading smiles and heartbroken little sighs. She would count to three and then intervene if Rae continued to harangue their father. One,
two . . .

"Oh, Father, we really must make the trip. If we don't, we
shall all wither and die here of old age," Rae beseeched,
smiling sweetly at the baron. It was a cajoling smile, and
one that was often effective. "How can we meet Prussian
Society in gowns at least two years out of date? Why, I
should probably be so melancholy that the men would
be miserable themselves. We can't do that to these poor
Prussian gentlemen." She sighed and bent her head
dejectedly, then peeped out beneath her thick, dark
eyelashes to note how her speech was affecting their
father.

"I am sorry, my child, but I have not the coin for such
expenditure," the baron explained again. He frowned
slightly, for he disliked the fact that his lovely little Rae
sounded more like her mother every day. Perhaps his
daughters *should* go to Prussia. "Be assured that if I had
the funds, I would be more than willing to rig you out."

Rae pouted prettily, contriving yet to bend her father to her will. "I must have the new gowns, Father. Truly. My beauty should be showcased in nothing but the finest. For all our sakes."

"I can spare enough for one new gown each, and perhaps a ball gown, that is all."

Rae's face flushed red, but Greta frowned and spoke up. "Rae, really you should be embarrassed by such wheedling. Just because you won't be parading around every day and night dressed as the finest of the fine, that's no reason to blame Father. There are things he has no control over. Like the weather, and diseased crops."

The baroness snapped, glowering at both her eldest daughter and husband. "Don't speak to your sister like that, Greta! Someday she will be of higher social standing than you. Her beauty *deserves* to be showcased, unless of course she stays here to become a drudge or an old maid. Or perhaps Rae should just go ahead and marry the butcher, Mr. Spratt, since he's asked her four times, even if he smells of raw meat and cheap tobacco. Or maybe she should marry the squire's fat, pimply son. He's been asking Rae since he turned sixteen. Your father and I could have fat little lumps with bumps on their faces as grandchildren."

No one responded to this melodramatic announcement, although the sisters did trade a smile at the passionately charged atmosphere.

Undaunted, Rae retorted frostily, "*Princes* should write odes to my beauty. Not a butcher, a baker or a candlestick maker." She was well aware that she rated herself highly, but then she had spent days in front of her mirror. Vain she might be, but Rae knew her own worth—and that was definitely a small kingdom, or at least a large duchy.

"Alas, if my dear Rae feels inclined to choose a spouse from her many local admirers, I imagine I will bear up to the challenge of squint-faced, grubby little grandchildren," the baroness said. "Even if Rae marries the stablehand,

Mr. Stilzkin. I know he's asked her at least twice, though he is twice her age and rather short of stature. I hear he wants to be a weaver. I can just imagine how clever their children will be. Perchance they will spin gold out of hay. And just think of it: dressing their brood would not be costly, not with their short statures. And if Rae deigns to marry the butcher, Mr. Spratt, we shall be well set in pork. Ever since his last wife died, he's been looking to remarry." Rae gasped, and the baroness waved her arms in the air, wailing. "Fetch me my vinaigrette! I am overcome with palpitations."

As the maid fetched the hart's horn to revive her mistress, Rae and Taylor both pouted. Faye picked up a book and began reading, pretending to ignore the rumpus. Greta and her father exchanged sympathetic looks.

Once revived, their mother, quick-witted when cornered, spoke tersely. "If we sent only two of the girls, they could each have more gowns. I think Greta and Rae should make the journey to Prussia." Satisfied, she sat back and smiled. "Yes, my loveliest two daughters will travel to Wolfach, and each will catch a fine, rich and noble husband. Then, with their new connections, they shall help find husbands for their less fortunate sisters." Yes, the baroness would worry about her other two daughters later. With Faye being a cripple, the season would probably be wasted upon her, anyway, and Taylor was barely eighteen. There was still plenty of time for her debut.

At first, Rae was overjoyed that she would have more new gowns, but glancing over at Faye she was suddenly struck with guilt. Her elder sister was disappointed, although she was trying to hide it. "I'll find you a husband once I'm married, Faye. Verily, I promise he'll be handsome and of the nobility. And you can come and stay in my fine castle with me. We'll have a lovely time."

Greta silently seconded the notion. She admitted that Faye deserved much more than she had been given in life. Instinctively, she knew that Faye was rather like Sleeping

Beauty: someday her prince would come and awaken her with a kiss, and she would become smiling and cheerful like she had been long ago.

There was some argument yet to come, but their mother's wishes held sway. Thus, Rae, the most beautiful lady in Cornwall, and her vivacious sister Greta, were soon to be off on a grand adventure to find fortune, fantasy and marriage. The baroness was in raptures, and could be trusted to remind each and every one of her acquaintances about "the trip" each and every time she saw them. She often boasted that nothing less than Prussian princes would do. Several likely thought this objective a bit overreaching, and wished to contradict her—but no one could contradict Rae's smile.

# CHAPTER THREE

## The Bully Aunt

Far away in Prussia, it was a lovely winter day, probably about twenty-nine degrees. Despite a few light snow flurries, a warm winter sun shone down, seemingly to welcome the Grimm sisters to Wolfach. Only, Rae wasn't smiling. Rather, she was giving her sister the evil eye as they traveled the last few miles to their destination.

"Seven bridges? Seven! I have never been so sick of looking under bridges in all my life. Another harebrained scheme of yours!"

Guiltily, Greta glanced away from her sister's dirt-streaked face and the muddied skirts of her gown. "We are in the Black Forest, where there are supposedly trolls. Who knew that last bridge would be a *toll* bridge?"

As her wounded dignity and filthy clothing made her stomach twist, Rae narrowed her eyes. "I would expect the family expert on fairy tales to know that trolls always require a fee of people crossing their bridges!"

Greta sighed in exasperation. "Those weren't trolls; they were thieves. And I'm sorry they took your new gown."

"And my ribbons and two pairs of my slippers!" Rae had tears in her eyes. "My favorite pair, and all they took off you were your gloves and cloak."

"My favorite cloak, and I'll give you my new gown."

"It's pink, not blue. I look divine in blue because it matches my eyes. Pink is merely tolerable. Evidently the thieves thought so, too, as they left it. I told you that shade of pink was wrong when you picked it out. Too reddish by half," Rae chided. "But what do you care? You just want to track trolls or whatever. Sometimes, Greta, you are not my favorite person."

Greta sighed. She was disappointed, too. She just knew there would be trolls under at least one of the Black Forest area bridges. Instead, they'd found a band of shabby villains, a motley crew with nagging wives. Hence the loss of their clothing.

"Oh, stop it. I said I'm sorry," she snapped.

It was at that moment the carriage pulled up at the Snowe residence, and the driver smiled. Never would he be so glad to get rid of passengers. The two ladies were queer in the head, having made him stop at all large bramble thickets, in case a castle was hidden behind one, and at all those bridges—including one where they'd been robbed. He'd lost his whiskey and his best pipe!

"Oh, will you look at that?" Rae breathed, her ire forgotten as she took in her aunt's magnificent home, which was beyond impressive. They'd known their aunt married a Prussian baron who was considered quite well-to-do, but such a prodigious display of wealth was comforting. Rae smiled brightly at her sister Greta, her blue eyes twinkling as if to say that she'd been born for just this lifestyle. "It's wondrous. I just know we'll find suitable husbands with our aunt's connections—men with fine, noble, *happy* last names."

Greta was busy scanning the entrance, her smile wide. "Very nice. I'm so glad I wrote her, and that Aunt Vivian decided to help us."

"Only to spite Mother."

"True," Greta remarked. "But that should be reason enough for you to forgive me for getting your gown stolen. If I hadn't written, we wouldn't be here." Greta had decided weeks earlier to come clean regarding the letter. Instinctively, she reasoned that if their Aunt Vivian was even halfway like their mother, she would end up revealing all in due course.

Rae shrugged her shoulders. "I guess I could forgive you, if it weren't for you choosing that stupid pink gown. I want to impress the Prussian gentlemen, not make them pity us."

Greta started to object, but was stopped as the carriage door swung forcibly open. "Here you are, my ladies!" the carriage driver said, hurriedly helping them down.

They were soon inside the massive home, and were taken straight to their aunt, who glared at them. "You're a day late."

Rae glanced nervously at her sister, who sighed. Their first meeting with their Aunt Vivian in many long years, and it was not starting well. The Baroness Snowe was rigged out in the height of fashion, with full stiff skirts, an elaborate hairdo and a multitude of jewels. She was a majestic woman, rather built along the lines of a clipper ship, with an abundant prow and cargo area. "My gracious, she's scary," Rae whispered.

"She certainly resembles Mother," Greta whispered back.

Still glowering at her wayward—and *late!*—nieces, Vivian inspected them from top to bottom. Finally, she expelled a harrumph. "So, you are my sister's gels, grown up?"

She walked around Greta, noting the lively intelligence in the girl's eyes. She shuddered. "Unmarried, and at your ages—why, it's ghastly! But with your mother, what can one expect? It's a good thing you wrote, Greta. Else you'd soon be leading apes instead of your little brothers." She eyed Greta severely. "I've been warned about you, gel. Your mother writes that you are always reading books! Books in Italian or French. Audacious chit! I won't have such silliness in my home. Why, I tell you that French and Latin books have been the downfall of many a young man and maid in those countries. Henceforth, I'll have no blue-stocking tendencies. Gentlemen prefer wives who have no thoughts and listen intently to their opinions. Remember that man's favorite subject is man, not woman, unless he's seeking she do her husbandly duty. Then you may be able to hold his interest for ten minutes or so. So, I am laying down the rules now. We will absolutely have no intelligent conversation or thoughtful airs in this household, nor more especially in public."

Greta smiled politely, keeping her thoughts hidden. She was quite masterful; after all, she had been practicing this particular look most of her life. "My, how astute you are, Aunt Vivian. But no worries. I've given up books for my complexion." To think, she had written to this woman for support. Her aunt was even worse than their mother!

Her aunt nodded, satisfied. "Wise gel. You might just have a brain in your head. You must get it from your father."

"Not from my mother's side, certainly," Greta replied, staring meaningfully at her aunt. Her aunt did not seem to take her meaning, which was likely best.

"Since you're at your last prayers, the burden of helping you husband-hunt now falls to me. You must allow one who is slightly older to guide you. Besides my proficient experience, I am a woman who is held in high regard in the upper echelons of Prussian nobility, and who knows exactly how to bring a wealthy and titled gentleman to heel."

Greta barely managed to hide a snort. Her sister continued to smile that pleasant, vacant smile which always made her wonder if anyone was at home. The men, however, absolutely worshipped Rae's smile, and were always looking to knock on her door.

Rae had been cataloguing the cost of the paintings and vases which lined the salon, listening with half an ear. Intelligent conversation was beyond her, anyway: she was an expert at flirtation. In her experience, one didn't need to know Plato's theories to succeed; all a lady had to do was look lovely.

"How fortunate we are to have you for an aunt," Greta replied.

Baroness Snowe looked disgruntled. "Are you being clever, gel?"

"I would never dare."

"You sound a wit," was her aunt's reply, and the woman wrinkled her nose in disgust.

"I beg to differ."

Raising an arctic brow, Vivian harrumphed and turned her eagle-eyed examination upon her other niece—the extremely pretty one. "Let me tell you right now, missy, that I will brook no vanity in my home, and no pouting or pretentious airs," she remarked. "Well, it's certainly easy to see whose side of the family you favor. Ravishing. You look much like I did when I was younger."

Both Rae and Greta managed to hide a smile at this comment, since they had heard it quite often back home. Their mother claimed Rae was the spitting image of herself.

"How your mother has failed to get you wed is beyond me. Pretty gels are usually the first to be married off, even with little dowry. With your looks . . . well, you two must be of a shrewish disposition like your mother," Vivian remarked.

*Uh-oh*, Greta thought silently. She bit back a retort on her and her sister's behalf. Discretion was the better part of valor, if a lady needed a husband—or to track down and research dark legends. So Greta kept her mouth firmly shut, enjoying her aunt's tirade. She would write home to Papa about it.

Not realizing that she was providing delightful letter-writing fodder, Baroness Snowe continued on. "I was considered quite the catch in my day. I was of course a diamond of the first water. Everyone wanted a drink. By your age I had taken London by storm and married the

Baron Snowe. How old are you, anyway—and why are you still unmarried?" The woman shook her head in utter perplexity. "Such a disgrace, to have a pretty girl who can't manage to attract the right man."

Rae took exception to the question, as it was a tender subject for her. "I am twenty . . . barely." Well, perhaps not *barely.* Twenty, and eight months.

"A veritable old maid," their aunt pronounced. "Did your mother teach you nothing of women's wiles?"

Rae's complexion reddened, and she did so hate the thought of that. Red was not one of her favorite colors. "I am certainly not a shrew. Why, many men have remarked upon my disposition. And wiles? I thought you disliked cleverness in a woman!" Rae snapped back, less politely than she knew she should, yet with much less rancor than she wished.

Her aunt glared at her imperiously. "I will have no tantrums in my home. Best you remember it now. A nobleman wants a sweet, pretty wife who will not cavil him when he spends his money gambling . . . or on other less savory things." Staring hard at her young niece, she persisted, which was something she excelled at. "Come, gel, it's time for the unvarnished truth. Why haven't you married? No one asked you?"

Rae drew herself up to her five-foot-six height and stared hard at her aunt. "I've had hundreds of proposals."

"Humph."

"It's true! Tell her, Greta."

Greta nodded, wanting to be helpful. "Suitors flock to our door like demented geese."

"Geese? Why, really Greta, my swains are more impressive than geese," Rae replied.

"Harrumph! Ineligible, every one I expect. Probably the blacksmith or some lusty farmer's get. Am I right?" Aunt Vivian asked, a rather gleeful cast to her voice.

Rae opened her mouth to lie and say her proposals were from barons and earls and so forth, but she wasn't thinking through the situation. If an earl had asked her to wed him, she would be wedded and bedded by now.

Greta, knowing her sister only too well, knew it would behoove her to make this reply. "You're entirely correct, Aunt. Rae's proposals were from men who smelled of the shop. Stank of it, really. But you really must be careful, Aunt. Your wit is showing."

Baroness Snowe shrugged. "Beware more of that pestilent tongue of yours, gel. Sit down and do try to keep it in your head. We wouldn't want it cut out for impertinence."

Greta smiled to herself but retreated under her aunt's admonitions, apologizing prettily. In the drawing room, she seated herself upon a large gold and red brocade settee, right beside a rather fat white cat who lay snoring on his back, his pudgy feet in the air.

Sitting down in her chair, the baroness fully enjoyed her power over her young nieces, and Rae's comeuppance. There was nothing worse than having a beauty in the house when one was aging. "I know you've attended society affairs, but it's preposterous! Whatever is wrong with your mother? A weak man needs only a nudge in the right direction to make a fine match, and as for the grander prospects, they too can be had, even if one must drag them kicking and screaming to the altar."

"That must make for a festive wedding," Greta remarked, and was pleased to see her aunt's jowls shake with irritation. "Still, we have met but few eligible gentlemen in Cornwall."

Their aunt pounced on that explanation. "What of those few? Why did they not offer for Razel or yourself?"

This time, Rae managed to beat Greta to the punch line. "None of my sisters wanted them. One was a widower with ten children. He also had a tendency to sermonize."

"Methodist, was he?" their aunt asked. "And the other?"

"He was at least in his middle years. All of thirty-eight or thirty-nine. And he had a large mole on his forehead."

"What's that got to do with anything?" their aunt asked

harshly. "Your mother is much the fool as ever, I see. Why didn't she push this match, despite moles, gout or whatever? If you had been *my* daughter, you'd be wedded, bedded and with a string of children at your knees."

"My mother wants my happiness, and would never have forced such a man upon me," Rae said.

"It was a very large mole," Greta added, throwing in her two pounds.

Another loud harrumph. Aunt Vivian pointed a stiff finger at Greta. "I said I wouldn't abide cleverness in this house, unless it is mine. Go up to your rooms at once while I consider how I can find husbands for such ill-raised gels. Dinner is served at eight."

The two sisters retired, feeling both humbled and rather abjectly depressed. Rae even cried a few tears once they were in the sanctuary of their rooms, though she was careful not to make her eyes too puffy. In a fit of temper, she vowed that she would not marry a man with a mole or gout or whatever other deformity age bestowed, no matter what their wicked battleship of an aunt commanded.

Greta's mind, however, was more deviously occupied. She was vowing to find other bridges. She'd cross them—and look under them for trolls—when she came to them.

# CHAPTER FOUR

The Pursuit of Happiness Is Not Easy

"A witch, you say? In the Black Forest, and she tells fortunes?" Rae asked the young man she was seated beside at the dinner party. Sighing, she guessed she'd have to tell Greta. Then Greta, being Greta, would drag her off for a visit. At least she'd get her fortune told, and would get out of her aunt's home for a while. That particular thought made Rae smile. Snowe Manor was downright icy, even though the baron ordered it to be well heated with blazes in many of the fireplaces.

To be honest, the home's discomfort didn't come from temperature. The snow was blowing outside, but the storm inside the manor was worse. Their determined and demanding aunt had evaluated the Grimm sisters' clothing and found it severely lacking. She had also judged the gels' manners countrified, their ages abysmal, and their fates indeed . . . grim. And if they didn't listen to her, the baroness warned, she vowed to wash her hands of them. Going back and forth in her mind, Rae couldn't decide whether to thank her sister for writing to their aunt or curse her.

Greta managed to do as she was told and also escape at times to search the baron's massive library for local tales of vampires and monsters. She even questioned a few of the maids, who'd looked at her as if she were mad. Rae bore the brunt of Aunt Vivian's corrections. Remarkably, she was able to seethe silently, holding on to her temper by a slender thread. In her three days at Snowe Manor, many a time Rae had wanted to tell her aunt to go to the devil. She had bitten her tongue until it was sore. Wisely, she knew that she couldn't tell her aunt exactly what she thought of her, or she'd be shipped back to England to die a lonely, but very beautiful, spinster—or worse, to be married to some imbecilic squire's son.

Yes, that was why Rae dutifully held her peace, even letting her aunt pick her gown for tonight's ball. It was her least favorite due to its pale color, yet her two dinner partners were both gazing at her with adoration in their eyes. Rae shrugged. Of course they were. Even in pale blue she was ravishing, and the cut of the gown happened to flatter her perfect figure, cinched in tightly as it was at the waist, and with its off-the-shoulder design that showcased her firm, high breasts. Still, as it was her first dinner and ball in Prussian society, she had wanted to look her very best.

She had entered the Count DeLuise's residence with excitement, harboring plans of being toasted by much of the Prussian nobility, only to discover that she was seated anonymously beside a rather young man who was merely Herr something-or-another. Her second dinner partner was a Baron Schmutz. No, that wasn't right, she realized. The man seated to her right was called Baron . . . something. Perhaps Baron Schook? No, that wasn't right either.

Baron Schortz! That was it! An odd name, to be sure. But then the great hulk of a man was rather strange in a way she didn't understand. He caused her heart to beat faster, like it did when she had danced three country dances in a row. She found this particular feeling left her a tad disconcerted. And his admiring glances and fulsome gallantry were becoming tedious as they finished the fourth course.

It was with discomfort that she suddenly noticed the heat coming from his body and his scent, which was warm and musky with the hint of some wild spice. Lowering her

lashes, she knew that she really should depress his attentions and nip them in the bud—but she did like having
admirers, even if they were rather hulking. Of course, Greta
would probably say the man was muscular and rugged.

Glancing down the table to where her aunt sat, Rae wondered if Aunt Vivian's dinner partner was a prince. She
shuddered, hoping this was not the case, since the man
was at least sixty if a day and rather stoop-backed.

A comment by one of her dinner companions caught
her attention once again. She turned to him, noting that he
was making sheep's eyes at her—and they hadn't even
reached the fifth course. She managed a coy smile, a look
she'd had down pat since the day she turned thirteen.

"Miss Grimm, you are a delightful surprise! Quite a lovely
girl. I do so hope you enjoy your stay in my country."

Rae glowed with happiness at the compliment, even if it
came from a mere impoverished baron. Her smile dimmed
as she studied him, however. His compliments were quite
nice, but the silly man was just too big. Though not fat, he
was large and very tall, with thick blond hair and a beard.
She had never liked beards. He had amazingly broad
shoulders and a chubby nose as well.

"You put Helen of Troy to shame," the man said sincerely.

Rae's smile brightened again. Although she hadn't yet
launched a thousand ships, Bertie Higgins, the candlestick
maker in Cornwall, had launched his boat and even named
it in her honor. Besides, she reasoned as she took a sip of
wine, everyone knew that Greeks had much more passionate natures than Englishmen. If she lived in Greece, she'd
probably have a thousand and one ships to her credit. Or
at the very least she'd be wedded by now.

Baron Fennis Schortz hadn't wanted to come to either
this dinner party or ball, but he had reluctantly sent his acceptance. He'd felt he had to attend, as his good friend,
Rolpe von Hanzen, had so insisted. Rolpe had been berating him for the past year, claiming Fen was burying his

head in the snow, refusing to live life. Rolpe had pressed
the point, saying that Fen's unruly brood needed a stepmother with a loving and guiding hand. To be honest, Fen
agreed that he could use a wife to help him recover his
good humor—and to warm his bed as well as his heart.

For that reason, Fen had responded to the countess's invitation. But never had he expected the vision of loveliness
he'd received tonight: a blonde beauty the likes of which
he'd never again thought to see after burying his beloved
wife. Seated by Miss Grimm and breathing in her scent of
lilacs and cloves, he'd sensed his heart immediately beating harder. He'd felt a tug at his groin in response; several
tugs, in fact. Apparently, Fen realized ruefully, his juices
were flowing again. His heart was no longer dead, but beginning to pulse with passion. Or at least one of his organs
was.

"I have envied Helen at times," Rae said softly. "To have
such devotion from an admirer, to have armies fight great
battles over her . . . that is every maiden's dream." And it
was just what she deserved herself. Who knew? Someday
historians might write of her great beauty!

"I can't believe you have cause to envy anyone." Fen hid
a grin. "I don't believe I have ever seen hair so gloriously
golden. It's like moonlight, and it must hang down to your
knees when unbound." The little ingénue would be a
wicked handful, for he could tell she was a bit vain; but
then, what woman who looked like Miss Grimm was not?

Rae preened some more, then realized she should dis-
courage the man's attentions somewhat. He was already
so besotted she could wrap him around her finger a dozen
times, and dessert hadn't even arrived yet. And he was
poor and a mere baron, even though he was correct: her
hair *was* glorious. Everyone told her so.

She adopted a stern tone. "Even though I'm English, and
unfamiliar with Prussian manners, I can't imagine a conversation concerning such personal attributes is entirely
appropriate."

"Perhaps not," he ceded. "I must admit you rather muddle my thoughts."

She nodded coolly, acting bored. "Do you know anything about the witch in the Black Forest?"

Fen choked on his wine. "A witch, what witch?"

"Not *a* witch. Not what witch or which witch, but *the* witch, and her whereabouts." Good grief, the silly man seemed a dunce as well as a hulking lout. And he looked genuinely startled by her question.

"Why?" Fen managed to ask after wiping his mouth with his napkin. Whatever had caused the ravishing beauty to talk about witches?

"Why what?"

"Why witches?"

"Why not?" She gave him a peevish look. "Are you dim?"

He blinked, then grinned.

"No, *Baron*. I meant are you dim in the brain. Of course, would you know if you were? Dim, I mean. In the brain." Rae felt more than a trifle annoyed. "See what Greta's started?" She narrowed her eyes. The baron had stopped giving her compliments, all because of some foolish old witch who told fortunes and probably turned princes into frogs. Perhaps she would make an exception and target a baron as well.

"Greta who?"

"Oh, don't start the who-ing again," Rae chastened him coldly. "You sound like an owl. Greta, over there." She politely dipped her head in the direction of her sister, who was sitting watching the room in general and surely plotting ways to discover all kinds of nasty little secrets.

"What exactly has she started?" Fen asked. He'd totally lost track of the conversation, but that wasn't entirely bad, because he could stare at the vision before him.

"Do you always ask so many questions?"

"Only when I'm interested," he responded, grinning at her cheekily. "What has Greta done? Is she a witch?"

Rae smiled. "At times, yes. You see, she's my eldest sister."

"Ah." Fen understood the tribulations of siblings, and the bonds between them. "Why witches?"

"She studies fairy tales." Rae wrinkled her nose. "Half my family does. She actually," Rae began and then shuddered, "*believes* in them."

Fen hungrily watched her wrinkle her nose, longing to kiss its adorable tip. "There's no witch," he said. "Only an old woman who tells fortunes."

"Greta will be deeply disappointed. She wants a witch."

"No witches here," Fen replied honestly. No, there were no witches; though many other supernatural creatures laid claim to the Black Forest region. He sincerely hoped that the sisters Grimm were not going hunting. The local creatures often valued their privacy, and dealt harshly with any who trespassed upon it.

Greta grimaced. Her first dinner party, and everyone was so secretive . . . or in denial. Here she was, deep in the heart of the Black Forest—well, not actually deep in its heart, but nearby, in the town of Wolfach—and yet, where was the danger, the intrigue, the legends come to life? Instead of people taking up arms against aggressive ogres, or big-fanged werewolves howling at the doors, or young fair maids with bite marks fainting all over the place, the whole locale was remarkably cheerful. It was most depressing. There were no dark shadows or castles of Dracul in the picturesque town, merely people, ordinary people, just like in Cornwall. Boring.

Also just like in Cornwall, Rae was being cosseted and admired. Greta noted her sister's expression as she glanced down the long expanse of white tablecloth. Rae's dinner partners were almost strutting like peacocks due to their good fortune at being seated beside her. As usual, Rae was enjoying the attention, flashing brilliant smiles all around. It was a sight Greta had seen a hundred times, and oddly she felt a wave of homesickness. The three days they had been staying at her aunt's seemed to stretch to months, and Greta wondered why she hadn't just stayed home. After all, she could have been insulted in England with less enthusiasm than Aunt Vivian showed.

Of course, tonight looked more promising. This dinner party away from their aunt's mausoleum of a home, their first dinner party in Prussia, was filled with the elite of local society. Their aunt had taken great pains to apprise the two sisters that this particular courtesy was due to her patronage. They were most fortunate to have her for an aunt, or so she kept telling them.

Greta turned her attention to the hosts, the grand old dame and her husband, the Count and Countess DeLuise. Their wrinkles matched their pomposity. They were both considerably older than even Greta's aunt, but they did seem to be the crème de la crème of Prussian nobility, with their pretentious airs and jewel-laden bodies. Greta had never seen such wealth. Again she calculated just how many gems were affixed to the intricate golden headdress on Countess DeLuise's head: well over sixty diamonds and rubies, she was sure. Greta had noticed that the lordly old dame rarely spoke a word, and that her lips were tightly drawn. *But then*, Greta thought, *if I had to wear something as heavy as my aunt's cat upon my head, I'd be grumpy, too.*

Turning back to the diner on her right, Greta held back a sigh. She was seated beside an odd little man with an unusual style of hair. He was reminiscent of a hedgehog, since his coiffure stood up in straight tuffs all over his head. "That Pied Piper in Hamloff is nothing, I tell you. Nothing!"

"A pied piper?" Greta asked. Hadn't she read something somewhere about that?

Herr Mozart didn't answer, just began humming and scribbling again: black marks all over the tablecloth. He had a strange little laugh, and was most definitely enjoying his wine. After a few moments of silence, he glanced at her, his dark eyes harsh with anger. "No real musician would play for rats. They say he can cause goats to follow him when he plays on his pipe, too. It's total rot!"

Having overheard the conversation, Greta's other dinner partner, Herr Nietzsche added quietly, for her ears alone: "Goats, all manner of goats, follow the Pied Piper's playing. It's an unseemly disaster. Whole villages lose tons and tons of milk and cheese."

"That must be rather vexing. Being stuck with cow milk and losing their kids like that," Greta replied.

She studied Herr Ronald Nietzsche, a jovial and round fellow of middling years who had introduced himself by saying he didn't care to have too many virtues because it was upsetting trying to maintain them all. She had liked him immediately; and when he proceeded to gossip about those around the table by saying they should not underestimate the privileges of the mediocre, Greta had to bite her lips from laughing aloud. He really was of a humorous bent, and he'd kept her entertained with the exploits of local nobility, both the great and the small. Yes, it appeared the people here were exactly like the English, with the exceptions of being Prussian and speaking a guttural language called German.

Herr Nietzsche chuckled. Leaning over, he whispered, "Herr Mozart prefers being the only talented musician in the region. He's jealous of the Piper."

Greta nodded, smiling. After a crafty pause, she led the conversation back in the direction she most desired. "All this talk of Pied Pipers makes me think of fairy tales . . ."

Nietzsche groaned. Whenever she'd mentioned fairy tales or monsters before, he'd swiftly changed the subject. But, undaunted, Greta tried again. "I had heard the tale of a young lady of royal birth who was bitten by something strange in the Black Forest and went to sleep for a hundred years. Thousands of rose bushes and bramble bushes grew up about her resting place. I heard some prince finally rescued her."

"Really, my dear, such a vivid imagination you have, and

so silly. The prince's attire would have literally been torn away, so he would have been naked and scratched raw by thorns. What princess would have wanted to wake up to a prince with a thousand pricks? Besides, it wasn't a princess; it was a man by the name of Rip Van Winkle. He wasn't nobility, either. And he only managed to sleep for two months, after he drank too much ale at the Oktoberfest."

Leaning over and inspecting the scribbles of Herr Mozart, Nietzsche deftly changed the subject again. He whispered to Greta: "Mozart is a musical genius, but as a conversationalist he leaves much to be desired. Just don't mention Tchaikovsky to him, because he goes absolutely berserk. Genius must be catered to and cajoled. I absolutely insist upon being fawned over myself."

"You're a musician, then?"

"Good heavens, no! I can't tell a *C* note from a *B*. Is there even a *B* note?" he muttered. Before Greta could answer, he went on to explain that he wrote not music but books. "It's always been my ambition to say as little as I can in as many sentences as will fill up a page. Where another man might write two pages, I will write ten."

"Then you subscribe to the school of loquacity?" she asked.

"*Nein.* I subscribe to no school. I just love to hear the sound of my own thoughts."

Greta tried once again. "Ah, excellent! Then I beg you to please tell me more about this mysterious area."

"It is . . . mysterious," Nietzsche revealed. Then he turned his attention back to Herr Mozart.

Greta couldn't help but laugh, but he truly was dodging the question. Shaking her head, she wondered why no one appeared to know anything, or wanted to know anything, about the supernatural world surrounding them. Although Greta appreciated the humor with which Herr Nietzsche had related the foibles of the local elite, she was rather disappointed by what she'd gleaned.

Wolfach was amidst the Black Forest—a land of fairy tales, blackish forest trees, black forest cakes, black magic, black lacquered cuckoo clocks, and black magic witches casting spells and causing women to sleep forever. (These witches also turned princes into frogs or other equally degrading things, Greta was told.) This was the land where werewolves feasted on human flesh by moonlight, yet wore a human form by day. This was the place where legend and reality met, and she would find out what everybody was hiding—even if it killed her. Though she hoped she didn't mean that literally.

Sighing, Greta fought her disappointment. This was her first outing in Prussian society, and her research was not going well at all; her brothers would be thoroughly disappointed when she wrote to them tomorrow. Perhaps she could embellish a bit and mention something about witches turning someone into a bird, or witches' houses made of . . . ? Greta thought a moment. She needed something which would make her brothers laugh. Then, glancing down the table to a *schnecken,* an elaborate gingerbread muffin, she had her answer.

Taking some of the *schnecken* and nibbling on it, she glanced over at her sister again. Rae's rather imposing dinner partner captured her interest. He was a very large man, not fat or stout but apparently heavily muscled beneath his black jacket. His eyes were a deep gray, the color of smoke. He was a plain man, his face a bit craggy, like the cliffs back home. Weather-beaten and creased, it was still a face that commanded attention. The man's attire was well made but rather threadbare, and he wore no jewelry of any kind except a large onyx ring. Greta had been introduced to him shortly before they took their seats. He was Baron Schortz, and from the looks he was giving Rae, Greta knew her sister had made another conquest.

It appeared, however, that Rae wasn't in the least interested in the baron. Now that she had found a chance to mingle among nobility, she might just find herself a prince, rather like that Cinderella character Greta had read about. Her beauty would draw them in despite her lack of coin.

Suddenly the Countess DeLuise, who had been silently sitting and glaring at her cherry strudel, sat up straight and cleared her throat. The guests turned to her. In firm command, Countess DeLuise, bedecked in jewels, loudly tapped against her champagne glass with her spoon. The table grew silent. The countess let the silence grow for effect, then in a bracing voice declared, "It's *schrecklichkeit!*"

Greta searched her memory and remembered that the German word meant *frightful.* Her blue eyes lit with interest, and she wondered just what it was that was being described.

Countess DeLuise continued, her substantial voice growing stronger with each word. "*Ja,* I must speak now! I can hold the forbidden secret no longer. The news is grave, very grave. One of you . . . is a *vampire.*"

A murmur rippled through the dining hall. Greta and Rae's eyes went wide with shock.

# CHAPTER FIVE

## The Countess Who Cried Vampire

"Yes, one of you at this table is a vampire," the countess repeated for effect. "My poor Wolfach is filled with *vampyr*. Evil, vile creatures they are, with extremely big teeth that suck the blood of innocents under the shadow of night," the woman declared, the fervid light of sincerity burning in her eyes.

Greta wanted to dance a jig. Finally! Someone was actually talking about something interesting. She drew in her breath and waited, giving Herr Nietzsche a speaking glance.

"They are everywhere, so beware!" the countess remarked, an odd twist to her features, her tone harsh with condemnation.

"Yes," Greta whispered, zealously scanning each of the guests' faces, wondering if anyone did have the urge to bite a neck instead of the delicious gingerbread. Unfortunately, as she regarded the various diners, she noted with disappointment that none appeared to be sporting fangs. Nary a guest looked discomfited by the countess's revelation, either.

Glancing over at Rae, Greta glimpsed her sister staring in rapt fascination at DeLuise.

"Alas, our fair town is brimming with *vampyrs*. It's clogged with the foul vermin, chock-full and just plain overrun by the nasty biting creatures. A stake! I'll trade my strudel for a stake!"

Herr Nietzsche caught Greta's perplexed look and spoke quietly: "Oh, my dear child, pay the countess no mind. It's all a bit of *unsinn*—nonsense. The countess is a bit eccentric, even if she does have exquisite taste in jewels. And I do so love her wiener schnitzels; her chef is a marvel. It's the main reason I put up with her odd quirks and kidney complaints."

On her other side, Herr Mozart roused enough to remark with a slurring of his words, "I'll write an aria to the dreaded *Nosferatu*. They will adore it in France. All that passion and bloodthirst, you know."

The Countess DeLuise cried out, "Fritz, get the garlic cloves!"

Her austere butler sighed and nodded uneasily. Then he shuffled off to gather the required herbs.

"Enough of somber tidings. It's time to enjoy life and dance away the fright," the countess commanded, and she then proceeded to the ballroom, where she would stand at the head of the receiving line with her husband.

As Greta watched the dotty old dame leave, Herr Nietzsche extended his arm. "Come, my child, let us proceed," he asserted, placing her hand on his arm. "*Nein*, we must not upset the countess. She becomes quite testy if her words aren't taken as law. If she commands us to dance, we must dance. But before we dance, we must wait in line like all good *Niederer Adels*." Upon seeing her confusion, he quickly translated: "Lower nobility such as myself. Alas, I have the brain of a king but the blood of a commoner."

He escorted Greta to the ballroom, where they stood like all the other guests. Introductions were made by Greta to her sister and Herr Nietzsche. Afterwards, they continued their conversation, this time including Rae.

"It's a shame, really," said Nietzsche, "but it seems we nobles spend half our lives waiting in some line or another.

Someone to wake us, someone to bathe us, someone to make our food and pour our wine . . . and they always keep us waiting. I think it's on purpose. Just think how we wait for those higher up to notice or befriend us. And now we must await the dancing, while the countess receives her guests for the ball."

"Waiting for our hair to dry, which in my case takes forever," Rae spoke up, her nose wrinkling. "Or waiting for flowers to come and tarts to bake and gowns to be made. It's really quite trying," she agreed.

Greta shook her head at her sister. She was also amused by the fact that Herr Nietzsche was trying to pull the wool over her eyes—in this case, keeping her focused on the mundane when the otherworldly was sitting in the room like a fat purple dragon.

She squeezed the man's arm. "Did I not hear the countess order her butler to fetch some garlic, Herr Nietzsche? Yet you have made not a single comment about that."

"Perfectly ridiculous. Fritz won't get within an inch of that herb. Did I mention that the DeLuises' chef is part French and guards his spices religiously?"

Greta let out a soft snort. "You are so calm. A rather canny sort of fellow, aren't you?"

"Canny? I have been called many things, but canny . . . ?"

"Wily. And disinclined to talk about a most interesting subject. Imagine, a vampire among us; and this pretty town could be brimming with vampires. Yet you calmly go on about this and that, jewels, dancing and wiener schnitzels."

"I am ever a practical Prussian. Jewels, food and fine wine, not to mention my esteemed valet, are what I concern myself with. Surely such a pretty little English rose can't be one of those monster-followers, always bouncing from one cemetery to another. Forever going on about men with pointy sharp teeth or hairy little men who chase their tails. It's preposterous, my dear, utterly preposterous. Such beings would clearly be superior, yet we humans are the dominant force on earth."

"I tend to agree that vampires and werewolves and other such things could rule us if they so choose, but perhaps they prefer the shadows. Vampires like cemeteries, which shows they lack sense. All that dirt and mustiness," Rae remarked. Her brow furrowed.

Nietzsche shook his head. "You two are too lovely to be filling your heads with all these superstitions. Legends are just so . . . plebian. They're for peasants who like to be frightened because their lives are dull otherwise."

Rae turned to her sister, confusion filling her face. "Did he just call you plebian? We're Protestant."

Herr Nietzsche chuckled while Greta explained; then Greta turned back to him. "We have legends for a reason, sir. There is more on heaven and earth—"

"Oh please, my child, not Shakespeare. *Nein.* I know the quote only too well," the author interrupted with a quick arching of his eyebrow. "Terribly overrated, that man. An atrocious dresser, and those tights! Why, a chicken has better legs. Confound it, why everyone should quote a man who couldn't dress himself is beyond me. My writing is of a much more serious vein . . . and I look smashing in a cravat."

Greta ignored his silly rambling. "Why are there so many legends in so many different languages about the same thing, if they are all lies and bedtime stories? There is never smoke without fire."

Rae shrugged her shoulders, shaking her finger at her sister. "Greta, leave the poor man alone. Just because you choose to believe in monsters doesn't mean they exist. And it certainly doesn't mean that we want such a topic to dominate the evening. It appears that Herr Nietzsche here is not a believer." This conversation was utterly dull, and she wanted to speak of more important topics, such as the handsome gentlemen all about the large and crowded ballroom. Hopefully the countess would soon finish with greeting her guests, and the dancing would begin.

"Not believe? Oh, my dear, sweet misguided child, of

course I'm a believer," Herr Neitzsche said melodramatically, patting Rae's arm. "This is the Black Forest, after all. Look into its depths . . . and it will bite you." And with those words, he excused himself to speak with another brightly dressed guest.

"What an odd little man," Rae said as the two sisters watched his small, stout figure depart.

"I knew it," Greta crowed. "There *are* vampires, werewolves and witches in Wolfach! And we're going to find them."

Rae frowned. "Make sure to ask Aunt Vivian's chef for some garlic cloves first."

"Yes, I'll be sure to do that," Greta said, nodding. "We're fortunate her chef is German."

Rae frowned. She would never understand her sister. Why would the chef's nationality matter? But she didn't dare ask, for she didn't want to extend the conversation any longer. Soon the dancing would begin.

The ballroom became a dreamily lit fairyland, swirling with colors from the twinkling chandeliers to the guests' attire, and it was truly a spectacle to behold. Women wore ball gowns bedecked in jewels and flowing with delicate rows of spidery gold lace. The men, not to be outdone, sported brightly colored jackets and breeches. Large jeweled stickpins flashed everywhere, as did sparkling rings, and the dancers twirled in frenetic merriment. Rae found the effect dazzling. She nudged her sister. They had both just finished dancing and were waiting for Herr Nietzsche to bring them some punch.

"Isn't Prussian Society just magnificent? Much more so than Cornwall. Although I can't say much for your dinner partners tonight." Rae glanced over at Herr Mozart, who was humming to himself and tapping a spoon on his champagne glass.

Greta glanced over and nodded at her sister. "It's true, he didn't offer much conversation. But he does hum most prettily."

"My companions were not of the first water, either. The poor young man on my left was terribly gauche. He could barely string two words together," Rae complained.

"Yet I noted that you smiled graciously and spoke with him quite kindly."

"My beauty made him afraid, I fear."

"So you eased his awkwardness by discussing the things he's interested in," Greta guessed.

"I hope so. And the next time he is seated beside a comely lady, he will remember his success."

Patting her sister on the arm, Greta shook her head in amusement. "Rae, my dear, you are a contradiction in terms."

Rae cocked her head. "Sometimes I don't understand you at all."

Laughing, Greta replied, "Nor do you understand yourself, I'm sure."

Rae shook her head, narrowing her eyes. "I should pout over that remark . . . but I fear you are right."

A lady danced by in a gown literally covered in sparking gems, capturing Rae's attention. "My gracious, Greta, look at the rubies sewn into that lady's gown! Someday, when I find my prince, I'll have a dozen—nay, a hundred—gowns with inlaid jewels," she remarked.

Greta barely nodded, recalling the Countess DeLuise's comments. As her mind raced with possibilities, she began to plot the best way to view one of the demented monsters. Vampires in town were a marvelous discovery. Now she just had to find them.

"Greta, pay attention. If you won't stare at the gowns, at least look at the gentlemen."

Greta smiled at her sister's one-track mind and then suddenly felt the breath leaving her body as she spied one of the most handsome men she had ever seen. He was talking to Rae's past dinner partner. "Oh, *my*." The man had dark blue eyes and coal-black hair, which was tied back in a queue, in the manner of many of the gentlemen there that night. "I wonder who that is with your dinner partner?"

Rae looked to where Baron Schortz was standing and noticed the handsome man beside him. "He is quite marvelous, isn't he? He certainly puts the baron to shame in looks. But, alas, he isn't titled. I was introduced to him right before I was seated. His name's Frank or Faust . . . von Hanzen or Hanzel, or something of that sort. You know recalling names can be quite tedious, and I've not the talent for it that you have."

Greta slid her gaze back to her sister, disliking the interest in Rae's eyes. If her sibling decided to set her pretty little cap for the handsome stranger, she herself didn't stand a chance. "It's not surprising he's not titled. The handsome prince is a thing of fairly tales, remember."

Rae sighed. "The handsome baron, as well. And to think! Our hostess had the gall to place beside me a mere baron, and a great hulking one at that. She must have windmills in her head. The man is smitten. All I did was smile, and he's like taffy in my hands. It's a shame, really, but he's too bold for my taste—and too poor and too homely."

Greta studied Baron Schortz for a few moments. "I don't know, Rae, I find the baron an attractive man. Maybe not handsome, exactly, but compelling. His face has character, and those gray eyes are remarkably lovely."

"You've had too much champagne."

"One glass." Greta continued to stare at both the baron and his handsome friend.

"Quit staring at them!" Rae complained. "The baron will think I'm interested, when that is the farthest thing from the truth."

At that moment, Baron Schortz caught the ladies regarding him, and he smiled. He nodded to his companion, and the gentlemen began to make their way around the crowded ballroom floor.

"Oh, Greta, see what you've done? Heavens, I had enough of his company at dinner. I certainly don't need to dance with him. I fobbed him off at dinner by saying my dance card is full. He's besotted enough already, and I don't want him hanging on my sleeve, scaring away any potential princes."

Greta merely shook her head. "Your smallness is showing, my dear." But inside, Greta's heart was beating loudly. The very handsome Mr. Whomever was coming toward them. If only her sister would suddenly vanish into thin air or miraculously contract a spotty complexion. Then Greta might have a chance to catch his eye and perhaps even dance with him.

"Mayhap," Rae concluded reluctantly. She knew she was rather vain, but she had just cause. Men had fallen all over her from the time she was twelve years old. "At least he's bringing his friend with him. With such a face and figure, there might be enough for some ladies to forget their desire to be a princess."

Rae risked a peek at the two towering figures making their way over, and noted how often the two stopped for brief chats with other guests. "Oh, Greta, I just can't dance with the baron! He'll probably step all over my feet. And I do so adore my new slippers. Besides, with his great weight he'd probably break all my toes, and then how would I dance the rest of the season?"

"Rae, get off your high horse and start behaving like the lady you sometimes are." Greta gave her sister a scorching look and shook her head. "Sometimes your swelled head is enough to try a saint."

"Well, you certainly aren't a saint," Rae retorted, embarrassed and annoyed.

The two objects of the Grimm sisters' glances returned their interest. Baron Schortz couldn't get over Miss Rae Grimm. He had never seen a vision as lovely, and he had learned discreetly from their hostess that she was related to Baroness Snowe. Much to his delight, the two sisters would be wintering in Wolfach. Miss Rae Grimm was a magnificent creature, and he wanted to get to know her better. She did so remind him of his first wife, Fiona.

Unfortunately, his crony, Rolpe von Hanzen, was also interested in the delectable Miss Rae. In their wild youth, they had sometimes hungered after the same female. Most times Rolpe won, but sometimes it was Fen. This would be one of those times, Fen vowed. Rolpe couldn't possibly understand the need he'd felt when he first beheld Miss Grimm's visage: a roaring of blood, a clouding of his mind and an unearthing of senses long buried. After four years of feeling hollow, he was suddenly fraught with emotion. The air smelled better, colors were more brilliant and his heart was singing in his chest. He would be the one to win Miss Grimm, not his friend.

The men bowed to each woman separately, and Fen introduced Rolpe to the elder Miss Grimm. Rae smiled prettily, causing Fen to lose his train of thought. She then interrupted the introductions by placing her elegant hand on his jacket.

"Baron Schortz, I hope you won't think I'm presumptuous, but could I be so bold as to ask a boon?"

Greta glanced quickly at her sister, then took a peek at the tall, dark man beside the baron. He had a daunting reserve, and from his rather formal manner, Greta would peg him for a duke at least.

"Of course," Fen said, honored to do anything at all for the lovely young lady before him. Her hair was aglow with light from a dozen chandeliers, and it burned like moonlit gold. She wore part swept up in some complicated style and braided with tiny seed pearls, but the rest hung down her back, thick and shiny. He longed to see that same hair gracing his body as she sat astride him, her glorious locks floating all around.

"How may I be of service?" he asked gallantly, though privately his thoughts were of ravishing her.

"My sister's favorite song is playing, and I wonder if you would do the honor of dancing with her?" Rae asked, manipulating things to her satisfaction. She was not about to dance with this great hulking oaf when the extremely handsome man beside him was available.

Greta was taken aback by her sister's forwardness, and wished to hide behind her fan. No lady should ever pose such a question as Rae had just done. It was unheard of and quite gauche. She smiled bravely at poor Baron Schortz, who looked vaguely distracted. She felt sorry for him, for it was evident that he'd been caught in Rae's glittering web. But he politely nodded and led Greta away to dance.

Fen was bemused. The delectable Miss Grimm had a kind heart, to make sure her sister was taken care of—and beauty in combination with a kind heart was irresistible. Although the elder Miss Grimm was not a stunner like her sister, she was still a comely lass. Even if, standing next to Rae, she did seem to shine less brightly.

Greta's thoughts of her sister were not so kind. In fact, she was livid with Rae for once again practicing her tricks. Making Baron Schortz dance with her instead of the handsome stranger—but, then, why should she be surprised? Rae was always arranging things and people to get her way.

Noticing Baron Schortz's quietness, she smiled politely. "I am sorry for my sister's lapse of etiquette. She meant well," Greta lied through her teeth.

He smiled back. "Please do not worry your pretty head. Although, the *wahrheit*—the truth—is that I would have asked your sister to dance first because I was her dinner partner. But as you are her sister, I would also have asked you."

Greta sighed. The baron had politely reassured her that he would have asked her to dance, but at the same time had told her it was due to her sister's influence. How tiring it was to be the less attractive sister!

As he twirled her around the floor, the baron asked more about Rae, gracefully maneuvering them around a slower couple. For a man as large as he was, he was quite agile, Greta saw. Up close, the baron's dark gray eyes were truly lovely, and his smile was contagious. He might be a poor baron, but he had manners and was kind. Those were two qualities essential in a husband, if one wanted a marriage of contentment and had a dollop of sense in the head—which, of course, her flighty sister didn't.

"I believe my sister has your admiration?" Greta asked gently.

He nodded, his expression sheepish. "I know I've only just met her, but she reminds me of someone I held in the greatest esteem. Is it so apparent?" His question was rueful.

"Only when you look at her. Which is a great deal of the time," Greta teased. "She has always had a great many admirers. I believe they have spoiled her a tiny bit." Perhaps he would take her hint and not be as besotted. "Because of her lovely features and hair, I must admit that Rae has had much made easy for her."

He smiled back politely and twirled her, causing her to question whether he heeded her words. If Baron Schortz stood any chance at all with Rae, he needed to change his approach and appear rather aloof, behaving with a mere modicum of civility around her. He also needed a new jacket.

As Greta danced, she caught a glimpse of her sister dancing with Baron Schortz's friend—clearly the most attractive man at the ball. Rae's face was bright with laughter, her two dimples showing. It made Greta sad.

She asked, "Does anyone ever appreciate the easy gain?" Her question was earnest. The more smitten Rae's swains became, the less Rae seemed to respect them. Most men fell for her at first look, and Greta had grown used to this situation. Still, just this once, Greta had hoped that this handsome man would have chosen her over her sister. There was something about his dark good looks and grand demeanor that called to her on a level she did not understand, even if she found his presence a trifle intimidating. If only one of her other two sisters had come instead of the magnificent Rae, then perhaps the daunting Mr. Whomever would have noticed her first.

But that was not the case.

# CHAPTER SIX

## Prussian Pride and Prejudice

Insomuch as Rae was unaware of her sister's dark thoughts, Rae was blithely enjoying her dance with the handsome Mr. von Hanzen. His face was well shaped, with high cheekbones and a fine nose that was neither too long nor too short but just right. His eyes were the color of bright blue sapphires, neither too light nor too dark but also just right. And he was dancing with her. Rae smiled up into his rather somber face, smitten.

"You dance divinely," he complimented.

"Thank you. I've had a great deal of practice."

*Fürst* Rolpe von Hanzen was not a man of many words. Highly intelligent and aware of his own consequence even more than everyone else, he was an arrogant soul who took what he wanted, lived life on his own terms and did not suffer fools gladly. Staring at Rae, he replied, "Indeed. Your dance card must always be full." He knew that this beautiful creature had enraptured his friend Fen, a remarkable feat in itself, since Fen had practically buried himself in grief the last few years. Yet this lovely girl had touched Fen's heart—and other regions, he was sure. From afar the lady was ravishing, but up close she was even more divine, and when Rolpe spotted her, he had instantly understood his friend's need. Her ploy, however, to get him to dance with her instead of Fen, had left Rolpe feeling vaguely uncomfortable. He didn't like being manipulated, and that was just what Miss Rae Grimm had done. Most likely, she had also unintentionally embarrassed her sister and insulted Fen.

"Of course," Rae replied, laughing merrily, "my dance card is always full." She flirted as effortlessly as she danced. And soon Mr. von Hanzen would be dancing attendance on her, his eyes alight with the fires of passion that she so easily invoked in men. She would, of course, have to rebuff his attentions. If only he were at least a baron; then she might swallow her pride and settle for less than royalty. She had to admit she would be the envy of any female under the age of eighty and older than fourteen if she could wed someone as handsome as Mr. von Hanzen. Yet his lack of a title settled it, so with ruthless efficiency, she quelled her interest.

"Yet, you danced with me," he pointed out.

"I didn't wish to appear rude. Besides, a clever lady always saves one dance or two."

"Baron Schortz will be gratified to hear this."

Rae's smile faded somewhat. "I'm afraid he'll be disappointed, for I have no dances left to spare."

"Fen's a fine dancer," Rolpe remarked, though he somewhat questioned his friend's choice. He found this woman rather shallow, her conversation dull and lackluster. He knew he was handsome; men and women had been riding his coattails—and other things—from the time he was fourteen. He'd lost his virginity in the Black Forest with a woodcutter's daughter by the name of Red Helga. He could steal a maiden's heart with a snap of his fingers, seduce her among the sweet fragrant clover with a simple smile.

Rae smiled politely, disinclined to respond.

"A good man, a widower," Rolpe continued.

Arching her neck and turning a little to the side to display her body to best advantage, Rae imagined his appreciation of her form. Smiling a secret smile, she let him admire her all he wanted and took great pride in his inevitable interest.

Irritated, Rolpe noted the woman's bland stare as she gazed past him. Her disinterest in his friend left a sour taste in his mouth. He tried one last time: "Fen and his late wife made a wonderful couple on the dance floor."

Rae was getting tired of all this talk about Baron Schortz. The buffoon should be complimenting her instead. "I'm sure he isn't as graceful a dancer as you."

Rolpe raised a questioning brow. "How so?"

She preened a bit before answering, letting him drink his fill of her beauty. "Well, to be honest, big men rarely are graceful. In fact, I can't tell you the number of times my poor feet have been trod upon by someone designed more for hunting than dancing."

And just like that, all interest in her was lost, washed away like the dirt after a hard rain. No matter how lovely she was, she was wholly selfish and thoughtless. Rolpe hoped Fen would recognize these traits and steer clear of the English beauty. "How tragic for you."

"Yes, it is, but one does what one must," Rae said coyly. "A lady must sometimes dance with persons she'd rather not."

"A cruel jest of fate, I'm sure."

"*You* understand," Rae said. "When a lady is sought after, she must share her attention among the many, even if she would rather it be among the few. But men so easily get their feelings hurt, and I don't wish to do that to anyone." She bowed her head modestly. This was too easy, once again. This poor besotted commoner was falling into her palm like a ripe plum. At least he was a well-to-do commoner, judging from the cut of his clothes and diamond stickpin. The diamond was at least a full carat. He was also notably high in the instep, which to Rae indicated good breeding.

"Well, I've heard people say that God has graced me," she continued. "Therefore, I must make the most of His blessing by appearing at my best at all times. I think I'm rather like a work of art, relieving burdens and easing the heart." Men were so easily conquered, it was almost not worth the effort trying, Rae thought smugly.

"How noble, to risk your toes for such a good cause," Rolpe replied, assessing and dismissing her again with his eyes. No matter how lovely she was, she was a useless bit of conceited baggage. Why, she thought so much of her worth that she didn't even realize he was being sarcastic! *Ja*, she was so vain, she probably thought this dance was about her.

"You, sir, most assuredly have your wits about you. Most gentlemen do not realize how difficult it is to pick and choose a dance card. I have no wish to break hearts," she added in a sweet, innocent voice. She knew men found women who thought of others quite sweet, that sympathy was an agreeable trait for a bride. Rae had learned at a young age, from her parents' marriage, what acrimony could do. Therefore, she well knew to show herself off as a kind, compassionate lady, which would further enflame this commoner's senses. Which she should not do, but she could not help.

Rae fluttered her eyelashes at him as the dance ended. He would call the next day at her aunt's house, she was sure, and she would be the envy of all for this extremely attractive man's interest in her. He would probably send two dozen red roses to her as well. And a sweet card praising her beauty would be enclosed. She looked forward to the look on her aunt's face upon the discovery that her niece was the belle of the ball.

"How difficult, indeed," Rolpe agreed. And with those words, he intended to return her to her sister; but another eager dance partner met up with them and led Rae away. As she left, she flashed him that lovely smile, her dimples showing. Ignoring it, Rolpe instead listened to the sound of footsteps behind him.

"I wanted to ask her to dance, but it appears she's taken,"

Fen remarked ruefully, staring hungrily after the younger Miss Grimm. "I should call you out for dancing with her first, Rolpe! I told you I want her."

"Have at her," Rolpe replied, giving a shrug as they walked to an alcove near the balcony.

Fen turned to stare at him. "I thought you were interested in Miss Grimm."

Greta, who had slipped into the alcove to compose herself after her sister's betrayal, heard the voices and recognized them immediately. She shrank back into the shadows.

"No. Miss Rae Grimm is too rich for my blood," Rolpe remarked. He stood, legs braced, arms behind his back, and glanced out at the dancing couples on the floor.

Inside the shadows of the curtained alcove, Greta's heart beat faster. Should she reveal herself and leave the alcove? That would be the polite thing to do; but somehow Greta's curiosity got the better of her, and she was fiercely glad that she had learned German as a young child from their governess. Her mother had called it a waste of time—and once again had been proven wrong.

Leaning closer to the shut drapes, Greta shamelessly listened to the two men's conversation, a grin growing on her face. It appeared that the most handsome man she had ever seen had *not* been taken in by Rae's charms. Could it mean that she might have a chance? She certainly didn't mind his lack of a title, as his mere presence sent her heart to pounding. His deep blue eyes, the color of a stormy sky, made her feel as if she were falling into a deep well. How she longed to drown in them.

Fen braced himself against a column on the other side of the alcove. "Too rich? Why, she isn't rich at all. I spoke to her aunt tonight, and she seemed almost proud to tell me that neither sister has any dowry to speak of."

"I meant vain, Fen. The female is all conceit and vanity." Seeing the look on Fen's face, he quickly continued. "Now, don't go and howl your head off. She's a beautiful handful,

I'm sure, but too vain for my wants. I want a wife who can talk of more than gowns and jewels. Miss Rae Grimm will want compliments—a daily litany, I do believe. She will run some man a ragged race. Besides, I'm much too young to take a wife."

Wounded by his friend's comments, Fen glared at Rolpe in vexation. "You merely danced with her. I ate dinner with her. It's true she may show some conceit, but what female wouldn't who looks as she does? And by the by, you aren't getting any younger. Youth is a *wahn* in your case."

"It's no illusion. And I am not that old. Plenty of time yet to settle down and create little von Hanzens."

"Hah!"

Rolpe shook his head and stared at Fen. His friend had been devastated by the loss of his wife four years ago, but to have Fen fall for a female so shallow was distasteful. His friend deserved better. "What about her sister? She seemed an amiable sort."

"She's pleasant, I guess, but she's not Rae."

"No, unfortunately she is but a pale imitation. Still . . . it must be hard, being an aging spinster with a sister like hers. Probably she is a shrew in private. Jealousy will do that to a woman." Rolpe spoke with the wisdom of long experience. His mother had been like that with his sister, whose beauty had grown to surpass hers. There had been pouting, temper tantrums and an unsettled household all through his formative years. Rolpe still cringed when he remembered.

Inside the alcove, Greta had been jubilant about the conversation up until that moment. But his words quickly brought her back to earth. Aging spinster? Shrew? She would show him just how much his words meant to her. She lifted her hand to part the silky curtains of the alcove, intending to go out and tell this too proud jackass her opinion of him: a few choice words sprang to mind that she had heard the stable master use when one of the horses had stepped upon his foot. But as her fingers touched the crimson drapes, she froze. If she denounced him harshly, then she would prove him right. If she showed her anger and wounded dignity, he would know that he had hurt her. That, she couldn't bear.

As she heard the two men move away from the curtain, she brushed a tear off her cheek and cursed her weakness. He was clearly an arrogant buffoon who—peeking out through the curtains, she saw—was taking his leave of the ball.

Outside, as Rolpe called for his mount, he shook his head, disgusted with both Fen and the conceited Miss Grimm. Poor Fen: he was in for a momentous hurt.

Back inside the sparkling ballroom, left to himself, Fen anxiously searched for Miss Rae Grimm. Even though Rolpe's warnings had struck a cord, he couldn't seem to halt his actions. He needed to be near his lovely vision. Spotting her, he quickly hurried over, asking for a dance.

"I'm sorry, Baron," she replied, stiffly polite. "My dance card is full."

As Rae glanced up at the big man beside her, she wished he'd just go away. She had recently met a Prince Gelb, and he had asked for a dance. It was true he was probably at least thirty-five years older than she was, and a bit thin for her tastes, but that was outweighed by other factors of grave importance. Prince Gelb lived in a palace where he had a golden room. Wondrously, everything inside was made of gold or gold gilt. He even had a golden harp! That was most assuredly enough to stir her interest.

"If you'll excuse me," she said as that very man came to escort her onto the ballroom floor.

Rae danced with the prince, who said he would call on the morrow. Then she danced with other men. Between each partner, Baron Schortz remained persistent, sticking by her side like a lovesick puppy. It wasn't until Aunt Vivian signaled that it was time to go home that Rae was finally shot of him.

Inside the cloakroom, Rae found that she and her sister

were alone, apart from the attendant. As the little maid sought their cloaks, Rae let loose her pique: "That stupid man would not leave me alone! I wanted to scream at him to go away, but fortunately I am a lady of good breeding. But really, Greta, Baron Schortz is so vexing."

Greta, not in the best of moods herself, snapped back, "Then tell him politely that his interest is not returned, and quit whining. I am sick of hearing it."

Rae glanced at her sister in surprise; Greta rarely snapped at anybody. Nodding to the maid, who handed over her blue velvet cloak, Rae said with a hint of censure, "Really, Greta, it is most vexing, and I would think I was plain regarding my lack of interest. I didn't grant the baron one dance, and I quite smoothly eased him into dancing with you when I knew he was about to ask me. I spoke little to him, and replied in a monotone. That should tell him my interest is not engaged, yet he's still smitten! At times my looks are a curse, you know."

"Oh, Rae, do grow up," Greta growled. "What you did tonight was very bad manners. You should never have tricked Baron Schortz into dancing with me. I was embarrassed, and it was not well done. If I were a witch, I would turn you into a worm."

Rae actually shivered at her sister's condemnation. Not to mention, she despised worms and all squiggly things that hid in the earth. "Well, at least you got to dance," she snapped. Greta had no cause to berate her. "And I saved you from dancing with Mister von Hanzen. Just plain *mister.* It's too bad he's not a prince; I would snap him up in a minute."

"I can manage to find my own dance partners!" Greta cried. Her sister was so self-involved, she didn't understand anything. Even now Rae had her head in the clouds, where all was silver and gold, and an entire contingent of male angels was spouting odes to her beauty. Perhaps she should relay what Mr. von Hanzen had said about her. Greta was sorely tempted, as her own pride had been lacerated by the man's rude remarks.

Greta thought hard about putting her sister in her place. A few hard truths and a cold dose of reality would work wonders. Still, Greta knew this was not the time or place; nor did she want to spend the rest of the night listening to her sister's tears. She remained quiet, remembering Mr. von Hanzen's cruel words.

Tying the bow of her scarlet cloak, she shook her head, fighting off her annoyance. "No, Mr. von Hanzen is certainly no prince. He's too rag-mannered for that!" she couldn't help adding. Then, thinking of the aging roué of a prince Rae had discovered, she shook her head. "But you did meet a prince tonight, didn't you? Prince Gelb. I found him to be rather sly."

Rae noticed the expression in her sister's eyes, and could read it as disgust. It hurt when Greta gave her that look, and she received it much more frequently than she felt she deserved. She knew she was a trifle vain, and she wanted to be more considerate, like her eldest sister. But it was very hard when one looked as she did. She also wanted to be cleverer than Greta every once in a while, since Greta was highly intelligent, and on the odd occasion to converse about something beside herself; but people rarely let her. "Well, he is a prince," she remarked.

"He's older than our father. If I were you, I'd think carefully. A baron in hand is worth two princes in decline. Besides, that old prince . . . I say, the way he looked at you was verily obscene."

"How so? He merely seemed smitten to me."

Greta shuddered. "Leering, pure and simple."

Rae giggled. "There is nothing pure about lechery."

Greta shook her head, amused. "*Touché.* But beware that old coot. His mind's in the bedchamber."

Rae gasped, then frowned. "Thankfully he's not the only prince in Prussia. And he is rather stooped. But at least he still has a handsome mien."

"If you discount his wrinkles and squishy lips."

Rae glowered at her sister. "I do beg pardon, but he still

has a full head of hair. Champagne-colored, it was. And he dressed well. Did you see the Baron Scwills's jacket? At least four years out of date. How he dared show his face in such a jacket is beyond me."

"Baron Schortz," Greta corrected. "And perhaps he is a wise but poor man who spends his money on his estate," she speculated. "He appeared to be a man of intelligence when I danced with him."

"Estates! Why would anyone spend their coin there instead of dressing as befits their station? Oh, never mind. Enough about him. I can hardly wait to see Aunt Vivian's face. I was the toast of the ball tonight. Men were eating out of my hand," Rae recounted.

"You make them sound like hungry hounds," Greta grumbled.

Rae glanced at her sister. "Men and hounds have many things in common: they like their dinners on time and adore being petted." Her voice quieted as they walked outside to meet their aunt, who was busy gossiping with several older ladies while waiting for their carriage.

Inside, a somber-faced figure opened the door to the smoking salon, which was attached to the anteroom where the cloaks were kept. His dark gray eyes were filled with anger, turning them an even deeper smoky color, and his lips twisted down; his soul was wounded. He had heard the Grimm sisters' conversation. It appeared that Rolpe had been right after all: Miss Rae Grimm would not do at all for his "great hulking self." Apparently his looks were dismal, his title unworthy and his fortune in question.

Once the Snowe carriage had left the premises, Fen walked outside, his scowl foreboding and his heart heavy. Miss Rae Grimm might think him stupid, but he was not. And he was certainly not some mongrel, forever to be at her beck and call.

"Why, for that comment alone, Miss Rae Grimm should be turned over on her pretty stomach and her bottom blistered till she can't sit for a month! Hound dog, indeed!"

Retrieving his massive chestnut mount from the stable, he quickly saddled it. His thoughts were as morose as the night sky was dark. He had touched the light briefly, and for one solitary night he had felt he might just begin to live again. But cruel fate had put him back in his place. Life was hardly a fairy tale when it involved the Grimms.

# CHAPTER SEVEN

## The Grumpy Guardian

Rae triumphantly waited for her aunt to compliment her on her popularity at the dance, yet the moments passed, and the only noise was the plodding of the horses' hooves outside as their carriage moved bumpily over the snow-covered road to home.

Never one to be overly boastful, she felt, Rae nevertheless thought her achievements of this evening should be remarked upon. "My dinner partners were rather dull, although I swear that Baron Schortz is quite smitten," she remarked. "I shall receive at least a dozen roses from him tomorrow. No; as besotted as he was, I imagine I shall receive two dozen—probably white roses, though, dull fellow that he is." Then, thinking about his worn jacket and the state of his shoes, she amended, "Make that *one* dozen white roses, with a note swearing his undying admiration. They shall probably get lost amongst the other flowers."

Her aunt acted as if she hadn't even spoken. Still, Rae persisted. She had been the belle of ball, and it was high time someone beside herself gave voice to it. "I swear, I have never been wearier than tonight. I scarce sat down a dance."

In the glow of the carriage lantern, Vivian turned to Greta, speaking stiffly. "I noticed you made quite the dash.

You scarce missed a dance as well. I must admit to being quite impressed."

Rae frowned, while Greta pondered how to respond. "Yes, I did," she said at last. "Tonight was quite nice." Evidently, her aunt had taken umbrage at Rae's popularity with the gentlemen; and yet, that was what the two sisters were here to do, to cause a stir. Rae by her beauty, Greta by finding out all she could about the truths of fairy tales surrounding the Black Forest.

Of course, Greta admitted now while maintaining a polite smile, she wouldn't mind a husband either, as long as he wasn't anything like Mr. von Hanzen. Although, as much as she hated to admit it, the man did stir her senses. Even if he was a pompous fool. It was really too bad he was such a jackass.

"Quite nice? Quite *nice*? Are you being impertinent, gel?" Aunt Vivian asked huffily. "Why, you foolish twit. Tonight you were amongst the cream of the crop of German nobility. Both the *Uradel* and *Briefadel* were there." She paused briefly before delivering a set-down. "I'm quite sure the two of you haven't ever rubbed elbows with the type of company you kept tonight. I must write your mother about your first dinner and *tanzen*." She said the last with a gloating smile.

Greta glanced at her sister and could see storm clouds on the horizon. Before Rae could lose her temper, Greta pinched her sharply on the leg.

"Ouch!" Rae hissed.

"What was that, Razel?"

Giving her sister a mean little stare, Rae answered stiffly. "I merely got a crick in my foot. From all that dancing."

Aunt Vivian settled back against the cushions, her nose held high in the air. "Perhaps," she conceded to Razel, vexed at her vain niece's popularity at the dance, "I might have noted a time or two that you were dancing as well. Of course, that was probably due to my great consequence. I was rather surprised to see that *Prinz* von Hanzen danced with you. Von Hanzen. Yes, he most likely danced with you knowing that you were my niece, since he is a man very aware of his own consequence and rarely dances at these events. Unless it is, of course, with his latest cherie amour."

Greta sat back in her seat, frowning. So, the hateful man was a prince after all? It wasn't surprising, and yet at the same time it made her even angrier. Well, apparently she had been fortunate to have been snubbed by German royalty. Perhaps she should have stayed in England, where the only person snubbing her was her mother.

Rae's bittersweet acknowledgment of the backhanded compliment was quickly shoved aside as she registered her aunt's words. "Prince, prince? Who's a prince?"

"Why, *Fürst* von Hanzen, of course. His father's side of the family is related to the House of Welf," their aunt informed them.

"Oh no. How absolutely ghastly! I shall just die, expire right on this spot."

"What on earth are you speaking of, Razel? Are you addled? I can't say that it would surprise me. Your mother never was too steady, always having fainting spells and predicting doom and gloom."

Rae had completely missed their aunt's rant, consumed by her utter stupidity and social faux pas. "Oh, how shall I bear it?" She turned pleading eyes to Greta, hoping her sister might devise a way out of her social blunder. "When he was introduced as *Fürst* von Hanzen, I thought that was his first name, and I called him Mr. von Hanzen. I thought it was a derivative of Frederic or Francis," she explained, putting her hands to her cheeks in embarrassment. "What a silly chit he must think me."

"You stupid gel!" her aunt scolded. "I know I explained the differences in the German nobility. Such disgusting behavior, and on a matter of such grave importance. My heavens! He will think my nieces totally lacking in polish and good breeding. Why did you not take what I said to heart? Are you a total dullard?"

Rae's face took on a mulish expression. She might not be as bright as her sister in those uninteresting things like science and literature, but she was not a lack-wit. When her aunt droned on for hours last evening about this and that and her connection to the local nobility, Rae had been busy doing something important. While her aunt flaunted her precious position, Rae had been planning her triumphant entrance into Wolfach Society.

But, daunted she was not. Just because she had made a slight social gaffe, that would not keep her from her target: a handsome, wealthy prince like von Hanzen. Someday she and the attractive prince would laugh about her mistake, ensconced in their huge castle with one child—certainly no more than two—running about the magnificent palace.

Narrowing her eyes, Rae prepared to give her aunt a chilling set-down. After all, when she married the prince, she would rank higher than her aunt.

As her sister opened her mouth to speak, Greta diplomatically intervened. "Now, Aunt Vivian, I'm sure the family honor"—Greta paused for emphasis—"to your great credit, can withstand Rae's little misunderstanding. After all, Prince von Hanzen did ask her to dance." She wisely left out the part about Rae forcing the prince's hand.

Her aunt settled her considerable bulk back on her seat, her harshness dissipating to a degree. "Perhaps. I did explain to the Countess DeLuise that the two of you were from some godforsaken place in England. Yes, you're right. I'm sure they'll overlook the social blunder as nothing more than a green gel's *fürst* mistake. I can't dare predict what he will do the next time he meets you, however. I suppose I can speak with him about your lack of polish."

Ignoring Greta's pinch, Rae took exception to this slight. "I am no green girl; nor am I some countrified milkmaid,

and neither is Greta. Both our dance cards were full, and
many a gentleman asked to call tomorrow. In fact, I danced
so much my feet hurt, and they may never recover! My admirers will be thoroughly devastated." There, you great
beastly woman, take that to heart, Rae thought.

"Your feet hurt because your head is so heavy from
swelling. Vanity has puffed you up, gel. And I told you that
you needed a larger slipper," Baroness Snowe reminded
her. "There is no sin in having big feet."

"Big feet?" Rae screeched.

Drawing back the curtain, Greta stared out the carriage
window with a slight smile touching her lips. Rae's remarks
to her aunt were amusing, as was Aunt Vivian's lack of po-
liteness. Despite her good intentions to keep the carriage
from erupting into armed warfare, she couldn't help but
enjoy the verbal fisticuffs. Here was vacuous, womanly
bickering at its finest. And their aunt was its paragon: apparently, Vivian wanted the girls to triumph so she could
show up their mother; yet at the same time, she dearly resented their small successes.

Squeezing her sister's leg abruptly and breaking into the
conversation, Greta pointed out the window. "Oh look,
there's a castle—or at least what's left of one."

The castle she referred to was situated upon a tall white
hill, its great glistening stones covered by snow. The rem-
nants of a blackened roof, half fallen in, gave a stark con-
trast to the snow's purity. "To whom does it belong,
Aunt?"

Vivian's attention was easily diverted, as Greta had
quickly discovered early on in their visit. "Oh, that belongs
to the Frankensteins," she said, glancing out the carriage
window. "They no longer live there."

"Obviously," Rae said, sotto voce.

Greta hid a snort, and apparently their aunt had missed
Rae's little jab, since the baroness added, "Which is a great
blessing in itself. They were dreadful people, really. Just
dreadful. Always wandering about cemeteries."

Greta's eyes lit up. "They were vampire hunters, then?"

"*Vampyr* hunters?" Baroness Snowe's jaw dropped open. "Oh, you foolish child! Surely you don't believe in all that *vampyr* folderol? The Countess DeLuise is simply a great lover of fairy tales, and enjoys macabre intrigues. *Vampyrs* overrunning the town? Pure poppycock!"

Now Greta's temper began to stir. Pointedly, she replied, "You did mention that the Frankensteins preferred cemeteries."

Their aunt gave a sharp bark of laughter. "The family is eccentric. Mad as hatters, the lot. They're not the undead at all, merely your common bunch of criminals . . . grave robbers, actually. Shameful business, really. And disgusting. All those dead corpses." Vivian gave a shudder. "And if it wasn't graveyards, then their mad grandfather was running around the roof of their castle during thunderstorms, flying a kite with a key attached. A key attached! Can you imagine? The whole lot of them stark raving mad. Thank heavens the castle roof burned and villagers rioted several days later, upset over the Baron Frankenstein's latest invention. The family moved away shortly after that. It's been a good seven years."

"They sound like an intriguing family. I wish they were still here."

"Nonsense, Greta. If you've seen one grave robber, you've seen them all."

Greta shrugged her shoulders. It *was* a shame. The Frankensteins sounded amusing, and she'd bet they believed in vampires, witches and werewolves. They were probably a hundred times more interesting than the supercilious Prince von Hanzen.

"Now the only madman we must deal with is Wee Willie Winkie, who runs through the village in his tattered nightgown and hollers that cows are jumping over the moon," Aunt Vivian seethed. "Winkie's wee willie? That, I can assure, is quite madness enough."

# CHAPTER EIGHT

## The Devil Wears Prada Petticoats

The clock was ticking. It had been two days, and though the Snowe residence held an abundance of flowers from both Rae and Greta's various admirers, not one bouquet had been delivered from Prince von Hanzen or Baron Schortz. Rae was in high dudgeon over this slight, while Baroness Snowe was a combination of two things: a trifle ecstatic that her shallow niece hadn't received a tribute from either Baron Schortz or Prince von Hanzen, yet wondering if her own social standing was diminished by this slight.

There did, however, remain *Fürst* von Gelb. He had recently left after a visit where he preened and boasted about his great wealth and complimented Rae incessantly. Scowling at the flowers she held in her hand, the Baroness Snowe tersely stuck them in the bouquet she was arranging. She was of two minds about the elderly prince's interest in her niece. If Rae married the prince, then Vivian would definitely get her sister's goat, having managed to marry off the child in one season to Prussian royalty—a grand and glorious feat that would most definitely put her sister's oversized nose out of joint for many a year. On the other hand, if Rae managed to marry Prince von Gelb,

Vivian would be her niece's social inferior and would have to curtsey to her. The thought was thoroughly repugnant.

She glanced up as the two Grimm sisters entered the room in quiet conversation about their last visitor.

"Prince Gelb is quite enchanted by me. He's visited twice since the ball, and has sent over six dozen roses so far. Aunt Vivian did say that he was one of the wealthiest men in Prussia. And he does have such nice thick hair," Rae added.

"For a man of his age," her sister pointed out.

Vivian remarked, "*Ja*. Prince Gelb comes from a respectably royal line. And though an older man, I imagine he will still be able to do his husbandly duty—too often."

Rae thought about wifely duties. They were mysterious things rarely discussed in good company, something to do with thinking of one's country and bearing up stoically like a good little soldier. She was not totally ignorant, however, and knew that the aging prince would be with her in her bedchamber while she was in her nightclothes. Did this mean that he would be in his robe? Were his knees bony and knobby? She did so dislike knobby knees. A frown filled her face.

"Rae can do better than an aging roué with gout," Greta protested. The thought of her beautiful sister with a man old enough to be her grandfather left her stomach rather unsettled.

"I daresay she might if other princes of the realm or dukes of the duchies were about. But most are in Berlin, Munich, Paris or Rome right now. Besides, you shouldn't worry about his age. Prince Gelb probably doesn't have liver spots on his stomach . . . and he is very wealthy!"

"His stomach? Why would I see his stomach?" Rae asked, repelled.

"Why, to undress before bedtime. Some men prefer to perform their husbandly duties without a nightshirt," Baroness Snowe remarked, smoothly adjusting a particularly

fat red rose to her satisfaction and thrilled to see Rae turn
a particularly unattractive color of white. Greta's eyes had
grown wide.

"Naked, you say?" Rae squeaked. The old prince would
be naked as the day he was born and probably looking a
lot less grand in the all-together. This was not good. She
spoke, trying to resuscitate her flagging ambitions. "I would
have a fine carriage with gold wheels and six white horses.
I would be a grand princess . . . and he said he owns a
solid gold harp!"

"You don't like harp music. A better question is: will he
make your heart sing?" Greta said, her expression trou-
bled.

"Singing hearts? Why such romantic foolishness! Marriage has absolutely nothing to do with romance. Your silly
mother has certainly done you a great disservice if she's
led you to believe otherwise."

Confused, Rae narrowed her eyes in thought. Was wedlock to Prince Gelb truly what she wanted? The marriage
would help her family tremendously. She would happily be
linked to royalty through marriage, and admired even
more for her connections, her gowns, her slippers and her
jewels; but this wifely duty thing might be a bit more than
she could swallow. "Naked, you say?"

"Enough of this talk. This isn't an appropriate conversation for unmarried ladies," the baroness scolded, forgetting her part in the indelicate conversation. "If—and I do
stress the word *if*—Razel can bring Prince Gelb up to
scratch, then it will be quite the coup."

"Are you sure that is what you want, Rae? I don't trust the
man. Verily, I say. Why he wants to marry at his age is beyond me, for I hear he has an heir already, and that heir
has an heir. Perhaps he's putting on heirs." Greta scruti-
nized her sister, noting Rae's paleness. Prince Gelb would
never be the right man for her sister, even if he were King
of Prussia.

"There are other noblemen seeking wives," Rae remarked. "Such as Prince von Hanzen, even if he isn't as wealthy as Prince Gelb."

"I have heard that *Fürst* von Hanzen sent a dozen posies to Fräulein Hilda, Baron Mueller's daughter," the Baroness Snowe spoke up. "A pretty gel, but certainly not as lovely as you, my two nieces. I wonder why he's dismissed Rae. That's one reason I don't go in for those long engagements, you know. Pure folly. A man might learn the character of his intended before the wedding, and then where would we females be? Men should have years to get to know our habits, both good and bad, but always after the ceremony. Ah, Rae, you take the cake. He meets you for one night, and now nothing," she remarked. "Perhaps your misuse of his title offended him after all. This I must say: Prince von Hanzen is a man of much importance. To be insulted by you, a little nobody from nowhere, must have been more than his dignity could stand."

"Then he's certainly not much of a man. Everyone makes mistakes," Greta said stiffly, disliking the prince even more.

Had she been paying attention, Rae would have glared at her aunt, but her mind was occupied with dour thoughts of Baron Schortz and why the big buffoon hadn't sent her a bouquet or a note telling how much he admired her. "Perhaps he is ill from bad oysters. Or perhaps he has fallen off his horse and frozen to death in the snow," she suggested. He would make a terribly big snowman, and she wouldn't get her flowers from him or hear him call her Helen of Troy again. Men could be so horribly unpredictable.

"Who's speaking of death? Poppycock! I'll have no more about the dead, lest Greta use it as an excuse for indulging more galling inquiry into the *Nosferatu*," their aunt pronounced. "Haven't you listened to what we were saying? How can a dead man send flowers? Are you deaf as well as dull-witted?"

Greta interrupted before Rae could retort. "Perhaps Prince von Hanzen is already interested in this Miss Hilda. Perhaps that is why he sent her flowers."

"Ha. The gel is a mealymouthed little nitwit. The prince couldn't possibly be interested in her. Besides, as I remarked, she is merely pretty. Von Hanzen, when he weds, will wed a sophisticated beauty of impeccable breeding and manners."

Rae nodded. "He's a handsome man, and a prince as well. He will want the best." And the best would be she herself.

Her aunt concurred with her spoken words. "But of course. That goes without saying. Now, if you or Greta had a title and a fortune to go with your looks, the prince might look your way. But even with your connection to my own august self, I fear it isn't enough for him to choose either of you." She continued, condescendingly, "However, Baron Schortz would be a good catch for you. Not too handsome, not a prince, and he's a widower needing a wife for his children. But of course, Baron Schortz must have been disgusted by you as well. Perhaps you shall manage to keep your mouth shut at the next dinner party we attend. In fact, I insist, for I have always maintained that the saying is true: Familiarity breeds contempt."

Rae, who was sitting on the blue brocade couch, began tapping her foot upon the floor, her nostrils flaring. "Do you know how many swains I've had? And of course I do not allow them to become too familiar with my character! Good breeding requires this. But I can assure you quite firmly that they all adored me."

Greta bit her lip to keep from giggling. Rae was rewriting history just like their mother.

"Furthermore, I do not want that great oaf for a husband, baron or not. He's ugly and poor. I thought he would never leave me alone."

"Ah, yes, so interested in you that he has shown no interest beyond that night," their aunt retorted. "Whatever have you done to make these men change their minds so quickly? And Baron Schortz is not poor. In fact, he is more endowed with lands and coins than most princes. The money comes, of course, from his mother's side. They were related to Norwegian royalty, and had some Viking blood or some such thing. And we all know that Vikings were well off. Always have been and always will be."

"We do?" Greta asked.

"Yes. All those ill-gotten gains from pillaging and plundering in their early years. Built empires upon it. I feel quite sure Baron Schortz's family got their money the same way. Still, gold is gold, however it was gained."

Greta would have argued the point, but Rae, having caught the gist of the conversation, was shaking her head. "Baron Schortz is royalty as well? But he seems such a common churl."

"He's not royalty," their aunt replied.

"But you said his mother is related to Norwegian royalty, which would make his blood blue as well," Rae argued. "How can such a buffoon be wealthy and royal at the same time?" And the fool man had been besotted, so where were her roses? Surely he had not taken her cool indifference to mean that she found him annoying! Although, at the time, unaware of all the circumstances, she had.

Their aunt waved her hand in dismissal. "His mother was related to *Norwegian* royalty. Which is certainly nothing like Prussian royalty."

Rae just shook her head. Royalty was royalty, whether one was a Norwegian king, a Prussian duke or an English prince. Her aunt was talking utter rot.

"He would have done for you. Such a shame that he's lost interest. The poor man loved his wife greatly. He suffered quite a bit at her death. In fact, the countess's dinner was the first time I have seen him so animated in some time. But if you've disgusted him, then you've disgusted him. And it can't be helped, although it puts me in an untenable situation. How am I to find a husband for you, Rae, if all men take a dislike to you after only one meeting? No wonder your poor mother sent you to another country for marriage. I'm sure you turned all the local men against you."

Oh boy, Greta thought, the blades were out. There would be battle over that comment. She opened her mouth to intervene as Rae came up off her seat and stood, hands on hips. At the same time, a maid came into the room bearing a vase filled with water. Rae bumped into the young maid, which caused her to lurch forward and trip. The maid spilled the water all over their aunt's ottoman, upon which happened to be resting the fat white Persian cat. The water splashed the cat, causing it to screech and leap upon their aunt. The salon was soon filled with their aunt's cries, mixed with the sodden cat's howls, along with the maid's terrified apologies.

Greta managed to hold her laughter to a minimum. Rae, however, was bent over like an old woman, hooting, her anger forgotten. Anything that made her aunt look foolish lifted her spirits, even more so than a dozen well-paid compliments to her beauty.

"You stupid gel! You may now join the ranks of the great unwashed and unemployed! My poor little Miss Muffet—all wet!" the baroness screamed at the poor frightened maid.

Rae, who had heard the maid earlier in the week talking about her sick mother and a house filled with younger siblings, knew why the maid's face was the color of fresh milk. Her giggles subsiding, she turned to her aunt. "'Tis my fault, Aunt Vivian. I tripped her accidentally."

"You foolish, wicked gel. And you stupid maid, quit crying and come clean me up. I still intend to let you go, but you can clean up your mess first."

Greta and Rae both glared at their aunt. Mistreating servants was something they were used to observing at home. Their mother often complained and yelled; at the same time, she never fired the help.

"Come, I'll assist," Rae said. "And I'll help you pack. I'll be sorry to see you go, since you have such a talent with hair. But I'm sure my aunt won't mind sharing her maid with me, or hiring me another hairdresser while I'm here."

Baroness Snowe stopped mopping her cat and glanced from the still sniffling maid to her least favorite niece. "Astrid dresses hair? Why didn't I know this?"

"Well, I needed help the other night, but your own maid was busy. Astrid volunteered to help, and you know what a masterpiece she created." Rae was lying. She had been doing her own hair for years, since she trusted no one to be able to duplicate the artful hairdos she managed to create herself. After all, her hair was her crowning glory.

"Yes, your maid is inspired," Greta quickly added, already understanding the situation. "Never have I seen Rae's hair look better. And as long as it is, why, it sometimes takes hours and hours just to do her hair. Perhaps, Aunt, you wouldn't mind your maid doing Rae's hair first. Or you could dress maybe an hour or two or three earlier than usual, so that your maid will have time to attend to Rae's hair. After all, knee-length hair must be washed and dried, and then just the arranging of it can be quite time consuming."

"I had no idea," their aunt remarked frostily, a deep scowl creasing her brow. "You should have said something sooner. Why am I just hearing about this?"

"Rae meant to bring it up, but Astrid solved the problem," Greta volunteered, her quick mind at the ready. Although she didn't lie all that often, a good deed was a good deed and a lie was a lie, and sometimes the twain did meet.

"Very well," their aunt sniffed. "I guess she may stay. Now, clean up this mess immediately. I must attend to my little Miss Muffet. Poor dear. I hope she doesn't catch cold. A cat with a cold is too much to bear. Do be ready to go on time tonight. I absolutely hate arriving at a musicale late. It is so plebian."

Their aunt then sailed from the room in a flounce of material, her soggy cat clutched to her ample bosom.

Astrid smiled weakly. *"Danke.* You saved my position. But I know nothing about coiffures."

Rae and Greta both grinned, with Rae saying cheerfully, "I know that and you know that, but Aunt Vivian doesn't know that. We escaped by a hair."

# CHAPTER NINE

## Mozart and Whalebone Corsets

'Twas the night of the musicale, and all through the house, people were chattering away while Rae listened, a frown on her pretty face. Greta stood nearby, spellbound, her mind working furiously.

"The corpse was gone."

"They opened the grave and no one was there!"

"What must Herr Choplin think? His mother's body is missing."

"The town's overrun by *vampyr*. We are doomed, I tell you. Doomed! Where is my vinaigrette?"

"Missing corpse, empty coffins and vampires. Oh my," Greta whispered.

Rae bopped her sister with her fan, and glared at her as they were ushered to their seats. The room settled down for a long and delightful winter's entertainment. Soon no one was stirring within the house, as all were listening in rapt attention to the odd little man with the bizarre hairdo. His mastery of the piano was riveting, and his nimble fingers skipped across the keys. Crashing sounds as well as soothing melodies poured forth.

Yet, Rae wasn't spellbound by Herr Mozart, for she had other things on her mind. Three other things, in fact. The first occurred when Herr Mozart sat down to play and

someone had the misfortune to request Beethoven. The
little man had jumped to his feet and begun to curse. At
least Rae thought he'd been cursing, but she didn't understand because he was speaking in German. The lady
seated next to her swooned, at any rate. Rae had decided
then and there that she really must learn the language,
since their curse words seemed pithier.

After the lady was revived and Herr Mozart placated, the
musicale had begun in earnest. The banging music quickly
turned melancholy and transported one to heights of fantasy. But another thing happened that kept Rae from thoroughly enjoying the music and the Italian singer who
accompanied Herr Mozart: *He* was there. The big lummox
with Norwegian royal blood flowing through his big, blue
baronic veins. And he actually ignored her very lovely self.
It was galling to no end! In fact, it didn't matter that other
men were admiring her and comparing her blue eyes to a
summer's day or her hair to spun moonlight. It didn't matter that a duke complimented her dress. Baron Schortz
had merely nodded at her once the whole evening, then
turned his back on her. On *her*! It wasn't to be borne. The
man was even stupider than she'd thought.

Rae tried to speak to Greta about her dilemma, but Greta
was busy concocting cemetery plans for later that night.
Cemetery plans that included Rae—though Rae wouldn't
go. Not on her very desirable life, Rae mused; and that was
the third and final reason Rae sat stewing in her chair as
the heavenly music flowed around her. She didn't intend to
go haunting cemeteries in the dead of night looking for the
undead. Just because some silly woodcutter's mother's
body had vanished from its grave and had the town in an
uproar, was not a good enough reason to be curious. Greta
could coax her till the cows came home, but Rae was not
blindly following her this time. Trolls under a bridge in
daylight were one thing; vampires and empty graves at
midnight were quite another.

When Herr Mozart and the singer took a break to sample

the buffet, Countess DeLuise took advantage of the moment to start her usual rave about rampaging *vampyr*. Hungrily, Greta listened to each and every word, and began to discuss the new occurrence with glee.

Rae glared at her sister. Verily, Greta's behavior was most vexing and unladylike. A missing corpse was most assuredly not a reason to frequent graveyards. In fact, it was decidedly a reason *not* to visit them. Unhappily, her big sister was just foolish enough to do so. Just curious enough to try and find one of the bloodsucking leeches so that she could write home about it. And to think: their father thought Greta was the clever one!

What a horrid surprise he would be in for when Rae wrote and told him that a nasty old vampire had bitten Greta. He would be horrified, and her mother would have apoplexy, and it would all be Greta's fault. Instead of concentrating on trying to trap a spouse, Greta was knee-deep in fairy tales, and at the pace she was going she'd soon be up to her neck. She'd never get married . . . but, then, she would be dead so it wouldn't really matter. Of course, their mother would blame it all on Rae, anyway. Her morbid thoughts caused her to send her sister, seated two chairs down, a look fraught with bitter resentment as the recital again began.

Greta had been listening to the piano's opening notes while at the same time plotting out her strategy to visit graveyards. When her sister sent her such a glance, however, Greta turned her attention to Rae. The girl was obviously annoyed with her plan, so it might be better if she didn't come to the cemetery. Yet Greta didn't feel entirely comfortable going alone. She didn't feel that either she or her sister would be in any real danger. Their parents had not raised a fool; a spinster, perhaps, who loved legends, but never a fool. With every practicality, she would undertake precautions to make sure that if they did encounter the undead, she would be more than ready. And she could hardly wait to write to her brothers and sisters about this startling and intriguing development.

Suddenly, Greta's plotting was interrupted by a pretty, plump young woman who scurried into the large salon and approached the piano, daggers shooting from her eyes. Greta had been introduced to the Baroness Wagoner and knew her to be the widow of some obscure lesser noble. Wrathfully she stopped and stood literally screaming at Herr Mozart, holding a woman's whalebone corset in each hand. Both corsets were of the finest make, with tiny emeralds sewn into the bodice and upon the hem. They were both ivory, and decorated with fine Belgium lace. Unfortunately, their appearance was ruined by big black musical notes. Row upon row of musical notes.

The audience listened unabashedly as the baroness berated Herr Mozart for ruining her lovely new undergarments.

"Philistine!" Herr Mozart shouted. He quickly grabbed the corsets and cradled them close to his chest.

"You mad little man!" Baroness Wagoner shrieked. "These are not the only undergarments you have ruined with your ghastly little sonatas."

Herr Mozart, who was several inches shorter than the raving baroness, still managed to look down his nose at her. "That is a little nightgown music. It's an opus!" He pointed grandly to his mistress's underwear. "Who cares for such inconsequential things as ruined garments when genius is at work? You should be down on your knees thanking the heavens that your corsets received such tribute."

Greta heard a man behind her whisper something to the effect of, "I've heard she's been down on her knees quite a bit. Only, I should rather think Mozart would be doing the thanking."

The two men chortled at the jest, while Greta pondered their words, wondering if it had something to do with husband and wife duties. But their mother had never mentioned being on your knees for anything besides praying.

Her musings were interrupted once again by Herr Mozart,

who was dramatically announcing to the room in general, "My nerves are overwrought by this demented and ungrateful woman. I can play no more." And then, waving his hands, he left the room in a royal huff, even though Greta doubted he had a royal bone in his body. Baroness Wagoner swiftly followed, finally realizing the folly of her rage. The room immediately erupted in gossip. Yes, tongues were definitely wagging tonight.

The girls' aunt, her nose in the air with disapproval, made much ado about protecting her nieces from such lewd and gauche behavior; but to any who looked, her eyes were alight with victory. How fortunate that they had attended the musicale tonight, which the baroness had almost not deigned to attend. What utterly marvelous gossip she would now have to discuss with her dearest friends, all twenty of them, on the morrow. And on that wicked little note, Baroness Snowe ushered the two Grimm sisters out into the chilly night.

Rae tapped her foot eagerly while waiting for the carriage to take them home. She should be enjoying another successful evening and boasting of her many conquests, but she was torn up by the exception of one man who was too simple to live. Unfortunately, Baron Schortz hadn't died in a snowstorm and been turned into a snowman as she had hoped. And he hadn't sent flowers or written odes to her eyes, feet or glorious hair. Instead, he had basically ignored her.

"Just who does he think he is? If the baron thinks being ignored bothers me . . . well, he's in for a big surprise," she muttered under her breath, glad that her aunt was gossiping with another of her cronies as the coach approached.

Greta stood to Rae's side, no doubt plotting strategies of how best to convince her younger sister to accompany her. Rae spoke up first: "I couldn't care one whit about some loutish Prussian—or graveyards." She said the last with a definite emphasis, just loud enough for her eldest sister to hear.

Their aunt hailed their conveyance, and Rae caught Greta's studious glance. It was one, she knew, that boded evil.

"That poor old woman's corpse is missing. Everyone was talking about it tonight," Greta coaxed, watching her aunt's plump backside disappear into the carriage.

"It was most likely misplaced," Rae replied.

Greta gaped. "The grave was opened, Rae, after the body was laid to rest. It was not *misplaced*. Vampires, I'm betting." She nodded emphatically, lifting her gown to step up into the carriage. "And I'm going to the cemetery tonight come hell or high water."

"High water? More like blood. What with all the deranged, undead men leaping out of coffins and trying to bite you. Well, just go ahead and be drunk to death," Rae hissed at her sister's back. She would be old and gray before anyone found her wandering around a cemetery at midnight.

# CHAPTER TEN

Everybody Loves Rae, Mon, Even Vampires

Several hours later found Rae neither old nor gray but standing in the middle of a cemetery glaring at her sister, with more than one smelly necklace of garlic around her neck. "How do I let you talk me into these things?" she asked. "Sometimes, just sometimes, I think I may not be very bright. And I smell like some week-old Italian dish. It's so unladylike."

Greta chuckled and moved slowly, looking for disturbances in the snow around the graves. Dense shadows lay beyond her lantern light, which was something of a ghostly glow. They passed monuments of black marble and white granite, and dense, shadowed ebony spaces in between. Thick snow covered the ground. This was definitely a dark fairyland made of mist, magic and hopefully a measly monster or two. Or so Greta hoped.

Turning to the left, Rae noted that several large crypts rose out of the darkness. Lantern light revealed their shapes, but no distinguishing marks.

"Nonsense, Rae. You smell like a good bowl of soup—and who says you aren't bright?"

"Me, since I let you prey on my guilt so I would come here tonight. I shall just die if anyone should see me dressed in my old gown, with my old boots and breeches underneath. No lady, especially one seeking a husband, would ever appear this way. What if one of my suitors should see me?"

"Oh, fiddlesticks. What would a suitable suitor be doing out here in the dead of night in a freezing cold graveyard? Unless he's a vampire," Greta admitted. "But then he's *quite* unsuitable. Besides, Rae, the better gentlemen have more on their minds than what you are wearing."

"Bite your tongue. Gentlemen have always admired my gowns."

"Not the gold gown," Greta remarked, "and not Timothy Sterne."

"Timothy's a dunce," Rae scoffed. She carefully made her way around a large marble tombstone, noting that the lantern barely kept the utter blackness away from them. "Greta, I really don't like this. I want to go back to our aunt's home now!" She stomped her foot angrily, and managed to merely sink deeper into the icy snow. "Dash it all!" Then, noticing her sister hadn't stopped, she hurried over the white bumps of snow-covered earth to catch up.

"I will never forgive you for this, Greta," she complained. "You know I don't like graveyards, even when I know somebody there! I don't like wearing breeches under my gown. I don't like monsters. I don't like big teeth. And I hate garlic!" Rae grumbled as she glanced nervously around. She hated the thought of the undead living in moldering ruins, hated the idea of crypts and eyes burning with the flames of Hades, staring at her while she was unaware. "Here I am, among demonic monsters, all because you're mad. Sometimes, family loyalty is too high a price to pay. I can feel their beady demented eyes staring at me behind those gravestones. Let's leave, please, before a vampire attacks us!"

"Do stop your grumbling," Greta snapped. "And stop whining about having to wear breeches when they are much more comfortable than skirts. We certainly couldn't have climbed down the trellis from my room in our gowns and hoops. Come now, sister dear, you would have been bored stiff staying at home," she added. "Besides, look on the bright side. This cemetery is very close to our aunt's home. So we didn't have to walk far in this weather."

"Pooh, I should be sound asleep," Rae groaned, her eyes continually searching the encroaching shadows that might hide big shiny teeth. A faint shiver of fear snaked through her. "And I certainly wouldn't be freezing to death in this graveyard. Of course, I won't freeze if I get sucked to death first. I can't believe I'm here. This is some mad dream, isn't it? Rather like when you dream you're naked and think you're dressed, but you aren't. And you're at some marvelous dance and everyone is staring at you . . ."

Greta stopped looking amongst the tombstones long enough to hold her lantern high in the direction of her sister, staring at her with an expression of dumb amazement. "How is looking for vampires in a cemetery like being stark naked at a ball? Really, Rae, sometimes you get the queerest notions."

"Must you argue philosophy at a time like this? We might be vampire bait at any time. I hope our brothers understand our sacrifice and feel guilty when I am dead or undead, sacrificed on the altar of their monstrous ambitions and your own. I hope they can't sleep at night due to nightmares of me haunting graveyards with really big horrid teeth. They had better appreciate how I gave my life's blood so that you may write to them of some silly fable or some such nonsense."

"I don't know why you're so worried." Greta sighed. "I've brought garlic, stakes, and we're wearing enough silver crosses to out-holy the Pope. I have taken every precaution for meeting one of the fiendish monsters."

"I only hope it impresses the vampires," Rae retorted, stepping around a pretty marble angel statue and anxiously fingering her garlic (all four rows of it). "I beg you, let's leave at once."

"I'll protect you, Rae. I promise you that."

Rae shook her head. "You'd better, Greta. I attract men

like flies. If there are vampires here, they are going to want to drink my blood first. Of course, after draining me, they'll probably be too full to attack you. So I guess I'm protecting you in a way."

With a modicum of civility, Greta managed not to berate her sister. The hour was late, the graveyard apparently empty of blood-drinking fiends, her feet were freezing and she was tired of Rae's conceit. Enough was enough. "Perhaps they'll be female vampires and ignore you altogether. Or, mayhap, the male vampire might prefer me to you. Not everyone falls at your feet, you know."

Rae was incensed. "How dare you talk to me like that? If there is a male vampire here, I know he's dying to drink my blood. In fact, I'll go so far as to predict he'll be in immediate bloodlust. That's why I'm so afraid. You're pretty, Greta, but alas, you are definitely on the shelf—and rather thin to boot. I highly doubt that any self-respecting, red-blooded vampire would choose you over me. I, on the other hand, am like a vampire beacon, driving them mad with desire and undead passion."

Greta would have laughed if she wasn't so annoyed. "Undead passions? What rubbish. Your conceit is really getting out of hand. In fact, I am going to tell you something that I wasn't going to reveal at all." She halted and stared hard at her younger sister. "I overheard a conversation between Baron Schortz and Prince von Hanzen the night of our first ball here. The reason the prince hasn't sent flowers is that he finds you a vain bit of baggage."

Rae halted dead in her tracks, her fears forgotten. "I don't believe you. You are as bad as Taylor, making up stories out of thin air."

"No, I'm not. I'm also not proud of the fact that I was eavesdropping and heard ill of myself as well. But I did hear, and now the words will always be there," Greta said unhappily. She would never forget the prince's caustic comments about her looks paling into insignificance beside her sister's. "Prince von Hanzen also warned his friend away from you. He asserted that you were shallow and would make the baron miserable."

"You're lying; you have to be. Men don't speak ill of me. They worship me." Rae's expression was thunderstruck, but that quickly changed to hurt. Suddenly the baron's defection made sense.

"No," Greta replied, starting to feel a twinge of guilt at her sister's expression. Rae looked deeply hurt. Surely she didn't really care for the prince beyond his royal blood, his antecedents, his handsome looks and his coin.

"How dare he say I'm shallow? Why, I'm a very deep person. I have even forced myself to read Shakespeare on occasion."

"Yes, I remember. Whenever you wanted to impress your more scholarly or poetic swains."

Rae nodded, uttering, "A lady has to look impressed when they talk about all those dead Greek philosophers or that Donne character who's always writing about man is an island. Why would anyone want to be an island? I bet the nasty old Prince von Hanzen reads Shakespeare. Just who is he to criticize me when we met on such short acquaintance? Why, he doesn't know my character at all! Just because he's royalty, he thinks he can insult a gentle lady with a pure and kind heart and genteel manners. Bloody hell, may the devil take his rotten little soul!"

Greta lowered her lantern, feeling even more guiltily. Despite her discomfort and her fears, Rae had come out tonight to find this blood-sucking monster with her so that Greta wouldn't have to go alone. "Forget his words, Rae. The man is of no consequence to you."

"That handsome prince . . . he warned his oafish friend away," she spluttered. "And though the baron is too big and all, I did admire his frankness. Now the big ox is ignoring me, all because of that abominable Prince von Hanzen. I'll show them both. I'll no longer allow any hint of shallowness in my character. Inside I'll be so deep, people will think I'm an ocean." Rae turned to Greta. The lantern light glowed softly upon her face, and her blue eyes were bright with unshed tears. "Just wait and see if I don't!"

Greta opened her mouth to comfort her sister, hating that she had allowed her annoyance at Rae to overcome her good nature. But before she spoke, a ghastly scream rent the air, causing both sisters to clutch at their crosses and garlic. Their flesh was creeping, and their hearts pounded in their breasts. The lantern swayed back and forth due to Greta's trembling hand, casting shadows upon snow-crusted tombstones and branches bare of leaves.

"Vampire?" Rae asked, her voice trembling in fear.

"It very well could be. But do remember, sister, that I've never heard a vampire before," Greta admitted, her breathing fast. She felt both jubilance that she might make the discovery of a lifetime, and a direness of spirit. If it were one of the undead come to life, she might have compromised her sister's and her own life with her unrelenting curiosity.

"We should leave now!" Rae's voice was filled with fear; it had flooded her system, leaving her shivering in utter terror. "I do so hate screaming. It upsets my nerves."

"But if the scream wasn't a vampire's, then it might be someone in trouble. Perhaps we should offer help."

"If anybody screams in a graveyard in the dead of night, Greta, you can be most assured that it means trouble," Rae pronounced nervously, her eyes wide. She held a small stake in one hand and her gown in the other, ready to flee at the slightest sound. She was suddenly glad to be wearing breeches and her riding boots. "It was a very scary scream. They most likely do need help."

"That would be the heroic thing to do," Greta replied, her face a mask of indecision.

"Yes, it would," Rae conceded, her eyes scanning the darkness. If they went to help, they might both die—and that meant she would die unmarried, which was unforgivable.

As the two Grimm sisters hesitated, wondering what to

do, another chilling scream rent the air. Greta had eight crosses lodged in various parts of her dress or around her throat, but after hearing this, she suddenly felt like she needed another ten. Or mayhap a hundred. She turned to her sister. "I'd never forgive myself if anything happened to you."

"N-neither would I," Rae stammered.

And with that, they sprinted down a path back toward their aunt's home, their footsteps crunching through the hard-packed snow. Those footsteps sounded very loud indeed in the silence of the graveyard.

They didn't run far before the two sisters paused to catch a much-needed breath, and it was at that moment Greta saw a shadow rise from the crypt to the right. This time, she herself screamed, and she placed herself in front of Rae. But her scream was of excitement.

Her heart was pounding. "A vampire. I've found a vampire! Just wait until Jakob and Will hear!" At the same time, Greta suddenly realized that the vampire might be hungry, and that they might not live to see the dawn. Most certainly they would not have the time to compose a letter home. She felt a bleak spear of despair. Poor Rae, she might have been led to her doom before she became a princess.

Rae squeezed her eldest sister's arm, closing her eyes tightly, hoping that by doing this cowardly but smart thing she would miss viewing the big-fanged monster. If she couldn't see him, perchance he wouldn't be real and wouldn't bite her enchantingly beautiful neck.

The shadow moved closer, followed by another a few steps behind. "Oh, gracious, I do believe that I've found a nest of them. This town is overrun with vampires like the countess warned," Greta exclaimed, her tone conveying both awe and dread. "I've found vampires. Forgive me, Rae."

Feeling Rae behind her shaking in fear, Greta fought the urge to scream hysterically and run headlong into the night. She had to protect her sister at all costs! And she also couldn't wait to get a closer look at one of the *Nosferatu*. Her fascination was unreasonable. It was foolish, most possibly deadly. Yet Greta couldn't seem to overcome her morbid curiosity.

With eyes squeezed tightly shut, Rae snapped, "You must be so proud. They could put that on your tombstone: *She found the monster that ate her*!"

"Oh, dear, it's actually quite thrilling. Quite the time of my life," Greta gasped, her breaths becoming jerky. "It's enough to make one swoon."

"If you faint and leave me alone with two fiendish undead, I'll kill you, Greta!" Rae replied. Then, realizing that with her eyes closed she couldn't help defend her older sister, she managed to open them slightly. Her heart pounded as if it wanted out of her chest. Tightly Rae clutched her stake, wondering just how one went about staking the undead.

Rae started bravely around her sister, feeling sick to her stomach, so that they could stand side by side in Grimm acceptance of their fate. They would fight with the armor of familial love, a helmet of the cross (or crosses), a shield of garlic and a wooden stake of a sword. "I wonder if they felt like this in the Crusades when facing the infernal."

"That's *infidels*," Greta remarked, amused in spite of the fear rising through her body like mist at dawn. Once again, she shoved Rae protectively behind her.

Then the remarkable happened, as it did in all fairy tales. The fickle fingers of Fate intervened, and in a good way. Before Greta could faint or Rae murder her eldest sister for leading them into this folly, the shadow came close enough for the lantern light to reveal the monster's features. Those features were pretty handsome.

# CHAPTER ELEVEN

## Ask the Dust (If It Answers Back, RUN)

"Ah, look what we have here, Fen, Tweedledee and Tweed-ledumb," Rolpe remarked to his companion with a studied insouciance.

Stunned, Greta gasped, and Rae quit looking through her fingers to stare hard around her sister's shoulders.

Why, he's not only an extremely rude prince; he's a blood-sucking monster, Greta thought to herself, pleased she had decided against him if still miffed by his rejection. Her mother might have welcomed the prince into the family, but she knew her father would draw the line at a vampire.

Fen shook his head at the sight of the sisters Grimm standing in a cemetery in the dead of night, both wearing apprehensive expressions. "What are you ladies doing here?" His heart twisted at the sight of Miss Rae; she did so remind him of his late wife. But his late wife had owned a heart of gold; Rae was merely beautiful on the outside, and tarnished on the inside.

Rae remained silent, mortified that the baron should see her in such a ghastly state. What had she been thinking, following her sister out here?

The men walked toward them, and Greta felt a chill of foreboding envelop her. Surely the most handsome man she had ever seen wasn't undead, she thought, already forgetting her intense dislike of him. Meticulously, as they walked closer and into the lantern light, she searched for evidence of fangs or bloodlust. This was no easy task, because she really wasn't certain what face bloodlust would wear.

"The baron just asked what you are doing here," Prince von Hanzen prompted. His tone was harsher than he'd intended, but he found himself infuriated by the thought of the elder Miss Grimm risking life and limb to haunt cemeteries at night. Surely she was not the grave robber they were after. That was almost too ludicrous to think, much less believe. Yet, here she was in a place where ghouls, vampires and other creatures prowled. Fortunately, in the Black Forest, whenever something strange was in the neighborhood, he and Fen were the men you were gonna call.

Several moments passed in silence, with all four staring hard at each other. Finally Greta spoke. "We were visiting the grave of a relative," she said. Holding her lantern high, she carefully searched the men's faces again for a hint of fangs or evil intent.

"Tweedle-who?" Rae asked, continuing to gaze past her sister's shoulder. "And what are *you* doing here?" She asked the question of the hulking oaf. Then, aside, she whispered to her sister, "I don't think this is good, Greta. Sane gentlemen don't walk around graveyards at night. At least, they don't in England. Do you think this is some queer Prussian custom?" She certainly wouldn't be surprised to discover that Baron Schortz was one of those creepy, cursed undead things. Even now he was glaring at her with his beady little eyes. Well, perhaps they weren't really beady or little. They were rather large and finely shaped.

Drawing her cloak closer, Rae shivered and felt as if the darkness was closing in around her. Next time Greta came up with one of these bizarre excursions, she was going to stay in the comfort of her own bedchamber, under the nice warm covers, and not humiliate herself in front of the Prussian nobility.

Ignoring the younger sister's silliness, Rolpe narrowed his eyes and glared at Greta. "Visiting a relative's grave at midnight, alone? Why, what an outrageous piece of nonsense!"

The man wore his arrogance like a second skin, and Greta's ire grew. "It seemed as good a time as any. No crowds to gawk," she replied carefully, fingering the Van Helsing-brand stake in her pocket and ignoring the prince's disbelief and scorn. She studied von Hanzen, deciding that he didn't look like a bloodsucking fiend; but then she had never met one face-to-face before. She decided that he merely looked displeased, and not in the throes of any passionate bloodlust.

"Where is your aunt?" Fen asked, his tone surprised. He couldn't believe the Grimm sisters were here. It was bizarre, odd and strangely fascinating. He'd have thought such a delicate flower as Miss Rae Grimm would faint at the thought of entering a cemetery at night.

"I imagine she's at home," Greta replied, edging back slowly and pushing against Rae, who was still peering around her shoulder.

"Where you should be," Rolpe retorted sharply. He extended an arm. "Come. We'll escort you home."

"I don't think so," Greta said.

"It's not safe here," Fen stated sternly, his eyes focused on the younger sister. "You'd be surprised at what can come out at night, especially here." He edged nearer to Miss Rae Grimm, only to see her frown at him. He halted abruptly, cursing his protective instincts toward the little vixen.

"I know. We heard a scream," Rae said, glaring mulishly at the baron. "From the direction you came." Let him get out of that one, she thought waspishly. Obviously the man was up to no good in a cemetery. Only someone with evil intentions would come out on a night like this. She'd completely forgotten her own haunting of the graves.

"We were riding home and heard the scream ourselves,"

Fen answered. But, how dare the younger Grimm question his honor? How dare she look at him as if he were dirt beneath her dainty foot? His expression becoming dour, he added severely, "Fortunately it was only the gatekeeper, who'd had a rat run across his toes."

The younger Grimm sister was eyeing him, and it appeared she was studying his teeth, obviously finding fault with them. "The gatekeeper?" she asked suspiciously. To her elder sister, she whispered, "Sounds like an unlikely story to me. Do you see any fangs?"

Rolpe snorted, and Fen cracked a grin. "Fangs?" Fen asked. Then, turning to his friend, he laughed. "She thinks we're *vampyr!*"

Rolpe acknowledged his good friend's words with his own sharp bark of laughter. "So it would seem, and so it appears that Miss Greta Grimm is not only a liar but also has a vivid imagination. As for her younger sister, she's just plain foolish. But I will be gentlemanly enough to admit that the Black Forest does that to people, filling their head with silly superstitions. I should also like to add that, if we were the dreaded *Nosferatu,* you two would no longer be visiting graves but in one."

With lightning-quick reflexes Greta pulled out her stake, saying, "I don't think—"

Rolpe divested her of her stake, a superior look on his face. He noted how angry she was, her deep gray eyes burning. He also noticed that her crimson riding cloak had fallen open, exposing the bodice of a gown which had slipped a bit lower. This revealed the tops of her breasts, which were very white. Rolpe grimaced as he ignored the reaction of his nether regions.

"That was very ungentlemanly of you," Greta remarked wrathfully, rubbing her wrist.

"Extremely," Rae agreed, stepping out from behind her sister and glaring. "Apologize to my sister at once, you big brute!" She slapped the prince's arm, but before she could hit him again, Fen stepped up and yanked her away.

As Rae stared up at him, a chill stole through her. The look the baron gave her was truly frosty. Glancing back at her gown, she wanted to cry.

"Oh, no!" she said. "This night has been a complete disaster. You've stepped on my gown and torn the flounce, you oaf." Then, turning back to the prince, she protested heatedly, "And you not only manhandled my sister, but you called her a liar. That is a vile accusation, since Greta is not the fibber of the family. That would be Taylor, our youngest sister. Greta is the bloodhound, always searching out the unexplainable. If there is a fairy or a troll or some fiendish vampire, she'll find it, have no doubt."

Pleased, Greta smiled at her younger sister's defense. She hated to admit it, but Rae wasn't the only one in the family who enjoyed compliments.

Startled, Fen let go of Rae, stepping back, and both men shook their heads in unison.

Vexed, Rolpe scolded harshly, "As I was saying, if we were the undead, you two would long be drained of life, in spite of your stakes and garlic and crosses."

"Of course," Fen added, "there is no such thing as the *Nosferatu,* so you ladies are safe from them. But not, however, from human men, the kind of ruffians who would take advantage of you, stake or no stake, garlic or no garlic."

"If they could stand the stink," Rolpe remarked. His sensitive nose had caught the smell of garlic long before he and his friend approached the sisters. "Besides, ladies—and I use the term loosely—in this cemetery, the rumors of undeath are greatly exaggerated."

"How dare you mock us? Everyone tonight at the musicale was conversing about that woodcutter's mother's grave being disturbed. Countess DeLuise announced boldly that vampires are everywhere in Wolfach. Yet you pretend an open grave and a missing body is just foolish nonsense? Well, I am no fool!" Greta growled.

Rolpe admired her profile, composed of a high forehead and an elegantly angled jaw that hinted at her determination, but he scowled at her assessment. "That remains to be seen, if you choose to listen to a dotty old woman with bats in her belfry," he retorted, arrogantly raising a noble brow. "But there is another explanation."

"What?" both sisters asked at precisely the same moment.

"Grave robbers," the prince answered.

"Death takes everything, but grave robbing is just bad manners," Rae remarked. When both men glanced at her, incredulous looks on their faces, she added petulantly, "Well, it is extremely rude . . . and probably forbidden by the church as well." She added the last comment, feeling ingenious for having chosen surer ground.

Rolpe gave Fen a look, then stated with authority, "Let us go. This is not my idea of pleasure, to stand around in the freezing snow with two lack-witted ladies who lie through their pretty teeth."

Greta stared at the handsome prince. He thought her teeth were pretty? For some strange reason, this made her heart beat faster. Of course, he also thought her a liar with a shallow sister. And that she was lack-witted. Still, pretty teeth were a nice thing to have. And this man would know, as he really was too pleasing to look upon for his own good—just like Rae.

"You cretin! We are not lack-witted! Why, back in England, men were lined up for miles to court our favors. At every dinner party, they fought to have the honor of being seated next to us because of our clever conversation," Rae announced, seething.

Fen managed to look less than impressed, and again Rolpe ignored Rae's comments. He took Greta's hand, pulling her along. "We need to pick up our horses at the cemetery gate."

Rae watched the arrogant prince drag her sister away, then waited for Baron Schortz to lend her his arm. He did not. He simply followed the others, and Rae was left to trudge after him, her anger growing. After a few feet of following in his footsteps, she stopped.

"I am not stepping another foot without some form of escort," she announced. "My flounce is torn, thanks to you, and my feet are frozen. My skirts feel like they weigh a ton, and a gentleman would not leave a lady to flounder in the snow."

Fen stopped, hesitated a moment, then turned back to Rae. She really was a little shrew. He was fortunate to have found out before he did something stupid like falling in love with her. Reluctantly, he held up his arm, saying, "Come along, then. My feet are cold, too. You aren't the only uncomfortable one."

"Really!" Rae huffed as she walked forward and placed her hand upon his arm. "I can't believe a Prussian baron is so lacking in common courtesy."

"What would you know of common courtesy?" Fen snapped back.

Abstractly he observed her expressions. The first was of shock, followed quickly by pique and then outrage. This told him quite plainly that the lady was unaccustomed to set-downs. His own expression remained grim, which seemed in keeping with the general flavor of events. If she expected him to grovel at her feet like some young pup, she was sadly mistaken. He was a grown man, forged in and hardened by the fires of lost love and responsibility, burdened at a young age with the gambling debts of his deceased father. It had taken Fen a good seven years to restore the estates, and another nine to make them prosperous.

For a moment anger crackled in the air between them, and Rae realized she had underestimated her adversary. "I don't follow what you mean. I have been brought up to respect decorum and society's rules," she said, her thoughts tumbling over and over. The baron was so hostile; it surprised her. She raised both brows, her mouth forming a perfect moue of distaste.

He snorted loudly and glanced around the graveyard. "Yes, I can see how well brought up you are."

"I see nothing irregular about my appearance," Rae lied through her teeth, cursing that the past hour had been such a sobering experience. Still, she wouldn't let the baron know that her nerves were stretched to the breaking point. She doubted he had the sensitivity to notice, and she certainly wouldn't give him the satisfaction of pointing it out. "I can't believe that you are so rude and so shallow."

"*Me*, shallow? If that isn't the pot calling the kettle black." Fen wanted nothing more than to turn her over his knee and give her bottom a swat. She was more than a shrewish witch; she was a completely vainglorious monster. He was not a vain man, and he knew he wasn't considered classically handsome, but women did find him attractive. Before he wed, he'd never lacked for lovers. Yet Miss Rae Grimm's comments had severely damaged his self-esteem, and he resented her greatly for it.

"Don't look so stunned. If the big boot fits then wear it—if you can wrench it out of your mouth." She stabbed a finger in his direction, her lovely blue eyes flashing. "Just because your friend warned you away from me by saying unkind and untrue things, well, I would have thought you man enough to think your own thoughts and feel your own feelings."

Almost stumbling, Fen caught himself, amazed at her pithy chastisement. His expression turned dark with anger. "What are you blathering about?"

"Greta overheard you two talking. Prince von Hanzen thinks I'm shallow and warned you away from me. You sent me no flowers, nor did you come to call at my aunt's fine home. You also ignored me tonight at the musicale."

"And you think Rolpe's warning is why?" Fen asked, shaking his head. "*Nein wahrheit.* This is not truth. I've ignored you because of your manners."

"My manners? Why, I have been perfectly amiable! If you will recall the night of the DeLuises' ball, I listened to your flattery with grace and admiration." Rae was incensed at the bull-headed lout. "I particularly liked your compliments about Helen of Troy."

Fen just shook his head at her self-involvement. "I, too, overheard a conversation I should not have heard. You were speaking to your sister. I am not rich enough for you nor noble enough, nor handsome enough for your fickle tastes. So, it seems we are in complete agreement and disinterest of each other."

"I . . ." She opened her mouth to say more, but for the first time in her life was at a loss for words. Just then, she stumbled in the snow quite badly. To her utter mortification, the baron grabbed her around the waist and helped keep her from falling face-first into the snow. She thanked him quietly, all the time feeling very small. She was ashamed of herself for hurting the big lout's feelings, and for once Rae understood the bitterness of regret for her vanity.

# CHAPTER TWELVE

## The Baron's Grudge

As they approached the cemetery gate, Rae saw the prince mount up behind her sister and turn his horse toward their aunt's palatial home. She could see the manor lights in the distance. Beside her, Baron Schortz was quiet. As he turned to lift her upon a gigantic white horse, she blurted, "I'm so very sorry you heard my silly comments. My words were not well thought out. They were really meaningless, meant little to me. Of course, to you they meant more, even though they were never meant to be mean, merely meaningless. If I incensed your sensibilities, I have regrets. Know this."

The baron's silence stretched into an eternity, but Rae decided to be magnanimous and ignore his ill humor. She cheerily took off her garlic clove necklaces and flung them into the snow. "I don't know what I'll tell the cook about her missing supplies," she remarked.

The baron's lips twitched. "I'm sure you'll think of something," he said. And with those words, he literally picked her up and threw her upon his horse, his manner briskly efficient. It was as if he didn't want to touch her any more than he had to, which hurt both her pride and her feelings . . . and her bottom, because her landing on the stallion was not gentle. For that reason, she changed her opinion on whether to remain silent.

"I am rather rusty on apologies, since it's rare I need give them. I'm afraid my apology didn't come out the way I meant. Of course my words about you meant something. I am just so used to being admired and cosseted that I find such treatment is rather irritating at times. You were so smitten that I'm afraid I took out my little vexation on you. But really, if you only knew how tiring it can be to always have men tripping about your feet like adoring puppies."

"Your life sounds a sad trial." Fen managed to speak without the harsh sarcasm he was feeling as he recalled her earlier words about men and hounds. The fool woman was obsessed with dogs.

"Yes, beauty can be a curse when a gentleman sets his cap for me, especially when I don't want his cap . . . or even his handkerchief!" Realizing that she had just insulted him again, she shook her head and added, "Not that I didn't want your cap. Although I notice you don't wear a cap, not even when it's cold like this. How strange."

Scowling, the baron mounted behind her and said nothing once again. Instead, he urged his horse forward. Its big hooves splattered snow everywhere as they galloped toward her aunt's house.

He knew he should accept Rae's apology gracefully. It was the polite thing to do, but he didn't feel polite. This young, vain woman had wounded him deeply, hurting not only his pride but also his suddenly reclaimed vivacity. It was difficult to believe that such a breathtaking angel was in reality a little devil.

Rae sat on the massive horse, stewing. The baron was not much like her other beaus. Schortz's callous attitude toward her apology infuriated her. She would have protested vigorously if guilt weren't nipping at her heels. Instead, she sat up straight in the saddle and tried not to lean against him in any manner. It was rather hard, as the gait of the horse kept throwing her back against his very broad chest. Glancing down, she noticed how far away the ground was.

"This is a very big horse," she noted.

"It fits my big, loutish body," he replied. She had stolen something special that night from him by her cruel words, and he didn't know when he would gain it back again. Glancing ahead, he kept his mind off the subtle scent of fresh violets that always seemed to surround the woman seated before him on the horse. As he urged the steed onward, he noted with great relief that Rolpe was slowing down.

Prince von Hanzen was finishing his lecture on the evils of hunting monsters in the dead of night. It hadn't been an easy lecture, since the foolish female in front of him kept interrupting with her own opinions, which he found disturbing. She also refused to take off her garlic necklace. Thus, the ride had lasted forever.

The woman also felt too fine pressed against him, with his arm clasped tightly around her waist. He wanted to clasp her tighter, knowing that beneath the folds of her cloak were her firm white breasts. Instead he leaned back, glancing down at the chill gray mist upon the ground. He ought to tell her aunt what the maddening minx was doing, but he had given his word as a gentleman that he wouldn't. Of course, this only held if she promised she wouldn't go around haunting cemeteries anymore. It was quite a compromise for a man who didn't like to compromise.

"Stop here," Greta warned, and Rolpe pulled up his horse a little ways from the house. She'd thought the ride way too short. The feeling of his arms around her had made her heart go pitter-patter, and he smelled so nice: sort of woodsy and of bay leaves. She was sorry her aunt lived so near the cemetery; she could have ridden through the night with Rolpe, although she could have done without the lecture.

"You will give me your word."

"What word?"

"Don't be a pea-goose like your sister," the prince said,

glowering at her. "No more hunting for legends and *volksmärchen*—folktales. No more listening to Countess DeLuise and her mad ravings."

Greta borrowed one of her sister's smiles for the occasion: one that said, *aren't you just marvelous and so very clever, but I'll still do what I want and you won't care because of how pretty I look.* "A word is a fine thing, and very important. Why, the world would be in utter turmoil without giving one's word and taking another's word and so forth."

"I'll have yours," the prince pronounced, leaning over her shoulder and glaring down at her.

"My, you glower so well," she replied. He grimaced even more, which had her wisely hiding her smile. "Yes, I can see that my word is important to you, although I can't imagine why. But a word is a word, and a word given is a word given."

His glower disappeared, replaced by a wary admiration. "I see you dance around with the best of them."

"Oh, we're speaking of dancing now? I thought it was words of honor," Greta teased. Then, putting a finger to her chin, she added, "I do believe that anyone seeking something important would climb mountains and ford every stream until he or she found what he or she was seeking. Thus, a man or woman of determination would find it difficult to give a promise that compromised their goal. Don't you agree?"

"*Nein.*"

"Short and sweet—and contrary, but then I already pegged you for a man of few words. Actually, the less you speak the better, for I do believe that you have a tendency toward ill manners," she mentioned, remembering how he'd hurt her feelings.

To say Rolpe was taken back was an understatement. Women didn't criticize him; they adored him. "What in kingdom come are you prattling about?"

"The walls have ears, as do velvet curtains."

The prince's horse began sidling and sidestepping, disliking immobility in the bitter cold. Von Hanzen dismounted swiftly, clearly peeved at the elder Grimm. Then, with the barest of courtesy, he helped Greta dismount.

Baron Schortz followed suit, touching Rae as little as possible, lifting her from the back of his massive Clydesdale and placing her none too gently upon the thick blanket of snow.

With her feet planted firmly on the ground—and sinking up to her ankles—Rae glanced up at the baron, still feeling a twinge of guilt. She had foolishly hurt this proud man's feelings with her unkind words. "You simply must pay us a call tomorrow and let me make up for my silliness."

"Thank you, but I'm afraid I've got a full schedule."

"Then the next day," she tried, smiling, her blue eyes sparkling. It was a smile that had netted her thirteen marriage proposals in her past. As thirteen was an unlucky number, she had quickly garnered one more with a different smile, just to be on the safe side—although she didn't hold much faith in the superstitious nonsense that fascinated her siblings. Still, it never hurt a lovely lady to be absolutely careful.

"I'm busy then, too," the baron said. Turning back to his horse, he curtly bade her good night.

Rae watched him ride away, his big horse fading into the shadows with the prince's close behind. Giving him a withering glance, she then turned to face her sister. "What cavalier treatment from that oafish clod! To think I felt sorry for him."

"Rae, come along. Hurry." Greta grabbed her sister's arm and began dragging her toward the side of the manor with their bedchambers. "If Aunt Vivian discovers that we have snuck out of the house like some tarty maids, she'll ship us back to England without batting an eyelash."

"That would certainly be tragic for you. No more vampire hunting, I suppose."

Greta merely smiled. Again, her sister had supposed

wrong. Vampires were a delightfully decadent draw, but Prince von Hanzen had suddenly become her main attraction.

For everyone there is a season and a purpose unto heaven. Greta discovered this as the two sisters scurried toward the back of their aunt's massive house and Rae explained about the baron overhearing their conversation. Greta said little, noting that Rae criticized herself quite harshly for hurting the baron's feelings. Perhaps her little sister was finally growing up.

"I just wish the ground had swallowed me whole . . . or that I had met a vampire, and he took me away to be his undead wife," Rae said honestly. "I hurt that poor man's feelings, and if his feelings are as big as he is, that's a lot to hurt."

As they climbed up a trellis, Greta whispered, "The prince berated me all the way home. He said that all this vampire stuff was *unsinn*."

Rae stopped climbing and glanced at her sister. "Well, I guess being a vampire is a sin. But I don't think hunting them is."

"Oh, Rae, you never listened at our German lessons, did you? *Unsinn* means nonsense. The prince thinks vampires are a figment of very active imaginations. He said I was silly and childish for believing such nonsense."

Lifting a leg over the balcony rail in a very unladylike way, Rae shook her head. "The prince is the foolish one. After all, he thinks I'm a vain, shallow female and you are a foolish liar. Who cares what he thinks? He's only a prince. Only a handsome and wealthy prince." Her words made her feel worse.

Climbing onto the balcony, Greta followed her sister inside. "Who, indeed." But she was a liar, as the pompous prince had already pointed out.

As she stepped inside her bedchamber, Greta heard Rae's gasp of shock. Glancing over, she saw a large stuffed

mink lying across the Persian rug. Her sister's words followed: "Good grief, what is Aunt's stuffed mink doing in
here?"

"I imagine Miss Muffet brought her to me," Greta answered, picking up the stuffed mink and setting it atop the
dresser.

"Why on earth would the silly cat do that? Aunt will be
displeased to have her mink toyed with and clawed."

"I believe the cat is mostly blind. She likely thinks she is
bringing me a nice plump mouse to admire," Greta replied,
untying her deep red cloak. "So far she has brought me a
perfume bottle, a rock, and now this lovely stuffed mink."

"How fortunate," Rae replied, wrinkling her nose as she
too unbuttoned her snow-dusted cloak. "Still, you'd better
put the mink back in Aunt's collection before she discovers its theft. Why she collects minks is beyond me, but I
guess it is better than collecting old pipes, as our father
does. I wonder if that hulking oaf smokes a pipe? His cape
didn't smell as if he does."

Greta stopped pulling off her boots to give her sister a
stern glance. "I thought you weren't going to denigrate the
baron anymore? Especially since he heard your last unkind comments."

"I didn't delegate anything to him. Nor would I!"

"Denigrate, not delegate, you illiterate creature. It means
criticize. It's a grand blessing that you don't wish to marry
a scholar. You'd drive him around the bend on your honeymoon."

"Don't be ridiculous, Greta. You know I can't drive a
team," Rae exclaimed. She halfheartedly threw her half-
frozen boot at her sister and, rubbing her cold nose, remarked wearily, "Say what you mean, then, rather than
using those fancy Latin words. If you don't quit these blue-
stocking pretensions, no man will marry you, even if we
do now have new wardrobes and brand-new cloaks. No
man wants a lady who spouts Latin at the drop of a hat."

"You sound like Mother."

"Bite your tongue," Rae retorted as she picked up her boots to go to her room. "You know, I apologized wholeheartedly to the baron, Greta, for all the good it did me. He barely spoke. And I even invited him to call."

"He declined?"

Rae stopped by the dresser a moment but didn't turn her head. "He declined, the big oaf—and I'm not denigrating him, just stating a truth. He's utterly huge, and a stupid man."

"I thought him quite well spoken when I heard him jest tonight with others before Herr Mozart began playing. He has a sharp wit, and seems a fine man with a fine character. He did not deserve your scorn, and I would have stopped you had I known he was listening."

This time Rae halted just outside the bedchamber door. "Eavesdroppers never hear good of themselves."

"I know. I will long remember every word that Prince von Hanzen spoke about us."

"Well, anyone who knows me knows that I often say things I don't mean, and a shallow woman's words have little import, anyway," Rae remarked. "If Baron Schortz was as clever as you say, he would have ignored my little outburst and would still be worshipping at my shroud." And with those words, she burst from the room.

"That's shrine, my dear," Greta said to the closed door, her voice filled with soft laughter. "Methinks the damsel doth protest too much. The baron has gotten under her perfect fair skin." Which was a feat in itself.

Even more surprising, Rae felt remorse for something she had done. Greta was heartily glad for this change in heart, and appalled that Baron Schortz, who seemed a good and fine fellow, should have heard her sister's thoughtless remarks. "This time, Rae, I think the shoe is on the other foot. I much doubt that the baron will become one of your besotted lapdogs."

"My, oh my, the Black Forest really is a place of magic," Greta said to herself. For the magic had touched her as well. She had ridden with and been held by a handsome prince who was neither charming nor gallant. But he did make her feel dizzy whenever he was near. Mayhap gallant was not all that it was cracked up to be. After all, who wanted perfection—besides Rae?

# CHAPTER THIRTEEN

## The Best Little Whorehouse in Prussia

Not so long after—in fact, only minutes had passed since they provided escort for the sisters Grimm—and not very far away, the two noblemen rode their horses from the cemetery. They were traveling in the direction of an exclusive brothel called Thor's Hammer, where the two planned to spend a night indulging in wine, women and song. Thor's Hammer would provide this more than adequately, for it was a place a man could feel at home by getting drunk and fornicating all night long. Or playing cards and fornicating all night long. Or just plain fornicating all night long. Like most brothels, the place was big on fornication.

At first both men were quiet, deep in thought; the only sounds were the footfalls of their horses crunching through the hard-packed snow. But finally Fen broke the silence. "Do you think it's a *vampyr*?" he asked. "If it is, it's most likely one of Dracul's brood. They hunt in territories not their own."

Rolpe studied the snow-crusted landscape before them. "I don't think it's one of the *Nosferatu*. I believe it to be simple grave robbers."

"But there haven't been any grave robberies here since those infernal Frankensteins moved to England."

"I rather liked old Vic Frankenstein and his son, in spite of his mad starts."

Fen shook his head. "They were queer in the head. Remember the dinner I held where all Vic and Victor talked about was reanimating dead flesh? My poor guests. Dr. Frankenstein's conversation definitely put them off their feed."

Rolpe chuckled. "I remember it wasn't a conversation suited for the dinner table or mixed company. But you must admit he and his family are intriguing characters, and I believe that Vic might someday be successful in his attempts at the reanimation of the dead." The prince admired Dr. Frankenstein for his great intellect and devotion to a cause. "Frankenstein is an honorable man."

"Why bother with robbing graves and working on corpses or even running about in thunderstorms trying to get lightning to strike?" Fen asked. "The *Nosferatu* are already the animated dead."

"But *vampyrs* require blood to survive. Look at Dracul's brood: they always kill their victims . . . unless they turn them."

"Nasty nest of *Nosferatu*," Fen agreed. "They really should be all put down—for the sake of all otherworldly species, not to mention humanity." He had no liking for the undead, as he had fought a small army of them in his lifetime and found them both exceedingly cruel and merciless. He much preferred the company of shape-shifters and an occasional witch or two.

"True, they are devious and utterly without conscience, which is why I do not think the woodcutter's mother vanishing from her grave is connected to one of the undead," Rolpe replied. "I caught no scent of them at the cemetery, nor did the doctor who examined Frau Choplin mention that she was drained of blood."

"Rolpe, you've been away too long in your travels. The good doctor is a drunk. Frau Choplin could have been dry as a bone—unlike himself—and the doctor wouldn't have noticed." Fen shifted slightly in his saddle. "He did mention that she had lost blood from the cuts on her arms and legs."

"Exactly," Rolpe replied. "Too messy for the undead. When they attack, it's only one or two bites."

"Unless it's one of Dracul's brood gone mad. Or mayhap he is trying to throw us off."

"*Nein*. I believe Frau Choplin suffered an accident with the falling woodpile, as the evidence suggested. This does not feel like a *vampyr* attack. Nor do I think she was turned into one and rose to haunt the town. No one has seen anything remotely like the woodcutter's mother running around in her shroud—and after the countess's comments, believe me, the people of Wolfach are watching."

"Still, Countess DeLuise was very specific. She said the undead were overrunning the town."

"The countess is . . . a trifle eccentric."

"That she is." But Fen did not give up. "If it is a *vampyr*, we can't let him hunt in our territory." He glanced at the forest: snow-gowned, white and glittery. The icicles' color at night, a vivid blue, reminded him of Miss Rae Grimm's lovely eyes.

"Agreed," Rolpe admitted. "No one shall hunt in our territory, especially the *Nosferatu*."

Fen nodded in satisfaction, then asked the question that had been bothering him for most of the ride. He found it annoying that he cared what Rolpe thought about the shallow creature who was the younger Miss Grimm; yet he did. "What do you think of the Grimm sisters being there?"

"A complication I don't need: two nosy females sniffing out mysterious happenings in Wolfach. And 'tis obvious that the elder Miss Grimm believes in the legends of the Black Forest and will probably continue to hunt for them." Greta Grimm was a complication indeed, for Rolpe found her far too alluring for his peace of mind.

"If it is one of the undead doing these things, then the Grimms could be digging their own graves. They are searching out legends, and they might meet the Grim Reaper."

"The same might happen if we're dealing with grave robbers. There's good coin in bringing corpses to medical universities for study, and with coin involved, the type of men who rob graves . . . Well, there would be danger."

"Yes. It's dangerous and a stupid thing to do, to haunt cemeteries at night. Most females wouldn't dare." He still couldn't believe it of the flighty Miss Rae Grimm.

"Miss Greta Grimm isn't like most females," Rolpe pointed out. "No, I rather believe she is of a different cut altogether. If we are lucky, she will soon find a husband. That will keep her occupied with weddings and other such nonsense."

"The elder Miss Grimm doesn't seem as interested in capturing a husband as the fairy tales of our region," Fen remarked.

Rolpe nodded, his expression stern. The elder Miss Grimm would be a problem.

His sternness softened somewhat as he recalled how delightful she'd felt in his arms. She might be a trifle slender, but she had a very womanly shape, with well-rounded hips that he had brushed against while placing her on his horse. She was a tasty handful, and he would have already had a nibble if she were not an unmarried woman of virtue.

"Yes. She's clever, and she has a sharp wit. A curious cat," he remarked. A cat with such remarkably fine eyes, irises of pewter gray with slivers of icy blue entwined within; they were eyes a man could stare into forever.

Startled, Rolpe almost dropped his reins, wondering where that last thought had come from. Miss Grimm was merely an annoying acquaintance, he quickly reminded himself.

"Yes, the elder Miss Grimm does seem to have a fine head on her shoulders—nothing like her younger sister," Fen said, his tone clipped.

Taking note, Rolpe glanced over at his boon companion. They were just pulling their horses up in front of a large manor house a little over a mile from town. "Do I detect a note of discord? I thought you were interested in the younger one."

Pride prevented Fen from telling Rolpe about the conversation he had overheard between the two sisters. Instead he said, "At first I found her to be enchanting—quite the most beautiful woman I have ever seen, even more lovely than my dear departed Fiona. But you were right. She's too shallow, and I doubt she would make a good stepmother for my children."

Rolpe leaned over and slapped him on the shoulder, dismounting from his horse. "Glad to see you've come to your senses. You are much too good and generous, my friend, to end up leg-shackled to someone of that caliber."

Fen nodded, but his heart still felt dark as he handed his horse over to one of the stable boys. Even knowing what Miss Rae Grimm thought of him did not ease his desire. She popped into his mind at odd times, though he fought the intrusion. Hence, the visit to Thor's Hammer this very night.

Rolpe laughed, a sharp, brisk sound, as he clasped a hand on Fen's shoulder. "Come, the rest of the night is for *wein, weuband* and *gesang*."

Fen managed a lopsided grin. "Indeed. And I hope the wine is warm, the women hot, and the songs . . . I can do without." He would get that blonde-haired vixen out of his mind one way or another.

As the madame of Thor's Hammer greeted them effusively, Rolpe glanced over at the group of ladies present for his selection. Without realizing it, he was looking for a female with remarkable gray-blue eyes. When he did realize it, he cursed himself silently and picked a voluptuous redhead with a jade gaze instead.

Smiling, he took her hand as she led him toward the stairs. "You're lovely," he complimented, eyeing her nearly bare breasts with less hunger than normal. He found that totally exasperating. Yet hope sprung eternal, and he hoped that this particular soiled dove would make him forget vain peacocks and dodos of the Grimm family.

Fen and his chosen companion followed a scant few minutes later. Unlike Rolpe, who had tried for someone very different from the elder Miss Grimm, Baron Schortz had picked a voluptuous, blue-eyed female with extremely long blonde hair. Upstairs, the blonde undressed quickly, letting the baron eye her large, firm breasts, but she sensed he was not as interested as he might be in her ample charms.

"Like what you see?" she asked.

"Of course," Fen remarked, his cock rising to attention. Yet in his mind he was wondering what Miss Rae Grimm would look like standing naked before him. Grunting as he pulled off his boots, he chided himself for even thinking of the maddening female.

Unbeknownst to Fen, Rolpe was experiencing much the same dilemma. But arrogant and self-assured as he was, the proud prince did not let it stop him. He did not curse himself for being intrigued by the elder Miss Grimm; Cupid's arrows might be deadly sharp, and lust's heat as consuming as hellfire, but he was too wily a wolf to be trapped by a pair of fine breasts, eyes and an unseemly curiosity. Yet after he'd climaxed, Miss Grimm's features filled his mind.

His crude German curse was heard throughout the cathouse, and it woke a good number of those sleeping in nearby beds. Next door, Herr Dumpty was reminded of what had happened last fall, and he came apart. And none of the Thor's whores, and none of the king's men, could help to put Dumpty together again.

# CHAPTER FOURTEEN

## Cock-a-Doodle-Didn't

One winter night a short time later, with snowflakes a-falling, a grand and aging prince gave a ball to proudly display his great wealth and treasures. The sisters Grimm and their aunt were of course invited, since the elderly prince had wedlock on the mind with the younger Miss Grimm.

Inside the ballroom, Greta was demurely if anxiously standing near a massive mirror that covered half a wall. She had been standing there for over an hour, declining to dance as she observed the many guests both in the reflection of the glass and upon the dance floor. Suddenly, Rolpe appeared behind her and addressed her in a haughty manner.

"You will grow roots if you stand here much longer."

As usual, whenever the pompous prince popped by, Greta's heart beat faster and her stomach felt as if a thousand butterflies were vomiting there. Prince von Hanzen made her yearn for hearth and home, made her forget momentarily her quest for the vampire in their midst.

"I am resting," she said.

"You haven't even been dancing." Glancing from the mirror and back to her, he smiled wickedly. "Strange, I didn't realize you shared your sister's fascination with mirrors," Rolpe remarked, his blue eyes gleaming.

"Don't be absurd," she replied curtly. "I am not studying *my own* reflection." Then, realizing what she'd just revealed, she swiftly shut her mouth. A frown formed on her brow; the man was too clever by half.

He scowled. "You're looking for *vampyr*."

"If I am, 'tis my own business."

Rolpe chuckled. "What a droll and foolish woman you are. *Vampyrs*, indeed. May I take it that this, your impression of a statue, means you haven't spotted any? No undead lurking around *Fürst* Gelb's home, bloodthirst in their eyes?" This woman vexed Rolpe, made him laugh, but also made him impatient and excited. Her imprudence could get her in serious trouble. Fortunately there were none of the undead lurking about; he had made sure of that fact. There were, however, other creatures in the Black Forest just as deadly.

"I'm not foolish, but I have been known to be droll upon occasion. When people understand my jokes."

Her anger darkened her eyes to the color of misty bottomless lochs, and he stared at her in fascination. Then, annoyed with her magnetism, he stepped back a pace. Since the cemetery incident, he had thought upon Miss Greta Grimm more than once, and that irritated him. She was a virgin of a good family, and he was a hardened rogue, a sensuous lover and a hardened (and hardheaded) bachelor. And this infuriating beauty made him, or parts of him, even harder.

His scowl deepened. "Come, admit it, you've spied nary a vampire in Wolfach. Simply one missing corpse."

Greta fought back annoyance. She had been staring hard into the mirror and then back out into the sea of dancers, trying to spot someone, anyone, whose reflection was not shown. Now she had a headache, and the ball was only beginning. "Not yet, but the night is young."

"What do you really want to find?" he asked crisply.

She gulped, staring back at the handsome prince, wishing with all her heart that fairy tales could come true. "In

Wolfach? A legend come to life, a good man, and mayhap a troll or two. I also wouldn't mind seeing an ogre."

He shook his head. "You should be dancing and hatching plots to wed some unsuspecting gentleman, not searching out supernatural secrets," he chided, licking his lips as he stared at her mouth. Her own lips were quite lush, firm and full and pink, and more than a little inviting. Leaning over, he chucked her gently on the chin. "You don't make a very good wallflower. Too pretty, and much too spirited. Go dance." And with those words he strolled arrogantly away, leaving Greta to stare after him.

"He's a maddening, cocky fellow, I do declare."

Hearing her comment, Herr Nietzsche, who had just arrived with a cup of punch, followed her gaze. He shrugged his shoulders delicately. "He's a prince. They're all like that."

Herr Nietzsche wasn't the only one who had noticed Greta's interest in the handsome prince. Her Aunt Vivian, who was chattering jovially away in the midst of the dowagers, was watching both her nieces like a hawk. She had noted that Greta had not danced as of yet, and had been speaking with Herr Nietzsche again, a friendship she did not approve of. The man was nothing but a frustrated writer, and an old gossip who stirred Greta's interest in all that unseemly fairy-tale nonsense. Alas, just what she didn't need if she was to encourage her niece to marry. If the baroness hadn't grown a little fond of her eldest niece, she would have washed her hands of the whole affair.

Yes, she had found that she did like her eldest niece, and noting the girl's interest in *Fürst* von Hanzen, the Baroness Snowe shook her head, her chins wobbling. The prince was too high in the instep to marry Greta. Still, if Greta was interested in that man, she might find she could be fond of another. Perhaps a writer would be a good match, so that the two would have something to talk about after their marital duties were done. Just not a writer like Nietzsche.

One of her companions made a comment about Rae's

gown, and the baroness turned her attention in the direction her companion was staring. She said, "Of course Rae looks radiant tonight. I picked the gown myself. Cost a small fortune, but then what could I do? The gels arrived on my doorstep practically without a stitch of suitable clothing. It's to their great fortune that I am older and wiser. I also happen to have splendid taste and am much admired for my style, if I may dare boast."

The other Prussian ladies murmured something back, something appropriate, and Baroness Snowe turned to see *Fürst* Gelb ushering her niece, Rae, along with Lady Lentel, an old family friend of the house of Gelb, down the red hallway that led to his treasure room. At this sight Baroness Snowe sniffed disgustedly, her heart freezing. Evidently the old scoundrel was intending to show off the many gold odds and ends in his famous Gold Room. It was more than obvious that he was trying to impress Rae with his wealth, and that could only bode ill. She was torn between arranging such a smashing marriage—Gelb *was* part of the upper nobility of Prussia—and protecting her niece from his lechery.

Gloating, she imagined the years of boastful letters she could write. Yet, as Rae walked with the aging prince, Baroness Snowe suddenly recognized that she absolutely could not allow Prince Gelb's suit to be pressed. Not with her niece, of course. She'd leave it to the dry cleaners.

Unaware of her aunt's feelings, Rae entered Gelb's Gold Room with a sense of wonder. Her mouth opened and her eyes went wide. The room was almost blinding in its splendor, with every manner of ornament made of gold, many encrusted with rare and monstrous jewels.

"Oh," she gasped. The prince was obviously a very wealthy man. Perhaps knobby knees were not so high a price after all. Not for such glittering beauty. After all, she did not do poor well: it was so unbecoming.

Enthralled, she walked to the large glass shelves that housed more than sixty golden objects of every description and from every land. There were golden elephants from India and golden vases from China. Another whole row was filled with eggs: golden eggs, jewel-laden Faberge eggs from Russia. She examined them in awe, unaware that Lady Lentel had excused herself.

"I take it you like my pretties?" Prince Gelb asked.

"They're wondrous. I've never seen anything like this in my life. Such lovely baubles."

Her response made his sly little heart beat faster. "Yes, those *bubbies* are quite pretty," Prince Gelb commented. A leer covered his face as he stared hungrily at her decolletage, which pushed up her breasts. Tempting morsels they were, surrounded by delicate ivory lace. She was mouth-watering. "*Quite* pretty."

Not paying attention to the older man's words, Rae nodded absently, still admiring the collection.

"Come, you must see my harp." The prince took her hand and guided her to a shadowy corner where the harp sat alongside a couch done in gold brocade. "It's solid gold. I bought it from a collector in Greece. He says it dates back to Spartan times."

Rae nodded eagerly and reverently touched the golden harp. "It's lovely."

The prince leaned in closer, his breath caressing her shoulder. "Not as lovely as you, my little goose, so plump and pretty. Perchance you'd like to pluck *my* strings."

Fortunately, Rae was not enraptured by the harp, as she had never been a big fan of harp music; thus, she caught his tone and words, which were absolutely fraught with lecherous intent. She gasped and glanced over at him, noticing with alarm how his eyes were burning with that fire men sometimes got around her.

Oh, drat! she thought, irked. Now she would have to cut her viewing of his treasures short, for she was certainly not going to be plucking anything of his on this night—or on any other night. Of this she was quite certain.

The old man counted to three, then tried to play patty-cake on her dimpled knee. Rae had played it as a child with her sisters and brothers, but this old roué didn't have innocent games in mind; rather naughty ones, she suspected.

Glancing desperately about the room, Rae looked for aid from Lady Lentel only to discover that the lousy lady had left. "We're in here all alone. That isn't proper in English society, and I doubt it is in Prussian society either." She had never really thought long or hard on May–December romances, but as the prince puckered his lips for a kiss, she found herself repelled. She moved to step back from the old randy goat, but was prevented as he grabbed her shoulders.

"You must not flee, my pretty little goose. So soft and plump and fine. I just want a small kiss to make my heart sing."

"I prefer to remain on speaking terms," Rae replied. Shaking her head, she added forcefully, "We must leave before my aunt realizes I am not in the ballroom." She did not want Prince Gelb's thin dry lips to touch her own. Greta, of course, had been right all along: This decrepit prince was too old to be her husband, even for a hundred gold carriages and a thousand golden eggs.

Ignoring her protest as one of maidenly modesty, the prince leaned down to kiss her. Rae jerked back, knocking into a large fern that was nesting in the corner. As she did so, a large cockroach scurried up her leg, and all at once she found the strength to shove the prince back. Leaping and screaming, Rae leapt upon an ottoman sewn with Turkish designs in golden thread. "Help, it's on me! Oh no, this is horrible! I have something crawling up my pantaloons!" she shrieked.

Though no Prince Charming, Gelb valiantly came to the rescue, lifting her skirt and hoop to search for the offending insect. His eyes lit with lustful glee as he took in the fine lace underthings and the shapely legs they encased. Forgetting the bug, he leaned forward to bestow a kiss.

Shocked and half-crazed, Rae screeched. First the skittering of the little bug's legs, replaced by searching fingers and lips on her legs—it was all too much. She cried out for the prince to leave her be, trying desperately to force her skirts down over the despicable lecher's head.

It was at that moment that Fate played its hand, and Baron Schortz hurried into the room. When he took in the scene, his expression turned to an angry scowl. After three steps, he routed the prince by throwing him across the room, lowered Rae's skirts and threatened to tear the prince's rotten head off if he remained present even a moment longer.

The dazed Prince Gelb quickly left the room, tottering a bit as he did. Once outside, he hurried down the hallway, straightening his jacket. His ruffled appearance caught the attention of Baroness Snowe, who only moments before had seen Baron Schortz entering the hall. A scheme popped into her mind, a scheme to make sure her niece did not marry above her.

While the baroness was busy plotting, Fen glanced up at the vision in blue damask silk before him. Instead of the gratitude he expected to find upon her lovely visage, he instead found disgust and horror. Disappointment filled him, but then he reminded himself sternly that this was a shallow woman.

"He's gone. You are safe now," he said.

"No, he's not. He's there, and I can still feel him crawling up my leg!" This said, she began a strange little dance on the ottoman, jumping up and down. "Oh, do something, you big oaf. He's climbing higher, and I can't stand it one minute more."

The poor English lady was a bit overset. "*Nein,* Prince Gelb is gone!" he said.

"Oh, you ninny! Before the prince accosted me, a cockroach accosted me first. From that dusty fern over there. It ran up my pants!" Rae snapped. Then she went silent and started weeping, raising her skirts, hoop and all, hastily over her head once again as the scurrying bug came preciously close to the slit in her drawers. "It's so crawly and creepy. Please Baron Schortz, you must get it off me!"

Finally understanding the awkward situation, and rather valiantly ignoring her offhand insults, he gallantly began the search. His eyes quickly caught the brown bug scuttling across the slit in her Parisian pantaloons and back out of sight. In the back of his mind he noted the shapeliness of her legs and the other flesh exposed. His mouth watered.

Courteously he reached inside the pantaloons and grabbed the offending bug. Unfortunately, as he tried to bring his hand back out, his onyx cufflink caught on the lace of the slit in the pantaloons. He cursed. She cursed. And pandemonium ensued.

The pantaloons ripped. Huffing and puffing, Baroness Snowe scurried into the room, her own matrimonial plans in mind. Fast on her stylish heels were seven of her bosom beaux, gossips one and all. Greta was also there, for she had noted her aunt's look of evil intent, which was the same look their mother wore when she was scheming. Prince von Hanzen also arrived, having noted the crowd and decided to investigate the commotion. And last but not least was the proud owner of the Gold Room, Prince Gelb, who couldn't stand to miss anyone's reaction to his impressive collection.

One by one and one and all, they stood enthralled, or titillated, or scandalously appalled. Yes, to a one they stood inside the magnificent Gold Room, staring at a most magnificent sight—and that sight wasn't the golden harp or any golden eggs. No, the particular golden goose cooked here was Baron Schortz.

Miss Rae Grimm was standing on an ottoman, her skirt over her head, and Baron Schortz's head was half under that skirt, his hand coming out of her pantaloons. Yes, the baron's goose was royally cooked—as voiced by Prince von Hanzen's bout of pithy cursing.

Greta, stunned, glanced from her sister and the baron to the handsome prince, still so shocked by the compromising situation that she took only a mild interest in the curse words she'd never heard before.

Prince Gelb frowned, shaking his head in regret. Rae would have made him a fine wife. Alas, fate was against him—as well as Baron Schortz.

Rae stared wide-eyed at the group before her, feeling more humiliated than she ever had. This couldn't be happening. But it was.

Swinging back around to face the music, and whatever else awaited him, Baron Schortz forced himself not to shudder. Everyone was staring at a piece of lacy drawer in his hand, still attached to his cufflink, and his own pants were somewhat tented in front.

"You cocksure son of a . . ." Baroness Snowe trailed off, her chubby finger pointing, denouncing him as a lecherous bounder he wasn't.

"Cock*roach,*" he tried to explain, but his mouth was dry and he felt a disaster of momentous proportions overtaking him. What a cockamamie mess. He was cocked up for sure.

"Ha!" the baroness snapped scornfully. Secretly, she was delighted. Her vain niece would marry the baron, and their social standings would be equal. As well, Rae would soon be out of her hair. And the marriage would be high enough—especially since Baron Schortz had blue Norwegian blood—to cause her sister, the Baroness Grimm, to see red. Oh, happy days were here again. Never was she more relieved that she had followed her instincts, gathering her companions and hurrying here. She'd hoped that luck would be with her and she would catch the baron in a compromising position; but never had she thought she would find them in *such* a compromising position. As compromising positions went, this one was deliciously wicked.

This couldn't be happening to her, Rae thought again. She stood looking like a dazed doll, the picture of perfection, perhaps excepting her pantaloons. This was a horrid, heinous and hideous nightmare, and soon she would wake up. Perhaps she ought to swoon.

One of Aunt Vivian's companions commented, "Impetuous young men have been leading innocent and foolish girls astray from the beginning of time."

"And witless, don't forget witless," Baroness Snowe added, enjoying her natty niece's discomposure.

Glaring, Rae snapped, "I am not witless. It was the bug that's stupid." Then, turning her attention to the pale-faced nobleman, she added, "Baron Schortz only tried to help."

"Help himself to your womanly delights," Gelb said.

This time, Rae's glare pierced the prince. "Talk about calling the kettle black, you old roué."

Prince Gelb ignored her outburst, and again accosted the baron. "How could you—seducing a young innocent in my home? And all in the guise of lending a hand." How he wished he'd had the foresight to stage a compromising situation so that the delightful Miss Grimm would have been his. She would have fit in beautifully with his gold and his Gold Room.

"It really was a huge cockroach," Rae said, her voice high and unnatural as she tried to explain again. She stepped off the ottoman. "It was the biggest roach I've ever seen. A king cockroach, or some such thing."

"I imagine so," one of the older ladies said, with a glint in her eye. She had noted the baron's rather impressive bulge. "A giant to be sure."

"Do something," Rae urged the baron, adjusting her skirts, which had been lowered some time after the offending insect had been squashed beneath the baron's heel. Yet the baron remained silent, his face pale. If she were not mistaken, he was praying, his usual aplomb deserting him.

Greta came to her side, and Rae was glad of her sister's support. She was horribly embarrassed and annoyed, and her face was a shade of bright red bordering on scarlet. "A horrible, awful cockroach—truly, Greta."

One of Aunt Vivian's companions, who was rather deaf,

shook her head sadly. "Never mind, my dear. They're all awful at first, but you'll get used to them. Some ladies even find them awe-inspiring, I've been told."

Greta stepped closer to her sister's side, and Prince von Hanzen moved to stand nearer the baron. The prince said, "If this hasn't all gone cockeyed. He might as well cock up his toes. Fen's done for now. Wedded, without the bliss!"

Greta turned and gave him a fierce glare.

"Enough! No more cocks or cocking or cockroaches. It's marriage we speak of," said the Baroness Snowe.

Greta scowled at their aunt and her entourage of busybodies, while Rae looked embarrassed and dazed. Fen wasn't in much better shape, but he nodded abruptly. Von Hanzen's scowl matched Greta's.

Baroness Snowe clapped her hands with glee. "Prince Gelb, may I ask a boon? Perchance, may we borrow your study to discuss this rather odious situation? Youth is impetuous, but we must outlast the stink."

"I must give the girl a point for her imagination," said the baroness's youngest friend, a woman of a spritely sixty-five. "A cockroach as a wedding trap! What won't they think of next?"

The conversation disintegrated from there, leaving the elderly Gelb to quickly agree to the baroness's plan. Soon both sisters Grimm, their aunt, their uncle, Baron Schortz and Prince von Hanzen were all on their way (if not merrily) to an ornate, severely overdecorated study. Everyone was pleased to see it was well stocked with brandy.

# CHAPTER FIFTEEN

## Beauty & the Beastly Baron

"Undone by a bug. I shall never live it down," Fen whispered miserably.

"I think the roach had little to do with your downfall," Rolpe replied. "The blame falls more squarely in your lap."

Fen glanced down at his trousers. Fortunately the flag of his excitement had lowered to half-mast. He shook his head glumly.

Rolpe jested, "Who could foresee that a roach in the hand looks like one in the bush?"

Fen shot him a look of true displeasure. "I have never liked this cruel streak in you, Rolpe." But that only caused the prince to laugh again.

Ahead, the weight of the world had settled upon Rae. She walked, eyes downcast. "My life is over."

"It only appears so now. Tomorrow things will look better," Greta said, taking her sister's hand. "Surely the baron will be a good husband."

Rae gave her sister the evil eye. "You marry him then."

"I wasn't caught with my skirts over my head."

"Bloody fool bug. Bloody fool baron."

The study remained heavily silent for a moment; then Baroness Snowe proceeded to suggest the arrangements necessary to save her niece's tarnished reputation.

"Marry Baron Schortz? I can't! I mustn't!" Rae cried. "I should be marrying a prince at least. Certainly no less than a duke!"

The expressions in the room offered varying degrees of disgust. Even Greta looked appalled, which hurt terribly. But this was all so distressing to contemplate. Even if the others didn't understand Rae's position.

Her aunt, face red, trembling in rage, exclaimed, "Rae, you addlepated gel. Are you bent on ruining us? Your reputation is in tatters, and by association mine will be too. I'll be dragged through the mud with you unless you wed the baron! Now, I won't stand for any shilly-shallying. You *will* marry, and marry within the week, you ungrateful, spoiled child." Then, recalling that Baron Schortz had not done the honors of asking for her niece's hand, she reluctantly amended, "That is, if he should choose to honor such an undeserving gel with the option of being his wife."

Fen nodded stiffly then turned to Rae, his expression as somber as hers. He would not balk at this jump, though he longed to do so and race headlong off into the night. But as a gentleman, he could not. He too understood he had tarnished her reputation, however unintentionally. As that was the case, he could not let her live in unmarried shame and ostracism.

"Miss Grimm, may I have your hand in marriage?"

Rae studied her aunt's face, which was a rigid mask of fierce determination. Prince von Hanzen looked as if he had swallowed something repugnantly vile. Greta appeared sad, but gravely nodded.

Rae turned her attention to the baron. He did not look at all like a jovial man contemplating a lovely bride, a happy future and a fairy-tale wedding. In fact, he looked as if he had eaten something even more repugnantly vile than his friend had. Swallowing hard, Rae pleaded with tears in her eyes, knowing that when they wetted her eyelashes her eyes sparkled even more. If ever there were a time she needed all her feminine wiles, it was now.

"We can't possibly marry," she said.

"You can and will, you obstinate gel," Baroness Snowe declared, her tone as harsh and cold as the winters in Russia. Her husband, the baron, took his wife's side—as he always did to ensure peace in his household, whether he agreed with his temperamental spouse or not. But this time he did agree, wholeheartedly. Honor must be preserved.

"You will marry Baron Schortz without delay. I must say that it disgusts me to know that I've nursed a viper in my home. Baron Schortz is a noble man in every sense of the word, and for you to seduce him is shameful!" he proclaimed.

Rae's tears dried up immediately. "I did not seduce anyone!"

Coming to her sister's defense, Greta retorted, her blue eyes bright with anger, "How can you be so unfeeling? Rae would never have attempted to seduce a mere baron." Then, realizing her defense was rather condemning, she quickly added, "Rae would never seduce anyone. She has too much good breeding!"

"Yes, and good breeding does tell," their aunt replied. "How do you think your mother managed to get your father to the altar when it was me he was courting?"

The room grew silent as its occupants processed what Baroness Snowe had unwittingly revealed, each person having a different reaction. For Fen, he noted how quickly a woman's tears could dry, leaving behind a hard brittleness. Such was the case with Rae. And as her mother had trapped her father, so now was the daughter following the same path. Blood would tell. Only, to be perfectly honest, he knew Rae had not intended for him to be this sort of victim.

Rolpe gritted his teeth in rage, feeling certain that the younger Grimm had deliberately set out to trap his friend.

Baron Snowe gazed in disgust at his wife, realizing that she still held a torch for the Grimm girls' father.

But it was indeed the two Grimm sisters who were most

shocked of all. Greta, feeling terribly embarrassed by this public announcement, also felt relief. It explained so much about her parents' less-than-harmonious marriage. Rae felt as if the world were spinning wildly and she would fly off into the heavens. Her rather spoilt and shrewish mother had tricked their good-natured father into wedlock? The thought was detrimental to her entire sense of self-worth.

Observing her sister's pale face and somber eyes, Greta leaned over and whispered, "Be glad. Can you imagine Aunt Vivian as our mother?"

Greta's quick wit caused Rae to smile, and that smile Fen found rather enchanting. He did so in spite of his better judgment, but he had no choice. Just as he had no choice about his future: Honor did not care that he would be marrying a woman who would never offer him the slightest bit of affection, it simply demanded he make the little pea goose the offer. If she declined, then she would pay the price. She would no longer be accepted in polite society.

"Miss Grimm, will you marry me or not?"

Determined, Greta nudged her sister's back. Rae managed to whisper an acceptance, albeit a breathless one. And just like that, her dreams of being a princess or duchess blew away like dust in the wind. Baron Schortz was not even on bended knee or begging for her most lovely hand! This time, the tears dotting her eyelashes were real.

Nodding abruptly at her reply, Fen announced coolly, "Then it is done. Baron Snowe, I will call on the morrow to discuss the particulars."

"Yes, Fen, that will be agreeable. Come, Vivian, let us leave the betrothed coupled alone for a few minutes," their uncle said.

As the others left the room, Fen shook his head, muttering, "*Immer schlimmer.*"

"I don't know what you just said, but I don't think I like the tone," Rae snapped. The room appeared to shrink in size, as if some giant had entered the room and was breathing fire. Baron Schortz was so large and so very muscular.

Standing before the large mahogany shelving, he poured himself a stiff drink. "Bad to worse. Things have gone from bad to worse." He threw the drink back, letting the burn slide down his throat. It eased the headache at the back of his eyes. Fate had been both kind and cruel to him. The irony was absurd. He had fallen head over heels for a beautiful vision who was all he'd wanted for a brief period in time. Now that he had her in hand, so to speak, or had her hand, he knew he would long live to regret being forced into this marriage. Honor was a grueling taskmaster at times, and the results could be devastating. He had a soon-to-be-bride who would be no wife. Who would be no stepmother to his brood. Yes, irony was at its best tonight, and at its most cruel.

Rae was not thinking clearly, or else she would have been even more insulted by her betrothed's lack of response to his great good fortune in her accepting his suit. Embarrassment, shame and guilt made her feel quite unlike her normal self. "I should never have agreed to see the golden eggs and harp. But a golden harp and golden eggs—it all sounded so lovely."

"Yes, your *strofftriels*—your love of material wealth has led up to this hideous farce!" Fen muttered harshly as he poured himself another drink. Swallowing it, he began to stalk the room like a hulking giant. "You, Rae Grimm, haven't the good sense God gave a goose. Golden harps? Bah!"

Rae pouted very prettily, deciding to turn the other cheek, especially as that was her best side and she wanted to show it off to advantage. Seating herself gracefully on a slender Louis XIV chair, she held back any temper she might be feeling and did her best to hide her overwhelming shock at this marriage. After all, an innocent maiden needed all the help she could get in such a trying situation. Hence, she would look her best.

"I will have you know that I have more than ample intelligence, and certainly more than that of a vicious, fat bird. Now, as to your other charge, of course I love beautiful things. Most people love wealth; that doesn't make us wicked or foolish. We just enjoy owning the rare and beautiful. Perhaps it's not even about the owning, but the appreciation of that which is beyond the mundane. Although, you'll soon own me. That must bring you some pleasure."

It brought Rae little.

"I weep for joy." Standing with his back to her, staring morosely out the window, Fen searched for something.

Patience, perhaps.

Wisdom.

A call to arms in Russia.

Rae sniffed, her delicate feelings hurt deeply. "If you think I am happy about this, well . . ." She sighed dejectedly. "I can assure you that I'm not. If I were in Cornwall right now, I'd marry Timothy Sterne, even though I didn't want to be a Sterne after being Grimm for so long. So there." And with those words, she turned on her heel and started to leave the room.

Resolutely she stood tall and proud. She had a beautiful chin and would keep it held high, even though she felt like crying and screaming. Most of her life she had believed that she would marry well; her husband would adore her and grant her every whim. Now her dreams were gone. What she had long striven for and depended upon happening was no longer possible. What did a person do when their dreams died? How could she go on? Did she even want to carry forth, carry on, carry a load, and carry a tune in her heart? She thought hard. Yes, she did, she realized reluctantly. She was no quitter, and though her life's journey was now a rugged one, she would face it proudly. Well, as proudly as she could with her broken heart and teary eyes. Still, she would persevere.

"I suppose we must make the best of a bad situation," Fen mused dejectedly, causing her to pause in the doorway. "Marriage can last a lifetime. I'd prefer not to be constantly at sword's length with my wife."

"I'd prefer to marry a handsome prince and live in a fairy-tale castle," Rae replied, and with that said she exited the room. To herself she whispered, "Whatever shall I do? I have hurt his pride again, and now he will shame me. Everyone will expect him to be deliriously happy at having the good luck to marry me; only he's not deliriously happy. He's miserable. Why did I ever open my big mouth to Greta in a place that we could be overheard? Foolish, foolish bird-wit! He did not deserve my words then . . . although he does now."

Down the hall, Greta spoke heatedly with Prince von Hanzen, who in his utter arrogance had shown the gall to denounce Rae. Greta furiously defended her sister, and they'd taken their argument into the conservatory and out of the way of prying ears, but not so far in as to constitute impropriety.

"If we are to bicker like a couple of fishwives then let us do it here." He raised his eyes to the ceiling, his expression thunderous. "*Undank ist der Welt Lohn,*" he added.

Understanding the remark, Greta quoted it back to him, her scorn more than apparent by the lift of her chin and the tautness of her mouth. "'Ingratitude is the world's reward.' You think my sister ungrateful?" His hair was as dark as endless night, she thought, as she watched him brush a lock off his forehead. Like a raven's wings or the midnight hour when all grew quiet and witches flew.

"Not only do I *think* her ungrateful; I heard her remarks to Fen this night. Fen is a proud, generous man of great conviction and courage. He deserves so much better than a shallow, vain widgeon who cares only for herself and her clothing. I find it an utter tragedy that his good deed in saving your sister from nothing worse than a nasty little bug backfired. Verily, I say, Fen must now sacrifice his happiness for your sister's worthless reputation."

Seething, Greta gaped. "*Veritas vos liberabit.*" She narrowed her pretty gray-blue eyes at him and quoted, "The truth shall set you free. But do you know the truth? Or do you just assume you do?"

"You speak Latin as well as German. Unusual," Rolpe remarked, studying her closer. She was an enigma, unpredictable, and that made him uneasy. She intrigued him, and he didn't like that one bit. "But you also speak in riddles. Your sister is what she appears to be, no more and probably a great deal less than an ideal wife and stepmother to my good friend and his *kinder.*"

"There is more to Rae than meets the eye," Greta replied. "Yes, she is vain, but that is not all her fault. Beaux have always flocked to Rae."

"But did she keep them? And while many men prefer a lovely stupid wife, Fen does not number among them."

The prince was shrewd, Greta would give him that. "It's not Rae's fault that for most of her life people have cosseted her and admired her beauty. But she is also brave, and loyal to those she loves, and fiercely protective of them. She does have a kind nature, even if at times it is buried beneath a shallow exterior."

"Such a glowing recommendation from a loving sister," Rolpe retorted. But he was fascinated as he watched her color mount. What a fine passion, he thought lustily. Her blush extended down the front of her chest and beneath the frothy green confection of a gown she was wearing.

Hands on her hips, Greta breathed deeply, her anger making her wish to slap the prince's supercilious but handsome face. Although his resolve was daunting, she would not be intimidated by the fact he bestirred her heart unlike any other. In fact, he stirred her heart like a rip-roaring good fairy-tale prince could do. "I'm sure there will be difficulties, as with all newly wedded couples, but my sister has a good heart. If Baron Schortz is the intelligent man I think him to be, he will treat her with kindness. And she will return his kindness in kind." And, having said her piece, Greta turned to leave.

Rolpe watched her go, her back stiff and her manner rigid. Her parting shot made him admire her more. She was angry with him for criticizing her shallow, selfish sister. Most women would have been jealous of such a beautiful sister, but Greta not only defended her sister, she genuinely cared about the younger Grimm's happiness.

"We really must do this again sometime!" he called after her. He heard her footsteps rapping angrily down the hallway.

"What a little wildcat," he muttered appreciatively. Greta Grimm was, he decided, an intelligent woman, well-learned, and with perhaps the most remarkable gray-blue eyes he had ever seen.

He shook his head. She was intriguing, but he should not be intrigued. Still, he would have to watch her carefully, since he had overheard more than one of her conversations tonight about the woodcutter's mother, Frau Choplin. Miss Greta Grimm did fit her name, for she had an unhealthy and grim determination to ferret out the secrets of the Black Forest—and many of those secrets would love to get their teeth into *her*.

# CHAPTER SIXTEEN

## The Gushing Bride

Soon there would be a church. Soon there would be a steeple. Rae would open the door and see all the people staring at her, gossip running rampant; and worse, her husband, the hulking giant, would be there as well. Mayhap if she were lucky she would break out in measles. Perhaps if God were listening he might send a great flood and wash her out to sea.

Rae put her head down on her arms and moaned. Alas, there wasn't a single rain cloud in the winter sky. Nonetheless, with nary a cloud in sight, Rae's wedding day was a wet one. Not that it rained or snowed or even sleeted, but the sisters Grimm spent the early morning together crying.

Although Rae continued on, her tears soaking her nightgown, Greta finally managed to halt her crying long enough to dress; after all, she wasn't marrying the big oaf. Rae's tears remarkably dried up when the maid mentioned her eyes would be bloodshot and puffy at her ceremony. Cool cucumber compresses were then applied, to relieve the puffiness, and she rested for a bit, then the younger Grimm sister was ready to be dressed.

As the maid fussed about her, Rae managed to hold back the new tears that threatened to fall. This was her wedding day, a day she had dreamed about since she was a small child. She had known even at that young age that she would be a beautiful bride in a lovely gown with rows and rows of pearls. There would be hundreds of fragrant red roses, and her groom would worship her with his eyes as he pledged her his troth. And everyone who was anyone—and even those who weren't anyone—would be envious of the happy couple.

Rae shook her head sadly. Reality was certainly nothing like her dreams. Her aunt had been writing letter after letter to their mother, letters of long length, each boasting of the grand success of marrying off a Grimm daughter to a Prussian baron in less than a month. The groom was minor nobility, it was true, but nobility nonetheless. After writing her dozen or so missives, Baroness Snowe had done her aunty duty and explained the wedding night to Rae: something about a man's large pickle being shoved into a lady's jar. Since Rae doubted that her groom would much relish his wedding night, Rae decided that her aunt's advice was useless, and she wanted no part of it.

After her aunt had left Rae to finish dressing in peace and blessed quiet, Greta arrived, tears in her eyes. She wished her sister much happiness. And the gushing of tears commenced again.

Rae soaked two handkerchiefs before she finally got herself under control enough to speak. "I have no wish to marry," she said, "but with Aunt and Uncle acting like fire-breathing dragons, I must marry this obscure baron."

Greta took her hand. "Rae, you deserve to be happy, and I think you will be, in spite of the way this wedding has come about. I'm sure lots of forced marriages have become love matches."

"If you are trying to cheer me up, please don't bother," Rae groaned. "I still don't see why I must marry the man."

"Rae, you've got to stop this. You know as well as I do that a lady's reputation is fragile. People are always willing to believe the worst. And of course the worst they could have believed is what they actually caught you doing."

"I was doing nothing but being attacked by an old lecher, a bloody bug and an overgrown lummox."

"Well, just think of the positive side of this marriage. You are marrying nobility."

"A mere baron!"

"He's very wealthy."

"Probably a clutch-fisted miser. Look how he dresses, without a thought for style or his place in society."

"Well, he doesn't have to pad his calves or his shoulders," Greta remarked, patiently cheerful as she did up the last of the pearl buttons on Rae's gown.

"That's what I'm afraid of. He's so very large, and he doesn't like me much."

"That shows his sound judgment," Greta teased. "After all, you've insulted him time and time again. Would you want a stupid man for a husband?" she asked. "But he finds you beautiful. Didn't you say he likened you to Helen of Troy?"

"I would settle for a less clever man if he truly wanted me to wife. Baron Schortz hasn't smiled at me once since we became betrothed. In fact, he's spoken very little to me. I don't think this a good sign for connubial bliss."

Placing both her hands on her sister's shoulders, Greta stared down into Rae's pretty blue eyes. "Rae, I've seen you make grown men tremble when you give that come-hither smile of yours. If you can overcome your habit of vanity and always searching for compliments, I think the baron and you will do nicely."

Rae shook her head. "I wanted to marry very well indeed, to a grand prince or even a duke, but even more I wanted to marry a man who would cherish the ground I walk upon—not curse it. We aren't even going on a honeymoon. What kind of man marries a woman and doesn't take her touring around the Continent?"

"A widower with estates and children, I expect," Greta answered. "Besides, there wasn't much time to plan such things."

"And that's something else. I'm to be a stepmother, and I don't even like small children. They remind me of little hairy dogs, all smelly and into everything. Stepchildren are the root of all evil—I believe I saw that on a sampler somewhere." Her years of helping to keep watch over her two wily and rapacious brothers also came to mind.

"Please tell me you haven't given the baron your opinion on motherhood and children," Greta said.

Pinching her cheeks as she gazed into the mirror, Rae frowned. "Really, Greta, do you take me for a silly green girl? Of course I didn't tell him. He might take exception. Besides, if I'm lucky, he'll never know."

"He'll never know you don't like children?" Greta confirmed, confused as she stared at her sister's reflection in the gilt-framed mirror. Yes, Rae definitely had more hair than wit.

"Of course not. The children will have nurses and a governess enough to keep them busy. I shall go up and visit them once a week, and if they are very good, twice a week."

Greta shook her head, changing the subject to a more positive note. "Remember we came to Prussia to make good marriages, and you have. Baron Schortz not only took you without a dowry, but has sent funds to Papa as well. The money will help out a great bit, so you do not marry in vain. Well, the way you marry is no more vain than usual. Meanwhile, you have brought great peace of mind to our parents."

"Yes, I suppose that's true," Rae remarked.

"Keep in mind that I will continue to look for a husband as well."

"Ha! You're too involved with your old legends to worry about wedding. It's unfair; I wanted a prince but got a frog baron instead."

Kissing her sister on the cheek, Greta advised, "Make the best of this marriage, Rae. You only do it once."

"Once is quite enough, thank you." She sniffled piteously.

Brushing her cheek, Greta coaxed, "Please do smile. This is your wedding day."

Before Rae could respond to her sister, their aunt called out through the open doorway. Her voice was both loud and commanding. "It's time, Rae! Come along!"

Then their aunt ushered her out of the hall, and Rae repeated what the baroness had told her. As an older woman of much experience, Vivian likely knew all there was to know. "Duty, duty and duty." The words kept repeating themselves in her brain, and Rae heard the "Wedding March" being played quite beautifully by that odd little man, Herr Mozart.

Gathering her Grimmest courage, Rae proceeded down the aisle with her uncle, a smile so sweet on her face that surely the good angels above were weeping. She would do as Greta had suggested. It might not be the wedding of her dreams, but this was, after all, her wedding day. She smiled at her groom and willed him to look at her.

No smile lit Baron Schortz's face. He stood morosely, dressed in the deepest shades of black and gray, a testament to his lack of appreciation at what fate had generously bestowed upon him. Rae stepped upon his foot as her uncle gave her over, letting him know that he should show the world his delight at having such a magnificent lady for a bride.

Despite her slippered attack, Fen remained distant and gloomy, so Rae stepped upon his booted foot once more for good measure. Even dainty and fragile ladies knew when enough was enough and strong persuasion was needed. The man should be down on his knees thanking the lucky stars that they were to wed.

The groomsman was not smiling, either. No, Prince von Hanzen narrowed his eyes as he took in Rae's appearance, then switched his attention to Rae's sister, who had preceded her as maid of honor.

Greta glanced up and caught Prince von Hanzen staring at her. Despite her infuriation at the annoying but handsome prince, she smiled briefly, thinking how marvelous he looked in his dark jacket and white knee breeches. He didn't have to pad his calves or his shoulders, either.

She turned her attention back to her sister and the groom. Although she quite liked the baron and thought he would make her sister a wonderful husband, she could have kicked him for his somber expression. Not once had he smiled at his bride. This boded ill for marital harmony. Perhaps she could speak to the prince about his friend's lack of interest in both his wedding and his bride.

As the ceremony began, Fen couldn't help but feel utterly lost, made to bear witness to his own grim fate. Yes, he'd be married to a Grimm until the Reaper of similar name did them part. Stoically, he stood tall . . . ignoring the woman by his side. Clearing his throat, he tried not to recall the happy occasion his first wedding had been, and how he had yearned for the words to bind him to Fiona. His first wedding had been the happiest day of his life, and then the wedding night and births of his many children.

His erstwhile bride had similar thoughts, pondering deeply how going from a Grimm to a Schortz was an improvement. Wistfully, she sighed; she just couldn't see much difference.

To the great relief of all concerned in the improbable marriage, the ceremony passed quickly, and the unhappy couple was soon seated at their wedding breakfast. The pair barely managed to speak to each other, unlike the bride's sister and Rolpe.

Riveted by the striking woman beside him, the prince couldn't resist fanning her ire. Something about her made him want to nettle her needlessly, and his friend's marriage to the shallow, vain creature that was Greta's sister had not done much to improve his bitter mood. Over the past few days Rolpe had been deviled by a growing sense of . . . something different in the air. Whatever it was, it wasn't exactly evil, but it was definitely disturbing, as if air currents through long-dank chambers were suddenly set free. This awareness made him testier than usual.

"Ah, see the happy couple. Makes one want to run right out and find a bride. Shall we propose a toast to them? A fine grand toast—to years of misery and malcontent!"

"How lovely to find an optimist seated beside me," Greta replied. She turned regally toward the obnoxious but attractive man and raised a brow. Her face became a cool, distant mask.

"Miss Grimm, I am not an optimist, I assure you."

She pursed her lips. "I've said it before and I'll say it again: My sister may end up surprising you and the baron."

"I shall wait with bated breath."

"Prince von Hanzen, I think you need your ears boxed," Greta remarked. Her head held high, she made a move to rise and leave, but his hand on her arm stopped her. She also recalled just where she was; her aunt would literally lock her in her room with gruel and water if she made a scene.

His fingers seemed to burn through her arm, and she sat back down, her breath quickening. Managing to gain control over her feminine sensibilities, she said with some aplomb, "Do you know, I believe that you were raised in the castle barn, for I have yet to see you exhibit any good manners whatsoever. If I judged all Prussian nobility by you, I would have to believe them all snarling, rude little creatures."

"Some might say it's quite the fashion," Rolpe replied.

"And others might say it's your puffed up consequence. And the man who falls in love with himself will, in the great scheme of things, have no rivals."

Rolpe found himself chuckling. "I concede the point. But still, if I'm rude, it's because I find this whole wedding a farce and unmitigated disaster. Fen deserves better."

Greta narrowed her eyes. "As my sister deserves to be loved."

"She loves herself quite enough for everyone. In fact,

that affair is what has me worried," Rolpe retorted. It was with disgusted fascination that he watched Greta's lovely blue-gray eyes deepen in color and her pink rosebud mouth purse.

"She may be vain, but she will be true to him and give him support in whatever he needs. Just as she has supported me in my pursuits, even putting her own fears aside when I ventured into that cemetery."

"Ah, yes. The infamous cemetery. I'm surprised you aren't there now. The curiosity must be killing you. Oh, where, oh where has the woodcutter's mother's corpse gone? Oh where, oh where can she be?"

Greta sniffed. The prince could go hang himself, him and his unsought opinions. She would persevere in her quest for knowledge, and her sister would turn out a bride worthy of a king.

She addressed Rolpe: "I find your humor crude. And, alas, I felt my attire today would be inappropriate for a trek in the graveyard. Besides, it's not night yet."

Eyeing the lacy, blue crepe gown cinched tight at her waist, trimmed with tiny seed pearls clustered around the edges of her décolletage, Rolpe felt a stirring of desire which was inappropriate in this place and inappropriate for this particular woman. Her very lovely breasts, which had caught his attention the other night at the cemetery, made him want to explore them at leisure. And he found that particular desire, like this woman, discomposing.

He replied mockingly, "Yes. It might be rather difficult to maneuver around in a dozen petticoats and lace."

Greta gave him a rueful stare. The prince was an arrogant rogue, and had probably known many female conquests—so many that he could probably fill her aunt's manor home with his discarded *amours*. It was disgusting. It was intriguing. It was definitely beyond her concern, even though he made her pulse flutter and her knees sway. Oh, yes, the man brought out her primitive side.

Glancing over his shoulder, she regained some of her

composure. "You shouldn't speak of such things. Why, I'm shocked at such frank talk—mentioning a lady's unmentionables!"

"I shall keep it a secret that I know about them." He grinned. "And you needn't feign shock. I'd bet my best barouche that you've never needed smelling salts. Stop pulling my leg."

Unable to help herself, Greta glanced down at the strong leg muscles showcased by the cut of his breeches, and she swallowed hard. "I wouldn't dare," she said. Glancing up, she warily noted the heat in his eyes blazing like blue flames as he stared at her.

"I would insist, *must* insist," he responded, wanting her desperately.

Fanning her face, Greta looked away, feeling the power of his seduction and knowing that a gently bred maid would leave. "Have you perchance heard of virtue? It's its own reward," she remarked.

"Virtue I find very dull, and difficult to maintain. To be honest, it's a terror."

"I would think you incapable of fear. Being as awe-inspiring and knowledgeable as you are."

"My capacity for fear is the same as any sane man's," he replied. "As for my pride, to which you obviously refer . . . I find humility a waste of time. I am no more puffed up than any other man who is wealthy, wise and titled," he replied. "But back to the point. I know this region stirs the imagination, but *vampyrs* and werewolves and such in Wolfach . . . those are a preposterous, Canterbury tale."

"In your *worthy* opinion," she snapped. Her tone was full of sarcasm. "But there are other opinions. Take for instance the Countess DeLuise and Herr Nietzsche and even Herr Mozart, all of whom believe in the unbelievable. And explain this: Where do legends and myths come from, if not some form of reality?"

He studied her quietly for a moment. "The imaginations of the feeble," he replied. He'd found her to be a rational woman . . . until she was no longer rational. Now she was a danger to herself and those around her. He couldn't have Greta Grimm messing with things that bit in the night, hid under bridges or harassed innocent travelers. Or more deadly, wily witches who practiced black magic deep in the heart of the Black Forest.

She chided him. "Millions of spirit creatures walk the earth unseen, both while we sleep and when we wake."

"Very good. Milton, I believe." Once again, she had impressed him. She was what the English called a bluestocking. Oh, how he would love to see those stockings. And while her intellectual curiosity and aptitude intimidated most men, they did not deter him. He loved how she kept him on his toes.

"Miss Grimm, let us suppose that you are right. Do you not think that such legends, if found, could be extremely deadly? You would only be bound for trouble. However, you are *not* right. No, grave robbers are behind that cemetery incident, I'm certain." And before she could protest, he finished, "And as grave as that fact might be, it would be far graver should your legends be true."

Greta frowned, then retorted, "Perhaps, but my brothers are putting their trust in me to discover all I can about the Black Forest."

He studied her. "Just remember: Curiosity killed the cat."

"Ah, but the cat had nine lives." Her heart was beating faster, for she thoroughly enjoyed his attention; he had that something special which called to her. Blinking her eyes, she regained her wits. "And if you are right, then these legends are just so much smoke in the wind. If that's the case, there can be no danger. I am perfectly safe."

He snorted. "You are far from safe."

"And you are a boor."

Herr Nietzsche sauntered over to take a seat next to Greta. Having heard her latest comment, he chortled. "How well she knows you, von Hanzen. What have you done to inspire such plain speaking?"

"Hello, Ronald," the prince said, his high brow arched in query as to why Nietzsche was interrupting.

Greta answered: "Prince von Hanzen insists that there are no vampires in Wolfach."

Nietzsche narrowed his eyes. "Then where have Choplin's remains gone?"

A sneer formed on the prince's lips. "Grave robbers."

Greta shook her head. "If it was grave robbers, then why only the one grave? It makes no sense."

"Perhaps they only needed one body to sell. Perhaps there's a glut in the market. Mayhap they'll come back when the market levels out."

Greta's eyes widened.

"But we have prepared for that. There are two guards now placed at the cemetery," he explained, taking a sip of beer. "I spoke with my uncle, the magistrate."

"I hope those guards are wearing plenty of crosses," she remarked.

"My, my, you are like a dog with a bone," Rolpe complained.

"It's part of my charm."

Rolpe leaned closer to Greta, his gray eyes full of something beyond irritation. "That's debatable. What's not debatable is that you are on a fool's errand. Once and for all, *there is nothing supernatural in Wolfach.*"

"So you keep protesting. I, however, shall continue to believe in the unbelievable, and nothing you say can tell me otherwise."

Fighting his frustration—and the urge to kiss her so passionately she'd never think of vampires again—he remarked, "Have you ever heard of the two great tribulations in this world? The first," he said as he held up one finger, "is not getting what you want."

"And the other?" she asked, her eyes drinking in his masculine beauty, even if it was partly obscured by his scolding finger. She wanted to slap his face and then kiss it to make it better.

"*Getting* what one wants," Rolpe replied in a huff.

Taking a sip of beer, Herr Nietzsche choked on laughter. He sputtered, "Von Hanzen, what taradiddle is this? Of course there are monsters in Prussia! Always have been and always will be. We Prussians are the stuff of which fairy tales are made."

Rolpe stood up impatiently, his chair scooting backwards with a slight screech. Leaning over the table, he grabbed Nietzsche's collar. "I have the sudden urge to pummel someone's face. Have one to spare?"

The shorter man sputtered and shook his head no.

The prince turned his attention back to Greta. "Just be careful what you seek. You might just find something you don't want."

"Whatever doesn't kill me only makes me stronger," she replied, unmoved.

Shaking his head in disgust, Rolpe stomped away from the table. Herr Nietzsche jumped up from his chair, eyes bright with enthusiasm. Excusing himself from Greta, he bowed once. "I'm going to find a pen and parchment. By gads! I'm going to quote the prince. In spite of his ill temper, he does have a way with words. And you as well!"

Amused by the little man, Greta tried to put some order to the questions tumbling around her head. Von Hanzen had warned her quite thoroughly away from her quest, which only made her more determined. His warnings were too stern to not be grounded in something interesting.

Taking a bite of wedding cake, she turned her attention back to the unhappy couple. Her sister sat silently beside her new husband. To Rae's right, Herr Mozart was busy scribbling something on the tablecloth.

"My, who would have thought this wedding would inspire artistic creativity?" Greta remarked. Too bad it didn't inspire joy.

Taking aside the new Baroness Schortz, Greta cheerfully reminded her, "At least you're now nobility."

"I must have been cursed by a witch unawares," Rae blabbed, not finding any comfort in her new social standing.

At her wits' end, Greta stumbled around for something else positive to say. "Now that you are a married woman, with a home of your own, you no longer have to listen to Aunt Vivian's lectures! Nor will you have to put up with Mother's constant harping on your lack of matrimony. And just think how the gold Fen sent will help Papa. It was a far, far, better thing you did today for your family than you'd ever done before. Our family is quite proud of you, Rae. I know it. I most certainly am."

Rae finally managed a smile. "Yes, there is that." Perhaps her marriage wasn't a fairy tale, or her husband a prince, but at least there was some small comfort in knowing her family's financial woes had been lightened. Her heart was lightened as well.

# CHAPTER SEVENTEEN

## Yours, Mine and Outrageous

Well, she was certainly a fair maid all forlorn after her dismal wedding and even more dismal wedding breakfast. Rae frowned as her imposing and non-fawning husband helped her into the carriage. Rather dazed, she tried to compose herself as she sat down and arranged her lovely wedding gown with a twist of her gloved hands, then tucked a slender curl up under her lacy white bonnet. She looked the picture of a beautiful bride, except for the slight downturn of her lips.

Her grimacing groom looked less the perfect picture of a gentlemanly bridegroom. He stretched out his long legs and settled back against the cushions, looking very much more comfortable than she was in all her wedding finery. Somehow she found herself resenting him all the more. He certainly didn't appear put out by this farce of a ceremony.

Patiently, she waited for her brand-new husband to make some comment, but after seven miles or so she began to suspect that he wasn't going to break the silence. Well, if the big lout decided to be boring and petty, she would show him that she was made of sterner stuff. "Is your home of Durloc very large?"

"Yes."

"Is it very far?"

"Another eight miles."

"Will the children be there?" Rae asked, hoping that they might have been sent elsewhere for the duration of the honeymoon. The children were just another unpalatable fact of being forced to wed an ox, even if this was an ox with some Norwegian royal blood.

"It's their home," he replied without much inflection.

Drat, the children were at home. Still, she could plead a bride's nerves and probably avoid them for at least a month. She remembered her mother talking of nerves, and of how she had run home to the vicarage for a week after her wedding night.

"I believe you said you had three children. All girls?" she asked.

It was strange, Fen thought. The night he met Rae, he had considered her a perfect angel come to earth, so beautiful that it hurt the eyes, and he had mistakenly bestowed upon her all the radiant qualities of kindness, compassion, wisdom and wit that his beloved Fiona had possessed. It seemed he had been a bit overhasty. "I do have three girls. But I distinctly told you the other night that I have four boys as well."

"Seven? Seven!" Rae actually screeched like a fishwife. Something was fishy, even though she had only been a wife for a few short hours. "Stop this carriage immediately and turn around. We must annul this marriage at once!"

He stared as if she had gone crazy. "What the devil are you talking about? Your reputation would be in tatters if I annulled this marriage, and I won't be made a laughingstock in front of all of Prussia. Imagine, annulling a marriage of only a few hours."

"But seven children," she wailed. "I'm too young to have seven children. I know nothing about being a stepmother," she pleaded, her eyes filling with tears. "Well, I mean I do know a little about stepmothering, since Greta is always reading some fairy tale or another. But I don't think I should use those tales as inspiration, since all those stepmothers did was make the children clean chimneys and wear sack-cloth. Although, I do rather like the idea of glass slippers. Do you think the cobbler in town can make some? I'd like half a dozen in colored glass. I must admit to having a slight weakness for sartorial splendor."

Fen stared at his wife as if she had two heads. He had the strongest urge to lock her in a castle tower. On second thought, he would let his children do it for him.

"No, I don't imagine the Cinderella stepmother approach would work," he agreed. She wasn't going to make his life a hell and his children's life a misery. Glass slippers be damned. What did the fool woman think: that he was made of gold?

His golden brows lowered over his eyes. However had he managed to get into this predicament, to become married to a shallow, shrewish spendthrift? But as he studied her golden loveliness, his expression lightened somewhat. Fortuitously, as her husband it was his duty to see that Rae changed. Her days of her excess and vanity were over. She would toe the line, and if he didn't make her, his children certainly would.

Rae was nodding her head up and down like a broken jack-in-the-box. "Good, then we are in agreement. This is a horrid mistake of a wedding. At first I thought you too pig-headed to understand, but now I know you can be reasonable. I know you don't want this marriage any more than I. And I feel perfectly correct in saying that your children wouldn't want me for a mother. Well, perhaps that's a bit too harsh. They would love to have a mother as lovely as I, but I'm much too young, and they would most likely see me as an older sister . . . which wouldn't work. I have been a sister to boys and it is a most difficult and distressing undertaking. My brothers made my life a misery. Frogs in my bed, tadpoles in my tea, moss in my bonnets, snails on my mirror and ink in my perfume bottle. The perfume was from Paris, too! So our wedlock will never work. It must be annulled at once."

Her words caused his mood to sour further. She was only managing to rub salt into a wound that was already raw. "Our wedding won't be annulled. I take my vows seriously; for richer, for poorer, for sickness and in health. Till death us part, which if you don't stop your whining, might be very soon." She had insulted him and his children with her words; he wanted to throw her out of the carriage and annul *her.* But he couldn't, and that was the rub. He was stuck with this vain, selfish female until he shucked his mortal coil, and he didn't know if he had the patience to teach her a thing, even if it was his husbandly duty. He sighed, a low sound. With his luck lately, he would probably live to a hundred and seventy.

Rae did not notice his reaction, since she was so busy justifying all the reasons this wedding wouldn't suit, including her fears regarding her wifely duty. "But nowhere does it say that I pledge thee my troth *and seven children.* I really must protest. I was led astray!"

"No more than I. Why didn't you listen to me the other night when I explained about my wife Fiona's death and my children? Obviously, you weren't listening."

"Of course I wasn't listening! I was planning my wedding gown, since we rushed to get married. A lady only gets married once . . . unless, of course, she becomes widowed and remarries."

Closing his eyes in dismay, he wondered if he could just ride away into the daylight, pretending he had never known her. He could send for his children, and they could travel the country without his whiny bride.

"Seven. That is most definitely six too many. Have you never heard of moderation? My sensibilities will be taxed beyond bearing. No wonder you were still unconnected when I arrived. No sane woman would wed you, not with a parcel of children not her own!"

"And no sane man would wed *you,* except if he were compromised, because your vanity and selfishness are monumental."

"You're comparing my vanity to seven children? Oh, no sirrah! I am the loser here, not you. My vanity you can walk away from, but how do you escape seven children?"

Fen leaned over and set his arms on either side of his bride's legs, his dark gray eyes stormy. "I am going to tell you this once. I love my *kinder.*"

Kindling? The man was upset about firewood at a time like this? She could only gape at him.

"My *kinder*—my children—are everything to me. I expect you to be good and kind to them. All of them. All seven, or else you will regret the day you stepped foot into my country and let a bug crawl up your drawers!"

Rae sniffed, letting one tear slip down her cheek, but her dratted lout of a husband didn't even notice. What a brute! Making her cry on her wedding day and making her a mother to seven little oafs. "I shall probably die young, mothering your brood. And I hope my sacrifice on the altar of motherhood smites your conscience."

Fen leaned back. "I shall endeavor to erect a lovely marble monument to your ability. Just think, when Greta visits the cemetery in the dead of a night, she really will have a relative to visit."

"Oh, you beast! You have no care for my sensibilities. I am doomed, and it isn't even the second day of marriage."

He laughed.

Rae pouted. She wheedled. She beseeched. She even tried her limpid gaze. All to no avail, for they arrived at the castle and her arguments were forgotten.

Her first glimpse of the castle had her changing her opinion slightly. The Castle Durloc was magnificent, with four large towers, two of which were guarding the arched entrance to a large courtyard covered with snow. A dozen or so fir trees lined the entryway. Long tendrils of ivy and other foliage climbed the pale gray stone of the castle walls.

With bated breath, Rae noted that many of the windows were stained glass. It was a fairyland, she thought, dazed. She might be locked in wedlock to a big churl, but he did have a wonderful home, and she was now mistress of this lovely place. "Is this your principal estate?"

The carriage stopped and Fen opened his door before the footman could, and quickly descended. "Yes," he replied, helping her outside. His body blocked her line of sight until he had deposited her upon the terraced steps to the front entrance.

Rae's smile of pleasure faded. "Oh, no!" she muttered as she stared at the frankly grotesque scene. Her breathing actually hitched, and her skin felt all clammy. It was hideous, worse than one of Greta's fairy tales. It was monstrous, an abomination. It was . . . her stepchildren: seven of the grubby little blighters, with their dirt-encrusted nails, muddy and torn clothing—and the littlest two were dripping snot as they touched her, leaving slimy and muddy handprints on her wedding gown.

At that moment, Rae did what any female of delicate sensibilities would do: She fainted. It was with graceful dignity, and she fell at the feet of her husband and his grubby little urchins, who surrounded her. The children all stared with wide-eyed interest at their new mother's spectacular greeting. And instead of picking her up, Fen shook his head and called for his butler to bring the smelling salts.

The oldest of the baron's children, Nap, nodded his head approvingly. "She's going to be easy to scare," he remarked with pleasure.

Nods of satisfaction came from the rest of the group, with the next oldest son, one of the twins, saying enthusiastically as he peered at this new mother, "*Ja,* she will. What grand fun I expect!"

Cheers arose as Fen brought smelling salts back to his downed bride. Ignoring the noise, and the happy faces of his brood, he felt particularly morose at the despicable turn his life had taken. Still, at least his children seemed happy with their new stepmother.

# CHAPTER EIGHTEEN

## Behind Enemy Lines at the Schortzes

If every painting tells a story, then this particular picture was straight from hell. As the swirling waves of blackness left her, Rae heard a voice calling to her. She knew that voice, and at the moment hated it. What a fine way to start a marriage, scared of one's husband and his brood! She shuddered, recalling the faces of the children before she'd fainted. What she had seen in their eyes chilled her blood. Her new stepchildren were utterly lacking in mercy.

Cautiously, Rae opened her eyes and stared up at a large wooden plaque. *Beware of Stepmothers* was prominently displayed across the fireplace mantel. She closed her eyes tightly.

"She'll make us dig potatoes in the snow," one of the twins predicted.

Fen shook his head at Ernst. "It's too cold for potatoes."

"Stones, then," Ernst insisted.

"You're not giving her a chance. And get rid of that foolish sign," Fen ordered as he stared down at his bride.

Rae sighed dejectedly, and sneaked a peak. It was bad. Worse than bad. It was absolutely horrible. Here she was, laid out on a hard settee like a slab of roast beef for their perusal. Well, she could certainly say that stepmothering was not the least bit dignified.

"Come on, Rae, I know you're awake."

She moved her lips soundlessly in a prayer for deliverance, but God seemed to have abandoned her. A triumphant growl assaulted her ears, and the voice came back with forceful persistence.

"I never took you for a coward, Rae," Fen continued, a tiny bit amused. He stood from the position where he'd been kneeling. The scent of lilacs which wafted from his new bride had his imagination running wild. Briefly he wondered what it would be like to bury his face in her pale golden locks. On the heels of this betraying thought came regret. He should not regard this unwanted bride as anything but a duty, a bitter pill to swallow.

"Are they still here?" she asked out of the corner of her mouth.

"What do you think?" he answered.

*That I'm cursed.* But wisely she kept this thought to herself. Reluctantly she managed to open her eyes to "them"— the children. Fen helped her sit up slowly, then stepped back, and Rae managed to paste a smile on her face. She faced her stepchildren, all seven of them. How could seven small children fill the room with so much menace? She didn't know, but the children hated her upon sight. Yes, here were the seven little Schortzes, staring at her with a mixture of resentful curiosity and devious intent. This was not good; she knew from her own childhood years.

Watching Rae, Fen couldn't help but admit that she did look ravishingly beautiful, seated on his sofa with slightly mussed hair and wary eyes. If only she were a different sort of woman. Of course, being a red-blooded creature with a healthy appetite, he did appreciate her looks, but he would have settled for someone less spectacular who could be a good mother to his brood.

A prodding at knee level caused him to look down upon his second youngest child. "Yes, Poppy?" Thank goodness it was Poppy, and not his youngest, Alden, who was still teething and had the unfortunate habit of biting ankles. If

Alden wasn't biting ankles, he was rubbing his "magic" lamp. Every boy has a treasure. The lamp was Alden's, given to him by his beloved mother. Not so pretty now, the lamp had a few dents and was in need of a good polishing. But to Alden it was solid gold.

"Who's that strange woman?" his little darling asked.

"Why, Poppy, I told you. She's your new stepmother." With a rather sick smile plastered on his face, Fen faced his fearless children. "Isn't it marvelous? Isn't she pretty?"

"Yes, she's pretty," his second eldest daughter remarked. "But my hair is curlier. So mine is prettier."

Hearing the baron's child's audacious claim, Rae started to argue; then she realized how foolish it was. The little curly-locked girl was only a child. And she *was* pretty, Rae decided as she briefly studied the brat. She clearly took after the mother's side of the family.

"*Nein.* Don't want a new stepmother," Poppy remarked. A chorus of equally negative responses followed from the other children, filling the air.

"We don't need a new mother." This from Fen's oldest, a clever lad with an impish bent. "She looks really mean," he remarked. "I can tell." Ernst was always trying to be important.

"I bet she hates pirates . . . and baboon tarts." Quinn, who loved playing pirates, added his thoughts to the conversation. "She'll hate dogs and cats and squirrels and horses and . . ."

"We get the picture, Quinn," Fen said flatly.

"She'll make us eat all her cabbage—and I hate cabbage." This came from Merri, the contrary one.

"She may be pretty, but I think she's a witch in disguise." Shyla did love pretty things. Maybe that would eventually be a stroke of good fortune in so far as her new mother was concerned, Fen thought hopefully. He stared at the child who looked most like his late wife.

Merri interrupted. "I'm hungry." She was always hungry when she wasn't grumbling about something.

Embarrassed by his brood's lack of good breeding, Fen told them to hush immediately. Turning his attention back to Rae, he recognized her look. She was clearly bewildered, staring at his passel of children, and she wore the glazed stare of a woman who was thinking of running. He reassured her firmly, "They don't really mean what they are saying. They're just a little upset over our marriage being as quick as it was. They're just a little *ver worren*—confused."

"Aren't we all," Rae replied, glancing from belligerent face to belligerent face.

"We do too mean what we're saying," Ernst stated, quickly backed up by the grumbling of his sister. Merri was complaining about wicked stepmothers and evil witches.

Fen shook his head. "We will have no more of this. Come, it is time for introductions. What will your new mother think of our *sittens?*"

What did Rae think? Sittens? Glancing at the horrid little monsters, she wondered if they were supposed to sit to be introduced. That seemed a strange custom, but then, from what she had observed so far, this was not your normal household. However, she certainly didn't want them sitting on the pretty striped French sofa next to her. Not with her lovely wedding gown and their grubby nasty little fingers.

As she started to protest, she was interrupted by her loutish husband, who quickly explained, "*Sittens* are manners." He must have caught her look of confusion.

However, at his explanation there were gasps of outrage. "She doesn't even speak German?" his eldest asked.

"*Nein,* Nap. Rae speaks very little German. But then, she was brought up in England," Fen replied, his tone abrupt.

"We live in Prussia, but we speak English," Merri pointed out.

"Well, now we have a stepmother who doesn't speak one speck of German," Shyla said, her little face scrunched in disapproval. "What will my friends think? What will Grandmother Schortz think?"

"She'll be mad and send her to bed without her supper," Merri predicted with a cheerful glint in her eyes.

"Grandmother can't do that. She's in Paris right now," Ernst spoke up.

"How fortunate for me," Rae remarked. "And most people in England speak French not German, anyway, since French is the civilized tongue."

Nap's face got a crafty look. "Then, you speak French?"

Fen had begun to interrupt, but when Rae disparaged the German language as well as his country, he stood and let his little darlings work their magic. Rae frowned, realizing a trap had been sprung, and decided to ignore the fractious lad. Ernst got a crafty look in his eye, tapped his brother on the shoulder and whispered. Nap's crafty expression took on a wicked cast.

Rae noted the two boys' evil intent immediately, and couldn't help but feel a chill creep over her soul. Her wedding day wasn't even half over yet, and she felt not only weary in spirit and body, but leery as well. "I will *learn* German," she announced boldly, forgetting that she had a terrible time with languages.

"Like you've learned French?" Nap questioned. A few snorts followed, all of disdain.

Rae lost her temper and replied snidely to the ugly little mob. "How hard can it be, if you all speak it?"

And with those few words, her fate was sealed. War was declared. It would be a bitter, winner-take-all battle, her against them, filled with wanton carnage, diabolical pranks and crafty maneuverings. There would be no flags of truce, no surrender. This was war at its most elemental.

Ignoring the ugly stirrings in the air, Fen proceeded to introduce his children. Pointing to a tall, lanky lad of twelve, with pale blond hair and deep gray eyes, he told Rae this was Napoleon—Nap for short. And Nap was dynamite. The child was a natural leader and quite intelligent, and the pride was evident in his father's voice as he praised his oldest son and heir.

Next he introduced a chubby child with light brown hair and pale blue eyes. His eldest daughter, Meredith, was called Merri for short. She had just turned eleven. After Merri, Fen leaned over and straightened the jacket of one of the blond-haired boys. He then presented his twins: Quinn and Ernst, who were nine. The two were almost identical, with the exception that Quinn had light gray eyes and Ernst's were a vivid blue with dark gray specks. (It would be much later that Rae took the time to notice the difference.)

Fen boasted of Quinn's interest in living things, while Ernst liked to invent things, including stories. Ernst, it seemed, wanted to be an actor when he grew up. Rae made a mental note to keep that juicy tidbit in mind. Her sister Taylor could act, and the pranks the girl had pulled were downright scary.

Before he could finish introducing a girl named Shyla, a very pretty little eight-year-old with golden curls and eyes the color of sapphires interrupted. "My name's Poppy." And the incorrigible five-year-old climbed up her father's leg.

Rae merely nodded. She was weary, and the restlessness of the child was not only distracting; it was tiring. Glancing at her new husband, she commented dolefully, "That child has been hopping, skipping or swinging her arms in constant motion ever since I opened my eyes. It makes me quite dizzy." Why couldn't the girl be still, like the littlest child, a boy, who was sitting quietly by the desk leg, playing with what looked to be like a dented lantern?

"I don't *yikes* to be still."

Shaking her head, Rae asked, "Why on earth would you saddle a child with a name like Poppy? It sounds like something someone would call their grandfather. Isn't it bad enough she has to bear the surname Schortz?"

The room erupted with shouts of anger as Fen sucked in his breath at her rudeness. And he had worried about the effect of his children's ill manners on Rae's feelings? What a witch!

"I see. Poppy is a strange name, while Razel is nothing odd, even though you're named after a member of the lettuce family."

"An herb. A healing herb," Rae cried out.

"Well, I see little difference. And what's wrong with the name Schortz? It's a fine, distinguished name! Schortzes have been in Prussia since the tenth century. And they have been barons for the past seven centuries. Can you say the same thing about your family name?"

Before Rae had a chance to defend her familial honor, she was rudely interrupted by Poppy, whose face had turned a deep red. "It's my grandmother's name, Schorz, and I *yike* it!" And with those words, the little girl jumped down from her father's leg, ran over and kicked Rae in the shin.

"Ouch!" Rae squealed, and glared at Poppy. She turned her accusing glare at her husband. "She *kicked* me!"

Nap interrupted, his face flushed with anger. "You wouldn't know a worthy name if it bit you on—"

"Nap, that's enough," Fen warned. He cut his son off and pulled the little warrior Poppy away from his new wife. Then, shrugging his shoulders, he turned to Rae and replied, "Some might say that you deserved it."

"How dare you!" Rae was beyond being incensed, since even a new wife knew that a husband's duty was to protect his wife from harm, even at the hands of his children.

"I dare anything I please," Fen retorted, eyeing her with no love lost. This proud, vainglorious woman would never be a good mother.

"We don't have to keep her, do we?" Merri whined. "I don't like her. And she doesn't like our name!"

"Father, we can't have her for a stepmother. She'll shame the Schortz name!" Nap exploded, his narrow features tightening as he glared at his new stepmother. "You could get an annulment."

"She is pretty, but our mother was much prettier," Shyla declared.

They already despised her, and she hadn't even been in their home for an hour yet. Which just went to prove that Rae had been right, which she was now thinking. "An annulment is a fine idea. What a smart boy!"

Rae smiled winningly at Nap, who, noticing how the smile lit up her eyes, narrowed his own. With a calculated gaze he switched his attention back and forth from his new mother to his father. His father was still scowling, but Nap had to admit that Ms. Rae was a fetching thing, and his father liked a pretty face. They were all doomed, unless he could get rid of her. The sooner, the better, too. His brothers and sisters needed a real mother, like the one they had lost. And this cold woman on the sofa would not a good mother make.

Hearing his son's words and Rae's agreement set Fen's teeth on edge and fired his temper. "There will be no annulment!" he bellowed.

Nap and the twins glared at their father. Poppy stuck her thumb in her mouth, while Shyla primped her curls and looked bored. Merri bitterly grumbled about evil stepmothers.

Not to be outdone, and expressing his outrage at being ignored, Alden attached himself to his father's strong right leg and began to bite. As Fen felt his son's sharp little teeth, he leaned down and plucked him off his leg and lifted him up in the air. With a sarcastic flourish, he introduced the mite. "And last but not least is my youngest, Alden. He's not quite four."

Rae's gasp was filled with undisguised horror. "Let me guess—an ankle-biter. Good grief. My youngest brother William was one, and I have a scar to prove it." She had not only not married well, she had married into hell.

She fled to her bedroom.

Meanwhile, while Rae was dealing with her new stepchildren by hiding in her boudoir, Greta was handling her own issues. She used her aunt's joyous celebrations to slip away unnoticed, and to confront the doctor who examined the old Choplin woman's body upon death.

"The time has come to talk of many things," Greta said as she stared at the doctor. "Of the woodcutter's mother, her missing corpse and bite marks on the neck."

The doctor just stared at her as if she were mad.

The man's a disgrace to his profession, Greta thought disgustedly, for he stood there, his jacket askew, with red-dened eyes, sagging jowls and a pasty coloring. He stared at her as if she were something strange. His house, which served also as his office, was filthy with discarded bottles of Schnapps littered here and there.

"Come, now, 'tis no time to be shy. I am asking about the corpse, and the fact that no body was in the grave."

"You're wrong. There was somebody. Frau Choplin."

"I know the body was hers, but there was no body in there." Impatiently, Greta stared at him, smelling the alcohol he'd clearly recently drunk.

"Of course nobody was there. Her corpse was stolen, which means that no body was there where it should have been. For that is where the bodies are buried—any old body—in the cemetery," the grumpy old doctor exclaimed.

"I wonder, do you take lessons from my sister?" Greta asked, bemused. This was not going as smoothly as she had foreseen. "Never mind. Just tell me if Frau Choplin had bite marks on her neck or wrists."

"My child," the doctor began. "She was not bitten by wolves or bears. A cart of wood fell upon her as she was traveling home one night."

Greta's eyes filled with displeasure. "I know a cart fell upon her, but before it fell, mayhap she was bitten and drained of blood."

"She lost blood due to the falling logs hitting her," the doctor allowed.

Greta shook her head, exasperated, and glanced up at the clock over the mantel. Her aunt would soon be leaving the after-wedding-breakfast dinner that the Countess De-Luise was hosting. She would be back any time now, and this idiot was not helping by hedging. "Did you even check for bite marks?" she demanded.

"Why would I check for bite marks when she was attacked by logs?"

Slapping a hand to her face, Greta glowered at the man. "You are a doctor! It is your duty to see what causes the deaths of the persons entrusted to your care. How can you do that if you don't thoroughly check over each corpse?"

The disheveled doctor glared back at Greta with distaste. "Do not presume to tell me how to do my duty. I'm the doctor here, not you!"

"Ha! I bet you don't know a shin bone from a thigh bone. How could you, drowning in liquor as you are?"

The doctor drew himself up to his very impressive height and pointed to a diploma by the door. "I graduated from the University of Munich twenty-seven years ago. I've been tending to bodies both alive and dead since before you were even born."

"That may be, but the facts are clear. Frau Choplin's body is not in her grave. Therefore, it is possible to conclude that she rose from her grave after being bitten and drained by a vampire."

"Oh no! You don't happen to be one of those Fairy Tale Fundamentalists?"

"No, I am merely a concerned citizen who has extensively studied legends such as those of werewolves and vampires, and of other things that fly by night," she stated proudly.

"Oh, good grief! Another one of those graveyard gatherers!" the doctor sneered. "Sticking your nose into cemetery business and other otherworldly concerns. I should have known. You're putting the cart before the *Nosferatu*. There is no such thing as *vampyrs*. Now, go away like a good girl and leave me to my work."

"You mean to your Schnapps."

Pointing at the door to his office, he eyed her with distaste. It was ugly. "You have overstayed your welcome."

Head held high, Greta left the room in a royal huff, muttering, "What in the bloody hell does he know, anyway? He was probably too stewed to make anything but a soup of the details."

As she carefully made her way around an icy patch of snow, she wondered how her sister was faring. Rae was probably right now ensconced in her new home. Greta hoped that Rae was at least enjoying explorations of her new castle. She also hoped her vain little sister would soon come to acknowledge that she was married to a good man.

With her thoughts focused on Rae and her wedding night, Greta rounded the corner to the main street. Then she saw *him* across the cobbled street. Prince von Hanzen was escorting a lady inside—if "lady" she could be called. Her gown was an outlandish scarlet, and her cheeks were painted. Still, if the prince wanted to parade a hussy up and down Wolfach for all to see, who was Greta to care?

Glancing down the street, the prince espied her and gave her a mocking bow. Greta fumed. "He's too arrogant by half, too assured and too stubborn," she muttered.

The so-called lady said something to him, and he turned his attention to her. Greta responded by turning and ignoring him, feigning great interest in the shop window.

"Imagine, escorting a soiled dove in broad daylight," she mumbled disgustedly.

However, she unhappily found herself angered by her concern that the pompous, promiscuous prince would be spending the afternoon kissing that hussy's too-red lips instead of her own.

# CHAPTER NINETEEN

## Bless the Beastly Little Children

In later years, Rae would always remember two things about her wedding. First: that the brood of seven little Schortzes, with their beady little eyes and grubby little fingers, were scamps one and all, pests pure and simple. The second thing she would remember was that she did not have a wedding night. Though, for the first few days of her marriage, this problem did not bother her a whit. It was only later, when she began to see her husband as virile and handsome, that his lack of interest in his husbandly duties bothered her.

No, on this night—her wedding night—she was praying for a reprieve from her wifely duties as she was seated at the dinner table by one of the footmen. Nodding briskly at her husband, she turned her attention to the room in general. She and Fen were dining by candlelight, as a newly married couple should, but without the intimacy or rapport. The atmosphere was very tense. The whole subject of children remained just out of sight, like a giant fire-breathing dragon watching from the shadows. The abysmal meeting between the children and Rae was not mentioned, but nonetheless the dragon eventually raised its ugly head, by way of a loud banging sound from above.

Rae glanced up and heard a shout of pure glee. Her husband remained silent, even though it sounded as if demented little goblins were breaching the castle walls. Enough was enough. She spoke. "I see your children have not heard of the golden rule."

Fen lifted his head from his contemplation of his plate. "The golden rule?"

"Children should be seen and not heard."

Fen didn't know whether to laugh or cry. "That's not the golden rule!"

"It's not?" she asked, genuinely surprised.

He shook his head. "Do unto your neighbor as you would have him do unto you."

"That's a fine rule, too," she agreed. "Shall I go make faces at the children as they did to me this afternoon, or make wooden signs, or perhaps a tapestry celebrating the dubious joys of being a stepmother?"

He actually cracked a smile. "It takes time, Rae. This situation is new to us all."

There wasn't much she could say to that, so she sourly took a bite of sauerkraut and began to study her surroundings. It was more than obvious her husband was wealthy. The dining area was a very spacious room with a high, vaulted ceiling. Watered silk covered the walls, with delicate tiny floral patterns. Placed about the room were several large paintings, and she noted a Rembrandt, which she knew to be very costly. A Venetian chandelier hung high overhead, with hundreds of etched glass pieces hanging from its center.

The silverware was gold, most probably real. All in all it was a perfectly divine dining room, Rae saw—with one exception. Fen had not ordered for her place to be set next to his own; hence they were separated by a vast expanse of polished cherrywood table, making conversation necessarily loud.

The bleak atmosphere seemed to affect everyone in the room, too. The butler's countenance was stiff, and the liveried footmen went about performing their tasks in solemn silence. Her bridal supper reminded Rae of a wake, rather than a bride and groom's first intimate meal.

As the silence drew on, Rae became aware that she needed to do something to lighten the atmosphere. She had never been seated with a gentleman who was not trying to win her affections—most especially not alone with one. The morose man was slowly sipping his wine, ignoring her presence.

He was certainly not the man she would have chosen to be her husband, yet he'd become exactly that. Regrettably. Nonetheless, she vowed that she would not let him ignore her. Her feminine vanity would not allow it.

"You truly have a lovely home," she remarked.

He glanced up at her, taking his attention off his food. "How fortunate that you appreciate my home, since you dislike me, my surname and my children. We must toast this fortunate turn of events!" So saying, he lifted his glass. "To my loving bride, who is overcome by good fortune. To Rae, with her gentle, demure and kind nature, who will always strive to make my life a veritable feast. My little Rae of sunshine."

Though she was not usually astute at discerning sarcastic comments, Rae realized her husband was mocking her. She narrowed her eyes, responding as she lifted her glass. "How thoughtful of you. Shall I propose one to you as well?" Not giving him time to answer, she continued with a sweet smile plastered upon her face. "To my very thoughtful husband, who has made my welcome here one I shall never forget. To his patient understanding of a new bride's need to feel welcome inside a strange home. To his gallantry in making his wife feel special on her one and only wedding day, giving constant attention and compliments."

Fen frowned, giving a signal to the butler, and the footmen and butler departed quietly. He had married a too-proud and disagreeable woman, and she had the gall to suggest he was the one at fault? He vented his shock: "You are taking me to task over my performance as a groom?"

Staring into her husband's eyes, Rae decided that honesty was the best policy. It was a tactic she rarely used with males, with the exception of her brothers and the vicar's brother, Timothy, but she was going to tell the whole truth and nothing but. "Yes. You have made it plain to your staff and to those who attended our wedding that you are not happy with your choice of bride. It's both ungentlemanly and ungallant of you. People will criticize and revile me, the bride whose groom was not besotted but instead felt she was beneath his notice. I shall be a figure of pity among society and servants alike. I hesitate to remark on it, but this will not do your consequence any good; nor your children's."

His outrage faded somewhat. She did have a valid point, he ceded, regarding her meaningfully over the rim of his wineglass. "I must say, in my own defense, that it has been a rather unsettling day."

"For us all."

"Touché." He set his glass back down. "It appears that I must give an apology for my ungallant behavior."

Rae nodded her head regally. At least the big churl could manage a sincere apology. "Thank you. I would hate the world to know that we are at drawn daggers."

"No. I would not like the *Freiburgs* of Prussian nobility to know, either. Most especially my mother."

"*Freiburgs?* Did I meet them at the wedding? Oh, wait. Are they that horrid grave-robbing family?" Had she married into a clan of corpse-coppers?

A smile stole over his face. "No, dear. That's the Frankensteins. A *Freiburg* is more important in Prussian society—as my mother's side of the family is."

"How important?" Rae asked, the status of his familial connections making her feel a bit better.

His reply was much less friendly, as he took her interest as avarice. "My mother is a relation to the King of Norway, distantly."

Rae smiled happily, oblivious to her husband's irritation.

At least her children would have royal blood. Thus, when she traveled back home to Cornwall to visit, she could truthfully boast of her connections. Also, since she was now part of a royal family, she should certainly be dressing better. "How lovely! I shall need at least ten new morning dresses, eight new ball gowns, two dozen new slippers and sets of jewelry. I simply love sapphires and emeralds. They go so well with my coloring."

Finally, she would be able to indulge herself in buying the many things she wanted for herself and others; they would be *de rigeur* for a lady of her rank. Faye would look divine in an emerald choker, and Taylor needed a whole new wardrobe, as she was usually tearing and ripping her gowns. Even her rapscallion brothers could do with a few new fable books. She thought of a few she'd seen with gilded pages.

Fen sat back heavily in his chair. But his ever-darkening mood went unnoticed by Rae, and she made a mistake many new brides make: asking for the moon before knowing if their husband could reach it. Swiftly, for she was fleeter of mouth than she was of foot, and faster even to join the two, Rae listed her demands, concluding with a brand-new carriage in white pulled by a team of ivory horses.

"Rae?" Fen interrupted.

Hearing more than a simple discordant note in his voice, she stopped in the middle of asking if she could have a muff lined by white ermine fur. "Yes?"

"I am not King Midas."

"Well, who said you were? You're Baron Schortz."

Angry and exasperated, he replied, "I am saying I am not made of money. Though I am well-off, I do not intend to spend it all on a vain little wife who asks for everything but gives nothing in return."

"Asking for everything? I think not. Why, I have asked for very little!" Rae cried. "And how can you deny me my right to attire myself as benefits a member of royalty? I just want to look my part, to do honor to you and our connections! Also, I have everything to give, if I so choose. My . . . loveliness, my glorious hair and perfect complexion. My—"

"Your complexion will not warm my children's hearts; nor will your glorious hair make my nights any less lonely. And as for your beauty, it is a fleeting thing. In the December of our lives, it will be faded away, and what will I have but an empty-headed wife? No, I fear your beauty is a curse rather than a blessing."

Stunned, Rae sat back in her chair. The baron couldn't mean what he'd said! But he certainly looked as if he did. "Of course my beauty is a blessing," she argued. "Why, my mother has harped upon it for years. Even my father, who is a truly clever man, said that my beauty would make my fortune. And it has. And others' fortunes, too. Now that I'm a member of royalty, I feel sure we can help my sisters find suitable husbands. Of course, Taylor and Faye both need dowries so that they may marry well . . . ." While she wouldn't be happy in her marriage, she would see to it that her sisters were.

"You are not a member of royalty," Fen snapped. "Your father is a baron, and your mother a vicar's daughter. Just because you married me does not make you a member of the royal house of Norway. And I'm sorry for your sisters, but it is your father's duty to provide for them."

Rae sniffled. "How can you be so cruel—and on our wedding night? So penny-pinching. All I need are a few trifles. And worse, you deny my sisters a chance at wedded bliss!"

"Trifles? Why, your shopping list would bankrupt a small country," Fen retorted. "And if your sisters eye marriages like ours, then I imagine they are better off unwed." He couldn't believe that she'd had the nerve to ask him for dowries for her two sisters when he had already sent a handsome sum to her father for the dubious privilege of her hand.

"You sound like Greta!" Rae snapped, remembering all

the times her parents and sister had argued along similar lines. "And my father, at times."

"He must be a wise man. Wiser than you, at any rate. Your sister Greta must take after him," he growled.

At first Rae didn't take his meaning, but when she did, she picked up a *sauerbraten* and threw it. Sadly, she missed.

Fen leapt to his feet, hissing, and reached his bride in a few long strides. He stood proudly, hands on hips as he glowered at her. "Rae, I've had about all I can take from you for the day. I suggest you go to your room and prepare for bed."

Chest heaving, eyes flashing, she glared at him. Knowing the best defense was a good offense, she pointed at the mess she'd made and said, "This is all *your* fault! I have never thrown food in my life. Except at my brothers," she amended. "I threw peas at them once. But then they had thrown Taylor's mud pies at me. You are a maddening man, and you are driving me to act like a veritable hoyden. I hope you are happy." She did not mention his filthy little beasts, sensing instinctively that the man was at the end of his tether. Then she stormed to the door.

His voice caused her to stop, her heart beating rapidly. "I shall be up directly," he said.

She spun around and stared at him, blushing. Noting her discomfiture, he proceeded to taunt her. "Are you turning missish on me? This is our wedding night. What did you expect—your gold-digging would come without price?"

She managed an answer. "I assumed that, since you aren't that fond of me, you would forgo the bedding."

"I am not fond of you; it's true. Nor are my children. That matters not a whit to you, of course, but it matters a great deal to me. They are a blessing to me, and are the very best of me and my late wife, Fiona. She was all that was good and kind and lovely."

"If they are the best of you, I most certainly do not wish to see the worst," Rae snapped. For some reason, his devotion to his dead wife rankled. She herself was lovely and good, or could be at times. And she was kind of heart whenever she thought of it.

Fen's scowl grew. "Well, you are correct in one thing. Unhappily, this is my wedding night—and farther from my first wedding night than I can describe. No, I do not want to bed you. Not on this night or any other. You disgust me." And so saying, he turned and went back to his seat.

Rae gasped, both hurt and relieved. She wasn't ready for any wifely duty, though she at least wanted Fen to want it. She certainly wasn't ready to become in the family way, not when they already had so many little monsters running hither and yon throughout the castle. But how dare he say that she disgusted him? She marched away, her eyes brimming with tears.

As Rae hurried up the stairs, her thoughts were dark. She was married to an ogre, with a houseful of beastly children. He didn't want her in his bed? Well, he certainly did nothing for her womanly affections, either.

As she entered her room, it was to find one of Fen's twins sitting upon the pale pink French settee before the fireplace. Fen's eldest son was there as well. Both eyed her arrival with a less than friendly demeanor. Rae halted abruptly, staring at them. "What do I have to do to get some privacy in my own bedchamber?" she asked.

"It's not yours. It's my father's," Nap responded.

Narrowing her eyes, Rae glowered at him. Yet Fen's eldest son did not seem impressed, as her suitors had been, falling all over themselves to make apologies. For that reason she had to say, "I beg to differ. This is now my room, and I do not want bratty children to enter without my express permission."

While Nap sneered, Ernst scowled. The younger boy said, "Come on, Nap. Forget trying to warn her. She wants no favors from us."

As the two boys leapt up from the settee, Rae's curiosity got the better of her. My, she thought, I must be more like Greta than I realized. "Wait! What warnings?" Ignoring the smug expression upon the elder boy's face, she stood, tapping her foot impatiently. Nap had the look of his father, though his jaw wasn't as square and his eyes were a lighter gray. Yes, his father's eyes were prettier. "Well? I'm waiting."

Nap glanced at his brother, then nodded.

"It's about Papa," Ernst began. "It's a secret. A big and bad secret."

Rae almost laughed. What could be worse than a churl with seven children, not to mention a pinchpenny? If she didn't have new gowns soon, she would have to begin wearing things a third or fourth time. If she did that, how could she ever impress Prussian society?

Ernst began to pace. Truly a virtuoso actor for his age, his faux nervousness was very convincing. "I don't know, Nap, perhaps she'd be better off not knowing."

Nap shrugged his shoulders, speculating, "She does look a bit delicate. Still, it's something a wife should know."

"Well, if you think so . . ."

"Oh stop this dilly-dallying!" Rae snapped. "Despite my delicate and lovely features, I've got a strong constitution. Now, either tell me this big bad secret or leave."

Her words spurred Ernst on. "Well, you know how huge my papa is?" he asked.

She nodded. Of course she did. She was married to the big lummox.

"Well, my father's an ogre."

"I already know that!" She almost laughed, though it wasn't funny. "He refuses to buy me a single new gown!"

Nap snorted, a harsh guttural sound. "That's not an *ogre*. That's just plain sensible. Why should he spend his coin on you?" His expression darkened.

Ernst interrupted before any real bickering commenced, since both his brother and his new stepmother were glaring as if they'd like to tear each other's heads off. "My papa is a real ogre. The kind that drinks Englishmen's blood and grinds their bones for bread. But he got rid of the sign in front of the castle."

"What sign?"

" 'Beware of ogres,' " Ernst explained. "He burned it last week. He didn't want you to know."

She blinked. "That's preposterous. An ogre? Besides, vampires drink blood, not ogres."

"Prussian ogres do. They look human, but on nights of the full moon they turn into hideous ogres who thirst for human blood. Of course, I must admit it's only the blood of the English." Ernst clasped his hands, the picture of youthful innocence and concern.

Rae, however, didn't buy it for a moment; she had used that look upon her father a time or two herself. "You are a liar, and a bad one at that."

Nap shrugged his shoulders, shoving his brother toward the door. "Why waste our breath. She's not worthy. Let her find out on her own, as she will when Father starts with the *fee, fi, fo-ing.*"

Rae opened the door for the two, glaring at them warily. "You're telling fibs."

Nap shook his head. "Well, don't say we didn't warn you."

After the obnoxious pair left, Rae said, "A blessing? These brats? Ha! More like the devil's own brood. Heaven has nothing to do with them."

She slumped against the closed door and locked it, but as she did, she heard one boy remark rather loudly, "Who knows, maybe Papa will start grinding the bones of Englishwomen as well. It'd be no skin off my back. I don't like her, and I don't want her for a stepmother."

Rae leaned closer to the door, trying hard to hear the fading voices. "We can only hope," the other boy replied.

Rae pressed her forehead against the door. The wretched little cretins were lying. They had to be, she hoped. But if they weren't, then, horror of horrors, she really was married to an ogre. She would write Greta at once and apprise her of the unhealthy alliance. Of anyone, Greta would know how a girl could protect herself against a Prussian ogre.

She remained awake that night, long after the castle had settled down to rest, wide-eyed and suspicious of every crackling sound. The only positive thing was that at least she'd been spared those humiliating wifely duties. Oh, she did hope those two beastly boys had been lying. And if so, well, her revenge against the duo would make the wicked stepmother of Cinderella look like a sweet fairy princess.

# CHAPTER TWENTY

## The Halls Have Eyes (Beady Little Ones)

The mirror on the wall lay across from where Rae awoke. The first thing she did was take a look at her reflection, and then she frowned. She was slightly pale and felt misused. Nonetheless, she had made her bed and now she must lie in it, either with or without her big ogre of a husband.

In a matter of minutes, a maid brought her morning tea. As the shy servant helped her dress, Rae reflected upon her wedding night, which had been a disaster. There was no sugar-coating that fact. She, who had been admired and cosseted from birth, had been totally ignored by her husband. It was a situation she would not—could not—allow to continue, and thus she quickly instructed her maid to fetch the most becoming and newest of her gowns. It was a soft white, with deep twining leaves and dainty pink rosebuds decorating the hem in a wide swath. Tiny seed pearls with pink rosettes striped the bodice and sleeves.

Staring into the mirror, Rae knew she looked absolutely lovely. Only a blind man would not notice her in this outfit; and her husband was many things, but blind was not among them. Ogre or not, she would win his favor. Then she could get him to open his tight fists and see that her sisters had dowries. Otherwise, what was the point of being Baroness Schortz?

Once downstairs, Rae soon discovered a disconcerting fact: the master of the house had already eaten and was out riding across his estate. Thus, she ate her breakfast alone and in a fit of pique. Next, she wandered the castle feeling horribly neglected. Even the housekeeper, who was older than dirt, had no time for her. But then, Rae mused glumly, that was not surprising. If a groom basically ignored his bride and treated her with contempt, the servants would follow suit.

As she explored her new home, in the distance Rae could hear the raucous sounds of merrymaking. It was the little Schortzes. Their noises were welcome, however. She wisely ventured far away from the maddening cries of the little monsters, and from the relentless patter of their stampeding feet.

Coming to a large room done in pale shades of blue, she noted that the furniture was mainly French and more delicate of nature. A small mahogany desk adorned the room, and across from it was a large and full gold-framed mirror. "This must be Fiona's sitting room," Rae guessed, and she walked over to the ornate mirror and studied her reflection.

Her hair was perfect.

Her face was perfect.

Her new gown was also perfection.

Everything about her was picture-perfect. Rae smiled in spite of her dismal mood.

"Mirror, mirror on the wall, am I not fairest of them all?" she asked, feeling foolish for talking to the inanimate object but wishing *someone* would converse with her. To her surprise, the mirror answered.

"Our mother was prettier than you."

Rae gaped, staring hard into the mirror until her dazed mind recognized a nasty snicker. For a moment she had actually thought she was in one of her sister's stories, and that the mirror had spoken.

She turned, moving past a massive pot of ferns, and found her husband's eldest son, along with his pretty sister—Sylvia or Shavia something or another—and the little ankle biter, all playing with Alden's much abused lamp. "You shouldn't spy on people," she accused.

"You shouldn't talk to mirrors," Nap responded.

Rae blushed. "I was only being a bit silly. I never talk to mirrors." Then, seeing the derision in the boy's laughing eyes, she added quickly, "In fact, I don't talk to inanimate objects at all. I find it as enlightening as speaking to brats who belong in the nursery."

The boy shrugged his shoulders, and his sister Shyla stared at her. "Napoleon's right. Our mother was much more beautiful than you."

Narrowing her eyes, Rae shook her head in pity. It would be terrible to lose a mother. But still: "You would think so. After all, she gave birth to you."

"My sister doesn't lie," Nap vowed.

The little ankle-biter, with his wild mop of hair, lurched to his feet and nodded enthusiastically. "My mama pretty."

Not about to be baited, Rae pasted a polite smile on her face. "As you say." She hadn't been born yesterday. The little mop-headed boy had a wicked set of teeth. She chose wisely not to dispute the facts of the matter with him, since she was partial to her ankles.

Shyla pointed to a door. "Go look and see. That's Papa's study."

Rae sighed. Then, doing as the girl asked, she went over, opened the door and found herself in an elegant but definitely masculine study. Large oak beams crisscrossed the ceiling, and painted friezes with Cyprian nymphs adorned the stone walls a foot or so below the ceilings. Above the arched green marbled fireplace hung a huge portrait of a very beautiful woman with deep golden-red hair and greenish-blue eyes.

The woman was dressed in a regal-looking gown with inlaid emeralds. Her ornate emerald and diamond necklace was worth a queen's ransom, Rae imagined, and she automatically wondered if she would look prettier if she herself wore such finery. But there was no question: The woman was beautiful, a true princess.

There was more to the painting than just the woman's loveliness, however, and Rae felt the sharp sting of betrayal. You see, Fen's late wife bore a strong resemblance to Rae herself. They both had the same expressive eyes, though the color was different. Their noses were similar, as well as the shapes of their faces. And their figures were very similar. This unwelcome discovery caused a flare of jealousy to shoot through her like a falling star: here and then gone before Rae had time to even recognize the green-eyed monster.

"That's our mother," Shyla said quietly. She had come to stand by Rae's side. "Papa says I am as beautiful as my mama, for I'm his golden princess."

"Beauty's not everything, Shyla. Watch out, or you'll grow too vain and no one will like you—like some other people I know," Nap warned. "Besides, what Papa loved best about Mother was not her beauty, but her nature. Mama was sweet and kind and laughed a lot. She never judged anyone, and she loved us with all her heart. She made Papa feel like a king, and she was always proud of him and of us, even on our bad days. There was none better," Nap boasted. His tone made it clear that his mother was an angel, while Rae wasn't even in line for lesser sainthood.

Suddenly pensive, Rae managed a slight nod. Their mother did sound like a fine woman, even if it stung to admit it. Fiona's children and husband thought the world of her. And that was a situation every woman could aspire to but few would reach, Rae mused dejectedly; most especially Rae herself.

Noticing the way Rae stared at the picture, Nap added, "Mama didn't even mind that Father was an ogre on the nights of the full moon."

Rae observed that the boy's expression was serious. She began to become worried again. Nap acted like he believed what he was saying. But still, could the baron really be a real ogre? That was foolish nonsense, fairy-tale stuff. But then, the Black Forest was renowned for its dark legends . . . well, and cakes. She really needed to speak with her sister. She would send Greta a note immediately, and ask her to come posthaste; she needed an expert.

Shyla, previously rather quiet, remarked, "See those jewels on Mother's gown and in her necklace? They're part of Papa's ogrish stash. He keeps it hidden away in the tower—where Englishmen can't steal it."

"Or a greedy English wife," Nap added.

"I'm not greedy," Rae replied. "As your father's bride, I should be allowed to see what gems he has. I intend only to look—for future reference, for when I go to balls and such." The jewels in the painting were magnificent. They would suit her admirably.

"I don't think so," Shyla said. "Papa wouldn't like it."

"He might grind your bones," Nap warned. The ankle-biter, Alden, vigorously shook his mop of golden-brown curls. "It is *verboten* even for us to play there—even in the daytime."

"*Verboten?*"

"Forbidden," Nap translated, a superior expression crossing his face. It reminded Rae of Fen's look last night when he'd mentioned he wasn't interested in performing his husbandly duties.

Rae scowled; then, seeing the answering scowls on Shyla's and Nap's faces, she decided to turn on her charm. She was after emeralds and diamonds, and she remembered her father telling her mother that one caught more "ice" with honey than vinegar.

"I promise not to tell your father. I only want a quick look," she said. Sticks, stones and ogres would break bones, but an emerald necklace worthy of a queen was something one didn't sneeze at. Besides, her husband couldn't really be an ogre. That was impossible and foolish. How silly did these children think her?

Glancing at her big brother, who nodded rather reluctantly, Shyla answered. "*Ja*. I guess it would be all right. We'll show you the way if you promise not to tell our papa."

Keeping her exaltation to herself, Rae nodded. If her big oaf of a husband thought he could outwit her, he didn't know Rae Grimm Schortz. She would look the jewels over and pick one or two, maybe even a dozen to wear, since she deserved to be decked out in them. Once the baron saw the pieces on her person, he'd recognize how they enhanced her beauty and how that same beauty was a credit to him. Even if he indeed was an ogre . . . Well, who if not an ogre—unless perhaps a troll—needed more credit? Yes, she decided, monsters truly did need the most beautiful wives to compensate for their monstrous selves.

With such thoughts filling her head, she paid little mind to the muskiness of the far tower to which she was led. As she and the children climbed the spiral stairway, so enraptured was she with her dreams of grand entrances, the dust and cobwebs filling many of the nooks and crannies didn't disturb her at all.

At the end of a wide corridor filled with large vases and grandfather clocks, she waited impatiently while Nap unlocked a door. "It's in there, he said, "by the golden hearth."

"Golden *hearth?*" Rae asked, rather breathless. Surely the baron wasn't so well off that he had a fireplace made of gold? She had married much better than she'd thought!

"*Ja*. It was done in my great-grandfather's time," Nap said, and he ushered her inside the room.

"I can't see anything," Rae complained. "It's too dark."

"Then open the shutters," Nap replied. "You can open a shutter, can't you?"

"Of course I can," Rae snapped. She didn't need to placate her stepchildren any longer; she had found their treasure.

She walked over and did just that. But as she opened the

shutters, which revealed a large set of windows with beveled glass, she heard the slamming of the door and the turning of a key in a rusty lock. These sounds were followed by the thundering of blood in her ears and her heart. She suddenly realized she had made a very serious mistake.

Whipping around, Rae found that she was alone in a filthy room filled with cobwebs, broken clocks and furniture. She sneezed, looking around in dismay. Half the dust of the earth must be in this one room. She sneezed again, then ran to the door and began to beat upon it, screaming shrilly.

"You hideous little savages! Let me out this instant! You lied to me! Your father isn't an ogre, and there aren't any jewels or even a golden hearth. Just wait till I tell the baron on you!"

Her cries met with resounding silence, so she resorted to more violent means: "You devil's spawn, just wait till I get my hands on you!" Then, realizing threats might not be the best way to extricate herself from this fiendish situation, she changed tactics again. "This is a fine jest. Quite a jest!" She managed to laugh heartily, but it was interrupted by another bout of sneezing. No one laughed with her.

Over the next hour and more, she tried cajoling the children with promises of tasty treats and late bedtimes. Everything she could think of, she offered. But to no avail. And the time continued to drag along.

At last, the key in the lock finally turned. Rae had red eyes from sneezing by this time, and her fine new gown was now a dusty mess. And she was beside herself with rage. She was going to find the little terrors responsible and make them pay. Their little black hearts would soon fill with dread for their stepmother.

Violently Rae shoved open the heavy oak door, her eyes wild and red and her fingers clutched into claws. But as she charged out the door, a chamber pot filled with flour and suspended from a rope crashed down. The flour covered her from head to toe. This time when she sneezed, instead of dust bunnies filling the air before her, white specks fanned out. Her shriek could be heard throughout the tower, excruciatingly loud and banshee-like.

"Ach! You demon spawn!"

Rae shivered as she scanned the area. The halls seemed to have beady little eyes watching every move she made. Letting her fear show would be a fatal mistake—a mistake she would not make, having learned this particular lesson more than once from living with her demented little brothers. Or mayhap she had learned that time when she was fifteen and a huge vicious dog had chased her and Faye. Faye had fallen behind, due to her injured leg. Fear had almost paralyzed Rae, but somehow she had found a small bit of courage to stand and face the dog. She'd stood her ground with stick in hand, like a steadfast tin soldier, and kept the dog from doing damage until the gamekeeper arrived. She would find that same courage now.

"I will personally see to it that each and every one of you little demons is placed in the dungeon," Rae shouted, fuming at the diabolical cleverness of the seven little Schortzes. Her face was scarlet and her eyes bulged. "I will make you bob for poisoned apples."

A voice called out as she thundered down the stairs, "We don't have a dungeon."

"And we don't like apples," another voice shouted.

More mad laughter followed, along with the pitter-patter of tiny feet. It made Rae see red. These were the sounds of happy feet—demented, deranged, diabolically happy feet—because their owners had won this particular battle with a flair that would have done Machiavelli proud.

Rae scurried down the last of the staircase, then slowed in her chase of the maddening monsters. She hadn't come close to catching even one of them, not even the littlest fiend, Alden. And alas for poor Rae, the shadows had another surprise in store.

Taking the last step, she felt insatiable little jaws clamp

upon her ankle with sharpened teeth like those of a badger. Rae gave a startled yelp. Lifting her full skirts and shaking her leg, she screeched, "Let go of my ankle, you little mutt. Ouch! Alden!"

Flour filled the air, swirling off and around her as she hopped on one leg and shouted in pain. The boy with the teeth hung on like a persistent rat terrier, and suddenly Rae had visions of turning old and gray with this ferocious child still latched to her limb.

Just when she thought she would have to drag the youngest Schortz outside and into the main part of the castle, the little boy let go and lurched over, playing dead. Rae shook him once, but he remained silent, his beady little eyes closed, his mop of light curls falling wildly about his face. He looked like a fallen angel.

"You're not dead. I didn't hurt you, so stop scaring me!" she snapped.

Yet the child remained unnaturally still, which surprisingly caused her more than a moment's concern. She might not like the ravenous little barbarian, but she didn't want to see him hurt.

Pushing her floury, tangled mess of hair out of her eyes, she leaned over to pick up the ankle-biting demon, but was surprised to find the little body grabbed and pulled through a dark hole in the wall.

"Oh no, you don't!" she shouted, grabbing the little child's legs. But the stealthy little beasts on the other side of the wall were quicker. They spirited Alden away, then slammed a wooden panel in her face.

She knocked to no avail. She shouted curses at the demon brood. She tried threats, also to no use.

"Oh, go bite your bums," she finally yelled, recognizing defeat. It was bitter ash in her mouth.

In the background, behind the wood panel and safe from her wrath, she heard whispers. "She said bum!" The voice was very young. Rae deduced it was that of the littlest Schortz girl, Poppy.

"I'm telling Papa," another voice added gleefully. It was Merri, the contrary, Rae guessed.

"He'll wash out her mouth with soap, like he did mine," one of the twins said.

Rae shook her head. "Not if I get to him first," she muttered. Then, without a thought for her appearance—a first for Rae Grimm Schortz—she practically flew out the tower door in a mad dash to find her husband. He really wasn't an ogre, she knew, and he didn't really own a golden hearth. But he did lay claim to seven villainous little dwarves.

# CHAPTER TWENTY-ONE

The Snow White Dress and the Seven
Little Schortzes

Up the stairs and down the stairs, Rae chased several scampering, shrieking children until she finally had to concede. As she bounded into Fen's study, she halted abruptly. Determined to hold together the last shreds of her battered pride, she stood poised in front of his desk. Alas, the wrath in Rae's bosom boiled over.

"Baron. I have come to discuss the disgusting and criminal behavior of Nap and his merry miscreants. Look at me."

Fen glanced up from studying the estate records and took in her flour-streaked face and dusty, white gown, also spotted with smudges of dirt and ash. As the winter sun shone through his large leaded windows, he noted in an almost abstract way how the sun made her golden-silver hair shimmer. Even though she was grimy and her hair a tangled mess, even though her pretty blue (if red-rimmed) eyes sparkled with ire and her firm little chin trembled with rage, she was utterly lovely. He sighed softly. The woman would be beautiful even in a flour sack—which her dress resembled at the moment.

"*Ja?*" He was no fool. He knew a woman's ire when he saw it. He also knew Nap, Merri, Shyla and Ernst's handiwork when he witnessed it. He came out from behind his desk and braced his foot against the fireplace grate.

Rae actually screeched as she stomped her dainty foot. "Do you notice something different about the way I look today?" Her new husband needed to smother her with apologies and try to make amends.

"Why, I believe, I do. You are so . . . *messe.*"

"Of course I'm a mess. That's why I've come to you!" Rae explained. How dare he sound so critical when her appearance was his fault! If he hadn't played Sir Galahad and rescued her from that cockroach, she wouldn't be here. Adding to that was the fact that he obviously hadn't been able to quit doing his husbandly duties with his first wife, over and over and over again. The result? A castle full of Satan's spawn.

Fen really tried to contain his mirth. "*Messe* means fair. You still look very fair, in spite of your less than pristine condition. I must say that I'm very impressed. I had no idea that I married such an inventive and clever puss. You have found a way to entertain my *kinder* since their governess left—shall we say for greener pastures?—and still manage to look lovely in the bargain."

For a moment his words hung between them, and he had the satisfaction of seeing her speechless.

Her husband had complimented her very nicely, and yet Rae could see mirth lurking in his eyes and in the twitching of his lips. Her eyes narrowed to mere slits, and she spread her fingers through her disheveled and gummy curls. "I was not, absolutely, in any way, in any fashion, in any manner, entertaining those unnatural little creatures! My brand-new gown is destroyed beyond repair by the vicious dwarves. They are a plague, a pestilence. As for your compliments, they are too few, too far in between and too late!"

He picked up the fireplace poker and jabbed at the logs burning in the hearth, his grin disappearing. "I forbid you to call my children unnatural," he remarked. "It's very natural to have high spirits and play pranks. Besides, there is no use in crying over spilt flour."

"Pranks! Spilt flour!" Rae shouted, forgetting that a lady never shouted or told children to *bite their bums*. " 'Pranks' is too light a word, sir. 'Vicious, bloodthirsty and deranged shenanigans' might be better. Attila the Hun would have run in abject terror from your children, and I wouldn't have blamed her."

"He."

"He?"

"Attila the Hun was male."

"Did his mother know?"

A bark of laughter was forced out of him. She was either totally witless or a total wit.

"I find no humor in this situation," she remarked. "I feel like that old woman in the shoe, with all those screaming children hanging off her apron strings." Glancing down at her ruined gown, she added sharply, "And I look like her, too."

"I must say, you have been in better looks, but I rather like this grubby urchin style. Very natural." Her beauty would have felled a giant, Fen thought in amusement, even covered in gook.

And his children could be a handful at times, but they were a delight and a challenge. All were clever, and they had good hearts. They had suffered terribly at the loss of their mother. It had taken over a year for the last of the nightmares to subside, and for Fen to finally sleep through the night without one of the children crying out for him. Though Fiona's loss had devastated him personally, he had never allowed himself a collapse, since his children needed him desperately.

"I have never looked like one of those creatures." Glancing down at herself, she revised her statement. "That is, not until I met *your* benighted brood. They are little monsters, each and every one of them."

He threw the poker against the grate and stood, hands on hips, glaring at her. "Wife, you go too far!"

"Me, go too far!" she shrieked. "I think not. Last night,

two of the little wretches came to my bedchamber. Your
eldest and one of the twins. The twin said you were an
ogre that turned during the full moon."

"Nap? Ernst?" An enigmatic smile settled across the baron's rugged face, and in that moment Rae was surprised to
discover he was not homely at all, but rather intriguing
and manly. Just like Greta had said.

"Well, yes, they were *both* very earnest, making it difficult to disbelieve them," she replied, hating the fact that she
had caught amusement in her husband's voice. It did sound
rather stupid in the clear light of day, especially after being
attacked with flour and the ferocious little ankle-biter.

"No, Ernst. The twin."

"Yes, I know. Most especially the twin," she agreed.
"Though they both were earnest." The big lout was rather
dense, it seemed. At least he couldn't expect her to go
around spouting Latin and Shakespeare.

Fen snorted. "No. Ernst. It's the name of one of the twins.
Remember? I told you that he wants to be a writer when he
grows up . . . or an actor. God knows he's good enough at
both."

"You mean he tells great big fat fibs."

Fen shrugged, enjoying her discomfort. For once Rae
didn't seem to be a seething mass of vanity. "You could
call it that."

"Of course I call it that. They told me you were an ogre,
and then this morning locked me in the far tower. When I
escaped, they dumped a bucket of flour all over me."

He grinned again. "Ah, the ogre bit. Rae, I find it hard to
credit that you believe such *unsinn*—nonsense. Why,
you're as bad as that English footman we hired last year.
The children took a thorough disliking to him, and they
told him that I ground the bones of Englishmen to make
the bread we eat. The poor fool lost a stone, declining anything made with flour. When the full moon arrived, he
locked himself in his room and carried on crying hysteri-

cally. I finally had to let him go, given that he was a ghost of the man I first employed."

"Why, how utterly horrid! What punishment did your children receive for tormenting the poor man? Did you spank them all harshly and put them to bed without supper for a month of Sundays?" Rae asked, appalled.

Fen remained silent momentarily, enjoying the sparks in his wife's eyes. "Actually, the man was proven to be a thief. He'd been stealing from me for quite some time. The children called for his unconditional surrender, which he gladly gave. My brood can be quite without mercy when need be. They were only looking after my interests."

"That may be, but on this point I insist," Rae began, her eyes flashing pure blue fire. "They must be punished for treating me this way. The youngest bit my ankle."

Fen glanced down at her ruined gown, with the flour, grime and many small tears. "I will reprimand them, never fear," he agreed. "Does it hurt?" And was that actually smoke coming out Rae's ears, he wondered, or just the fire in the hearth?

"Of course it hurts, you big oaf! I was bitten, attacked like I was a choice piece of roast."

"Alden is merely going through a stage. Besides, be glad that my children did nothing worse. You haven't exactly endeared yourself to them."

"Worse?" Rae couldn't imagine anything worse than being locked in a dusty, spider-ridden room, doused with a bucket of flour from a chamber pot and then attacked by a small child with razor-sharp teeth. Not to mention that she hadn't found any jewels and had ruined her new gown. She stared at her husband warily.

"Why, yes. Worse." Assuming a relaxed pose, Fen crossed his arms on his chest and planted both feet firmly apart. "The last governess was subject to having frogs placed in her *topfchen*."

"She was Chinese?"

"No, she was from Bavaria. The frogs were placed in her chamber pot. The silly woman would forget, and when she was, well, ah . . . the frog would unfortunately jump. After the last such episode, she decided to go back to Bavaria."

Rae scowled. The children appeared to have an unhealthy interest in chamber pots. "What else did they do?" she asked. Better to be forewarned.

"It seems," he replied, scratching his chin, "I recall they took her captive, tied her to a tree and then made her eat baboon tarts."

Rae gasped. "How depraved."

"It was summer, and they were playing pirates and she was their prisoner," Fen explained, his voice tinged with amusement. "They had captured her ship and the tarts were really lemon."

She shook her head in stunned disbelief. Obviously the house was lacking in discipline. "How can you be so blasé about all of this? How can you be so disobliging when I have suffered such appalling acts of violence against my person? I insist upon a new gown for the one they ruined."

"I'll take it under advisement," Fen offered. Then he turned to go back to his desk and his real work.

"You're dismissing me just like that? Why, we've settled nothing. What about my gown? My ankle? What about my sensibilities? I am quite overset with nerves. A husband is to never deny his wife's requests," she snapped, perfectly serious. "He is to pamper her and keep her in style and luxury, no matter the cost. When she is this unsettled, he gives her trinkets of his affection—like a diamond necklace or a pearl brooch."

He stopped and looked her over carefully, from top to bottom. "You do look nothing like a baroness should look. Whatever will the servants think? They might call me a pinchpenny and accuse me of beating you with a sack of flour." He stopped and put finger to his lips. "Why, anyone seeing you as you are right now would think I wedded a hag."

Staring at him with a stricken look, she acknowledged his words as truth. If anyone saw her, they would never believe such a ravishing beauty could be made to look such a fright. Till now, only her immediate family had ever seen Rae looking less than her best, but now her new husband had seen her at her worst, and somehow she didn't think he was talking about her appearance. She hurried from the room to address the problem as quickly and quietly as possible.

Fen watched the conceited bit of baggage leave the room as if her skirts were afire. But, then, he had speculated that his words would work, since he had appealed to her rather shallow character. He shook his head with more melancholy than amusement. "Vanity, thy name is Rae."

Already in the long hallway, Rae heard the words, which outraged her as well as leaving her self-conscious. "Why, if anyone walked a mile in my shoes today . . . they'd be heartbroken, weeping with self-pity," she said to herself. "And if these rowdy ruffians think I will let them walk all over me, they are very much mistaken! I learned from masters the art of terrible tricks!" Raising her fist high in the air and shaking it furiously, she made a solemn vow. "They think they have won the war, but I've only just begun to fight! If I have to lie, cheat or use stealth, I'll get those wicked little dwarfs if it's the last thing I do."

# CHAPTER TWENTY-TWO

## Greta's Red Riding Hood

As Rae dealt with devilish little imps, Greta was searching for information on Frau Choplin, the woodcutter's mother. After traveling for quite a distance, she at last arrived at her destination. Glancing out the window of her carriage, she dismally noted the small threadlike path, thick with snow, which wended off and disappeared in the heavy foliage of the woods. "It looks like I'm on foot from here," Greta told the driver.

As she left the warmth of the carriage, attired as she was in her scarlet cloak, plaid scarf and scarlet woolen gloves, she nonetheless braced herself against the weather. The narrow path ran beneath the ancient trees, which towered tall with their snowcapped leaves, and she breathed in deeply the scent of pine and snow. She had told her aunt's driver that she would be a while, and had bribed him with gold coins so that he would not mention this stop before she returned to Snowe Manor. She had tried bribing him to stop by Baron Schortz's house as well, but the driver, unfortunately afraid of her aunt, had declined.

"What an old biddy she is," Greta griped. Aunt Vivian had expressly forbidden Greta from visiting her sister for the next few days, to let the newlyweds get to know each other. Normally Greta would have agreed, but Rae's marriage wasn't exactly normal.

As she trudged along, she tried to stop worrying about Rae. Instead she would concentrate on monster hunting. It helped keep her worries at bay and made her feel less lonely. Besides, she was cursed with an overactive curiosity. At least it kept her overactive imagination company.

High above, birds chirped in the trees. As Greta walked, the air was full of a fine mist that couldn't seem to make up its mind to be either fog or rain. Still, a little bad weather would not defeat her. She would climb every snowbank, ford every frozen stream, or skate across it, till she found her vampire. Thus, she needed to speak with Herr Choplin, the woodcutter, about his mother's death. It's a vampire, she thought; nothing but a vampire and nothing less than a vampire. She was certain.

As her feet crunched in the snow, Greta pulled up her cloak around her head. She was hurrying as fast as she could. Just when she thought she couldn't go much further, the woodcutter's cottage came into view, right where Herr Nietzsche had said it would be. Sighing with relief, she knocked on the door. No one answered. Although smoke was coming out of the chimney, alas, no one was home.

"Well, isn't this a fine mess," she said as she contemplated her options. She could go back to her aunt's carriage and go home, but she was terribly cold, and her feet felt frozen in her soft kid boots. Perhaps, she thought, she could go inside for just a little while and warm her feet and hands. Perhaps there might be something hot on the stove to drink, neither too hot nor too cold.

"*Carpe diem,*" she muttered, thinking that she would indeed seize the day and go inside, despite the fact that it was rude.

Once inside the small cottage, her curiosity got the better of her. Although she did warm herself for a few minutes beside the fire, she forgot about the hot drink of tea she had been hoping for and began to search. She wasn't quite sure what she was searching for, but perhaps she would know if she found it.

"If his mother is a vampire, surely there must be some sign of this. Perchance he's been bitten and is lying covered over by a blanket of snow awaiting his transformation," Greta mused thoughtfully. "Maybe she has even visited him? Maybe that's why he's not here?"

As Greta searched a drawer in a small dresser by a bed with an enormous bearskin, the door came crashing open with stunning force. Gasping, she looked up to see Prince Rolpe. Undergarments clenched anxiously in her hand, and with a mildly abashed expression on her face, she asked, "What are *you* doing here?" He must have ridden up without her hearing.

Slamming the door behind him, Rolpe advanced on his nemesis, noting that she had the look of someone on a mission. He knew that the woodcutter Choplin was in town at the tavern and, after speaking with the Snowes' carriage driver, he'd learned that Miss Greta Grimm was here and unaware of where exactly the woodcutter was. Perhaps that was for the best.

He stopped abruptly, standing a scant few feet away, and fixed his darkest, most arrogant stare upon Greta's determined face. "What am *I* doing here?" Mentally, Rolpe counted to ten in Latin, trying to cool his temper at the silly fool's rash act of rushing into danger.

She nodded, clearly seeking an answer.

"Might I ask what *you* are doing here, in the woodcutter's cottage?" he said. "Are you here to eat his food and sleep in his bed, or is your only interest in getting into his drawers?" The prince kept his voice low, but there was no mistaking the underlying anger.

Affronted, Greta asked, forgetting momentarily that she was an uninvited guest, "You are angry with me?"

"How astute."

"How dare you be angry with me for having the gall to be angry with you!" Aggravated by his haughty stance and haunting presence, she mentally counted to ten in Spanish.

"That's not why I'm angry, and you well know it," Rolpe said. She was too lovely to be running around the woods where any manner of man or beast might feast upon her.

She contended, "I have not slept in his bed or eaten his food."

"But you *are* in his drawers," he accused. Then, realizing what he'd said, a slight grin twisted Rolpe's lips. Greta could search his drawers any time she desired, she with her clever gray-blue eyes and brownish-gold locks. She looked remarkable.

"Reckless. I charge that you did come here alone, which was highly foolish. You don't need to be traipsing about these dark woods without a chaperon, you and your bright gray eyes and scarlet cloak." She was everything a big bad wolf, of the human persuasion or otherwise, could want.

Greta retorted, neither too harshly nor too softly, "And what business of that is yours! Why are you here? Are you following me?"

"Apparently," he conceded. "Although it was not my intent. I saw your aunt's carriage where the path narrows."

"So, you came to rescue me from the woodcutter, who is fifty if he is a day."

"No, I came to rescue you from your own folly. Don't you know that 'tis dangerous for you to come here alone, prying into secrets that don't concern you?"

Pulling her gloves back on, she shook her head. There was a certain gleam in the prince's eyes that made her heart beat faster and her throat tighten. "Ah-ha. What secrets?"

"I was speaking in general terms, not particulars. Do you think Herr Choplin will be happy to have you invading his home? Do you think he would appreciate your questions about his mother's death?" He moved nearer, wanting to strangle her, wanting to shake her, wanting to kiss her full pouty lips.

She glanced up at the ceiling, as if her answer rested there. Finally she spoke. "I know this must look strange, but you must not leap to conclusions."

He stepped closer to both the flames within the hearth and those this woman engendered in his soul. "This is no leap. But it *is* a very firm step."

"I only wished to ask about his mother's death. That drunk you have for a doctor in the village is really rather stupid. I don't think he can tell an ankle from his elbow. Or an asp bite from a vampire bite."

Rolpe shook his head. "Greta, Choplin said his mother died when a bunch of logs fell upon her after her cart tipped. Such an accident would cause blood loss. If that's what you're thinking . . ."

"Exactly," Greta remarked. "And a vampire could have easily tipped over her cart. Besides, what person in their right mind travels with wood in a cart at night? The whole story is fishy."

A shuttered look came over Rolpe's features, masking his feelings. "Do you know, Miss Grimm, that before you came to Wolfach, the grave was a fine and private place to rest?" Before she could counter this strange comment, he held up his hand. "I really need to talk firmly with you. *Very* firmly. Perhaps this time you might try and listen."

"Oh, I hear you," she replied. "So far in our discussions I've found you to be abundantly honest to the point of rudeness. But I know there is a vampire out there, and I don't give a farthing if you believe me or not. The *Nosferatu* are real, and when a corpse goes missing in the Black Forest, it is most definitely because of a vampire!"

"There are no undead around!" Rolpe shouted in response. Then, softening his voice: "But there are other things. Do you know there are creatures hiding in the Black Forest that could eat you alive? *Vampyrs* are not the only things with big teeth. Walking alone in these big, dangerous woods is beyond foolish. And you are making a nuisance of yourself. I want it to cease, all this mucking about in things that are better left in the dark."

He continued to glower at her, his loins dangerously hot. To be honest, Miss Grimm was not only endangered by what lay outside the woodcutter's cottage, but what lay within. Eyes like hers accounted for the ruin of many a good man since Eve first bewitched Adam with that damned rotten apple. In the back of his mind, Rolpe's instinct was telling him to run, for love was trying to catch him with a well-sprung snare.

Greta shrugged, noting how Rolpe's dark eyes flickered with emotions she found both disturbing and delightful. Suddenly but not inexplicably, she found it hard to breathe. The man was just too virile and attractive for her good.

"Fools rush in," he warned, his tone becoming less strident, instead filled with seductive hints.

"Grimms rush in where sterner men have halted," she replied.

"Are you too thick-headed to note danger when it is knocking on the door?" he exclaimed, grabbing her fiercely by the shoulders. She looked so good; good enough to love, good enough to eat. She was neither too tall nor too short for him, neither too stout nor too thin, but just the right everything.

"You mean, grave robbers?" As she stared into his beautiful eyes, her pulse pounded. He could charm the pennies from a dead man's eyes, she guessed.

"No. I mean me," he growled. And then he kissed her lips. They were hot and very sweet, like his favorite apple cake.

Greta sighed in delight as he clasped her to him, enjoying how perfectly she fit against his body. As their kiss deepened, she opened her mouth and breathed into his, felt his tongue touch hers. A tingling began in her body, her veins rushing with fire. She loved the way his arms clasped her closer to him. He made her dizzy with emotion. She had been kissed before, but never as the prince was kissing her now. Von Hanzen kissed as if he had been doing it all his life. His lips were demanding, fiery, earth-shattering. Greta grew light-headed, and her senses reeled. She clasped the back of his neck with her hands, her fingers massaging through his thick, dark hair.

She started a little when his hand settled naturally on the curve of her breast, finding the nipple and causing longings she could not explain. The titillation created a riot of emotions and an exquisite trembling deep within her core. She shivered in delight as heat flooded her and her heart raced, threatening to beat out of her chest. "Oh, Rolpe," she sighed.

Her passionate response aroused the prince's male instincts and lust, but a tiny voice of reason in his head called to him to halt this folly. Rolpe had not intended to kiss her. He certainly had not intended for his hand to slide under her cloak. Nor had he expected his treacherous fingers to clasp her soft breast and begin to caress her with a lover's touch. He was enflamed by this person, though she was obsessed with fairy tales and grand delusions—well, delusions of monsters that were not delusions. Groaning passionately, he pressed closer, his body aching for hers.

"*Nein*," he managed to protest. He couldn't do this, else he be doomed. Greta Grimm was a virgin of good family, and any debauching would only end in marriage, just like his good friend Fen's. And he was too wily a wolf to get caught in the marital trap, leashed for life.

Panting, Greta drew his head back down for another kiss. Acknowledging that he was doomed to surrender if she continued to kiss him, Rolpe shoved her away a little more forcibly than he had intended. She landed on the bed, bouncing, a look of surprise crossing her face. The sight of her kiss-swollen lips and skirts rucked up about her calves caused his heart to race. His nostrils flared. She smelled absolutely wonderful, like honey and musk.

Steeling himself, he snarled, "Pull your skirts down and let's get you to your carriage."

Taken aback, Greta stared wide-eyed at Rolpe. What had happened to the passionate lover of just a few moments ago?

"I will not make the mistake of Baron Schortz."

"Mistake," she repeated. "What mistake?" She hastily adjusted her skirts.

"You cannot make me compromise you so that we must be married," he explained.

"Why, you filthy beast! I did not compromise you; *you* kissed *me*. Or is that too much for you to remember? Nor did I ask for you to follow me here." This time she counted to ten in French. When that didn't work, she tried German.

*"Nein.* That is true. But you took advantage of the fact, just like your crafty sister. And your mother. A family goal is it, craftiness?"

"My, how clever *you* are. My mother, always unhappy with her situation in life, is certainly my inspiration. As is my crafty sister, who is overjoyed to have been compromised and married to a man who despises her. Why, I want just the same thing, and in my own devious way I have somehow tricked you into coming here and forcing you to kiss me," she retorted, hiding remarkably well the fact that her heart was breaking once again. When would she ever learn? The prince and she were like oil and water. They did not mix.

He eyed her with distaste. "We did more than kiss."

"Barely," she acknowledged, looking away as a faint blush tinged her cheeks.

"Are you so experienced that you know the degrees of sexual congress?"

Her temper stirred, and she responded without thinking. "Why, yes. I've known dozens of men. And I must say they had a bit more finesse about the whole thing. And as for degrees—they were all hotter than you."

His eyes narrowed and he stepped forward, jerking her

into him. He branded her with a searing kiss, stealing into her heart against her will, making her weak, making her despise them both for his mastery.

When he was finished he drew back, an arrogant sneer on his face. "*Nein*, there is none hotter."

"Why, you top-lofty prig! You arrogant goat! And you call my sister vain? Ha!" And with those words, she slapped him. "*Wurst wider wurst!*"

Surprised, he rubbed his cheek and watched her flee. "Tit for tat," he mused. She was certainly all woman. Unfortunately, she most definitely, most decidedly, could not be *his* woman. He led a bachelor's life few men dreamed of, filled with bevies of beautiful women in countless beds. The thrill of the chase, the blissful release of victory and the ever changing array of conquests was too precious to give up just because he had stupidly and momentarily lost his head. He might yearn for Greta, he might burn for her—but ultimately, he must continue to spurn her.

Greta grabbed her cloak and valiantly kept her tears at bay as she hurried to the door. "Never fear. I will never repeat your rakish indiscretion to anyone. You may be assured of your eternal bachelorhood!" she snapped, then turned and stomped out into the slushy snow. How dare the prince assault her, then thrust the blame on her? It was the height of royal arrogance: to accuse someone else for one's own less-than-noble deeds!

Rolpe followed. "I'll take you up on my horse and drop you off at your carriage. You'll catch your death of cold." In spite of his desire to flee, he held his ground. He had indeed behaved less the gentleman, more the rogue. But, in his defense, she stirred his blood and made his good intentions fly into the wind. She was everything a woman shouldn't be—and everything he desired.

"Don't bother!" She did not stop walking.

Urging his horse forward, Rolpe quickly caught up with her and reached down to help her mount. She ignored his outstretched hand and turned in the opposite direction.

"What are you doing?" he asked.

She at last glanced up at him, her pretty blue eyes sparkling with tears of anger. "My grandmother always told me to take care of myself. She gave me hugs and loved me. So . . . I am going to the carriage. By myself. Not on your horse, and certainly not in your foul company. I am hurrying down this path. No matter how long it takes me, and no matter where it takes me, I'm taking it because it takes me away from you."

Rolpe halted his mount and shook his head in confused frustration, and the red-hooded woman soon disappeared down the shadowy footpath. Alas, he realized after she was gone, he had lost an opportunity to draw her close again, even for a short while. His arms might be bigger than her grandmother's, but they were the better to hold her with.

# CHAPTER TWENTY-THREE

## Hickory, Dickory Dock... and Cuckoo Clocks

Morning had broken, along with a Chinese vase, matching emerald Egyptian cats and an old pipe, which Ernst, while testing the theory of gravity, had dropped on an unsuspecting footman. Shaking his head in resignation, Fen wondered what the total tally of damages would be, seeing as it was only morning. Wisely, he decided that he really should put his new acquisition away. No telling what the children would do to his clock, since Nap and Quinn loved to disassemble things to see how they worked.

"I will put it in my study, away from prying little eyes and fingers," he said to himself. Then, glancing over at the fireplace mantel, he sighed in satisfaction. "*Ja.* I won't let my impish pack get their inquisitive little hands upon this."

He sat at the head of the large Darly table, taking turns glancing at the fireplace and his food, and he took another bite of his breakfast. If truth be told, he barely tasted his food. He nodded slightly as Rae entered the room and took a plate from the Sheraton sideboard. "A work of art, and such beautiful lines," he remarked.

His compliment made Rae feel a bit less surly. She politely smiled. She did look rather elegant today, in a gown of pale green silk with gold leaves bordering both the hemline and sleeves. "Yes," she acknowledged. "It is a nice dress." And

joy of joys, the seven little rag-mannered dwarves were nowhere to be found. Her polite smile became one of radiant
beauty.

Sadly for the state of their marriage, the baron didn't
notice, as he was again staring at the mantel. "Quite magnificent." Then he turned his attention to Rae. "One of a
kind, and fit for a king."

She had always thought highly of herself, and a compliment was a compliment, so Rae nodded. Mayhap her loutish husband was not such a dunce after all.

"I hope it tells time accurately."

Rae was confused. "What, my dress? Besides, why
would it need to tell time? You have enough clocks about
the place to supply the whole village of Wolfach. Perhaps
even all of Prussia!"

Fen glanced again at his newest purchase: a Thomas
Johnson clock. The timepiece was decorated with six small
cuckoo birds nesting in various places around the ornate
cherrywood design, and it was one of a kind. Reluctantly
Fen looked back to his bride. "I collect them."

"Dresses? Brides? I knew you had one other bride, but
really, sirrah, one cannot go around collecting women. It's
just not done in polite society."

He shook his head. "I was speaking of *clocks*. I happen
to have a rather large and impressive collection."

"I know. Oh." Humiliated, Rae realized that her husband
had been speaking all along about the silly clock, and not
about her looks or attire. The big churl! How could he not
realize that she had dressed especially to please him this
morn? How could her new husband not understand that
he was supposed to be showering her with gifts and attention?

Realizing that she had remained silent for too long, and
that the baron was still staring at her, she managed to say,
"It's pretty . . . for a clock."

Fen grinned. "I see you've tired of your sulks."

She sniffed delicately. Yes, she was indeed tired of moping

about, feeling sorry for her blighted plight. "Sulking when no one notices isn't any treat," she muttered. Narrowing her eyes at him, she managed another wounded sniffle. Her husband had not tried to placate her; he had not even come up to her room to check on her last night, after she had pointedly declined to dine with him. Hence, she'd ended up taking her supper in her room alone, where she had remained with nothing to do. Bored, Rae finally had made a trip to the library, only to find that her husband didn't have any of the Gothic horror novels that her sister so loved to read. She was missing Greta dearly.

"Well, it is such a lovely day, and you are my husband," she explained. "I was under the impression that the morn should always be broken together with one's husband, and with some good cheer, I suppose."

Fen was surprised that she was conceding. He would have guessed that Rae was a weeklong-sulk person. Even his beloved Fiona had pouted for a good day or two when angered. Amused, he teased, "I see you are trying to worm your way into my good graces."

Rae's jaw dropped open. "Surely you are jesting. Why would I want to do that? You are supposed to worm your way into mine! Do you know *nothing* of marriage?"

"I *was* married before," Fen managed to say, hiding a grin. "But please do explain."

She shrugged elegantly. "In a marriage between a man and woman . . ."

When she paused, he interrupted. "*Ja*, that's what we have here."

Rae's mouth formed a moue of displeasure. "As I was saying, in a marriage between a man and a woman, a man shall make certain that his wife is treated gently and kindly, and shall give her gifts. All kinds of lovely gifts."

He smiled wickedly. "Did you know that *gift* in German means poison? Are you sure that is what you wish me to give you?"

Rae was taken aback. "Poison? Of course not! How silly. A good husband would never give his wife poison. I very much fear that you Germans are lagging a bit behind in this whole marriage business. I want presents—English presents—and for you to lavish compliments upon me. Especially when I'm feeling out of sorts, as I did yesterday. Fulsome compliments about everything from the tips of my hairs to the bottoms of my toes."

"Alas, I have not seen your toes. But I think I begin to see. You want compliments," he stated.

Taking a sip of hot, strong coffee, he ignored the blush that stained her face. Almost abstractly, Fen studied his wife, trying to see beneath the superficial mask she showed the world. Was there anything more than surface beauty? He most fervently hoped there was, for both his peace of mind and the well-being of his offspring.

"What else did you say? Presents?" he repeated. "I am to 'lavish them upon my wife.' What will my wife lavish on me?" Her shallow remarks about praise and presents annoyed him, but he still wanted to know what she thought a wife's duty was.

"Why, she looks beautiful for him. She is an ornament he can proudly show to his friends. She is a lady of gentle manners who does him credit. She looks after his home, and he looks after her needs with proper presents—"

Fen interrupted, "*Ja*, and compliments. I got that part. But what about her other duties?"

Oh drat! He was speaking about those wifely duties in the bedchamber, Rae realized. Still, he didn't look like a man who enjoyed playing with pickles. Perhaps she had some chance left. "Well, yes, I suppose."

Fen watched his wife, managing to feel both irritated and amused at the blush that spread across her cheeks. She blushed so charmingly. And she was a vision today, with her long silvery-golden hair streaming down her back. "Yes, what?"

Lifting her chin high, she said, "Ahem. Yes, those duties too." Anxiously she wondered how she could do those things with him. He was so big. She wondered what size pickles he'd want to jar.

Sneaking a peek at her husband, she couldn't help but notice that Fennis had intense gray eyes and a lovely, healthy crop of thick blond hair. He also had a full-lipped mouth, and she wondered for an instant just how she could have overlooked these pertinent facts when she first met him. He might not be the most handsome of men, but he had an interesting and rugged face, very manly. Yes, one that was quite pleasing. It appeared that Greta had been right about one or two things, possibly even three—much to Rae's chagrin. But then, her big sister usually was correct.

His wife's answer surprised him. He had thought Rae considered him too repugnant to even think about bedding. His loins heated instantly, making him aware that, in spite of her shallowness, he still did want to sleep with her. "What about a wife's duty to her husband's children?" he asked, trying to regain control.

Ah, the fly in the ointment. The seven little dwarves in her fairy-tale castle. Noting Fen was studying her speculatively, Rae gave a slight but ladylike shrug. "What about them? What about a governess or nurse?"

Fen hid his disappointment in her answer. Yet, what had he expected? He had made his thorny bed; now he must lie in it alone—or with a conceited and thoughtless shrew, a vain and shallow creature, a fairy princess of great external loveliness but an ugly interior.

"Their governess, as I told you, left. I have not replaced her, since they have a new mother. Their beloved nurse died last year."

Rae shuddered. "Did they do away with her?"

He couldn't tell if she was being facetious or not, but he did not like her tone. His brood might be a ramshackle lot, but they all had kind hearts, and he loved them dearly.

"She died in her sleep, peacefully. My *kinder* were very up-set. They loved their old nurse."

Rae sighed. "I don't understand, Fen. Why haven't you replaced these incredibly important positions?"

"It's quite simple. My children were too upset over their nanny's death and didn't want a new nurse at the time. The governess only left six weeks ago, and then business kept me occupied until our hasty betrothal happened. I de-cided that before I hired a new governess I would let them get to know their new mother."

"Oh-ho, no thank you! I will begin looking immediately. I'm sure my aunt knows someone who can fill these positions."

"I said I wasn't hiring," Fen remarked firmly, conviction in his eyes. "I want you to get to know my children and befriend them."

Clearly infuriated, Fen leaned closer to her. Rae caught an enticing scent, a combination of pine, rich dark choco-late and the cold frost of winter. She blinked as she stared back at him. Her husband smelled delicious.

Returning her attention to the argument, Rae threw down her napkin and stood. "Befriend them? They locked me in a tower and dusted me in flour!"

He frowned, ignoring the sudden widening of her eyes and the way her nostrils flared. If this had been Fiona, he would be kissing her senseless right about now.

"The day I become a friendly companion to your obnox-ious little brats will be the day that the sun ceases to shine," Rae finished, stepping back from him and his intoxicating scent.

"Then it is a good thing you are so lovely. Perhaps peo-ple will notice your face rather than the rags you will be wearing, because I will not purchase anything for you un-til your attitude changes."

"Ohhh, you . . . Fennis Schortz, I despise you!" Rae grabbed her skirts and turned, the hem swirling about her ankles as she stormed out of the room. But his voice shout-ing her name stopped her dead in her tracks.

"Rae! I did speak with them about the flour debacle."

She turned to face him. "What punishment did you give—no supper until they're old and gray?"

"No. In fact, I had dinner with them last night, since you were indisposed."

Rae made a slight moue of distaste. That was punishment for him: supper with his beastly brood.

"I told them to stop playing pranks on their new mother, that it wasn't nice, and to be the good little Schortzes I know them to be."

"That's it? After all the abuse I suffered? Not even a slap on the wrist?"

"*Ja.* Well, I patted them on the head." He said the last just to annoy her.

Rae spun out of the room. "Oh, go bite your bum, you clutch-fisted tyrant," she muttered.

Fen couldn't help but crack a grin. His children had tattled on their stepmother's other "go bite your bums" remark. She might be vain, but she was also spirited, and had a colorful vocabulary for a gentlewoman. Would she be so spirited in bed? If so, then this marriage might not be made in hell but merely purgatory. More and more he wanted to find out.

As Rae started out the doorway, she was halted in her tracks by the approach of the very band of rampaging villains she so opposed. Trying to step aside, she was almost knocked over by the rag-mannered crew as they poured into the room, all pointing at her. Fortunately there were only three of the little barbarians, and three were easier to deal with than seven.

"What is it?" Fen asked, noting warily his children's grubby little faces and fingers all directing outrage at his new wife.

"She's going to make us eat pea porridge soup, nine days old," Ernst cried, his little face a mask of abject misery. "With a peck of pickled peppers."

"Pickled *pointers,*" Merri corrected, holding up her fingers and lying through her sweet little teeth, then contrarily added her two cents. "She's making me and Shyla wear sackcloth and ashes!"

Fen merely raised a brow, while Rae turned livid. "Never in all my life have I heard of pea porridge soup—one day old or a thousand!" Ernst snorted, so Rae pointed a finger back at Merri. "I said that if you were going to work in the garden, as is your wont, you need to wear something less dressy so it would not get so dirty. But never did I mention sackcloth or ashes, although it certainly seems appropriate now."

"Did you hear her, Papa? She wants to make me a hag?" Merri screeched. Alden simply burped and began rubbing his lamp, which Rae believed was to call forth a genie to send her to perdition . . . or at least back to Cornwall. "Wicked old stepmother. She made me polish her pearl brooches."

"I do not have a pearl brooch," Rae snapped. "Even if I did, I would not cast pearls before swinish children." Tearing her gaze away from the terrible trio, she stamped her foot. "Although, a dozen new brooches would be a good gift for a new bride. Most especially one who has to put up with wild accusations and pillaging little Viking children. A wise husband would take note."

Ernst could see indecision in his father's eyes, so he quickly added—rather judiciously, he thought—"This morning she gave Nap a poisoned apple."

Rae gasped in outrage. "Do you know," she began, putting a finger to her chin, "my sister once loaned me a book. *The Importance of Beating Ernst.* It was a wild book, and I find it now is a jolly good idea."

"Enough! I will hear no more about poisoned apples or beatings," Fen shouted. He was absolutely certain that Rae would never poison his children, even as angry as she was. He also knew that if anyone could drag Rae down off her vain high horse and make a woman and mother out of her, it was his unruly but devious little scamps.

Rae turned and stared at the brats. "Eating pickled pointers? Poisoned apples? I wouldn't give your new stepmother any ideas, you little scalawags," she snapped. Then she stomped out of the room, forgetting her genteel upbringing long enough to let out a few choice words she'd heard her brothers use. One of them started with *peck*.

# CHAPTER TWENTY-FOUR

## The Unmagnificent Seven

Having no one to carp to, Rae stormed down the long hallways, seething with ill usage and giving the Schortz family portraits the fish eye. "How dare he take their side against me? How dare they accuse me of such atrocious doings?"

Rae's vengeful musings were cut short by a loud crash. A crash, in her opinion, could only mean one thing: More little monsters were about. If she were sensible, she would turn tail and run. Still, she slowed down and peered into the room where the noise had originated. In the gloom of the shadows, she could make out a bust in pieces on the floor, and three of the little Schortzes staring down at it.

"I'm glad it was a bust of Caesar. Papa never really liked it," Quinn said.

Poppy nodded. "We could says our new mama doned it."

Shyla shook her pretty little head. "No. I feel bad about what I helped Nap and Ernst do yesterday. Our new step mama is very pretty. I like her."

An expert at eavesdropping, Rae eased further into the shadows by the door. Even though she despised these little scourges, Shyla was a beautiful child—like Rae herself had been. Perhaps they had something in common, and she could groom the little girl to be the toast of Prussia one day. The thought of being stepmother to an upcoming toast spread a jellylike feeling across her. It was odd—a sense of pride in something other than herself.

"I bet she can't put a worm on a hook," Quinn remarked.

Rae wrinkled her nose. Of course not! She wouldn't touch a worm with a ten-foot pole; they were almost as disgusting as her new stepchildren.

"We should tell her about the ghost," Shyla ventured, peeking up at her brother.

"No, Nap and Ernst wouldn't like it," Quinn replied. "And I don't like to make my twin brother mad."

Ghost, what ghost? Rae wondered. Was there a ghost here in the castle, like in Greta's books? Rae bent down to hear better. Of course, yesterday she had been made a fool, so why should she believe what they were saying now? Still, they didn't know she was listening, so what would the sly fiends gain by making up ghost stories?

Shyla seemed to read her mind. "She wouldn't believe us, anyway," the little girl said. "Not after we fibbed about Papa being an ogre."

"I saw it once," Poppy remarked, her voice rather high. "It's a bad old ghostie, and I cried."

"Oh, silly, you've never seen it," Quinn replied, his eyes rolling.

"Well, I heard it."

Patting her little sister's head, Shyla nodded. "I've heard it too."

"And Nap's seen it," Quinn added. "The night he saw it, he couldn't sleep. He sat up all night with his dagger. It clawed him."

Poppy nodded, rubbing her arm. "I *knowed* it. The scars on his arm. It probably kilt our nurse."

Rae leaned back against the wall. Died peacefully in her sleep? Fennis had lied to her! He was as devious and diabolical as his children. Yet, she was not only married to him, she was married into this ghastly family in an admittedly beautiful home that had specters gliding through its shadowy halls. Unlike Rae, her sister Greta would be ecstatic in this situation. She'd probably even get along with the brats.

Creeping away from the door, Rae shook her head. If there was a ghost in the castle, she would lock her door every night. Solemnly she vowed she would never go out of her room at midnight, since that was the dreaded hour when witches and ghosts roamed the earth. Even, she imagined, in fancy little castles.

Of course, if this ghost was so utterly horrible, why hadn't it gotten the children already? With her brow furrowed, she pondered the question for a while.

"Of course! They probably have protection. The demon spawn probably made a pact with the Devil. They are probably related," she muttered softly.

As Rae hurried down the corridor and far, far away from the wicked little dwarves, she didn't hear the little giggles turn to raucous laughter. Nap stepped out from behind the velvet drapes, where he'd had an excellent and unrestricted view of the doorway due to a large mirror hanging to his right.

"She fell for our ghost story! Again!" he cried. Their laughter turned to hooting calls and shouts of victory, and downstairs, the passing maids and footmen shifted uneasily, glancing warily about them. When the Schortz children laughed like that, prospects were grim for their poor beleaguered targets.

After dismissing her maid for the night, Rae sat down at her dressing table and unbuckled her house slippers. Lonely and bored, she picked up her silver-backed brush and began to brush her hair, which was so long that she had to fold it over her lap as she worked. The maid had brushed it earlier, but Rae had nothing else to do. Fennis had been called into Wolfach on some business dealing with Prince von Hanzen. She had discovered this by overhearing the butler tell one of the footmen. As a new husband, Fennis should have let her know himself, she believed, not hear it secondhand. This husband of hers had much to learn.

In another part of the castle, she heard a door slam. "It's probably one of *them*," she said to herself, and shuddered. She would get even with the children as soon as she devised a villainous enough plan. "One worthy of Macbarancle, or Macduff, or Macbeth or whomever. One of those Macs anyway. The big one."

Glancing at the mirror, she found herself frowning. As it would make lines, she immediately stopped. "One hundred and three, one hundred and four," Rae counted as she stroked her hair. The shadows deepened. Rae yawned slightly and set the brush down. "I might as well go to bed."

Her third night as a bride, and she was still as innocent as a lamb. The insult piqued her vanity, yet at the same time she felt a smattering of relief. And there was a tiny part of her that felt discontent, along with mild curiosity at the mysteries of the wedding night.

Rae crossed the room, passing several tables on her way to the oversized creamy-white sleigh bed with its lace coverlet. Suddenly, she heard a noise outside in the hall. Halting abruptly, she turned slowly toward the door. Was it the brood?

She heard a low moaning. Cautiously, she crossed to the door. "Hello?" Was someone hurt, or was this those sneaky stepchildren? "Is someone there?"

A low moan was the only answer.

"Oh, drat! This is a fine pickle." She couldn't help being reminded of her husband and the wedding night. "And it's just what I need to complete my list of woes—a haunted castle."

She cautiously unlocked her door and stuck her head out, muttering, "Surely a ghost wouldn't moan. According to Greta's Gothic novels, they rattle chains and boo at people. At least, I think that's what they do."

Outside, the corridor was empty. But the moaning was louder.

"Can one of the little toads be sick?" And if they were, should she do anything? If Nap were sick, or the fibbing twin or the grumpy Merri, she would let him or her nurse him or herself back to health. Still, if it were the pretty one, Shyla, or the little one, Poppy, or maybe even Quinn, perhaps she should take a look. The youngest, the vicious little biter, was on his own.

Taking a cautious step into the hallway, which was lit by a half-dozen wall sconces, Rae then followed the sound down the stone corridor, passing three sturdy wooden doors before she came to a turn. Inching forward, Rae cautiously stuck her head around the corner . . . and stopped short as a skittering noise accompanied the faint creaking of chains. Fear flooded her system. Clinging to the wall, Rae held her candle high in one hand.

The massive hallway was long and dark, with thick black shadows hiding whatever was making the noise. "Who's there?" Rae called.

Another low moan sounded, followed quickly by the sound of rattling chains. She took a step back, her spine pressed to the wall as she watched a figure emerge from the deep shadows. She was stunned, her mind refusing to believe that she was facing a ghost. If only Greta was here, she would know what to do.

"Go away!" she cried.

The ghostly specter did the opposite, skittering across the ancient stone floor and coming ever closer.

"No," Rae gasped, fear filling her. Her head grew dizzy with terror as the shadows receded and she caught a better glimpse of the ghastly phantom. The figure was covered in a white shroud, with dark red stains crusted upon it. Rae's breath quickened, and she could feel her heart racing. Something wicked was unquestionably coming her way.

"Go away. Shoo!"

The shrouded form raised its chains high in the air and shook them, emitting a horrible screech. And behind this heinous spirit of the grave, there was a scrambling sound, and rattles of more chains, as if they were striking the floor.

Finally Rae's instinct to survive overcame her paralyzing fear. She screamed, running down the corridor as fast as her dainty feet would carry her, with her lacy blue dressing gown flying behind. As she groped for her door, she felt something grasp her ankle. Lurching across the threshold, she shook off the grip of the evil thing that seized her, then slammed the door.

Outside, she heard a scratching on the hard wood, and a tiny voice asked, "Come pway wiff me."

Her eyes grew round with horror. "No," she murmured. "Anything but that." She had barely survived the attack from the living ankle-biter.

"Let us in!" several little howlers demanded.

"Not by the hair of my chinny-chin-chin."

"Then we'll huff and . . . put a gypsy curse upon you!" a voice threatened joyously.

The sounds of chains rattling in the hallway outside her door, and the now recognizably demented laughter of the seven little living Schortzes, had Rae's blood boiling. She didn't know how they had done it, but somehow they had managed to make her eavesdrop on a conversation. It was diabolically clever. She would use this lesson and file it away for future reference, in case she ever needed to do something so dastardly. Their execution had been perfect. Wait until Greta heard about this night's antics. Her eldest sister would probably laugh a little, but would also console her. Most importantly, Greta would help Rae come up with a grand plan for revenge

Rae yelled, hands clenched into tight fists, feeling fairly secure since the door was very thick and latched tight. "See if I come to check on you next time I think you're sick! You can die ranting and raving in fevered delusions, while I'll stand by with a merry smile on my face."

"Fooled again!" Nap shouted back, and he threw off the shroud, laughing as he jangled the chain. "You're so easy to trick." A chorus of laughter filled the air.

Rae shouted back, their shameless mirth grating on her nerves and self-esteem. "I'm counting to six. If you know what's good for you you'll flee, else I'll beat you with a big old stick!" Glancing about, she spotted her empty chamber pot. With fierce determination and quick hands, she quickly dumped all her face and body powders into it.

Outside, staring at the door, the youngest Schortz girl shook her head. "She was awful scared," she said thoughtfully. "Maybes we shouldn't've done it." Alden just growled.

Suddenly, Rae flung open the door and threw the contents of her chamber pot upon them. Four of the children were close enough to get the full blast, sputtering as white dust flew everywhere. Hands on hips, momentarily victorious, Rae commented, "If you want to play ghost, you need to be white!"

Seeing the fires of anger spring to life in several sets of beady little eyes, Rae made a quick and wise decision. She slammed the door in their faces once again, and shouted through the door, "Now you *look* the part."

This time, the last laugh was hers.

# CHAPTER TWENTY-FIVE

The Would-be Princess and the Peas

The children's hour was every hour at the baron's castle, as Rae could regrettably attest. Just this morning she had awakened late, feeling as if she had slept on hard little pebbles. Reaching beneath her sheet, she found a large scattering of peas—and not the cooked variety, either. Her temper boiling, Rae quickly went in search of the legume-loving brood. She was not a lady to be trifled with, and her future seemed to be war and peas.

Besides, she had come up with a fine plan to frighten the nefarious little urchins, a scheme worthy of her sister and her wicked little brothers. She smiled and handed her maid another letter to be delivered to Greta, this one describing her ordeals. Shaking her head, Rae pondered why her elder sister hadn't already written. She hoped that Greta wasn't sick. This time, if she received no note from her sister, she would go at once to Aunt Vivian's and check on her herself. Greta loved her, unlike Rae's oafish husband and his nasty little children.

Straightening her shoulders, she went in search of some much-needed help. If her wily plan was to succeed, some of the servants would need to be pressed into service, and from the short while she had been at Castle Durloc, she believed that the butler and the first footman could be trusted to keep a secret and aid her vengeance. Much of the staff would likely help, as they had for some time borne the brunt of the children's pranks.

After questioning several servants, Rae hurried to the study to find the butler. There he stood, a great mess in front of the fireplace. Ashes and dust were everywhere, and the butler was busy dusting it off his jacket. Rattled, he glanced at the fireplace with an expression no longer stoic.

"Let me guess," Rae said. "The baron's bratlings?"

He nodded, wiping gray ash off his dark brown mustache. "Yes, madame. Now, may I help you?"

"I assume this nefarious trap was laid for me?" she guessed.

Again, the butler nodded. His face took on a long-suffering expression. "You know, they were not always this bad. After their mother died, the baron was mad with grief. Later, though his grief lessened, he found it hard to discipline them because they were still grieving for the baroness."

His words touched Rae. But while the children had suffered, there was no excuse for letting the prickly pack run wild. "I understand they were hurt, but they need boundaries, else they shall tear the castle down around our ears," she stated. "Do you know where they are?"

This butler merely looked up and trembled. Warily, Rae joined him in his study of the ceiling, and she soon heard shrill cries and stamping feet, like a rampage of stampeding elephants. Then came the sound of *that* laughter: a noise no sane person would challenge.

The hairs on the back of her neck stood up. "I know I should see about the beastly little dears, but I must talk to you about something," she said.

The butler leaned against the wall, still shuddering. "I would hide beneath the settee, but the last time I did, they trapped me there. They placed spiders around the sofa. I have never been fond of spiders."

Rae placed a comforting hand on the butler's arm. "I can just imagine the terror you've borne. Now, now—Heinrich, isn't it?"

Tersely, he nodded again, and more ash fell from his forehead.

"Well, Heinrich, their reign of terror shall be brought to a swift end. I will not back down, since I have more backbone than that. Nay, nor will I sit still for their backbiting—or ankle biting. I tell you there will be a backlash from all their backwards, forwards, and sideways sneakiness, and an overhand slam for their underhanded dealings." She paused for effect then added dramatically, "I have a plan. But it is a secret plan. Where is the baron? I don't want him getting wind of what I am about to say."

It was then that she discovered Fen hadn't returned last night, though the butler was embarrassed to relay such information. It was inexcusable, Rae thought, seething. Her husband was doing his husbandly duties with some tart. It was a souring idea.

She didn't understand why she was being so maudlin, of course. Just because Fen stayed out all night in a drunken, debauched orgy was no concern of hers. Just because her new husband didn't care for her very much, there were still plenty of others who did, besides her family. She just couldn't think of any at the moment.

"I'd like to lop off his ears with a butcher's knife," she muttered. Then, realizing what she'd just revealed, she shook her head at her own foolishness. Revealing her humiliation to the staff was never well done.

"Horror of horrors, what if my aunt finds out?" she suddenly whispered, considering. Then, noticing the butler, she commented in a more normal tone, "The only thing worse than being gossiped about, is not being talked about at all." Still, if her groom was already practicing infidelity, what would happen when he got it down pat? She would never live down the infamy.

Was the tart prettier than her? Rae pondered momentarily. Then, realizing what a silly thought it was, she mentally shook her head. How could anyone be prettier if she was the fairest in all the land? Yet, another little voice nagged at her. If she were so perfect, why hadn't her husband come home to do his husbandly duty? And while he was playing, she was praying, spending her nights in deadly dread of what new pranks her stepchildren would perpetrate next.

Seeing the embarrassment on the new baroness's face, the butler took pity on her. "The baron was called away to business on one of his other estates. Plus he had a meeting with Fürst von Hanzen. He will be gone again this night, but should be home on the morrow," Heinrich explained. He was surprised to find his feelings softening toward her. He had heard that Rae Grimm was too full of herself, yet she had seemed concerned with the baron's happiness.

"Thank you, Heinrich. That relieves my mind," she said. So, her husband of only a few nights wasn't out tarting just yet. Yes, she was vastly relieved.

"The baron is a busy man. He looks after his own, cares for all of us. My family has served the Schoitzes for the past five generations. Though I've known the present baron's father and grandfather, both good men, the baron is still the best by far. He's loyal and true to his vows."

Rae was glad of the words, although she had already seen and judged much for herself. Fennis *was* an honorable man, and one capable of deep and abiding love. In the short time she had been around him, she had witnessed his love for his late wife and his children. He took his responsibilities seriously, and his servants were a mostly content and well-treated lot. Their clothes were also clean and of good materials, and they worked with a song in their hearts and smiles on their faces. Except, of course, when the savage seven were on the warpath.

Yes, all bespoke a manor ran by a fair and firm hand—the firm and fair hand of her husband, who had yet to lay said hand upon her. Would it be gentle or fiercely tender with passion, as she had once dreamed? Or would Fennis remain forever locked in the self-imposed prison of his dead love?

"*Ja,* the baron is a fine man, and Durloc is a fine place to live—even with *them* running about."

"Yes, the fly in the ointment is the baron's brazen brood," Rae agreed. Stiffening her spine, she stared the butler in the eye, trying to impress upon him the urgency of her request. "Heinrich, I have a proposition for you. One, I think, you may just well find not only helpful, but rewarding." Her eyes danced with wicked intent as she explained her plan. Then the first footman was called and the whereabouts of the children ascertained, for she wanted none of the wily little imps to know of her plot.

Upon learning that the children were ensconced in the stable yard, where they were most likely practicing dark rites, Rae preceded to speak. The butler and first footman were soon adding their own thoughts, and the scheme was hatched. From the baroness's study, their long and loud laughter could be heard.

Yes, they all agreed: "Tonight will be the night that the seven little dwarves get their well-deserved comeuppance."

Rae's determined footsteps rapidly *clip-clapp*ed as she made her way to the door, then turned back and pointed a dainty finger at the beleaguered butler. "And be sure that the little culprits eat all their peas from now on! Have cook buy pea porridge soup, nine days, old. We'll feed it to them for the next week. No, make that two weeks!" And with that, she left the room.

The two servants were beaming. Heinrich glanced over at the first footman with a thoughtful expression on his face. "The new baroness may be a match for those seven youngsters," he said.

"That she might. She'll give them a dickens of a time." The footman wore a look of great expectations.

Sometime later, the first footman espied the children returning from the stable, and he hurried to join Heinrich. The game was afoot, and peaceful living was at stake!

The baron's older boys passed by the butler's pantry, where the first footman and Heinrich, their backs turned, conversed earnestly. "Hush, lest someone hear," the butler warned, wanting exactly that.

"But it's so frightening. Do you think the curse is real?" the first footman asked. Too often he had been on the receiving end of the children's pranks.

"The new baroness received word today from her sister. It seems that their family has indeed been cursed by a gypsy. Alas, the letter arrived late, and tonight's the night. *Ja,* this very night—the thirty-first—this hellish rider will ride!"

Nap, listening intently, put his finger to his mouth to warn the twins from speaking. Quickly they darted behind the doors of the pantry, their greedy little ears listening.

"It's a bad curse. The worst! Do you think it's really possible?"

Heinrich sighed. "I do. Baroness Grimm's family made the gypsy very angry, so she cursed all children in the marriage to suffer the fate of the Headless Horseman." The butler knew he should feel a twinge of regret, but he didn't. Not at all. The baron's benighted brood had become near impossible to deal with these past few years, and someone needed to set them straight. It appeared the new baroness was just the fräulein for the job.

Narrowing his eyes, Nap moved closer to the door to the butler's pantry, motioning for Quinn to step back a few paces so they wouldn't be seen. Ernst's eyes were wide.

"But a headless horseman is a fearsome thing. I've heard tell they ride by night with sword in hand, carrying their heads beneath their arms. And whom they seek, they find.

And when they find them, they . . ." The first footman trailed off, his voice full of doom and gloom.

"Whack, whack," Heinrich finished. "Yes, I would warn the children at once, if the baroness hadn't made me promise to keep silent. She said that she would find a way to defeat the curse."

Nap's eyes narrowed even more. His new stepmother would leave them to the wolves—well, in this case the wolves were a headless demon.

Ernst started to protest, to cry foul at their new mother's plan, but Nap kept him to silence by a hard jab in the ribs.

The first footman scratched his chin. "I don't know how smart that is. The baron's brood is a hardy and canny lot, and so is the new baroness. If anyone can end the curse, they can . . . but it'd be easier if they were working together. Of course, they'd not believe you. And they certainly wouldn't believe their new stepmother, so where does that leave us?"

"We must watch and take care. The baron would never forgive me if something happened to any of them."

"'Tis true, Heinrich . . . It's a shame really," the footman remarked after a moment, shaking his head.

"What?"

"The baroness wouldn't have any children if she hadn't married the baron. Do you think the Headless Horseman will take all seven?"

Heinrich managed to hide his smile. The devil himself couldn't manage all seven of the Schortz swarm. "*Nein*. Probably only two or three."

Realizing that the conversation was about to end, the three boys departed, but not before the job was done. Worry was etched on their little faces, while laughter filled the servants' hall.

"Headless horseman?" Quinn gasped as they ran down the hallway to find their sisters.

"Two or three? I don't want it to be me," Ernst remarked. Then, seeing his elder brother shoot him a look of disgust, he adjusted his statement. "I mean, I don't want it to be any of us."

"What shall we do? We're doomed. If only Papa were here. He'd save us and lop off the horseman's head."

"His head's already chopped off, you fool," Ernst scolded his twin. "Nap, what will we do?"

"Fight." Nap spat out the words. No one would hurt his family. "Then we deal with our stepmother. How dare she bring her vanity and shallowness into our home along with a curse! What kind of family did my father marry into?"

"A Grimm one," Quinn replied.

"*Ja.* Indeed he did," Nap said. He'd brought home the Grimm Reaper.

# CHAPTER TWENTY-SIX

## Heads Will Roll

There was a quote in the Bible about mischief following, and who were greater mischief-makers than the brimstone brood? It went something like "a tooth for a tooth, a foot for a foot, and a headless horseman for a flouring animosity." Rae hid her snickers as she watched from her hiding place in the tack room; this prank would really satisfy her.

The hour was late and the little monsters were sleeping in the barn, thinking to avoid the headless horseman by not being in bed. Rae's smile grew wide. Afraid of the false curse, the children had banded together this night. They had giggled and plotted, hatched devious little schemes and so forth until the hour grew late. Shadows deepened and dark night was now upon them. They lay asleep. They had also left the candles burning, clearly afraid of the dark.

Peering through a crack in the door, Rae noted that in sleep the brood was almost human, almost cute, almost innocent.

Shivering, she drew her cloak closer. She had been stuck in this tack room for hours with no fireplace. Yet her frozen nose and feet would be worth it once the little imps were put firmly in their place. Besides, now that the children were all peacefully sleeping, Heinrich should soon arrive.

She did not have long to wait. The butler's approach was heralded by a loud banging. Next, the first footman suddenly threw open the doors of the stable. He was dressed in black, and hid in the shadows so as not to be seen. The children awoke with a start and a few screams. But neither the stable master nor the grooms would come to help this night, for they had been forewarned.

A demonic cry filled the air. Rae shifted, opened the tack door wider and saw the butler on horseback, riding a massive black beast. Heinrich was dressed in a long flowing cape that covered his head. With the shadows and the inkiness of night, he appeared to be headless. Beneath his arm, he held a pumpkin with a face carved into it and a small lighted candle within. In his other hand he held a large sword.

Another harsh cry rode the wind. Elbows and arms tangled as Nap and Quinn tried to jump up and defend their siblings. Alden, lamp in hand, flew beneath a hay pile, while Poppy climbed the ladder to the upper loft.

Hand to mouth, Rae tried to stop her giggles. This was marvelous. This was no horseman of the Apocalypse, no Headless Horseman of Sleepy Hollow, but a sneaky butler with a hint of the thespian bred into his blood. Finally, and with great finesse, the little Schortzes were getting their just desserts: a pumpkin-headed pie in the face.

"Be you the children of Rae Grimm Schortz?" Heinrich asked, his voice much lower than normal.

A chorus of *neins* filled the air.

"You lie." The butler raised the pumpkin head high, along with the sword.

Bravely Nap reached for his father's sword, which he had laid by the pile of hay upon which they had been sleeping, only to discover it gone. Nap was unaware that his crafty stepmother had crept from her hiding place and hidden it elsewhere. Rae had also made sure all sharp implements were locked away, along with the baron's dogs. She didn't intend for Heinrich to get hurt while doing her this favor.

Dumbfounded, Nap turned back toward the threat. His mind searched for a way to protect his siblings. "Run out the back door and go to the house. Rouse the servants!" he called.

Shyla obeyed. Screaming for all she was worth, she ran. Merri, snatching Alden from his hiding place, was not far behind, with Ernst on her heels. "Run, run," Merri screamed.

"Oh, Heinrich's good, he is," Rae muttered, watching the whole bizarre scene unfold. The little imps were running about like chickens with their heads cut off. The pumpkin was an inspired touch, she realized; it was driving the kids out of their gourds. "My, but the taste of revenge is sweet."

"Quinn—run, you fool!" Nap ordered.

"I can't find the kittens," Quinn cried. "I can't let him hurt them."

"Forget the kittens. Go, now! Where's Poppy?" Nap asked fearfully. Scanning the barn, he quickly spotted Poppy at the top of the ladder. He cried out, "Get down from there! We must flee!"

The Headless Horseman waved his sword and screeched long and loud. "I must have my vengeance." The sound caused Poppy to lose her footing, and she began to fall.

Seeing a potential for disaster, Rae slipped from the tack room, heart pounding. Swiftly she ran the short distance to the ladder, holding out her arms. She took most of the brunt of Poppy's fall. Unharmed, she handed the child to Nap, saying, "Run, before he gets you!"

"What about you?" Nap asked, securing Poppy's hold about his neck.

"He's after my children, not me."

"We're not your children!" Nap argued.

"Tell that to him," Rae replied. The daunting sight of a headless man upon a huge horse apparently made her suggestion distasteful to the child.

The horseman urged his horse farther into the barn, and Nap, Poppy and Rae retreated.

"Where's Quinn?" Nap asked. Then he saw his brother

holding two kittens in his hands. "Run, Quinn! Run for your life!"

The twin did as his brother asked, and Nap, seeing that, ran hard with Poppy. All would have been well, but Quinn tripped. One of the kittens flew out of his hands and landed near the massive horse. The horse reared. Quinn jumped up to recover the kitten before it was smashed beneath the horse's hooves.

The scene slowed, Rae frozen with terror. The hooves came down close enough to send dirt into Quinn's eyes. "No!" she screamed. "No." Without a thought for her safety, she dodged the flying hooves and pulled Quinn out from under.

Heinrich tried to calm his mount, the pumpkin discarded, but again the deadly hooves came close. At last, Rae dragged Quinn and his two kittens from harm's path.

At the back entrance, Nap, Merri and Poppy stood silent. They had seen their stepmother rescue their brother. They had also seen the pumpkin head burst as the horse hooves landed on it, and Heinrich threw back his cloak, desperate to calm the horse.

Rae knew the jig was up.

Dusting off her skirt, she handed a kitten to Quinn. "It seems we've been found out," she said to the butler.

"How could you?" Nap asked. "And you, Heinrich, it's a foul trick you played us!"

The butler having dismounted, the first footman appeared and took the horse away, and Heinrich stood staring at all seven of the children. "Is it worse than pig bladders dropped on the footmen's heads? Or being trapped under a settee with spiders? What about frogs in the chamber pots?"

"Or ghosts in the hall?" Rae added. "Admit it. You children have gone to the dogs. You're incorrigible."

"So you frighten us half to death? I lost my best pair of slippers running for my life," Shyla retorted, her curls bouncing in her anger.

"You endangered us!" Nap accused, his eyes dark.

Rae nodded. "That I did. And I'm very sorry," she admitted. "I meant no harm to any of you. I just wanted to make you think before you prank."

"I'm telling Papa," Shyla said.

"He'll send you away for this," Ernst remarked cheerfully. His smile faded somewhat, and he glanced at the butler. "I guess Heinrich will have to go, too. That will be sad. He makes such great faces when he sees a spider."

Drawing herself up to her fullest height, Rae stared hard at each child, her finger pointing at each one of them down their line as she counted them off and made sure of their safety. Looking at the little faces before her, she saw some change. She thought that Quinn looked grateful, along with Merri. Poppy smiled brightly. Yes, she had made some headway in this headless plot. But her scheming could have cost Quinn his life, and that was hard to stomach.

"I shall tell your papa myself. It is past time that you savage seven be taught a lesson. Your papa, in his grief and your sorrow, has let you get away with nothing less than murder. It's time for this tyranny to end. I'm sorry it frightened you as badly as it did. I'm sorry that Poppy almost fell and Quinn was almost hurt. But I'm not sorry that you got a taste of your own medicine. You have terrorized Castle Durloc for too long. How do you think the servants feel when you play your nasty little tricks on them? They work hard and serve this family proudly, yet you treat them so. They are afraid for their positions, so they don't dare complain. That . . . is unfair."

Staring hard at Nap, she shook her head. "Someday you will be master here. Your servants deserve better. Heinrich stays."

Her words angered Fen's eldest son. But they also had the ring of truth. Ashamed, he nodded.

Satisfied, Rae took her leave, along with Heinrich. Once inside the castle, she instructed the first footman to go and rouse the cook. "Tell him the children will be hungry."

As they walked back through the castle, the baron's brood discussed the repercussions from the night. Most wanted their stepmother's head on a platter, but a few thought hard on their new mother's words.

"She saved my life and the kittens," Quinn said adamantly. "It was very brave."

"She's the one who put you in danger," Shyla argued.

"I say we think up something worse than a headless horseman to scare her back," Ernst suggested, his eyes alight with sly determination. "Heinrich as well."

"We could always tell her the truth," Merri remarked. "That would scare the daylights out of her." But then she stopped herself, remembering how their stepmother had risked her life to save Quinn.

"We tell her *nothing* about the secret," Nap protested heatedly. "And Quinn, the next time you do something so stupid, I'll beat you to a pulp. You could have been killed!"

"I'mma tell Papa," Poppy said. "You're not supposed to hit each other."

"I hope he makes our new mother leave," Ernst grumbled. "That headless horseman plot was just plain mean."

"I hope Papa doesn't," Quinn disagreed. "And her plan was pretty sly."

"Wish I'd thought of it," Nap said through clenched teeth.

"I think our new stepmother's plan was wicked and nasty and horrid," Shyla pouted, her lip stuck out.

"I'm hungry," Merri announced.

This remark sent the seven little Schortzes into the kitchen, where they all did what they did best—bickered—until they were fed. Rae had been right to suggest Cook prepare a meal.

Rae peeked in on the children before hurrying up to her warm, cozy bed. Pranks were exhausting work. She wearily climbed the stairs while saying a quick prayer of thanks. She was lucky the children hadn't been hurt; Rae didn't know how she would have faced Fennis if Quinn or

Poppy had been injured. Or worse . . . She shuddered. This would be her first and last prank, and she hoped the children would end their reign of terror as well.

Suppressing a yawn, she entered her quarters and carefully locked the door. She might have won tonight's battle, but the larger question still loomed: Had she won the war?

# CHAPTER TWENTY-SEVEN

## May the Schortz Be with You

The morning after the night of the Headless Horseman was a quiet one, which surprised Rae. No menacing little footsteps rampaged above. No shrill shrieks or devious laughter. Yes, all was quiet on the Prussian front.

Rae had slept late, exhausted as she was from the night's madcap adventures. She also felt a bit guilty. The children's faces when they'd beheld the headless rider would forever be imprinted upon her mind. Perhaps she had gone a bit too far. But then, what choice had she had? It was either her or them. Naturally she had chosen herself.

Staring into the mirror, she shook her head. This morn, she did not feel the fairest in all the land. The children might never hold her in affection, even though she had saved Poppy from a bad fall and Quinn from being trampled. Shuddering slightly, she wondered what her husband would say when he found out. Fennis would not be happy that she had played such a prank: one that had exposed his beloved *kinder* to danger. She only hoped he would listen to her explanation before condemning her to a life of bread, water and no new gowns. Desperate situations required desperate measures. The meek might inherit the earth, but the devious and wily were going to make her earthly stay a hellish one in the meantime.

Dressing, she decided to thank the servants for their help in last night's plot. She would also assure them that the baron would not hold any of them responsible for what she had asked them to do. She would take full responsibility, and the wrath of her husband would all fall upon her own lovely, delicate shoulders. Just because she might soon be tossed out into the wintry night didn't mean they should be.

Yet her concerns were soon forgotten, as Rae finally received a note from her sister. Greta was coming to visit. Today! Rae smiled happily. Greta would understand why she had done what she had done. She might also help her devise a way to tell Fennis without Rae losing her own head in the bargain.

As she walked along the stone corridors, Rae happened to hear voices discussing her husband's recent absences. In spite of her good intentions, Rae halted and remained motionless, listening to two maids inside the large library.

"The baron will be home tonight. What he will say about this whole horse and decapitated man mess is beyond me," the first maid said as she dusted.

"I wouldn't want to be in the baroness's shoes for all the cuckoo clocks in Wolfach. The baron sets a fair store upon them children. This won't endear the baroness any to him," the elder maid responded, shaking her head, her gray bun bobbing. "At this rate, they'll never consummate the marriage. There'll be no more little babes in the nursery."

"Thank heavens for that!" the first maid exclaimed, relief obvious in her voice. "Seven is too many as 'tis."

A woman after my own heart, Rae thought.

"Still, a man's got needs. I imagine the baron is tending those needs even as we speak." The older maid lifted a vase and dusted beneath. "Since he's not getting those needs tended at home."

"I wouldn't mind him tending *me*," remarked the first.

Oh, I'll tend you, Rae promised, a fiery gleam in her bright blue eyes.

"Shush now, silly cow. The baron's never been one to

dip his wick where his ink's stored, especially not as he loved his first wife as he did. Nor would he do so now and discredit the new lady of the castle. Now, get up those shelves and finish dusting."

The conversation died, and Rae retraced her footsteps to the portrait gallery. Once again, the ghost of the saintly Fiona hovered above her. Fen would never cheat on his first wife, yet with his second spouse, he spent his nights away from home.

Feeling miserable, Rae had a sudden need to see her lost husband. The thought of Fennis with another woman, so shortly after their wedding, cut deeply into her soul, like a sharp, heated knife; and, angry that he'd left her for wild nights of deranged debauchery, she resolved to curse his portrait, as his face was not available. Within moments she was walking down the long hallway where his particular portrait was hung. Trying to study it in a detached manner, she pointed a finger at him as she let loose her rage.

"I do not share well! I have been thus, even as a child. So beware. If you are dipping your wick in another candle, know you'll soon be in hot wax!"

The portrait remained silent—just like her mirror, except when Nap was around. But that did not stop Rae; not when she was on a tirade. "How dare you not like me? How dare you leave me here alone? I'm a new bride, and I deserve to be respected and cherished." Yet as the words left her mouth, a nagging inner voice asked if she really deserved to be cherished.

"Of course I do. What right does he have to commit adultery when he is married to someone as beautiful as I?" But as the words left her lips, she really listened to what she was saying, and was stunned by a sudden realization.

Staring hard at Fen's portrait, she noted the way the light from the colored glass of the windows shone down, bathing him in light. Even portraiture caught the deep goodness in his eyes. He was an honorable man who loved his children and estates and worked hard to provide for the many dependent on him. He had asked for little from her, just to be a good mother to his children. Guilt suddenly weighed down her words as well as her spirit.

"He doesn't like me. But can I blame him?" Rae wondered aloud. Then she prayed, "Dear Lord, I'm stuck here until the day I die with a man who doesn't respect me and children who despise me. What kind of life is this? I miss my family, their love, their gentle chiding, and yes, even those fairy-tale dinners. I don't want to be alone forever."

In that moment the light bathed both her and the portrait, and Rae felt the foundation of her world shattered. Suddenly what her limited world and experiences had taught her seemed foolish. The world did not revolve around her, as Greta had often expressed.

"My beauty truly means little to him. But . . . that's all I know how to give: my enchanting looks. Yet he cares not, and he's unhappy. Alas, I pledged him my troth, to love and care for him through good and bad. I pledged this before God and gave my solemn vow, and I fear I have broken it already." Glancing heavenward, Rae winced. "I doubt that You take broken vows lightly."

Drained, Rae sat down upon a low bench and took stock of her life. The process was painful, the discoveries less than flattering. She had been spoiled and cosseted, oftimes taught to ignore how others were feeling; her mother and nurse had told her that she was special and deserved special treatment. Although she'd done a few good deeds, those acts were more than cancelled by her thoughtless ways. God had given her many wonderful blessings. Foolishly, she had thought them all her due, never realizing that she should have thought less about how she appeared and more about how she acted.

With brimming tears, Rae glanced at the portrait of her husband. "I shall do better, I promise. I'll transform. There's more to me than meets the eye. I know this to be true. I also promise not to play any more tricks on your children. Even if they hate me to my dying day."

As she made that statement, a creak came from a panel in the wall beside her and out popped Poppy, swiftly followed by her brother Quinn, who was carrying one of the small kittens from last night. Merri was not far behind.

Rae gasped, clutching her hand to her chest. "You scared me!"

"We're even then," Quinn replied, an impish grin on his face. "You're talking to portraits now, huh? Nap said you liked to talk to things better than people, because you admire them more."

Quinn's words stung. "I was merely voicing some thoughts aloud."

"To Papa's portrait?" Poppy asked. "Talk to *him*."

"I would, if he were here," Rae replied, wrinkling her nose. "And what is that smell?" Looking them over, she noted the source immediately. "Quinn, you are a mess and your stench is offensive. You look more like a stable master's son than the son of a baron. You remind me of my brothers."

Quinn looked down at his pants, which were black with encrusted dirt. His hands were not in much better condition, and his boots were covered with the muck of both horse and cow. He shrugged. "There was a dog with a hurt leg."

"Quinn fixed it," Poppy informed Rae. "He's good with aneemals."

"That was sweet. I've always liked animals—even sheep," Rae said.

"Well, we don't have any sheep," Quinn said, his disappointment obvious.

"But we've got cows," Poppy remarked happily.

"I'm sure I'll find them divine as well," Rae replied in earnest. These three were really rather cute when they weren't being obnoxious. "Why are you carrying around that kitten? Is she part of some potty plan of yours to play another trick on me? She looks rather young to be away from her mother."

"We came to say that we are sorry for playing jests on you," Poppy answered. Merri nodded, too, though she wore a cross expression.

"What kind of fool would I be if I fell for that old chestnut?" Rae remarked. "Just how silly do you think me?" Yet, their little faces truly looked sincere.

Quinn shook his head. "No, we mean it. Not all of us, of course, just the three of us. When Papa scolded us the other day, he made me think. You're a stranger here, and we haven't been very nice to you. Kind of like when Papa brought a hound here who had been beaten. He growled and bit Ernst, and Papa wanted to get rid of him. But I talked him out of it and took care of the dog. It took a while, but finally he grew to trust me."

"He's a good hunting dog now. Never bites anything but the foxes," Merri added.

Quinn looked embarrassed. "Last night you saved me from that horse. It was a brave thing to do. Papa says we must always respect and honor courage. I think you were magnificent."

A smile blossomed on Rae's face as affection bloomed in her heart for this freckle-faced boy who tended those weaker than himself. Even though he had more or less compared her to a dog, she felt flattered by his compassion and wisdom. A child of nine had it, and she didn't. What did that say about her?

"What a grand apology, and what a noble thing to care for those in need," she remarked. "Your father must be very proud of you, Quinn. You are noble of heart, and that's a rare thing. And I need to make an apology also. I did mean to play the prank, but I didn't mean to frighten you all as badly as I did. I hope you can forgive me. I certainly never meant to put either Poppy or Quinn in danger."

Quinn blushed, shrugging his shoulders. "Here," he said, holding out the small gray and white kitten. "It's for you. A wedding gift. Her mother died, and only two of the kittens survived. I've got one, and this one I wanted to give to you."

Rae stared hard at the three children before reaching for the kitten, a slight sheen of tears in her eyes. "Poor baby. I do love cats and dogs." She cuddled the tiny creature close to her chest. "You all are truly sincere, aren't you?"

The three faces nodded enthusiastically. "We want to call a truce. We forgive you the prank. It was a grandly cunning plan, worthy of a Schortz. Nap's just mad he didn't think of it first."

Rae hid her smile. "So . . . no more devious little tricks?"

"Not from us," Poppy said, shaking her head, her little gold braids swinging. "Will'd you climb a tree now with me?"

"No," Rae answered. Then, seeing the little girl's crest-fallen expression, she amended her statement: "I've decided that I quite like your name. It reminds me of spring flowers and cheery smiles. Regrettably, I don't climb trees . . . but I'll play dress-up with you."

Poppy had to think this over carefully. "Can I's dress up yike pirates?" she asked after a moment.

Remembering their past capture of their governess and the baboon tarts, Rae shook her head, thinking that would not be best. "How about a princess or a fairy?" she suggested. Seeing the child's mulish expression, inspiration struck. "How about a queen or a king?"

The little girl nodded enthusiastically, while her elder sister's almost permanent frown lifted. "Will you let me be the princess?"

"Yes. We'll dress you in something pink, I think, to go with your coloring," Rae replied as she closely studied the girl. Merri was certainly no beauty, with too big a nose and too round a face, but every little girl should feel pretty, and so Rae would find a way to accomplish just that.

Snapping her attention back to Quinn, Rae looked him up and down, trying to hide the mischievousness she was feeling. "You would make a grand knight."

"I'd rather be a pirate."

Rae sighed and considered a compromise. "No baboon tarts and no prisoners?"

Quinn thought about it for a moment, then nodded.

"I wants to be one too," Poppy said.

Rae sighed again. "Fine."

"I still want to be a princess," Merri said.

"And so you shall." Clutching tightly to her chest the sweet little kitten Quinn had given her, Rae let out a peal of happy laughter that filled the hallway. Then she and the Schortzes went to play.

Yes, for the first time in many a long year, Rae felt happy. Three of the children accepted her, even appeared to like her. It was a miracle. And just in time to celebrate, Greta was coming to visit. Rae could hardly wait to see her.

The tiny kitten purred in her arms, and Rae thought about what to name it. Perhaps she'd name it Greta or Faye. That way, even though she was now married, her sisters would always be with her. At least in name. Or, she thought with an odd pang of sadness, she could name it Fennis. Then she'd finally have a Fen in her bed.

# CHAPTER TWENTY-EIGHT

## My Life Is No Fairy Tale

Several hours later, Rae hurried downstairs to greet Greta. Joyfully the sisters Grimm embraced, each crying out glad greetings.

Smiling brightly, Greta held her younger sister at arm's length and studied her thoughtfully. "I wanted to visit sooner, but Aunt Vivian forbade it since you were newly-wed. She said the first few days should be spent with your new husband and stepchildren."

Rae scowled. "She would, the old bat. But why didn't you write me? I've written you almost daily."

"You did? But you hate to write—the ink stains on your fingers and all."

"I know. But I needed your advice," Rae replied.

"I never received one of your letters, and I wrote you twice." Greta's expression darkened. "Aunt Vivian! I should have guessed." She had been eager to speak with her sister about the prince, yet upon seeing Rae's face, her love life could wait.

Rae frowned. She had needed her sister, and her aunt had been playing spy-master: hiding letters, intercepting communiqués and issuing ultimatums. How she would love to fix Vivian's goose! "She really is quite monstrous."

Greta nodded. "You have no idea. It's not easy living there

with you gone. Now *I'm* her prime candidate for marriage.
I've been paraded about Wolfach like a fattened hog. She's
worse than our mother!"

Rae snorted elegantly, or as elegantly as a snort could be.
"I know. They're birds of a finicky and forever-complaining
feather," she replied, then hugged her sister tightly. "I'm so
glad you're here. I've much to tell you. So very much." A
worried look crossed her lovely face.

"What's wrong?"

Biting her lip, Rae confessed, "Almost everything." Motioning for Greta to take a seat, she managed a smile. She
was so glad to have her sister with her, for besides loving
her dearly, Greta was the only one, besides her father, who
represented security. Though it might be ridiculous to be
lonely in a castle filled with seven children and thirty-odd
servants, Rae was. Her sister's presence brought home just
how much she had felt like an unwanted interloper.

"Let me see, where to begin. Oh yes, most of the time
the children are cursed hellhounds subjecting me to indig-
nities that our brothers didn't even conceive."

"No!" Greta gasped. Her two brothers, of quite the mischievous bent, could turn a person's hair white in hours.
She'd seen them do so.

"Then there's my adoring husband. I've been a bride for
four days, and I know absolutely nothing about anything.
Fennis ignores me."

"No man ignores you for long," Greta said.

"Alas, it's true. He's not even been to my bedchamber."

"How can that be?" Greta asked, confused. "I wanted to
ask you about all that. No one ever really talks about it. It's
all so mysterious!"

"Well, sister dear, it's still mysterious to me as well. I feel
rather silly and inept, if at the same time a trifle relieved,"
Rae admitted. "Did you know that Fennis knows absolutely
nothing about giving compliments? I also discovered that
Prussian gifts are poison! What a barbaric country."

Greta realized that Rae was speaking of the German word *gift*, and she grinned.

"Anyway," Rae continued, "I much doubt I'll receive presents or gifts anytime soon. He despises me, I think."

Greta patted her sister's shoulder. "Give him time, Rae. I'm sure he'll come around. He seems a kind man."

Rae nodded reluctantly. "To everyone but me." Drawing a deep breath, she stared hard at her sister. "I must confess that much of my dismal start as a wife is all my fault. I have thought too long and too hard upon myself, my needs, my hopes, my reflection in the looking glass. I was brought up to believe that I would be the savior of the family fortunes, and it gave me a sense of power that should never be given to a child. I'm sorry, Greta, for the shallow things I have said to you. Today I took stock of myself, and what I found I did not like much. Do you remember Father's quote about how the world changes us? 'We are not only what we make of ourselves, but what the world makes of us.' I think it's past time that I grew up."

Greta's eyes widened in shock, but her disbelief was of a very welcome nature. She had always known that Rae had a clever mind and a kind heart, but it was oft hidden by her vanity. "Oh, Rae! I've always blamed Mother and Nurse for spoiling you. As a child you had such a sweet and unsullied nature."

Tearfully the two sisters embraced, and a world of hurts and slights slipped into the past to be buried. Greta began to praise Rae's new lease on life. Yes, they both agreed, the Black Forest was a magical land.

At last, Rae held up a restraining hand. "Please, there's more. Last night I played a prank on the children, hoping to teach them a lesson. Only, two of the children were almost killed. Poppy probably would only have fallen, mayhap broken an arm, but nothing as serious as having her noggin kicked in by the Headless Horseman's horse's hooves. I saw what those hooves did to that pumpkin, and it was not a pretty sight." She shuddered, thinking about the pieces of pumpkin mashed beneath the horse's massive hooves.

Eyes wide, Greta raised a hand in protest. "Rae, you're rambling again. What headless horseman? What pumpkins? Who are Quinn and Poppy? Do you have a headless horseman here at Durloc? If so, I shall never forgive Aunt for making me miss his dashing ride."

Rae rolled her eyes in exasperation. "Greta, this isn't some story to be told. This is my life! Let me explain about last night." And she did, telling her tale of woe and tribulation starting from her honeymoon. It was a story complete with ghosts, ogres, flour and the sly leadership of Nap and his mischievous mob of merry munchkins. The finishing touch was Heinrich's ride, the butler's head covered and gourd in hand.

While she explained her blighted existence, Rae watched various expressions flit across her elder sister's face. Some of the pranks had Greta laughing, but the smiles soon ceased. The children really had gone too far, and Greta's expression filled with indignation at several of the ill-conceived jests. And she clearly worried about Rae's part in the Headless Horseman fiasco.

"But, you see, I had just cause to act as I did. They needed to be taught a lesson. Their pranks just kept getting worse. You weren't around, and I felt desperate—but justified." Rae moaned, shaking her head.

Greta shook her head. The baron would probably be livid regarding Rae's prank. Yet, Rae was also correct. The wicked little beasts had needed to be taught a hard and fast lesson, and what faster lesson than a headless horseman? Staring at her sister in wonder, Greta shook her head once more. "Good gracious, Rae. How you've changed. Before, you would have been ranting, raving and in tears, but here I find you jesting about the situation. I'm proud of you. But I do council honesty about last night's escapade as soon as possible."

Nervously, Rae nodded. "I know. I only hope he can understand my reasoning. I can't even try to lessen his anger with me by flirting and batting my eyelashes! He'd probably just ask if I have something in my eye," she announced. "My whole life I was taught that my beauty would be a great gift to my husband, yet Fen cares not. How am I to cherish him if he avoids me and spends his night with mangled mockingbirds?"

"Er, it's 'soiled doves,' I believe," Greta corrected. "But surely the baron isn't consorting with them?" She was shocked. The baron had seemed nothing like the womanizing Rolpe.

"We've been wed such a short time. Yet, the past two nights he hasn't come home."

Patting her sister's arm, Greta replied wisely, "Make him want you. Besides, perhaps business truly called him away."

"I don't know, Greta. Fennis can be quite determined. And he seemed totally uninterested in me."

"Remember, for want of a horse and a carriage and a pair of slippers, a kingdom was lost," Greta said.

"Oh, do be sensible. Stop talking in platitudes," Rae chided gently. "And if you want me to flirt with him, I have tried. He seems immune."

"You underestimate your charm."

Rae sighed. "Since when? But perhaps the problem is something other than my attractiveness. He is much displeased that his children and I are not on the best of terms. What an understatement! With over half of them, I am still in open warfare. They despise me, these demon spawn . . ."

"Perhaps they have too much time on their hands," Greta suggested. "We shall have to come up with a way for you to win the war—or at least a flag of truce. Lest you end up living in armed strife all your married life."

"I am agog, and listen with bated breath."

"I'll do whatever I can to help. I love you dearly, you

know," Greta said, pleased that her younger sister seemed to have matured quite a bit in so short a space of time. For once she hadn't been deluged with tales of Rae's conquests. Of course, Rae really hadn't made any conquests.

Still, her sister needed help, as well as courage and a thick switch. She also needed to smile. Glancing around the room, Greta remarked with false cheer, "You at least got your castle. I must say, it is a fine one."

Rae leaned her head back against the soft cushion of her French-styled chair. "Yes, with a big frog prince and his seven warts. Just what I always dreamed."

Greta burst out laughing. After a moment, she said, "He's not a frog. He's a kraut." And her laughter finally elicited a bout of giggles from Rae.

Deciding to change the subject, as they could do no more for Rae in the nonce, Greta announced, "I'm going to see the old witch, Fräulein Hines. Why don't you and the children come with me? That way we can both spend some time with them, and I can come up with a strategy to win their devious little hearts. I'll stop by and pick you up tomorrow. I can hardly wait. I wanted to go sooner, but they said that the fräulein was away visiting family. So, tomorrow is the day."

"You're going to that witch's gingerbread house? Whatever for?"

"I want my fortune told."

Rae eyed her sister suspiciously. Greta had always been the most curious of the Grimm lot, but this was something more. "Spill the beans."

"Well, you'll think I'm foolish."

"Me? A woman who had flour thrown on her face, was locked in a creepy old tower and bitten on the ankle twice by a deranged four-year-old? Foolish? Methinks not."

"Well, I wanted to see if she was really a witch and all. I also heard that she was a close companion of Frau Choplin, the woodcutter's mother."

"Hmm. How is that investigation going? I take it you

haven't found any vampires wandering around yet?" Rae asked, half curiously and half in disbelief. "No, you would have written or come to see me about such a find."

"I did speak to the doctor who attended Frau Choplin's death. I was disgusted. The man is a notorious drunk. He told me there was not a single bite mark upon her, but I don't think he examined her body very closely."

"So you still believe she's a vampire? But if so, then where is she at night? Don't they have to feed?"

"I haven't figured that out yet, but I will. There's a vampire, or my name isn't Greta Grimm," she avowed, gravely pounding her fist into her palm. "If Rolpe wasn't so pompous and powerful, the magistrate might be willing to listen to my views—the views of someone who has much knowledge on the subject."

Rae sat up straighter. "So, it's Rolpe now, is it?" she asked, smiling. Her sister blushed. "You are calling him by his first name. How did this happen?" Rae was sharp enough to realize just exactly what Greta had been hoping, fairy-tale romantic that her sister was.

Greta confessed: "I saw Rolpe at the woodcutter's cottage when I went to speak to Herr Choplin about his mother's death. He . . . he kissed me." Finally, she had someone to talk to about that earthshaking kiss, and about her own response: her world crashing down around her.

"Greta!" Rae exclaimed in shock. "You have such news and you let me ramble on and on! What did you do? Did you like it? Does he kiss well? What did the woodcutter say?"

Greta was interested in Prince von Hanzen; that was as obvious as the nose on her face. Perhaps, Rae could arrange some matchmaking, since Fennis and the prince were boon companions. She nodded slightly. She could do that, and would do that, for her wonderful sister. even though Greta would be a princess while she remained a poor, neglected baroness.

"It was wonderful—and Herr Choplin wasn't there."

As Greta continued, her heart bursting with joy, Rae sat back and listened. This was just what the doctor ordered. Rae had been too busy worrying what underhanded plans the artful little mischief-makers were hatching around her, and about the baron ignoring her, to even guess that her sister had been finding romance. Perhaps, Rae thought, *one* of them would end up with a happily ever after.

# CHAPTER TWENTY-NINE

## Don't Throw the Baron Out
## with the Bathwater

Never trouble trouble, because trouble will eventually trouble you, as Rae well knew. Unfortunately, she'd had more than her share lately. Fen had finally arrived home, less than an hour after her sister left; only she, the new wife, still a blushing bride, had not been told. Fortunately, Heinrich had alerted her to her husband's presence. The canny butler had also announced that the children were at the pond, ice-skating. Thus, she would have time to tell her husband about the unfortunate misadventure with the headless horseman before they did.

Dressing carefully, she plotted her strategy and chose a gown of soft blue velvet trimmed with a darker blue to accent her eyes. It was important that she looked as lovely as possible before confronting her husband. Let him see what he was ignoring by ignoring her . . . if he could still ignore her tonight.

As she finished her toilette, her maid delivered a gift: the most divine gown of deep green, with seed pearls and tiny emeralds sewn into the bodice. She read the accompanying note.

*Since my children destroyed one gown,
I have decided to replace it.*

*My apologies,*
*Fennis.*

The gown was lovely, and wonder ate at her soul. He had thoughtfully brought her a present, and yet he denied her his presence.

Caressing the garment once more, Rae bravely, if with a little reluctance, marched to her husband's room. In her rush, she almost knocked over Fen's valet, who was leaving, a pair of breeches over his arm.

"Baroness Schortz, I'm afraid the baron is in his bath."

Rae stared at him. "I've seen a naked man before," she remarked. Seeing the shock on the valet's face, she quickly added, "Statues, of course." And with those words she hurried into the bedroom, slamming the door.

She halted about six feet from a tub that had been placed in front of a roaring fire. Fen was sitting in the overlarge bath, with water up to the lower part of his knees. His gray eyes were staring at her with a hint of curiosity and absolutely no modesty. She licked her lips, as her mouth suddenly felt dry.

"My, oh my," she whispered. Fennis had big shoulders, and his skin shone like bronze in the light of the candles and fire. He looked so hard and so smooth—like a statue. Yet no sculpture she had ever seen could compare.

"Did you want something?" Fen asked, feeling his manhood stir. His innocent wife's expression didn't look so innocent at the moment. In point of fact, she was devouring him with her eyes. If she had been Fiona, she would have joined him in the tub, and a fine time would have been had by all. The thought made him sad and cooled his ardor. Without thinking, he said, *"Nur wer die sehnsucht kennt."*

"What?" Rae managed to ask, forcing her eyes back to her husband's face from her study of his fine chest and glistening skin. She was glad he could not read her mind. She had been prepared to tell him of her little folly, which wasn't so very little, but his delightful body had sidetracked her good and honest intentions.

"None but the lonely heart," he answered, a bit embarrassed upon repeating the sentiment. After his wife died, he had thought he would be lonely forever. Now he was remarried, but not much had changed.

"Why would you say that, my husband? You have a castle full of servants and . . . your brood, all of whom adore you."

"A man can be lonely in a crowd. Lonely for his woman," he answered. Then, realizing what he'd said, he began to soap himself. He started with his arms, the soap gliding smoothing over his bulging muscles.

"But you have a wife now," Rae said. She was determined he would acknowledge the truth of this statement.

"Do I?"

"Yes," she managed, watching the water glisten on his skin, which made her pulse leap. "Although you might not wish it." Especially when she told him what she had done.

A sharp heat pierced her as she watched what could only be called pain pass through his eyes. Fen was lonely, terribly lonely, and she saw that now. He felt no connection to her. She was nothing to him, though he had begun to mean something to her.

"What did you want with me?" he asked when she just stood there.

Managing to regain her aplomb, Rae made a decision. But instead of blathering on, she decided to wait a few moments and silently enjoy the view. Once she told Fen of her misdeed, she might be ousted from his bedroom, perhaps even from his castle.

"I . . . the, uh, gown is lovely. Thank you. The color will look marvelous on me," she said at last. Her throat burned as she suddenly realized she wanted to kiss him on that wondrously broad chest.

"You're welcome. I hope it fits. The dressmaker in town had started it for another, but the fräulein had to leave suddenly. That's one reason I'm late coming home. She finished it so I could bring it to you. I know it's a bit dressier than your morning gown, but I thought the beadwork very fine."

"It's quite elegant. Verily, I appreciate you going to the trouble," Rae replied sincerely. He had gone to such trouble, all when she wasn't the helpmeet she was supposed to be.

When his wife continued to stand there and stare, Fen cocked his head and asked, "Was there something else?" He spoke in a suggestive manner. He knew he was playing a dangerous game, and yet he was helpless to put an end to her blatant admiration.

He waited for Rae to say or do something. Her face was lovely as always, but her eyes held something new: a warmth which was both vivid and passionate.

She was trying to decide how to begin when his voice interrupted her thoughts.

"Rae?"

She looked up at him, nervous.

"Is there something more you wish of me?"

"A great deal more," she said, and then was mortified to realize she'd spoken aloud.

Fen snorted. A sudden image of Rae caressing certain parts of his body was delicious torture. Still, he knew that he would be mad to make love to her. Rae would lead him a pretty dance: a promenade along the boardwalk of her self-congratulation, a gavotte of primping and pouting, a waltz through every fashionable shop for jewelry and clothing. Yet if he didn't take her to bed soon, he might just expire. Even now he could see an image in his mind's eye, a passionate tangle of limbs, satiny sheets and her glorious hair. She would whisper soft cries as he took her to paradise.

He groaned. This way lay madness.

Rae regained her scattered wits. "I wanted to remind you of your husbandly duties." This was met by another snort, only this time the snort sounded like the blast of a canon. Fen was shaking with mirth. "What do you find so humorous?"

"Husbandly duties. At this point, that's the last thing I need reminding of."

Rae's fascination with his naked body was actually making Fen feel rather special. She might have complained once about his size, but she certainly didn't seem to mind now. If he was not mistaken, his virgin bride was very aware of him. She even wanted him, but innocent as she was, she could only manage a blush and a stare.

Eyeing the hem of her gown, Rae hedged a moment longer. "I don't know if you are aware, but a husband's duty—"

Fen snorted again.

She glanced up quickly, then hurried on. "A husband should listen to his wife before he shouts at her. If she's sincere, he shouldn't shout at her. Even if she tells him something he doesn't like. A man should cleave onto his wife. And . . . and you didn't come and tell me of your arrival. I had to hear it from the butler."

Fen's self-congratulation faltered. Perhaps she wasn't as enraptured by his body as he'd thought. She had some other agenda here. He replied in a tone harsher than before, "You're right. I should have let you know when I returned. How much have you spent?" She'd likely come to tell him she'd spent his money—and to get more. But if Rae thought the minute he turned his back she could make promises to shopkeepers and live on credit, she had another think coming.

"Spent?" Rae gasped. "I have no access to any money!"

He paused, again stumped. "Then spit it out, Rae. What has you so upset? Has something happened in the past few nights that I need to be made aware of?" His wife was acting strangely; he could sense her anxiety. If she hadn't spent his hard-earned coin without permission, what was wrong? "Is it the children?"

"Of course not." Rae hedged again, though the time had

clearly come to talk of these things—things such as men at work, men without heads (or hats), pumpkins, and that the kids were ultimately all right. "But, now that you mention them, I do recall that they did me another vile turn. So I decided to—"

"Again?" he interrupted, vexed both at his children and his new wife. Couldn't she manage the scamps for a few nights without his help? What good was a wife who only stirred up trouble in the home?

"Yes, again! And you shouldn't sound so surprised."

"What on earth have you done to cause such animosity toward you?" He knew his brood could be a handful, but she was supposed to be their stepmother. Surely they weren't as bad as she made them out to be. They might be a trifle rambunctious, slightly sly and crafty at times, but there was generally a reason for their shenanigans.

Taking her eyes off his chest, she frowned. Verily, her simmering temper came to a rolling boil. The dratted man! "What have *I* done?"

He interrupted before she could go off on a tirade. "Yes. Tell me truthfully, and no ifs, buts or ands. No silly excuses."

"Silly excuses?" Rae asked.

"*Ja.* I've noticed that you ramble at times, often when you are trying to make a point." He began to soap his chest, trying to remain calm.

"I don't ramble! I get to the point exceedingly fast, at least when there's a need. However, since there is rarely a need, I sometimes might take an indirect route in some points I might be making. I've been known to talk about things in a roundabout fashion when there are other things to discuss that border the subject at hand."

Dropping the soap in the water, Fen shook his head and laughed. "I rest my case. Now, what have my little darlings done to you this time?"

As he slicked the soap over the taut muscles of his chest, Rae again grew fascinated. Then he rinsed, the water trickling down his flat abdomen. Just covered by the bath, she could see something large bobbing, the head breaking the water's surface every now and then.

She swallowed.

Hard.

Blinking, she finally managed to regain her wits. As her annoyance cooled, she remarked, "It would be easier to tell you what they *haven't* done. Peas in my sheets, ash-traps scattered hither and yon, and a ghostly haunting. Your ingenious, impudent imps, led by the lad Nap, dressed up as a ghost and frightened me half to death. Next in this line of heinous happenings, Alden bit my ankle. Again. Do you know how disconcerting it is to glance up from your tea-cup and see Death looking you in the eye? Those children want to do me in."

"You exaggerate."

She held up her hand. "Only a bit. They probably wouldn't do me in, but only because it would raise questions eventually. At least, I *think* you would begin to wonder if you never saw me again. Then again, with your nightly absences, you might not notice."

Fen couldn't mistake the annoyance in her tone, but it was a welcome annoyance. Rae had, unbelievable as it seemed, missed him. "I must do my best to avoid further absences," he remarked.

She wasn't sure what he meant by the words—whether he wanted to be around to protect her, or if he simply wanted to notice when she disappeared—but the suggestive look in his large, gray eyes made her throat suddenly very dry. She looked away to the flames dancing in the fireplace. "My, isn't it rather warm in here?" she asked.

Fen snorted. His wife couldn't seem to make up her mind. She seemed enraptured by his body, and he ached to have her touch it, but she also acted shy. With every advance he made, often against his better judgment, she started acting skittish. One wrong move and he was afraid she'd turn tail and run. Not that he wouldn't enjoy the view; she had a very nice tail. And he still knew that bedding her would be pure folly; madness. Regrettably, he had to get her to leave.

"I must give the little urchins points for imagination!" he remarked. "A ghost in the castle. What will you believe next? Perhaps they'll persuade you to spin straw into gold. I could use some extra coin."

Rae seethed. Instead of listening with sympathy, this maddening man was berating her? "I can see the little savages take after you," she snapped, momentarily forgetting her guilt, her desire to be a wonderful wife and wander her hands over those big, manly body parts, all wet and glistening. Dragging her eyes back up to his face, she shook her head. "I was terrified. I do not wish to live my life in a house of chaos and pranksters. Neither do your servants, I might add."

Rae hesitated. Her conscience urged her to tell him the truth, now, while she was righteously indignant; yet she couldn't quite do it. She began to fan herself rapidly, her breathing stilted. Once, twice and again, she fanned herself, pondering if it was rather inopportune that her husband was bathing. Or was opportunity knocking, waiting, bobbing just below the surface of the water?

Fen propped one shoulder against the tub and folded his arms across his very manly chest. "Rae, stop your fanning and listen to me. I'll speak to Nap. He will be punished. But this you must heed: life with children means mayhem. Nonetheless, the little scamps lift our spirits and our hearts. They spur our creativity and double our dreams. They are always a blessing, though sometimes a curse. I wouldn't give them up for the world."

"Of course not," she snapped. "But, then, they are not playing cold-blooded tricks on you. However, you have no need to punish them. I took matters in hand."

He sat up straight in the tub and stared at her. "What did you do?"

Twisting her hands, she summoned all her courage. "Fen, I had to do *something*, because doing nothing wasn't working. So I devised a scheme. Some might say it was a tad harsh, but none that live within these walls. If you ask the servants, you'll—"

"Rae, quit dallying!"

She opened her mouth and then closed it again. "First, promise me that you won't dismiss any of the servants."

His gray eyes turned to dark smoke, smoke from the ire burning intensely within. "What foul plot did you hatch?"

With great trepidation, Rae began at the beginning and explained. Fen's scowl grew, and his jaw muscles clenched. "How could you do this? My children could have been seriously injured or worse!"

Trying to regain some aplomb, Rae swallowed. Her husband was very angry, his large hands knotted on the edges of the tub.

He raged on, "I should dismiss the servants involved in this and give you the annulment you requested. Your prank was heartless, and if Quinn or Poppy had been seriously hurt, there would be no safe place for you on earth!"

"As if I wanted them hurt!" Rae shot back. "And if you would discipline them, I wouldn't have had to resort to drastic measures! The servants are helpless against your brood, and things are completely out of hand." She swallowed hard again, calming herself. Glancing back at her husband, she found him sitting still as a statue, his jaw muscles clenched. "What?" she asked.

"I'm afraid if I get out of this tub I'll strangle you, or at least put you over my lap and give you the paddling of a lifetime."

By all means, then, he could sit there forever. She hoped he grew gills. But she couldn't help but add in her defense, "Don't forget I saved Quinn's life."

"I would be eternally grateful—if you weren't the one who'd risked it in the first place."

"Well, the hooves didn't strike him. For that I'm eternally grateful. I would have done anything to save him." After a moment, she was overcome by a small pain, and she had to ask a new question. She just had to find the right way to ask. "You know as well as I do that accidents happen. What about when your children were chasing me around the tower? What if one of them had fallen? Would you deny your forgiveness to them—those children who were involved in the accident? It would have been their fault, seeing as they were the ones playing the pranks."

Staring into her eyes, he thought hard. "I would have been very angry, but I couldn't withhold my forgiveness."

"But you would withhold it from me, the woman you took to wife before both God and man."

Rubbing his face in annoyance, he shook his head. "I don't know, Rae. You are a grown woman and should know better." Glancing into the distance, he finally said, "*Nein*. I don't wish to hold it against you. But you must promise to do nothing like it again!"

Rae nodded, feeling tremendous relief. He might still be angry, but he no longer looked as if he wished to strangle her. "Fen, I didn't play the jest to be cruel. I just wanted to show your children how it felt to be on the receiving end of such a prank. And it is true, I am human and make mistakes. I did it in part for revenge. But *never* would I have intended to hurt them. Never. Most especially Quinn, Merri and Poppy. But your brood needs borders. They lack discipline. They are growing up wild and unruly, without thought to how their actions hurt others."

He started to argue, but with a fierce determination she continued. "I know you felt helpless when your first wife died. You and the children loved her greatly. Grief-stricken, you barely managed to get by. But eventually the children began to experience life again, as children do after great tragedy. Yet their pranks continued to grow, becoming at times mean-spirited and hurtful. Feeling guilt at their loss, you hesitated to punish them; it's understandable. But the time has come for change, before they grow too wild to control."

"You're a fine one to talk about hurting others. You, with

your shallow ways. How dare you tell me how to raise my children? Especially after what you did. Their mother never had any problems with them. She would never have put them in danger. She would never have been anything like you, you greedy, grasping—"

Rae gasped, and the baron realized he had gone too far. The hurt in her eyes was like a punch in the gut.

"Perhaps your children are right. There is a ghost in this castle after all," she said. Then, she seemed to summon all her strength. "I've asked you to help me. Instead, you've hindered me with your lack of interest and lackadaisical discipline, despite your children's pranks and how they speak to me." Tears filling her eyes, she stormed to the tub. Taking a bucket of water seated on the stool, she threw its frigid contents all over her large, manly, yet very insensitive husband. "Are you going to love only a memory forever, or your true wife?" Then Rae made for the door.

Gasping, Fen rose from the tub like some god of old, like Neptune coming to life. Leaping out of the tub, he reached her in two strides, sweeping her against his chest. He had not wanted her to wife, but now that he had her, his willpower weakened to the point of collapse. In his arms, she was irresistible. He would not, could not, spend years ignoring her ample charms. Thus, being the honest man that he was, he silently lowered his head and kissed her with all the pent-up passion he'd been feeling for weeks.

# CHAPTER THIRTY

## Sleeping with Beauty

.

If all the kisses in the world were only one kiss, what a great kiss it would be—and it would be just like this, Rae mused in amazement. She gasped as the baron's hot, searching lips claimed hers yet again. His was a kiss that made her senses spin.

As the kiss deepened, she felt her blood turn to fire and a place between her thighs began to ache. "I . . . ," she managed to gasp out between kisses. Her gown was wet in the front, since it was plastered to his deliciously dripping body. "My . . ." She trailed off as another assault left her breathless. Fen certainly knew how to kiss! "You're not mad anymore?"

Fen stopped momentarily, staring down at her swollen lips, and thought he had never seen anything lovelier. His foolish plan to ignore her in the bedchamber had been the height of folly. He had two choices. He could either continue to avoid her bedchamber, which in his opinion had been rather a trying experience so far: two nights of walking in the freezing snows to cool his ardor. Or he could bed her most thoroughly and nightly, resolving that even after bedding her, he would not let her run roughshod over him.

"Rae, I do know my pack can be an unruly bunch at times. I'm sorry. It's just that they're all I have left."

Rae traced his angular jaw with a finger and stared into those remarkably expressive gray eyes. "You have me now." And she meant what she said. "We're in this together."

Cautiously he leaned back and studied her face. Seeing the sincerity reflected there, he smiled. "That would be good, very good."

His boyish grin caused her heart to catch. Why, her husband was quite the charming rogue when he chose to be. She ran her hands up and down his arms, her fingers tingling from arousal. "My gown's wet. I take chills very easily." Her body corroborated, and she began to tremble with passion.

"Never let it be said that I don't take care of my own." So saying, the baron swept her up in his massive arms and laid her gently on the bed. He rapidly divested Rae of her clothes and lay down beside her, carefully moving her flow of long thick hair so that he would not lie upon it and cause her pain. She was breathtaking. The golden glow of her hair surrounded both head and body, a silent moonlit sheet. "You are truly one of the most exquisite creatures I have ever seen."

Vanity made her ask the question even as he was leaning over to kiss her: "Even more than your first wife?"

He halted a breath away from her tempting mouth. "You are exquisite. Yet she was truly beautiful, both inside and out. I cherished that all the more. For a beautiful face is God's present at birth, but a lovely character is something hard-earned and hard-won."

The words not only stung Rae's vanity but her heart, touching a place unknown before her trip down the aisle. "Oh." Lying with her husband for the first time and seeing the desire in his eyes without the love was crushing. But she did not give up. "Fen, I promise I shall do better as both wife and stepmother. I have come to realize that I'm not the woman I should be. I can be more, and I will be more, not only for you and your family, but for my own sake as well."

He smiled down at her, heartened to see the sincerity in her eyes. Apparently she could be reasonable, which was unexpected yet welcome. "I would be honored to have such a wife." He had been so furious with her only a short while ago, but upon reflection her words rang true. He had let his brood get away with more than they should have.

Pressing a kiss against her neck, he reminded himself he was a just and good man. Yet, he had failed not only his children but his bride. He had punished Rae for the compromising situation he had found himself in. He had ignored her because he feared his desire for her. He had been too lax with his children, resulting in beastly manners and reckless pranks. He had let his children, his servants *and* his wife down. Guilt bit him hard with teeth as sharp as Alden's.

He considered another aspect of the situation: Although Rae could have caused his children great harm, she hadn't. Instead, she had risked her neck to save Quinn. It was a brave thing to do, especially when the children could have harmed her as well. Change could come to anyone who sought it out. He would nurture this goodness, and make something strong and solid grow.

"Rae, I'm sorry, too. I have not been the best of husbands."

Head tilted back, she stared at him with starry eyes. "We shall both improve and grow together. I'll soon be deep as any abyss."

He laughed. Leaning down to kiss her thoroughly, Fen felt his heart expanding along with his world. He savored the sweet taste of her mouth and the subtle scent of lilacs. "And I shall plumb those hot and silky depths."

As their kiss deepened, Fen began to murmur sweet words of love—or at least Rae thought they were loving words, since she still couldn't speak German. Words such as *leiche*, which he later explained meant body, and *messe*, which meant fair. But the best one as far as Rae was concerned was *liebchen*, which meant sweetheart. Silently she vowed that she would learn German . . . and then forgot her good intentions as he caressed her.

He'd done something unexpected. He'd traced a pathway down her chest with his mouth and found her nipple. Rae gasped as she felt a sharp, fiery tingling, almost like a pain, shoot through her body, increasing the dull ache between her thighs. His free hand moved to touch that heated spot. Fingers stroking, he found the center of all her sensation and brought forth dew with a lazy touch.

"Oh, Fennis," she moaned.

"Call me Fen."

"Oh, Fen. This is wonderful. I never knew."

All talk was suspended as he continued to suckle her breast while moving his hand between her plump white thighs. It was delightful, how he felt her passion catch fire. She clutched at his back and began to move her legs back and forth. His little wife was a passionate thing, especially for an innocent. And if she could stir his blood this way as a virgin, she would be a terror between the sheets when she was more experienced. That particular thought had him hardening even more, which he'd believed impossible.

He disrobed and positioned himself above her. As he took himself in hand and guided his long-awaited entry, he groaned, his breath harsh as he felt her hot, welcoming wetness. "Oh Rae, you feel so tight, so right. What *genuss*—pleasure—there is to be found in your arms."

Rae felt something very large and hard probing at that aching place between her thighs which had begun to weep with want. She hugged him tighter, feeling emotions she'd never known existed. How she ever could have thought this man was graceless or unattractive, she couldn't fathom. She had been a fool.

"This will hurt but a moment, *liebchen*, then the pain

will fade into *genuss*." And with those words he thrust deep, tearing through her maidenhead.

Only twice in Fen's life had he taken a virgin, and both times it was an almost religious experience, being joined with a woman who was his alone, who welcomed him into her depths with tender yet heated passion. He was not only blessed with his children and fortune; he'd been blessed in his wives. Both of them.

Blessed with Rae? he pondered momentarily. But, yes. And the thought was swept away as desire consumed him utterly. It was almost as if he were drowning in passion. With lusty strokes he pumped deep into her body, feeling the snugness, the tightness, and overwhelming ecstasy drove him to the very edge of a deep abyss.

Fen's mighty thrusts took Rae's breath away, and instinctively she wrapped her legs around his back, urging him on. Over and over he thrust, until she was falling from a great distance. Her breaths became quicker and her hips began to arch, and it felt as if she were striving to reach something beyond this world. She didn't know what, but she did know that she must have it, and now. Like a new gown or a pair of pretty slippers.

"Oh, Fen, something's happening to me," she managed to gasp.

"Hush, my little bride. You're safe here with me. Let go and find paradise," he murmured as he kissed her ears.

Another hard thrust, and Rae felt something break within her, shattering her world as a bright purple haze filled her mind. It was comforting and strangely erotic.

Fen felt her muscles contract, and he recognized her climax. He thrust twice more and shouted, coming hard and long. He couldn't believe it; Rae and he had climaxed at the same time—a sharing of spirits, so to speak.

He rolled over, clasping her to him, placing her head upon his chest. He laid her hand there, too. "You drive me mad, Rae. You put me in a frenzy of desire and . . . and you make me smile."

She gazed up at his ruggedly appealing face. "I pleased you, in spite of my top-lofty nature?"

He smiled again. Bringing her fingers to his lips, he kissed them tenderly. "*Ja,* you pleased me beyond measure." In bed, she was all a man could want. More, even. Out of bed was another story; but she did seem sincere in her intent to change.

Of course, he was not blameless, and he reminded himself of this. Fen knew now that he should have given Rae more of a chance from the beginning. They could have been living in bedded bliss for a week.

"Is it always like this?" she asked, wonder evident in her voice.

"Rarely."

"Was it like this with your late wife?"

Holding her hand, he remarked, "I think for our marriage to be a truly good one, we should not discuss my late wife and make comparisons. You are as beautiful as she was, but different."

"I've heard it said that you loved her very much."

"*Ja.* A part of my heart will always mourn her loss. But you are here. You were right in what you said. While I shall cherish my memory of her always, it was unfair of me to compare the two of you. I promise to try not to do so again. The heart is a glorious thing, after all. There is always room for more people to love. We will make the best of a situation that started out badly. This is a good beginning, my fair Rae." And he patted her bottom with kind little taps.

Rae smiled up at him. Tonight Fen had been the most wonderful of lovers, introducing her to her wifely duties with a tender consideration and a passionate fury. He had intruded into her compact little world, expanding it greatly, along with her thoughts and feelings, which were suddenly more about him and his happiness than her own. She just might be falling in love with him. How lucky she had been on that fateful night she'd been compromised! Fen was a man she could easily grow to love; very easily, for she was already more than just fond of him.

As he stared down at his new wife, Fen knew something miraculous had happened. Rae was a different woman in her responses and the way she looked at him now. No longer was vanity her shield, her weapon and her gift. If Rae remained as she was this night, he knew that one day soon he would tell her the truth, the secret of his clan. But for now, that secret must remain hidden.

# CHAPTER THIRTY-ONE

## The Infatuated Wolfish Prince

The next morning found Rae shyly entering the breakfast room. To her dismay, her lusty husband was not alone. Three of the baron's boys were eating, too. Both Nap and Ernst scowled when they saw her enter the room. The little ankle-biter was sitting in his father's lap, one hand scrunching his *kolache*, the other holding his ratty old lamp.

Feeling more than a little nervous after her passionate night, Rae pasted a smile on her face. Shyly, she said, "*Morgengruss, husband.*" She had asked her maid how to greet her husband in his native tongue.

Her accent was atrocious, but Fen appreciated Rae's effort. "I did not think you were interested in our language!" he said. "But good morning to you, too."

"She sounds funny," Nap remarked, noting the way his father's eyes followed their stepmother to the sideboard.

"I think she sounds delightful." Fen glared at both of his older boys, then guiltily back at Rae. She deserved much better than he had given. "I have spoken to the boys about the other night's misadventures with the Headless Horseman of Durloc Castle, the ghosts, the peas in the bed and so forth. There is to be a ceasefire on all fronts. No more pranks. No more waging war within these walls. Servants and children and wives—all shall be safe."

Nap and Ernst glared down at their breakfasts, but both managed brisk nods of acceptance. Rae smiled at them. Her heart warmed, for her husband had defended her. He had also touched her over and over last night in ways that were surely scandalous, but were also oh so marvelous.

Depositing Alden on his chair, Fen went to his wife and placed his hands on her shoulders, whispering for her ears alone: "I would be willing to tutor you in German if you're interested." He knew she was embarrassed, and it tickled him: her innocence and the shy smile on her face.

Turning her head to gaze at her husband, Rae savored the thought, letting its sweet intimacy fill her completely.

"I enjoyed our tutoring session last night," he continued. Leaning down, he rested his cheek against her hair. "Can I tempt you with more?"

Rae caught her breath. There could be no doubt that he was flirting with her. Her harsh and unpredictable husband was making her feel very special after their forced and hurried courtship. Last night had clearly meant much to him, too. "Do I stand in need of much schooling?" she asked, batting her eyelashes.

"In *dire* need." His eyes were lit with boyish mischief.

"Then it seems I must place myself in your capable hands," she responded. It was odd, but Fen made her feel special in a way that had nothing to do with her appearance. Wonder at that made her blush.

"I shall be honored," he replied, gazing at her tenderly.

Before they could say more, Alden latched onto his father's leg, his little fingers sticky from honeyed pastry. "More eggs, Papa!"

Rae watched as Fen swung the boy up and filled another plate while she sat down. She was glowing with her husband's warm response. He really did want her here. And hopefully the trip to the gingerbread house would help smooth things over between the eldest children.

As the boys went upstairs to dress for their outing, a note arrived. Rolpe was coming to visit. Rae was delighted. It would give her husband a chance to informally invite him to their dinner party. She hadn't yet told Fen of her plan to play matchmaker, but she hoped he would be agreeable to the scheme.

While Rae went to instruct the cook about the day's menu, Rolpe arrived. He and Fen adjourned to the study, where Fen noticed his companion's countenance was grim.

"Although it's early, I do believe you are in need of a stiff drink," he suggested.

"That woman!" Rolpe replied, pouring himself a glass of brandy from the sideboard.

"What woman?" Fen asked. Rolpe rarely let a woman get him riled. He seduced them and then left; or they seduced him and he left; but few caused him to lose his famous von Hanzen calm.

"Greta Grimm," Rolpe spat. "She's a menace to society with her nosy ways. Doesn't she know dead women tell no fairy tales?"

Fen poured himself a brandy and leaned against the fireplace. "*Ja.*"

"If she's not staring into mirror reflections looking for vampires or ruthlessly grilling doctors, then she's out searching through woodcutters' drawers!"

Fen was shocked. "I seem to have gotten the tail end of this tale. This seems out of character. She was alone with the woodcutter?"

"*Nein.* Herr Choplin wasn't there—I told you that in town," Rolpe reminded Fen. He took a large sip of his brandy and savored the warmth that slid down his throat. Brushing back a strand of snow-wetted hair, he added rigidly, "She was only with me."

"I remember some sort of abbreviated conversation," Fen replied uneasily. "Yet I do not recall you mentioning that you and she were alone." He was starting to see just what had upset his friend, and the lay of the land. (Rolpe would likely say Greta was the lay of the land.) When he and his friend had last spoken, Fen's mind had been distracted by his bizarre marriage, or else he would have asked the question he should have asked sooner.

"Well, Rolpe, she's a very fetching woman, as well as a clever fräulein," he remarked, searching his friend's face for guilt. The prince might wish to remain footloose and fancy free, but his reactions to Greta Grimm looked right on track for a leg-shackle.

"Exactly. She's a managing type of female with a grim determination to rush headlong into trouble, with *vampyr* or whatever else might be hanging around. And now she's asking questions about other paranormal creatures. I've even heard she's going to visit Fräulein Hines today. No telling what that old witch will reveal."

Fen stretched back, shaking his head. "You know that fräulein is no witch, despite her boiling caldrons and that wart on her neck."

Rolpe began to pace, his emotions rolling. Fen could read them only too clearly.

"I know she's no witch, but she's lived in the Black Forest for over fifty years. You don't think she might know a secret or two about what goes on? Mayhap she'll let such secrets slip."

"Victoria Hines has kept silent all these years, Rolpe. Why should she reveal any secrets now, even if she does know them? Why would she reveal them to Greta, or even Rae for that matter?" Fen asked, calmly moving over to take a seat before the crackling fire.

"Because she hasn't met Greta Grimm yet. I swear, the woman could pry the secrets out of a priest and try the patience of a saint. As you know, I am neither!" She literally made him see red.

Fen paused cautiously, disliking the fact that he had to ask but knowing he must. His marriage to Rae Grimm now meant her sister was under his protection. "I must know, Rolpe, did you merely kiss her, or did you do more?"

Rolpe stopped pacing to stare at Fen, a guilty flush staining his cheeks. "I believe I did kiss her . . ."

"Again, I ask: Did you do more?"

"She has some strange effect on me, as if I've been cursed by gypsies. There's something about her scent. She smells like a fragrance I've known all my life, both sweet and spicy. Or mayhap it's the way she smiles, the warmth and mirth in her eyes. Her intelligence is there, too, for the entire world to see. Her jaw is too stubborn, but that's not a bad sign, and it fits with her obsession with myths and mysterious monsters and such." Rolpe stopped and looked up, a haunted look in his eyes. "You know I like women with lush bodies, and Greta is not lushly endowed. But, I swear . . . her breasts are perfection." He swallowed hard, his body afire.

Fen stood, his expression somber. "Do I need to remind you that Miss Greta Grimm is now under my protection? Have you come to ask me for her hand in wedlock?"

"Bloody bones. *Nein*, Fen," the prince retorted, appalled. "I may have fondled one breast for one moment, one tiny moment in time, but nothing more—I swear. I have not even seen those breasts, though their image haunts my sleep."

Fen narrowed his eyes. "I myself was trapped for much less, and my actions were completely innocent. I was merely hunting a cockroach."

"'Twas not the roach but the cock which doomed you."

A scowl formed on Fen's face as he gave a warning he'd thought never to have to give. "If you dally with her affections or any part of her person ever again, you will marry Greta Grimm or face my challenge." This wily wolf was soon to be caged, it seemed, for Fen doubted seriously Rolpe could keep his hands to himself.

The prince lowered his head momentarily, shaking it. Then he raised his eyes to his good friend, and they were strangely haunted. "As you say. I knew at the time I was behaving foolishly for a man with no desire to wed. I will not trifle with her again."

Fen nodded. Walking to the sideboard, he poured himself another drink. "Another?" he offered.

"*Ja.*" Rolpe picked up his glass from the large marbled sideboard. "She's driven me to drink, that blasted female." After a few sips, he went to sit in a comfortable chair across from Fen, and they began to talk about the things that men often talk about, such as territorial concerns and the price of wheat. Only when the conversation lagged did the prince note that Fen had the look of a man well pleasured.

"I take it marriage agrees with you. Yet, only two nights ago you were rather surly about the whole sorry affair."

A wide grin spread across Fen's face. "Rae is still vain as a peacock, but less so today than she was yesterday. Did you know she greeted me in German this morn, and has asked the children to accompany her sister to visit the gingerbread house? And it seems I have found a woman who dares match wits with my brood!"

Rolpe looked surprised, cocking an eyebrow. "Rae? Match wits? You are too easy to please, my friend. And anyway, this battling warms your heart?" After reading his friend's look, the prince said, "Oho! I can see that your heart is not all that's been warmed."

"Enough. It's my wife you're speaking of," Fen warned, although his tone was light. "I have not been fair to her. Though this is not the match I would have chosen, I find myself much pleased by the recent turn of events."

Rolpe slapped his friend on the back. "I'm glad to hear it," he said, and meant it. "It's nice to see that self-satisfied look on your face again. It's a sight for sore eyes."

"*You* should try marriage," Fen responded. "It's more than it's cracked up to be. You know, the best years of my life were married ones."

"I hope you can say the same next year." Rolpe nursed his drink, then gave voice to a fear. "I'm surprised that your wife is willing to change. Most women aren't. They often feel the need to transform us, rarely taking note that they too might need improving. It's a shame, really. Young men go out and seek their fortunes, and young women go out and marry the men who find those fortunes." He said the last with a grimace of distaste.

"Someone certainly has put a flea in your ear, and it isn't even the full moon."

"Leave it, Fen. You know I'm not ready for wedlock. I'm much too young to tie the knot. Not to mention, if I were to get married, think of the trail of broken hearts I would leave behind," he partially teased. He loved women, when he loved them; everything from their unique and varied scents, to the curves of their behinds, to the beauty of their bounteous breasts. He loved the way they moved when he thrust into them, and their breathy little moans and outright shrieks when their passions peaked. His pride and curiosity thrilled at their first glances of seductive intent, and the knowledge that soon he would ride an untried mount. "Variety is the spice of life—and I like my dishes spicy."

"Besides," Fen remarked, "when members of our clan find their mate, they instinctively know it—even if they are lack-wits who fight it."

Rolpe looked startled. "Surely you jest! You think Greta is my mate?"

"Only you can answer that, but I will say this to you: I have never, in all the years I have known you, seen you in such a state over a woman."

Rolpe's reply was cut off by the sound of a carriage pulling up in the drive. Soon to follow was the loud clamoring of a dozen-plus footsteps on the floorboards and stampeding down the stairs.

Standing, Rolpe moved to the large bay window and looked out to espy Miss Greta Grimm descending from the carriage. As she moved, he caught sight of a slender ankle that dropped down onto the terraced steps. Her scarlet hood fell back at the same time, showing Greta was laughing. Her gray-blue eyes sparkled, and her pretty bow of a mouth smiled prettily. The silly, curious woman really did have the most kissable of lips.

Noting his friend's consternation, Fen moved slightly and looked over the prince's shoulder. Seeing what had captured Rolpe's attention, he moved back to stand by the fireplace and remarked in an offhand manner, "As I said rather recently, marriage can be a fulfilling thing. Females may be difficult at times, since it's in their nature. At times a married man will wish to pull at his hair and howl at the moon . . . but there are times when what you share is beyond description. Both in bed and out. A fine wife gives a man a special warmth, knowing that she is waiting for him, bedcovers all toasty and clean. Or holding his hand, lending him her warmth and kindness as they walk life's path. 'Tis a blending of hopes, dreams, troubles and laughter. 'Tis this sharing of spirit that makes marriage a grand thing. At least, it is with the right female."

"Hmph. I'll buy a fur-lined cloak," Rolpe managed to say. But he didn't take his eyes off Greta as the children piled into the carriage. "I enjoy my bachelor existence and sampling the charms of each pretty new face. Alas, my old friend, I am not yet ready to be tied down. I like holding a different woman whenever I want, and taking my leave when I'm ready. No one female will ever be enough, not even her. Not even Greta."

Fen smiled. Rolpe was a ladies' man, charming all with his wolfish wit and intensity. Yet it appeared that, ready to be tied down or not, the trap had already been sprung; his good friend was just too stubborn to see he was caught.

"Did I mention I've acquired a new cuckoo clock?" Fen asked.

"I wonder what Greta's fortune will be?" Rolpe remarked. "With her propensity for stirring up trouble, I wouldn't be surprised if Fräulein Hines draws the Death card."

"It's very rare," Fen said, holding his clock and staring at it. "Only a dozen were ever made."

"She knows Spanish, did you know that?"

"It cost a bundle. The cuckoos are purple. With a drag-on's face on half of them," Fen added, amused by the prince's total obliviousness. It was evident to everyone but Rolpe that he had caught the scent of his mate and was on the prowl. "Probably should be called a dragon clock. It can actually fly at the witching hour, too!"

"Ah, that's good. Did you know that she was seen waltz-ing two waltzes with that Herr Mozart fellow last night? Of course, she is taller than he is, and the man never speaks of anything beyond sonatas and marches, so I think—"

"I'm going to say good-bye to my brood."

Rolpe watched Greta climb back inside her large travel-ing barouche; then his attention was drawn back to Fen. "What did you say?"

"I'm going to wish them good-bye."

"I'll come with you," Rolpe said. "I didn't get to say hello to the children when I arrived."

"Of course." Fen did not break stride, nor did he crack a grin. The older Grimm girl might be just the woman Rolpe needed . . . and wanted, as well. Yes, the charming, ro-guish prince's bachelor days were numbered. Fen could see the writing on the wall.

# CHAPTER THIRTY-TWO

## Are We There Yet?

"He was mad about my prank, very mad. But it all worked out in the end," Rae whispered to her sister as they rode.

Greta smiled. "I knew the baron was a reasonable man."

"That's debatable. He thinks I'm jealous," Rae said petulantly, wanting to spell it all out for Greta. But she was all too aware of the little ears here, there and everywhere. Of course, the little ears were most likely too busy listening to howls of complaint as the barbaric brood shoved each other around the barouche. "I've never had to be jealous of a man before."

Greta ducked, dodging another flying elbow. As she did, she wedged her body further back upon the seat. She was crammed in the carriage so tightly that she felt she was back at home with her mother lacing up her stays, but she managed to say, "Well, there's no time like the present. Besides, I do believe he might be worth it." Then she watched in rather stunned disbelief as Rae's hat was knocked from her head and her curls spilled everywhere. Instead of pouting or crying, Rae simply reached out and cuffed Ernst on his devious towhead.

Merri, sitting beside Rae, flapped her arms and complained for the tenth time, "I don't like it in here. It's too crowded, and I want a window seat. I think this is a stupid idea."

Poppy asked for the sixteenth time in the four miles they had come, "Are we there yet?"

Greta again replied kindly, "No dear, just a few more miles." She had hoped to sit back in the carriage and think of Prince von Hanzen. Her heart had leapt with joy today as he stood by the carriage with the baron and wished them a good journey. Ha! Good journey, indeed.

"Are you sure we aren't there?" Poppy asked, hopping up and down. Ernst stuck his tongue out at her. Nap rolled his eyes, along with Quinn.

"I notice that the prince watched you as we took our leave," Rae murmured, dodging a flying knee. "Poppy, the carriage is too small for leap frog. Ernst, stop sticking your tongue out at your sister. Nap, quit laughing and watch your elbows."

"Do you think so?" Greta asked. "He seemed to pay equal attention to all of us."

"Not quite equal, because he watched the carriage as we left. I think he finds you very attractive—which should make me pea-green with envy," Rae said as she pushed Alden gently back down on his seat. "Alden, don't chew on your lamp. It looks bad enough already." Turning her attention back to Greta, she added a tad sourly, "You do realize that if you wed with him, you'll be a princess. Everyone in Cornwall will think I've gotten my comeuppance. *I* was to be the one to marry royalty." A tiny frown turned her mouth downward.

The grin disappeared from Greta's face. "Whoever said anything about weddings? The prince is nothing but a womanizing rogue."

Rae regretted having embarrassed her sister with her silly complaint. "You'll make a lovely princess, and I hear that rakes make the best husbands once they find their way. And by the way he watches you, I do believe the poor prince is smitten."

Greta returned Rae's smile, then moved her knees so Ernst could step around her and look out the carriage window.

"Oh, do sit down, Ernst!" Rae demanded. "A view of your backside is not so pleasant. And please stop stepping upon my feet."

"I'm telling Papa you said backside," Shyla said. "And we don't like your backside, either."

Rae let out a chuckle. "That's perfectly fine by me." *Your father certainly does,* she didn't add, lust filling her heart. *He fondled it all night long.* For the first time in a great while, Rae was well and truly content with her life. Mayhap being a princess wasn't as exciting as it sounded.

Patting her sister's knee, she added sincerely, "You just wait. I see weddings—perchance a June bride?"

Alden, who had been born a little tyrant, took exception to being ignored by his siblings and pretty new stepmother. Crawling to her ankle, he tried to bite, only to encounter hard leather; so with a devious glint in his eyes, he leapt up at his stepmother's soft white hands. Just as quickly Rae jerked back from the jaws of doom, frowning down at the vicious little creature.

"So, it's now my hands, is it?" she asked. Evidently, since she was wearing sturdy boots, the littlest Schortz was looking for an easier meal. Apparently she would have to wear the boots morning, noon and night to remain unbitten.

Gently she tapped the child with her muff. "Don't bite the hand that feeds you," she said, giving the ravenous little creature the evil eye. "Even if she is your stepmother."

"If you act mean to us, Papa will send you to bed without supper," Ernst warned, relishing the thought.

Rae fought the sudden urge to stick her tongue out at the little heathen. "How wonderful. Then I can feast upon little plump children with blond curls in the dead of night," she replied, her expression intense as she eyed the little boy with a ferocious grin.

Unfortunately for both Grimm sisters, Alden's bite was

on par with his howl, and at Rae's comment he chose to do just that. Not to be outdone by his howl, Shyla squealed at the top of her lungs in false terror. Soon Poppy and Ernst joined in the merrymaking.

"She's going to eat us all up!"

Greta winced, feeling sweat form on her brow, her heart hammering in her chest. As another fist flew by her face, she shrank back against her seat, feeling as if she were under attack by a horde of pillaging Vikings or fire-breathing demons. As she did so, she noted that the little girl with the perfect golden girls and pretty pink frilly smock had some very formidable lungs.

"Don't wrinkle my pretty new smock. It has pink ribbons," the girl cried.

Greta wanted to howl with both annoyance and laughter. Rae's marriage was not only a financial gain; it was the making of her. Greta was actually in awe of her composure. She was handling this situation with great aplomb and cool daring. Military commanders could take lessons.

"Ouch! I'm not a pastry, Alden." Rae yanked a curl out of the child's grubby little fist, for he was attempting to chew it. Turning to glare at the deviant little feaster, she then shook her head and turned back to Greta. "I certainly hope no one of import is at the fortune-teller's, for my hair is a mess and my dress is wrinkled. But then, so is yours."

Greta had to shout to be heard. "How can you stand it?"

"What, all this? Why, sister dear, I fear for my very life, not to mention my sanity. This is some of their *better* behavior."

"But why in heaven's name aren't you sulking?" Greta asked. She'd been pondering that very question for the last five miles. Carefully, she studied her sister's content expression. "At any rate, I must say that your change of heart is delightfully refreshing."

Rae smiled a secret smile.

Poppy clearly wanted to comment. She leaned over

Rae's shoulder and patted her on the head, saying to Greta, "We've gotten a pretty new stepmama. She lets me play with her kitten that Quinn gave her, and she sleeps in Papa's bed now."

"Oho!" It hit Greta like a bolt of lightning that Rae had done her wifely duty. Which meant not only was her sister happy, but that she'd be perfectly able to tell all about the wedding night and wifely duties. Greta grinned merrily. Rae looked radiant.

Greta wanted to question her sister thoroughly about the mysteries of wedding nights and closed bedchamber doors; however, she reluctantly managed to restrain her curiosity, knowing full well that the carriage had ears. Underage ones.

"*Ja*," Rae whispered, smiling. "Better than *ja*. It's beyond wonderful."

"You're learning German? Will wonders never cease!" Indeed, it was a miracle. Her sister was changing, growing, and Greta would have clapped her hands with joy if the little girl Merri wasn't sitting on one of them.

"Come down from the window, Poppy, you wretched little monkey. A lady doesn't show her limbs," Rae instructed, pulling on the little girl's leg. Her command was firm if her eyes were lit with affection. "Remind you of anyone—such as Taylor?" she remarked to Greta. Both sisters grinned as they recalled their sister's youth.

"*Nein*. You'll eat me all up," Poppy teased, clinging to the window and enjoying her view. "I'z an eagle."

"I'm hungry. I'm tired and I think I'm going to be sick," Merri grumbled. "Carriage rides always make me sick."

"Merri, Merri, quite contrary," Nap taunted.

Leaning over, Rae patted the girl on the shoulder. "Just be patient. I'm sure the gingerbread house will have plenty to offer."

"I could eat the whole house," Ernst boasted.

"No you can't. But *I* can," Quinn argued, laughing. "My

stomach is bigger than yours, and Papa always says I eat more." Quinn patted himself proudly.

As Nap shoved Alden off, a number of complaints filled the carriage.

"Get your knee out of my rib cage, you tiny little blighter!"

"Stop biting my elbow, you little monster."

"Wipe your mouth—good grief, not on my new muff!"

"Nap, stop rocking the carriage right this minute!"

"Was that your foot in my backside, Ernst?"

"I'm telling Papa you said backside!"

"Are we there yet?" the second youngest asked again.

"Yes!" Rae and Greta announced in unison, for indeed they had finally arrived at the gingerbread house. One of the boys climbed halfway out the other window to take a gander, while inside, cries of "Stop pulling my hair" were heard by one and all.

Fräulein Hines, who had heard the ruckus outside her little cottage, bravely opened the door. She stood on the front porch studiously surveying the odd scene. Her companion and maid stood there wide-eyed, her mouth forming a perfect O.

From his lookout, Quinn called, "It's not real gingerbread, and there's no lemon drops!"

A great deal of shoving, howling and groaning accompanied this gloomy declaration, and then came a gradual unloading of the swaying vehicle. Fräulein Hines watched a small boy of no more than four crawl out the window and be helped down by the driver. Next a little girl exited, her skirts rucked up about her knees as she waved gaily. "Are you the wicked witch?"

"Don't be rude," said a stunning woman with a messy hairdo as she stuck her head out the carriage window. "I'm sorry about that," she apologized. "She has few manners. I've only been her stepmother a short while." The head disappeared back inside the carriage, and more complaints burst forth.

"If you'd move your foot I think I can manage to pry you loose, Sister."

"I want candied apples!"

"I think I'm going to be sick!"

At last, the carriage was empty. And Rae wasn't sure, but she thought the house cringed as the children approached.

# CHAPTER THIRTY-THREE

## The Death Card

For want of a nail, the shoe was lost. For want of a shoe, the horse was lost. For want of a horse, the battle was lost. For want of a good cookie, a temper was lost—and then the kingdom, which was Fräulein Hines's mantra. Thus her pretty little house was always filled with the smells of baking gingerbread and light fluffy cakes.

As her guests were seated, Fräulein Hines filled a plate with fresh gingerbread men and set it down, a sacrificial offering amongst a gluttonous horde of children. Greta had meanwhile pulled Rae aside, confiding, "I want to hear everything as soon as these prying little ears are out of sight."

Rae blushed, but nodded. "But, Greta, don't you mean out of hearing?"

Now that the children were occupied, Fräulein Hines seated Rae and began to read her fortune. Greta studied her as the woman shuffled her tarot cards. The fräulein was at least in her seventies, with very bony, long fingers and a thin pinched face scored by dozens of wrinkles. The first card she turned over was the Chariot. "This is the card of movement. Movement that has made you ill at ease."

"Well, I have had more pleasant carriage rides," Rae replied.

"That is not what I speak of. *Ja*, there has been great

change in your life recently, and I think you were not happy about this at first."

Both Rae and Greta glanced at each other, and then Rae shrugged her shoulders. "You could have heard this from gossips. I was recently forced into marriage."

"Ah, but there is no force involved anymore, is there?" the fräulein asked, turning over the Fool.

Rae blushed, and Greta smiled.

"This man you did not seek for a husband is exactly the husband you need. The baron is your destiny." Fräulein Hines glanced over to where the children were busy consuming another pan of gingerbread that the maid had set out. Two of the boys were rolling on the ground like demented raccoons, while the others were chattering and howling with laughter. They were making enough noise to make her glad she had never married. "These children . . . Their loss was great. Their mother was very special. But even broken hearts mend with kindness and love."

Rae smiled at Greta, then turned back to the table. The old woman turned over the last card. A frown appeared as she said, "This one is the Devil, and it warns of trickery, deceit and treachery."

Rae nodded sagely. "How true. You've just described life with *them*."

Fräulein Hines studied the younger woman, a strange glint in her eye. She opened her mouth to speak, then decided to remain silent.

"Is that all you can tell me? What of my husband—will he grow to love me? Will we be happy together? Will my sister, Faye, find a husband?"

The fräulein held up a hand. "Some things I cannot see, but I will tell you this. You must search your heart. All things are possible with hope and love. Baroness Schortz, you are more fortunate than most in your marriage. The baron is a man who will move aside to let his wife walk beside him if he feels true affection for her. And yes, your sister Faye will marry—in the not too distant future."

Rae sat back, smiling, and Greta was impressed with the old woman's words. Still, this kind old dear was not a witch, although she did have boiling cauldrons in the room—Greta knew this because in her first moments inside the cottage she'd managed to sneak a peek into them. But she'd been doomed to disappointment, for all they contained were little balls of rolled dough. Also, the old Prussian woman's cat was deep orange in color, not black.

Suddenly, Shyla and Merri appeared at the old woman's side. "Can you tell me if I'm going to marry a king someday?" Shyla asked. "I'm very beautiful; everyone says so. So I should marry a king or at least a prince, because he will want to marry the fairest maiden in the land."

Greta looked over the little girl's head at Rae. Her sister raised a brow.

Rae mouthed, "Surely I never sounded like that!"

Greta nodded.

The old woman shuffled her cards for the young girl and drew the Star. "You will marry well, and your husband will be of a royal house."

Shyla smiled, content. Turning to Merri, she nudged her. "See, Merri? I get to marry a king because of my golden locks and pretty blue eyes. You have brown hair and funny gray eyes, so you'll have to marry a blacksmith or a peddler."

Greta shook her head, her lips fixed in an amused smile. "My, my, just like old times."

Ignoring her sister, Rae corrected her stepdaughter. "That's not polite, Shyla. Fräulein Hines didn't say you would marry a king. Besides, kings want to marry ladies who are as kind as they are beautiful." Putting a gold coin on the table, she stared hard at the fortune-teller and said, "I would guess that Merri will marry a prince or mayhap a duke."

Fräulein Hines picked a card, laid it on the table and smiled. "This pretty one will marry her heart's desire. She'll not care that his name is not noble, for he will be a brave, strong man of great wealth. And both girls' husbands-to-be will be influenced by your new stepmother."

Merri beamed.

Rae ushered the children off, saying, "Go have some more gingerbread. It's Greta's turn."

Suddenly there came cries of, "Run, run, you can't catch him!" The three women at the table all turned and saw Ernst dash outside, Quinn following hot on his heels.

"Aha! *I've* got the gingerbread man," Ernst cried, and the boys and their brother Nap were soon scuffling over the now crumbling cookie.

"Do you think if we left some cookies in the woods, they might not follow us home?" Rae asked. Both Greta and the old lady laughed.

"No, Rae, I think you're stuck with them," said Greta. "Think of them as penance."

The old woman just smiled and reshuffled the cards.

"Will I find what I seek here in the Black Forest?" Greta asked, wanting to know if she would find any monsters. That was why she'd come, of course.

"Oh, don't waste time about that. Who is my sister going to marry?" Rae asked.

Greta shook her head, blushing.

The old woman drew a card. "The World. This is a very good card, foretelling much happiness. I believe you are destined to marry a prince as well. You'll travel and have grand yet dangerous adventures."

Rae rolled her eyes. " I should have come here before I was married. Then mayhap I would also have gotten a prince. It seems everyone else is getting one today. There must be a sale."

Greta grinned. There was only one prince she wanted, and that was von Hanzen. "It's highly improbable," she said. "We're like oil and water." No, they didn't mix very well—not until he held her close. Then her heart beat happily along with his in a shared pulse of savage attraction.

"He's too haughty and arrogant, too opinionated and too handsome for his own good." Yet, if she were completely honest, Greta knew that his presence inspired and intrigued her.

Glancing at the old woman, Greta hesitated, then asked, "Can you tell me who this prince is?"

"The cards do not say." Fräulein Hines drew another card and placed it face up. "You seek the truth to all things," she said, and turned over another card. It was Death. She drew in a sharp little breath and looked at Greta hard. "But the truth can be dangerous. Very dangerous."

Studying the Death card, Greta felt a chill of apprehension and asked worriedly, "Does this always mean actual physical death?"

"*Nein.* No. But it is not a card to take lightly. It warns of danger and dark secrets. It warns of endings."

Rae, who was seated by her sister's side, felt a foreboding like a dark spot on her soul. "You should leave off your quest about the vampire."

"*Nosferatu?*" the fräulein asked worriedly, deep worry lines forming upon her brows. "*Ja.* You should leave those evil creatures alone. They are dead men who have been brought back to life with wicked means. They have no souls. Do not seek them out, or the Death card may prove prophetic."

Rae's eyes were beseeching. "No mystery is worth your life. Promise me, Greta, you'll stop at once."

Patting her sister's hand, she shook her head. "I will be fine. I am always very careful. Besides, the card is merely a warning." Leaning forward in her chair, she continued with her questions. In for a penny, in for a pound. "I wanted to ask you about Frau Choplin. I know the two of you were friends."

"Greta! Enough!" Rae was shocked by her sister's stubborn refusal to play it safe. Well, she wasn't shocked, but she was disappointed. She didn't want the fortune-teller's predictions to come true.

"I shall ask now, or I shall come back later," Greta advised her. Seeing the conviction in her eyes caused Rae to shake her head.

Fräulein Hines answered carefully, glancing from sister to sister. "We were good friends."

"You must have been concerned when her body disappeared from the cemetery?"

The old woman nodded.

"I believe it was vampires."

The old woman weighed her words. Although she could often read the future, she could not change it. Heaven's will was Heaven's will, and not all the king's horses or all the king's men could always put things back together again. "I have heard tell that it was grave robbers."

"Is that what you think? What do the cards say?"

Reluctantly, the old woman shuffled her deck again and then hesitantly laid one card on the table. What she turned over was a special card in her deck: the White card. She breathed a sigh of relief.

"I don't understand. It's blank?" Greta asked, clearly disappointed.

"It means that we aren't allowed to see. Or that the answer is yet undecided. Though we travel a fairly certain path through life, there be a few little roads off the beaten path that we may take, that bring either great reward or great heartache."

Before any more could be said, a loud crash filled the room. All eyes turned to the boys, who were still wrestling over the crumbled gingerbread man. Ernst had kicked at Quinn, and he'd knocked over a small stool.

"Stop this wicked behavior at once!" Rae cried. "You are behaving like a passel of pests." She narrowed her eyes on the misbehaving urchins. Merri had her hand stuck in the gingerbread jar, while Poppy was climbing the mantel over the fireplace. Shyla, not to be left out, was busy instructing the maid how to wipe the milk mustache off her dainty little mouth.

Rae heaved a dramatic sigh. "I think we've overstayed our welcome."

As they took their leave, the sisters Grimm looked at each other, the carriage and the rambunctious bratlings, then steeled themselves for the ride home in the closed contraption.

"Forget the prince and domestic bliss and heated kisses. It's not worth this," Greta mumbled to herself as Poppy trod on her foot.

"For once you're wrong," Rae replied. "The 'wifely duties' part is very much worth it, even this."

Greta's jaw dropped open. Surely nothing could be *that* pleasurable. However, Rae's calm demeanor assured her it was. "Well, I'll be a monkey's uncle." She'd never expected this of her sister.

Rae laughed. "No, you're a monkey's step-aunt," she said, again tugging Poppy from the carriage window. And she gave her sister a smug smile that Greta was hard-pressed to interpret.

# CHAPTER THIRTY-FOUR

## Someday My Prince Will Come... to His Senses

She was thinking of dead bodies when he spied her, but that was unknown to Rolpe. A flash of tawny-colored hair and her infectious smile—to him, Miss Greta Grimm was utterly captivating, and so innocently demure. Although, recalling the first time he'd seen her face, he'd thought she came out a poor second to her sister. It had not been one of his finer moments. The first time he'd kissed her, he had felt the earth move. He had stupidly put it down to an earthquake in Wolfach, even though there had never before been an earthquake nearby. Still, the slight deception had helped, if only for a bit. Then he had discovered in her a heretofore unknown world.

Rolpe started swiftly toward her, drawn like a hawk to its prey across the snow-packed cobblestones. It had been five days since he last saw her at Durloc Castle. It seemed an eternity, but he had purposely kept away to see if his fascination would fade. Instead, it had grown stronger, just as Fen predicted. He had even weakened two nights ago and accepted a dinner invitation from Fen, only to bitterly discover that Greta was not there.

In the shop glass, Greta spied Rolpe behind her and smiled. While the prince might thwart her plans, she couldn't help grinning whenever she saw his face. Cupid's dart had flown fast and true the very first time they met. The prince had released in her a dark and fiery passion that was only growing stronger.

Taking a deep breath, Greta regained some of her poise and turned slightly. She had a mission to accomplish, and Rolpe would stop her if he knew it, just as her sister would. Still, her quest was too important to be halted . . . but she could be sidetracked for a while, if Rolpe was doing the sidetracking.

As she faced him, the prince elegantly lifted her hand for a kiss, lingering over it far longer than was proper.

"Your Highness, please. People will talk," Greta scolded.

Mesmerized by the little dimple in her cheek, he dimly realized she was right. He stepped back to a more proper distance and said, "I had thought to pay you a visit this afternoon at your aunt's."

"It seems I've foiled your plans," she replied, glad that he had caught her before her foray into the doctor's cellar. She now knew where the dead bodies were kept. "Rae wrote a note and said you dined with her and Fen two nights ago. I hope you found all well?"

"I was sorry to hear that you were indisposed and couldn't join us." He had been more than annoyed, arriving to be told that Greta was stuck at home in bed suffering a cold. "How are you feeling?"

"Much better, thank you," she replied.

He stared, admiring her. The cold wind had made her cheeks red, and her lips were a little chapped from the cold. A few loose hairs escaped from under her hood and blew in the wind. She was absolutely beautiful—and she made him feel like a prince among men. To many, this feeling would be an absolute marvel, but to Rolpe, who had always been a prince, it was less amazing. No, he decided, Greta made him feel a king. A warrior king. She brought out his protective streak. His honor-bound, loving streak, which had formally been reserved for members of his family and a few close friends. She commanded his attention as no other woman had done before. Greta made him laugh, she made him angry . . . and she made him extremely randy. He wanted to know everything and anything about her and her life, not merely whether she cried out in the throes of passion or liked slow leisurely lovemaking.

"What are you doing out and about today?" he asked. "It's rather blustery for shopping, especially when one has been ill."

Greta glanced up to the sky and tucked her scarf around her neck as a gust of bitter cold wind blew. "I thought to pick something up for my brothers," she explained.

Rolpe glanced at the shop behind her, cocking an eyebrow at her guilty expression. She really was lovely, but something in her eyes . . . What was she up to? What supernatural legend was she pursuing now? "They like puppets?"

Greta followed the direction of the prince's gaze to the puppets filling the shop window. Several of the front ones were the size of small children. Each puppet had a friendly smile painted upon its wooden lips. "Not really, but I couldn't help but admire the craftsmanship, although this one's nose is rather long and crooked."

"That it is."

"At first I thought I was standing on an uneven stone. Then I stopped, and I noticed that everything in Herr Bierhalle's shop is rather lopsided. Look at the crooked wooden stick against the wall—and there!" she cried as she noticed a thin yellowish beast with a crooked tail. "Even his cat."

Rolpe agreed politely, and added with a hint of humor, "You should see his crooked house." He watched, and her eyes lit up from within. He held his breath, arousal filtering through him. She was ravishing when she smiled, and her scent was beckoning to him, calling his name. "Herr Bierhalle is overfond of the taverns, and oft works while intoxicated," he explained. When she laughed, his heart began to pound.

He gallantly escorted her onward, and they walked down

the sidewalk, passing other shops filled with all manner of varied and colorful products. Their manner was that of old friends, and at the same time full of unacted upon passion. Both took pains to keep the conversation light.

As they passed Drosselmeier's candy store, which was lined with baked sugared almonds, marzipan trumpets and French horns, Greta stopped. Both she and Prince von Hanzen peered in the window, and she merrily pointed to a large candy nutcracker. Beyond lay a large baker's oven. "Isn't he a jolly fellow, with his rosy red cheeks and bright green eyes? My brother William would like him." Turning to face the prince again, she explained. "William has a large collection of wooden soldiers. They are one of his favorite things. And I imagine a candy soldier would be even better."

"And yours?" he asked.

"My what?"

"Likes, favorite things, *desires*."

Her reply, when it came out, was rather breathy. "So, you want to know what I desire?" Love had definitely bitten her; it had pursued her ruthlessly and sunk in its teeth. If only Rolpe felt the same way, life would be a fairy tale come true. She instinctively knew that he was fond of her, and the days of their animosity seemed a distant past, but still . . .

"Well, let me see." She couldn't very well tell him that *he* was what she desired most. "I love raindrops on my window when I'm reading. I have the most wonderful time when Taylor and my brothers are sitting around the fireplace telling fairy tales. I love quoting Latin with my father and his friend Sir Jahn. And it's certainly true that I live for the thrill of discovery, or learning new things." *And you,* she added silently, *I love you.*

He cocked his head to the side and studied her. "What of diamond rings, ruby slippers and a hundred ball gowns?"

"I'd settle for a glimpse of a vampire rising from its coffin or the big bad wolf at some poor old grandmother's house."

He threw back his head and laughed. "Greta, you are an odd, odd woman."

"You find me fascinating—an intriguing mystery of whom you are trying not to be overly fond." Once the words were out of her mouth, she could have bitten her tongue for her presumption. "I'm sorry, what silly teasing," she back-tracked.

Her words stuck him hard, and in his pride and mis-guided sense of bachelorhood, the prince retaliated. "*Ja,* I do. However, I don't want to marry anyone, perhaps ever." And with those words he crossed the street, fleeing as if demons from the underworld were hot on his trail.

Watching his retreating figure, Greta shook her head, vexed beyond belief. "Well, Greta Grimm," she said. "For someone whom everyone calls a wit, you've proven them half-right."

After thoroughly berating her stupidity, cursing herself as she watched Rolpe enter the stable yard, Greta turned her attention back to the game at hand. She had a piece of a fairy-tale puzzle to explore, and she had to do it soon, before her nosy aunt became too curious. Aunt Vivian had berated her up one side and down the other about galli-vanting around the countryside seeking a monster; she didn't want the woman going front to back on the next go.

Scurrying off through the snow, Greta turned the corner to the doctor's office. If all went as planned, she would soon be examining the body of Herr Humpty.

Not desiring to be caught snooping, she glanced through the small window of the doctor's office to ascertain that the doctor was indeed indisposed. He was: The old man was asleep in his chair, an empty bottle of Schnapps by his side. She would be safe.

Greta hurried around the back of the office cottage to the cellar door. Descending inside, Greta wrinkled her nose in disgust at the moldy atmosphere, which also smelled faintly of death. Lighting a torch in a wall sconce, she swiftly headed toward the body under a sheet . . . then gasped in shock when she pulled back the sheet and found Herr Humpty. A naked Herr Humpty. A naked, dead Herr Humpty. She had never seen a naked dead body before.

The dead man had a bluish tint to his skin. His neck and head were pushed up, due to the large hump on his back. Herr Humpty also had a very misshapen skull, and a broken crown, if she was not mistaken.

"Dead men tell no tales," she sighed. "If only you could speak."

Bracing herself against the sudden queasiness in her stomach, and against her embarrassment at his lack of attire, she finally managed to examine him. She found herself thoroughly disappointed. "Not one bite mark," she muttered to herself. "Not one single mark. Not even a nibble."

Pulling the sheet over his knees, she found her disappointment was soon replaced by abject fear. Yes, that was the voice of doom and the happily unmarried male she heard!

"First I find you in the woodcutter's cottage, rifling through his drawers! Now I find you ogling Herr Humpty, who is not a day under seventy! I really must take your aunt to task for allowing you to roam free in Wolfach." Regretting his hasty and overly harsh words to Greta, Rolpe had followed her in order to apologize. Only the trail of her scent had led here of all places. Now he was too angry to apologize.

Sheepishly Greta tried a shaky smile, gazing helplessly at him. "Rolpe. How . . ." She hesitated. She couldn't very well say how nice it was to see him again so soon, even though it was. Nor could she pretend that staring at a naked man was an everyday occurrence for her, even if the man was older than Father Time and was now a corpse. And she really hadn't peeked at *everything*. Well, maybe she'd had one quick complete glimpse.

"Damnation, woman! Has the cat got your tongue? Or is

this a case of finally mitigated gall and shame?" He was more than enraged by her continual disobedience, by her reckless dashing into dangerous situations. That fury made him restless. He began to stalk her, his expression beyond somber.

"I can explain," she said, backing up. "Though I have doubts that you'll like my explanation."

"That you are a perverted Peeping Thomasina? No, I don't imagine I will like that."

"I needed to see if Herr Humpty had bite marks on his neck," she said, wringing her hands as he backed her into a corner.

"Bite marks!" He spat the words out. "I told you there are no *vampyrs* in Wolfach. When will you get it through your thick head?" He reached out and grabbed her by her arms, pulling her roughly to him. "Shall I tell you what you found? Not bite marks. Not a single one, because Herr Humpty drank too much Schnapps with the good doctor, and he fell off a very high, very narrow wall." And with those damning words, Rolpe swooped down and kissed her.

Learning how Herr Dumpty died left her shell-shocked but, not to be outdone by this raging but handsome prince, Greta returned the kiss with all the passion and love she had. Her intensity struck Rolpe hard, causing his mouth to gentle, though he still held her tightly to him. Truly, they were a perfect fit.

As the kiss continued, reason fled, and before Greta could say "Jack Frost," she found Rolpe nipping at her nose, kissing her cheeks and laying her across a wooden bench, one nipple peeking from out of her dress. Her skirts were around her waist, and Rolpe's fingers found that place that had been throbbing ever since she met him.

"Oh, my goodness!" she gasped. "What are you doing?" It was certainly strange and erotic. She could feel his fingers sweeping through her curls and touching something moist and sweet and aching.

He leaned back from worshipping her neck and smiled wickedly, "Making you crazy—as crazy as you make me."

"But we're not married! And though I do not know exactly what husbandly and wifely duties entail, I imagine this might be on the agenda." Greta spoke earnestly, if a bit breathlessly. She was worried about becoming with child, unmarried, and yet she was hungry for something she could not define. Alas, she was truly and madly in love with the man touching her, the man she was now wearing almost like a cloak.

"This is scandalous—heavenly, but scandalous nonetheless." Her aunt would decry these actions to the heavens; her mother would faint over them, and no young virgin should allow such wantonness. She had been seduced by a kiss and soon found herself at a feast, a banquet, a wedding night without wedding guests, wedding cake, or even a ceremony. She could not continue in this vein without dishonoring all that she knew, even though her heart wanted it so badly. "I cannot."

Rolpe blinked, the madness of lust leaving him slowly. His nostrils flared as he breathed in the freshness of her unique scent, made sweeter by arousal. He withdrew his fingers, wet with her arousal, and let loose a string of profanity.

"Well, you're certainly not Prince Charming. Really, Rolpe, there's no need for cursing." But she smiled a secret smile, for he was unquestionably the one who'd awakened her with a kiss.

"The hell you say," he snarled, pushing himself off her. He would die if he didn't finish what he had started. Nonetheless, he forced himself to leave her body, her scent, her very being. He regretted the act, especially remembering Fen's words about a woman's softness being more than just physical. A raging hunger had beset him, and Rolpe wanted Greta with a passion like no other. Despite all his attempts to the contrary, he'd become all too fond of the delicious Miss Grimm and the enchanting spell she'd cast.

"*Danke,* for stopping," she said.

"I had little choice, since I do not ravish virgins. Nor do I intend to become a husband," he growled, his eyes dark with thwarted passion. "I may want you like the very devil, but I'll be hanged if I'll stuff myself into his very handbasket on its way back to hell."

She was no longer in peril from his seduction. The words he spoke ripped into her like slashing claws, tearing her heart and her pride to shreds. With a gasp she cried, "I can't believe I let you . . . I fear I am more than fond of you, and that has made me foolish."

"I am not ready to wed."

"But you are ready to bed," she snapped. "I shall go down on my knees and give thanks."

He interrupted her with a painful groan. He ached with want, but he was also frightened of his feelings. And yet, as a prince of the realm, fear was something he couldn't tolerate.

Greta cursed him. "I shall not spoil the good name of Grimm or Snowe by giving my virtue to a man such as you—a man who takes advantage of finding a lady alone with a naked dead man and has the nerve to try and seduce her. And then you accuse me of trying to entrap you! Again! Just who do you think you are, the King of Prussia?" Never had she desired a man so much. If she couldn't marry Rolpe, Greta knew she would never marry. Alas, her heart, once given, was given for life. Rapidly, she readjusted her skirts and glowered at him. Her heart was weeping, and she was dying inside.

"*Nein.* Not a king; just a prince of Prussia, and too wily a one to get caught in a virgin's snares."

"You are a very *stupid* man," she retorted. Shoving him away, she marched to the stairs, head held high like a steadfast tin soldier, her heart threatening to pound out of her chest.

"Stupid. perhaps. Unmarried, definitely." And quite content.

"And you call yourself a prince? Ha! You, sir, aren't even a gentleman!" With contempt, Greta turned and hurried up the stairs. She wanted to escape him forever.

Regrettably, Rolpe noted the tears in her eyes before she turned away. That wounded him. Cut to the quick, he shook his head, realizing that he regretted much of what he had said. He wanted her so badly. He should have just dropped down on bended knee and proposed. But pride and four long decades of debauched bachelorhood kept him silent.

At the top of the stairs, Greta turned to glower at him one more time. "I wish you joy in your lonely old age. You'll never touch these lips again." And so saying, she slammed the cellar door behind her.

No one had to knock Rolpe on the head for him to realize he'd been given an ultimatum, and, like a prince of any land, he growled and cursed. No prince liked ultimatums. Especially not from his ultimate mate, hmm?

# CHAPTER THIRTY-FIVE

## Where There's Smoke, There's Alden Schortz

Familiarity breeds, contemplated Fen as he awakened early and reluctantly left Rae's bed. Time was passing on the wings of angels. Looking down at his lovely wife, he noted how her impossibly long braid was hanging across her shoulder and down her hips to rest between her plump white thighs. He licked his lips, and his heart did a strange flip-flop in his chest. Valiantly he resisted the urge to crawl back beneath the covers and cradle her golden head on his chest. His new wife really loved his chest, just as she loved his eyes, his arms and another part of his anatomy. One much lower.

Last night Fen had instructed his bride very thoroughly in her wifely duties. One of those was to loosen her hair from the braid she generally wore while sleeping. Next, he had taught her all about riding "a different kind of stallion." With a passionate wildness Rae had learned, her muscles clenching him tight, her unbound hair falling about them like a silken veil. If he lived to be a hundred and twenty, he would never forget the sight.

Despite the fact that it was only the fifth night since her deflowering, Rae had bloomed in the bedchamber. A happy place now was his boudoir, where Fen religiously assured his wife that it was his husbandly duty to make certain that she enjoyed herself. They had also made love in the stables yesterday, when he had found Rae there busy helping Quinn with a sick dog.

Merri had been there, too, watching her brother, grumbling about the smell. Rae had glanced over at the rather precocious girl and told her: Of course it smells, it's a stable. Verily, if that was all she had to complain about in life, then she was a lucky child. Her comments had caused Merri to shut her mouth with a snap and look thoughtful. Then Rae had directed Merri over to two frisky little pups and asked Merri to name them, since she was the eldest Schortz sister. Merri had proudly complied, only voicing one complaint the whole time—which was a record. Fen had been extremely pleased. To be honest, his wife had done well with all the girls. Poppy seemed to have grown quite fond of her new stepmother in so short a while, with her sisters coming along as well. Ever since the trip to the gingerbread house, Shyla had seemed very thoughtful. Although she was not actually friendly to Rae, she had at least been polite.

Unfortunately, Nap, Ernst and Alden still held some aversion to their stepmother, but Fen hoped that would soon change. His own opinion of his wife was changing daily. What he felt for Rae was not the enduring emotion he held for his first wife: a grand love, a first love, so very special. And yet, Rae stirred feelings in him, deep feelings. She was exciting, sweet, thoughtful, thoughtless, spoiled, humorous and vain, all at one time. She also had a few characteristics that he found essential. Rae had the capacity to forgive, and her heart was big enough to take in even his rowdy brood.

As he watched, Rae sighed in her sleep. Leaning over, Fen kissed her cheek and gently tugged on her braid. He had arranged it himself last night after a bout of lovemaking, so they would not awakened entangled in the thick silken strands, and he'd loved every minute of the job. Her hair was a marvelous color and texture, and so very long. He actually shuddered as he recalled her standing in all her glory, like Venus rising from the sea, the long moonlit strands floating about her body.

Another soft sweet sigh caught his attention, and he glanced down at her with pride. She looked so innocent, yet had the body of sirens of old. One bounteous white breast was visible with its rose-colored tip. Again he licked his lips. He wanted to bed her now, but alas, he had taken her three times last night and once early this morning. She had gently complained of being sore; so, doing a different husbandly duty, he decided he would give her a day and night of respite. Well, a day, anyway, he thought ruefully.

She moaned a little more in her sleep and turned over, her thick fat braid falling to the floor. With her pink mouth pursed and her eyelashes lying against her cheek, she was absolutely adorable. She had surprised him more than once in this marriage, and not only in bed. She was trying to be a good wife and a fair mother. When he was first honor bound to wed her, he had foreseen only dark days ahead for Castle Durloc. Yet a miracle had occurred. During this past fortnight, the darkness in his soul, the gaping hole in his heart, had begun to heal. It was all due to Rae.

He got up and dressed, went downstairs and ate, then worked hard on the estate books, knowing what he needed to do and dreading it. Tonight was a full moon, so he had to confess all. Hedging, he decided to tell Rae at teatime.

While Fen was in the study below, still pondering just how to introduce the family secret, Rae woke. Getting out of bed, she was pondering the strange response she'd gotten back from her sister. Greta had rejected a dinner invitation for tomorrow night, a dinner with Rolpe as the other guest. Rolpe, too, had rejected the invitation. Something was rotten in the state of Wolfach, and Rae would not rest until she knew why. Greta was marrying Rolpe whether she liked it or not. She might be too headstrong and obsessed with her fairy tales, but Rolpe would manage her.

Lazily, Rae brushed her locks and stared into a mirror. But this time, it was not in vanity. Since her wedding, she had undergone a strange yet exhilarating transformation. No longer did she spend her days in idle dreams about her future as a bride, complete with prince and fairy-tale castle. Well, she admitted, she already had the castle; but her happiness was not entirely due to the stuff of Greta's Gothic tales. Rae had grown strangely fond of most of her stepchildren, in spite of their odious pranks. Remarkably, even though her husband was not a prince, Fen did have a princely bearing, a nobility of spirit that she had come to admire greatly. And Rae blushed as she thought of their heated nights together. Her husband was a superb lover. In fact, he was everything she wanted in a spouse.

Humming, she hopped up to dress but stepped on something pointed. "Owwww!" she screeched, stumbling, falling near the hearth, a few strands of her long hair catching fire. Foot bleeding, hair smoking, she hopped around the room like a madwoman. Without thinking, she tossed the object that had inflicted pain out her window. But as she did, her long hair whipped past the hearth and caught fire in earnest.

"Nooooooo!" Rae screamed, even louder. As she ran to douse her braid in a nearby basin, she heard a horde of footsteps approach.

Fen reached her first. "My dear, what's happened?" His heart beat rapidly, though he was relieved to see his wife alive and well, so to speak. He looked her over carefully. Her scream had made him realize just how important she had become to him.

He cocked his head, suddenly realizing that she stood somewhat comically, her hair sizzling in the water bowl.

"No, I am not all right!" she snapped. "My hair's on fire! Or was."

Nap appeared and laughed. "Rae, be nimble, Rae, be quick, Rae didn't jump the fire too quick."

"It's not funny!"

"I heard a crash outside the window downstairs," Ernst said, appearing, his eyes wide.

"What? Oh, yes. That was what caused this whole mess."

"Um, how did you catch your hair on fire, my dear?" Fen spoke up.

"By stepping on Alden's lamp."

"I want lamp!" Alden shouted. "I looked for it all morning."

"Well, it's out the window. I tossed it."

All the children ran to the window and looked down. They gasped in horror.

"You broked my lamp!" Alden screeched.

"You're mean!" Ernst shouted.

Rae looked at the lot of them as if they'd all gone off their rocker. "I nearly burnt in a fire and you are all carrying on about a dented old lamp? I'll have to cut off at least a foot of my hair," she complained.

Alden burst into sobs. "Now I can't bring my mama back!"

Rae looked at Fen, confused, then had a sudden realization. The lamp was more than just a lamp to Alden.

"Oh, Alden! I'm sorry. I didn't mean to break it. I wasn't thinking."

Suppressing the urge to comfort his youngest, Fen let Rae take the lead. The child blinked several times, holding back his tears.

"It was magic," he said.

Rae sat down across from him on the floor, something she hadn't done since her nursery days. Her eyes too held tears. "I didn't know." She longed to reach across and brush away a stray lock of hair that had fallen over his forehead. But she knew she would be rejected.

"You must miss her very much."

This time, several tears slipped down Alden's little face. "*Ja*. Even though I didn't knowed her. But my lamp was gonna bring her back to us." As he said the last, more tears began to fall, and he angrily swiped at them. "I want a mama. All my brudders and sissers had a mama. But I didn't."

Rae's heart broke at that statement, and despite his initial resistance, she swept Alden into her arms and gently rocked him back and forth. He cried out his little boy sorrows.

"Oh, my little one," she said as she stroked his thick head of curls, "I'm so sorry. If I could take back what I did, I would."

He continued to cry as if his little heart was breaking. Soon Rae joined in. Fen's heart swelled for her. There on the floor, singed hair and red eyes and all, Rae had never looked more beautiful.

"Oh, sweetling, please don't cry. I know I'm not much of a stepmother, but I will do better, for I very much want to be a mama for you."

Alden sniffled and wiped his eyes with his sleeves. "You can't be her."

Rae tipped his head back and looked him in the eye. "I don't want to replace her. I can't do that, for she was a very special lady who held a special place in all your hearts. But, do you know? The magic thing about any heart is that it is big enough to love more than one person." She looked up at Fen and smiled, then, sharing with him a special moment. The other children watched Rae, and Fen knew they realized she wasn't so bad.

Alden looked highly skeptical, however, and suddenly Rae saw a resemblance to his father. "You love your father, your sister and brothers, your dog and your lamp. Right?" she asked.

After thinking it over for a few moments, he nodded slowly.

"Well, then, you can love a stepmother too. Or at least grow fond of her." Rae looked over at Shyla, Poppy and Merri. They returned her smile.

Ernst and Quinn shuffled their feet shyly. Maybe their

new stepmother was right, said their eyes. Maybe they could at least like her. But Nap still met her gaze with a doubtful glare. She hoped one day she could touch his heart.

Glancing up at Fen, Rae knew she had to do something to fix what she had unintentionally wrought. "What if I took your lamp to the cobbler to get it fixed? How would that be?"

Alden nodded, his chubby face grubby and tear-streaked. Then, narrowing his sly little eyes, he asked, "Will you played pirates with me?"

"Bargaining, are we?" Rae studied him back. Then she smiled. "I promise to play pirates with you. Only, Ernst shall be the captive."

"Ernst?" He sounded intrigued.

"Nein," Ernst shouted.

But Alden insisted.

As Rae shook the little boy's hand, Fen smiled down on his wife. For the first time in a long while, he felt part of a whole family again.

# CHAPTER THIRTY-SIX

## Six Feet Under Is Six Feet too Few

Greta was staring into the mirror's reflections as she was wont to do, looking for vampires, and she frowned; Rolpe was not at the ball to scold her about it. He was probably licking his bachelor wounds and hiding from her righteous fury, the seducing scoundrel. She might love the arrogant and idiotic man, but she wasn't going to let him walk all over her.

Her frown deepened as dancers twirled by, and she examined the mirror once more—all in vain. It was quite vexing. Still, she would not give up her quest, especially not when Prince Nein-It-All had given an ultimatum. Somewhere in this town was a devious vampire; more likely two. There just had to be, for this was the Black Forest. The truth was out there, and she would be the one to find it and excavate it. She would exceed Rolpe's and her aunt's expectations and thereby exonerate herself.

A sudden disturbance at the door caused Greta to turn and watch as three men rushed into the room, all babbling hysterically.

"Herr Humpty's missing from his grave! Just like Frau Choplin!" one of the men cried out. His fat cheeks were ruddy, and his eyes widened with fear.

"The groundskeeper is dead. His neck's been broken,"

another man exclaimed as he searched the ballroom now full of horrified faces. "Where's the magistrate?"

"He's not here tonight; nor is his nephew," one voice answered.

Shouts of "Get the torches and pitchforks" filled the room, and the men began preparing to do battle with the forces of evil. Including, Greta would bet, a vampire or two.

Greta was ecstatic. Finally! Her moment had arrived. She would see the face of a monster. "I must find my cloak and my Van Helsing stake," she cried out. "Drat! It's at Aunt's house."

Suddenly another voice rose, high and shrill from the crowd. "The *vampyrs* are coming, the *vampyrs* are coming, and we're all doomed." Countess DeLuise's eyes rolled back in her head. Clutching at her chest, the old woman sank heavily to the ground.

Grabbing Greta by the arm, Baroness Snowe hurried over to her good friend and began issuing orders like a general. The last of these was to Greta. "Since I will be tending the countess, I'm sending you to your sister's. She'll make sure you're not off and about the graveyard like some demented Frankenstein!"

"But Aunt Vivian, everyone else is going—"

"You're not," her aunt warned her. "A cemetery is no place for a lady." Turning to a footman, she commanded, "Bring my coachman at once."

"I *must* go!" Greta actually whined, feeling her excitement drain away.

Facing her niece once again, Aunt Vivian shook her head. "My coachman will take you directly to Rae's. I will speak to him and warn him that if you set one foot into that cemetery, he will be driving someone else's coaches and certainly not mine!"

Greta's heart sank. She was doomed. Doomed to disappointment both in love and in her quest.

Her aunt was as good as her word. Within moments Greta was whisked off to Castle Durloc, despite all her protests. Above her, the full moon shone bright, highlighting the tracks the carriage was making in the hard-packed snow.

"I'm missing all the excitement," Greta complained. She kicked out with her slippers and hit the other side of the seat. "Ouch. I bet they're chasing the vampires now, and here I am, stuck in a carriage while everyone else is having a grand adventure! My aunt is a witch!" she swore violently. "And the coachman is a coward." She had tried bribing him, but not with much enthusiasm, as her conscience wouldn't allow him sacrificing his position for her quest.

"She's worse than Mother! Jakob and William will never forgive me!" she said to the heavens. "Oh, this is monstrously unfair! I'm the one who believes in monsters. I'm the one who should be leading the pack. Now I've missed it all! I wonder how large its teeth are . . . ?"

Greta sighed. She sat up straight and brushed her tears away as the carriage slowed down. Outside her window, she heard the coachman calling out to someone. Surely they hadn't arrived at Castle Durloc already.

Sticking her head out the window, she spotted a large overturned carriage in a ditch. A body lay in the snow, blood spattered here and there. "Stop, we must help!" Greta commanded, beginning to rip a strip off her petticoats.

The carriage halted and Greta jumped down, taking the carriage lantern with her. Kneeling in the snow beside the man, she briefly noted how he was dressed. His attire proclaimed him the driver of the coach. His neck lay at an unnatural angle. Also—Greta gasped—blood flowed from his neck. Leaning down to get a closer look, she muttered, "Those are bites!" And at the sight of the puncture wounds, her heart raced.

Behind her, Greta heard the harsh cry of her own driver. Then, suddenly, all was silent. The hair stood up on the back on her neck. Whirling around, she held the lantern high and felt her heart drop in abject terror. "Who's there?"

"Surely you aren't afraid, *Fräulein,*" the dark voice asked, "of things that bite in the night? After all, I hear you've been looking for me."

Greta's jaw dropped open. "O-ho, you're really real! You're not a figment of someone's imagination after one too many steins of ale. You're not some legend from long ago, but a breathing creature of flesh and . . ." She trailed off as she realized she had almost mentioned his dinner.

Backing away, she stared at the figure before her. He was taller than she, but slender of build. He had long brown hair which hung loose past his shoulders. His eyes were a bright red, and when he smiled he revealed two very sharp fangs.

Stilling her impulse to run very fast to a place far away, she took a deep breath. Running might incite his predatory instinct. "Yes, I guess I have, and here you are. I can't believe it, though. I should, I know, because I knew you existed even when others proclaimed you did not," she stated, still in shock. Then, more to herself, she added, "And Rolpe was so certain that the woodcutter's mother's corpse was stolen by grave robbers."

"It appears you were both correct," the vampire replied silkily, his teeth glistening in the lights of the full moon and her flickering lantern.

"I . . . don't understand," Greta said, fear making her legs quake beneath her cloak. Her breathing quickened.

"I am a grave robber as well as a *Nosferatu.*"

"You mean, Frau Choplin was not bitten by you?" Greta was both terrified and amazed. And she was both terrified and amazed that she was even thinking about legends when she was about to become a vampire's dinner. If she was fortunate enough to survive this night, she would write home at once. Jakob and William would be up in the boughs over this strange, deadly and exciting adventure.

"*Nein.* I did not bite her. I merely wanted her corpse, since she was six-fingered on her left hand. An oddity which medical universities will pay well for."

"How did you know about this oddity?" Greta asked, courageously keeping the conversation going while her eyes darted around for any chance of escape.

"The undead have their ways, and one of the peddlers who travels the area happens to be a great-nephew of mine. He tells me these things and gets a percentage of the profit. I'm known far and wide in the business of dead bodies as the man who delivers the exotic and unusual."

"How interesting." She gulped. "So, when you found out about Frau Choplin, you merely dug up her corpse?"

"It didn't take long. Six feet is not really all that deep. Why, I have risen from beneath more than sixteen feet of dirt myself," he boasted shamelessly, savoring the taste of her fear. Soon she would be his, but for now he was enjoying toying with her as a cat with a mouse. He had been curious to meet the lovely lady so determined to reveal him, and now that he had, he couldn't let go. He had a mess to clean up. But first he would enjoy a little fine dining—and a sexual conquest.

Slipping her hand around her neck, Greta found her silver cross. The cold metal felt strong and hard beneath her fingers. It reassured her somewhat. Although she was in a dire and dangerous predicament, she would prevail or go down trying. "Herr Humpty was taken tonight from his final resting place. I presume that was you?" she asked. Evidently no one rested in peace around this vampire.

His smile was beyond wicked, his fangs deadly and sharp. "Aye, I did. He's got a hump on his back, which makes him different, so I came back and took him. Except, I encountered some trouble when my coach crashed. But now I have yours to carry me and the bodies to safety."

Aha! He was getting out of Wolfach in a one-horse carriage, since the other horses were limping. It also appeared that the traces might be broken. If she could delay him, the townspeople might be able to follow his carriage tracks in the snow and rescue her before she became a part of a legend—a legend that she once would have loved to be included in. Not so much anymore.

"I've never heard of a grave-robbing vampire before. Wouldn't it be easier if you were to simply drink their blood like other vamps? In fact, if you made them vampires, they could dig themselves up!"

A sharp bark of laughter filled the night, the sound cruel and guttural. "Don't you think that the medical universities would frown on their experiments waking up at night and chomping on their students? Besides, my kind require secrecy. When we hunt, we hunt the stranger on the road or those that won't be missed. We rarely hunt in towns anymore, because people would soon wise up to us. Now we seem the stuff of nightmares. But we are real."

"Oh, I see your point," Greta hedged. "But why grave robbing?" She flashed a coy smile. In the very far distance, she caught glimpses of torches. Their lights darted in and out of the far trees like fireflies. If she could just keep this monster distracted, she might be rescued from a fate worse than death. "There are more lucrative professions," she added, both afraid and exhilarated as she plotted her next move.

"How do you think I became as I am? I was robbing graves when I dug up the wrong corpse," the creature explained to her.

Greta nodded, easing toward one of the horses that had become unhitched in the accident. "A thief never profits from his crimes."

The vampire's slender shoulders began to shake as he erupted in laughter. Taking advantage of his distraction, Greta inched closer to the untethered horse. She kept her eyes on the undead highwayman, who was still chortling. Her pride battled with her fear and, piqued, she retorted, "It's not funny. My Sunday school teacher taught me that."

He wiped blood-red tears from his eyes and just stood there, watching her try to sneak to the horse with all the stealth of a large ox.

Noting the bloody spots on his hands and speckling his greatcoat, Greta shuddered. "You bit your driver, and you killed mine," she accused.

"Why do you think I have such big teeth? All the better to bite with, my dear. Alas, my driver was already dead." He shrugged his shoulders. "I couldn't see letting his blood go to waste. I'll take yours with me when I leave."

His pride in his killing was more than obvious. She found his demeanor both repulsive and cruel, and she shuddered all the harder when he added, "And your driver was a danger. I've lived too long to be careless. I'm just doing my part to keep the roads safe."

He winked, causing her to catch her breath at the grossly inappropriate gesture. His eyes were truly appalling. "My, what red eyes you have," she remarked. But bloody hell—she shouldn't have voiced that thought.

The vampire smiled—an evil smile, where the fires of hell resided. "They match your cloak, my dear."

"I didn't realize that vampire eyes were red," she admitted. Then, hoping she hadn't insulted him, as that might not be the wisest of plans, she quickly added, "It is a nice red. Like an apple or bl—"

The vampire put a hand to his ear as he stepped closer. "What was that? I couldn't hear you, my dear."

"Nothing of great import," Greta hurried to say. Drat! What was taking those villagers so long? The lights still flitted in the woods behind the vampire, but if they were torches, they didn't appear to be getting much closer. At least, not as quickly as she desired.

Her foe laughed in delight. "You *are* a beauty," he said. "And with me, you'll be so forever. You'll make a fine companion for me. Much better than the last female I turned. She turned out to be utterly lacking in finesse and always smelled of the brewery."

Greta shivered with fear and revulsion. Though the vampire was not old or unattractive, she found his eyes cruel and his fangs very sharp and long. "You can't touch me.

I'm wearing a big silver cross," she said, wishing for garlic and her Van Helsing vampire-slayer, too. She was always missing something when things were at stake!

"Now, that could present a problem," the vampire admitted. "I detest silver; it burns. But it won't stop me," he said. "I intend to savor you with my big sharp teeth, my dear. Then I shall make you mine."

His intent finally set in and had her panicking. She bolted around the back of the carriage door and lunged for the horse. It bolted. And with it went all hope of escape.

In this situation, Greta did what any proper lady would do: screamed. She screamed for all she was worth, which at the moment wasn't very much. She'd forgotten to take out a life insurance policy.

# CHAPTER THIRTY-SEVEN

## A White Knight (or Black Wolf) to the Rescue

The vampire scrambled after her. Still screaming, Greta could feel his hot breath scorching her neck. Slipping and sliding in the snow, she tried to crawl out of the ditch where the carriage crashed. Just as she reached the top of the crest, her foe grabbed her from behind. Greta didn't think; she just reacted, jabbing backward with her cross and hitting the vampire in his groin.

The air filled with the scent of burnt flesh and the vampire howled as the holiness of the cross burned his groin. In his rage, he shoved her. Greta flew out and against an embankment, her head hitting the side of the hard, crusted snow with enough force to cause stars to float before her eyes.

Grabbing some snow, the vampire quickly placed it over the deep burn on his crotch and doubled over, screeching obscenities and a threat or two that dealt with intestines and thumbscrews. Greta was glad she was too dazed and dizzy to understand his German completely; but unfortunately, she was also too dazed to flee.

After several more moments of intense cursing, the vampire rose to his feet and came toward her. He was no longer graceful in his stalking. There was a blackened area of

clothing and flesh below his stomach, and his eyes carried
the wildness of a savage beast. His fangs looked deadly.

The vampire snarled at her. Claws extended, he lunged.
In mid-lunge, he was disrupted by a large beast leaping
over the crest of the hill. It was the biggest wolf Greta had
ever seen, and what a set of teeth he had on him! If she'd
thought the vampire's fangs were large, he had nothing on
this wolf.

Like a bolt of lightning, the Black Forest black wolf attacked the evil vampire with a feral growl. The pair went
down in a tangle of legs and paws, with growls, curses, flying fur and howls of rage emitting from the tangled mess.

Greta leaned back weakly against the bank. Closing her
eyes for a moment, she hoped to still the dizziness enough
for her to run. But suddenly a loud scream rent the air.
Opening her eyes, she saw that the vampire's head was no
longer attached to his neck. The big wolf howled in triumph.

Coming to her senses, Greta's eyes widened in fear. Was
she next? This was a huge wolf, clearly dangerous. Her
heart pounded. She had to leave this cursed place immediately.

Unsteadily, she regained her footing and staggered up
the snowbank, only to be brought down by a tug on her
cloak. Weakly she fell to the ground, awaiting the lunge
that would end her life. It never came. Instead, the wolf
circled Greta and began to whine. After this startling development, all she could do was stare, both stunned and
amazed. The wolf looked very familiar, and his eyes were
lit with intelligence. This was no mean and savage beast.

"No, you are far more," she said. Then the light dawned,
and she knew.

Taking the shaggy head in her hands, she stared into
those deep blue eyes, eyes she would know anywhere. Even
in the face of a heroic wolf or roguish prince. "It's you!"

The wolf nodded his majestic head, and she threw her

arms around his neck and hugged him to her. "You saved my life. You were absolutely magnificent. How on earth did you find me?"

Rolpe yearned to answer her. To tell her that he had felt a cold fear take hold of his heart and somehow he had known she was in trouble. It was then he knew that Fen was right: Greta Grimm was his soul mate. And so he had followed her scent and found her there in the dark woods. A few moments later, he might have lost her forever. He shivered in his wolf form.

As Rolpe leaned into her and she placed her arms around his massive wolf frame, Greta felt such a strong wave of love that it took her breath away. Leaning back, she petted his furry head. "You were so brave and strong." The love of her life had come bursting out like in a fairy tale, like the heroes did in her stories, to rescue the fair maid. So, maybe he hadn't ridden up on a white horse. Or even been a white horse. No, apparently her prince was a wolf in sheik's clothing. Well, not a sheik, but just a regular Prussian prince.

Greta sighed. Nobody was perfect.

"Now, I know that you believe love is better served in fairy tales, and not for someone like you . . . but I believe in the power of love," she declared firmly. "And I love you, Rolpe, and I intend to be with you."

He threw back his head and howled. Then he licked her face, tenderly took her hand between his teeth, and shook.

Greta laughingly petted him, then replied. "Yes, you have very sharp teeth. Very big teeth. They scare me so completely that I agree to your proposal. I will marry you."

He threw back his head and howled again.

"That howl was a proposal of marriage, was it not?"

His wolfish eyes held a wicked look, and she laughed. They would have a grand and glorious life.

She smiled at him adoringly. "That will teach you, Rolpe

von Hanzen, to accuse a Grimm of trying to trap a man. However," she added, grinning, "I'm not above trapping a beast. Especially a wolf."

Rolpe howled again, and she recognized the sound as his victory cry. Then Greta remarked teasingly, "I think we should have a nice long engagement—perhaps seven or eight months?"

He growled.

"Five?"

"Another low growl, rumbling from his furry chest.

"Three? Three is really a very short time to prepare a wedding. And I would like my family to attend. They will need some kind of notice." She stopped what she was saying when she noticed Rolpe look away with wolfish disdain. A tiny frown furrowed her brow. Apparently even three months was too long. "Fine, you may set the date when you are able to converse like a civilized human being about the whole affair. But I warn you now: you won't always get your way when we are married. And I intend to keep up my search for the paranormal. No matter how much you growl at me."

Rolpe grinned, and it was the same wolfish grin that always set her stomach aflutter.

"I mean it, Rolpe. You will have to learn the fine art of compromise."

He cocked a savage brow, and then winked.

She laughed. "I didn't know wolves could do that! My gracious, Rolpe, you're haughty even in wolf from."

He nudged her playfully, to let her know he agreed with her kind assessment. And with her proposal.

"You know, I really like you like this—all bark and no biting remarks."

He growled menacingly, then snapped at the air.

Ignoring his wolfish snit, she threw her arms around him, saying gaily, "I love you, anyway, pompous paws and everything else. You're also very warm, and my feet are freezing."

He licked her face tenderly as she gazed into his beautiful eyes, understanding the love he held for her. It was evident even in his altered form. He expression seemed to say: "Yes, my *liebchen,* let's do get wedded as soon as humanly—or otherwise—possible."

Greta snuggled closer to him for warmth, her heart filled with joy. She had not only exonerated herself with her discovery that vampires really did exist, but she had also found her true love. Her father would be so relieved. Their financial gloom would be lifted with two sisters wed so well and out of the house. Soon, she and Rae could introduce Faye and Taylor to upper society so they too could find such happy fates. She couldn't believe it. She, Greta Grimm, was marrying a prince! Her mother would be so delighted.

Yet, she also knew the news would be bittersweet. After all, it was her aunt's victory in seeing them wed, and not her mother's—as they all would be daily reminded, she was sure. But Greta would tolerate her mother's complaints with the patience of a saint. She had found her knight in shining armor. Or gleaming fur. But then, what had she expected? This was, after all, the Black Forest.

# CHAPTER THIRTY-SEVEN

## The Boy Who Cried Werewolf

Speaking of black forests, Rae was noting that the woods were far from lovely, but more dark and deep—as she had first thought. As the moon rose higher in the midnight sky, her surroundings were getting downright creepy. For every evil under the sun, there was always a remedy, she had thought. And to Alden, she had a promise to keep.

Rae had set out to the cobbler's to get Alden's lamp fixed. The cobbler had assured her that it would be done today and, since Fen had been called away to another part of the estate on business, Rae had decided to go into Wolfach after tea to fetch it. Every time she had seen Alden's sad little face, guilt had chewed on her nerves. Now she had the lamp, and the cobbler had done a remarkable job; the lamp looked good as new. He had even engraved Alden's name on the bottom. But only now was she headed back to the castle.

As the temperature dropped and Durloc was still nowhere in sight, Rae began to doubt the wisdom of her actions. Fen would be worried if he returned to the estate and found her missing. If so, then he was probably out combing the forest for her now. That eased her mind slightly. She should have gone in the carriage, Rae admitted as the full moon glared down upon her, and she certainly should not have gone alone. But she had really felt the need for some quiet time by herself. Even though things had been running much more smoothly with the children, the rowdy bunch still could be taxing to a new stepmother's nerves. Oh, and she definitely shouldn't have tried that shortcut.

As she urged the mare through the tenebrous woods, Rae shivered. The ever-deepening shadows appeared to host a multitude of malicious forces. Every crackling sound had her heart racing, whether it was the tree branches rubbing together or the sounds of a large predator moving through the low-hanging underbrush.

"Drat!" she cried. "I should have taken the carriage—or at least the sled."

Her mare, although remarkably lovely, with a hint of Arabian in its blood, was actually rather dimwitted; she appeared not to care in the least that they were lost. Instead, the silly steed kept trudging through the knee-deep snow in the same straightforward direction, even when Rae had given the mare her head and hoped it would instinctively lead them home.

They had miles to go before they could sleep. The thought of curling up in warm blankets with her husband by her side and the warmth of the fire in the hearth nearby was almost more than Rae could tolerate. Her nose was so blasted cold, she felt it might snap right off, like a tender branch weighted with too much snow.

Suddenly, Rae thought she smelled smoke and turned to head in that direction. Perhaps she could ask for directions back to the castle if there was a cottage nearby. Her feet were freezing off as well. Soon, she would be a snow lady . . . a beautiful snow lady, but frozen over nonetheless.

Glancing up at the thick foliage of the trees above her, she was relieved that she at least had the bright moon to light her way. Whichever way she was going.

Her mare shook a dusting of snow from its head. It found

what she hoped was a trail homeward, and she urged it on. In the next moment several things happened at once: Her horse shied, almost unseating her. A crow in the tree branches above looked down upon her and screeched. Rae screamed. And from the ebony shadows, a figure on horseback burst forth. His horse panted hard as it galloped into the small clearing. And its rider . . .

As the rider came into a spotlight of moonbeams, Rae noted with great relief that it was her stepson, Napoleon! He rode to her rescue with a scowl on his face that was an exact replica of his handsome father's.

"Nap, how wonderful!" Never had she been so thrilled to see her stepson's face. "You've come to escort me home. Thank you. It's a brave thing to do. You do your family name and your father proud by rescuing me," Rae gasped, relieved.

Nap's scowl lessened. He had been angry at feeling such a strong urge to go after his stepmother. Alden had spilled the beans by saying that she'd gone to Wolfach to fetch his lamp. Though Wolfach was not a great distance from the castle, the thick woods made it difficult to navigate for those new to the area. Since his father had not returned by supper, either, Nap felt he had no choice but to look for Rae. As the eldest, he'd understood it was his responsibility to see to his stepmother's safety.

A bit embarrassed and pleased by her praise, he nodded.

Rae rode up alongside her stepson. "I hate to admit it, but I got lost."

"It was a silly thing to do, going to town and back alone," Nap remarked.

"My gracious, but you sound just like your father. You even wear his scowl." If Rae now knew one thing, it was how to tell when a male was in a mood. Especially one of Fen's brood.

"Do you think so?" Nap asked, the eagerness in his tone impossible to hide.

"Definitely. You also have the same look about the eyes,

and his majestic nose. Your hair color is similar, if yours is lighter. But I imagine that will change when you're older. I surmise by your gallant efforts that your father has not returned home yet?"

"*Nein,*" Nap replied, and relaxed a bit further. He wasn't used to seeing this cheerful and complimentary side of his stepmother.

Rae sighed. She was tired and hoped her husband would reach home in time to greet her. She hoped everything was all right on the other estate.

Catching Nap's glance, she returned her attention to the boy. She remarked, "But you have your mother's mouth and the shape of her face." For Rae had spent much time studying the late Baroness Schortz's features, and knew that she spoke true.

Glancing over at his stepmother, Nap frowned. "I wish I took after her more."

Rae thought it was a strange thing to say. Most sons wanted to be exactly like their fathers; especially if they had a father like Fen. "I would think you would be proud to be as much like your father as possible. He is a good man. You probably couldn't find a better one."

Nap was rather surprised by this defense of his father. The enemy, she was. Although, lately, he was thinking less and less of waging war against her. He just couldn't be sure whether or not to trust her. They had all suffered so much with the loss of their mother. His father and younger siblings were just too vulnerable still. He feared they were all falling for someone who would leave them as well as soon as . . . He realized she was staring at him, waiting for an answer.

"I do want to be like my father, of course."

As he listened to the crunching of the snow under the horses' hooves, Nap realized this was the perfect moment to find out if he could trust his new stepmother. If they all could trust her. And perhaps, if they could even love her. He debated for a moment. His father would be powerfully angry with him for what he was about to do. He would probably get whipped for it, but Nap had to do it. It was time to give his stepmother another little test. If she passed . . . well, then maybe he would let her into his heart.

"Still," he replied nonchalantly, "I would like to have inherited my mother's werewolf tendencies."

His words burst into the dark night like a bolt of lightning. Pulling her horse up short, Rae stared at him. Her jaw dropped open, and she squeaked, "Werewolf tendencies?"

Nap reined in his stallion, glad to have shocked her so. Would the news send her packing? He was curious to see. She pretended to care about them, but did she really? If she really loved them then she would still feel the same after his wild announcement.

"Is this like the ogre thing with your father, or the ghost in the hall?" Rae couldn't help but give Fen's eldest son points on originality and determination. "Do you know you rival my brothers in their fairy-tale telling?" She was amused. Certainly her husband would have mentioned, at least in passing, that his seven little Schortzs were werewolf pups.

Staring her straight in the eyes, Nap replied with a sincerity that even the cleverest priest at confession would find hard to doubt, "I'm not jesting." He hoped his little test would give him the answer he wanted. Although he wasn't quite sure what that answer was. He had truly despised Rae in the beginning, but now . . . Well, she had fixed Alden's lamp. And for the first time in such a long while, his father was happy again. So were Quinn, Merri and Poppy.

"Good grief! What a grave, hairy secret. I'm surprised you'd trust me with such a startling confidence. Especially since you detest me so."

"I don't detest you. At least not now."

"I'm glad to hear it."

"I'm merely telling you since our father didn't. It is something a stepmother should know."

Rae hid a smile. Really, Nap could well surpass Ernst in

acting abilities if he continued in this vein. "Yes, you're quite right," she agreed. She smiled up at the moon. "I suppose since this is a full moon, your brothers and sisters will all be out howling tonight." She laughed.

Nap frowned, glancing over at his stepmother. She was taking this awesome news rather mildly. "My family comes from a royal werewolf line. The Beowulf ancestry is ancient," Nap remarked proudly. "That's the part of my mother I wished I had taken after. I have some of the blood, but will never change by the light of the full moon as others do."

Clutching her cloak around her as the bitter winds blew colder, Rae replied politely, "Then Wolfach is a werewolf haven, I assume. My sister will be surprised. She and Countess DeLuise were certain vampires inhabited the area, stealing corpses, drinking the blood of innocents." Yes, she could talk fable talk with the best of them. "So, your mother was a werewolf?"

"She was a lovely werewolf, full-blood and solid gold. When the full moon came out once a month, she changed. You should have seen her run. She could catch rabbits with the best of them."

"How delightful." Rae sighed. Really, the idea of a full-grown woman turning furry and chasing rabbits was ridiculous. This story was just getting better and better. "I must write William and Jakob about this. When they come to visit, I think you will be great friends. I must tell Greta, too. Won't she be excited that she's related to werewolves through my marriage? Just think, she's run herself ragged digging up dirt, trying to find vampires by haunting cemeteries and stealing garlic. All along she's had her eyes on the wrong type of fangs. The paranormal has been right under her nose. Close enough to take a bite out of her, so to speak."

Nap glared at her from the back of his horse. "You don't believe a word I've said."

Instead of returning the glare as she once might have done, she shook her head. "Why should I? You've lied to me from the start. And now this? Why, it's just too ridiculous. Your mother a werewolf? What poppycock."

Nap's eyes burned with ire, but he couldn't really blame his father's new wife for disbelieving his words. He had done much to trick her again and again. Still, he persisted in his interrogation. "But suppose *Papa* was a werewolf? What would you do?"

Rae reined in her horse momentarily, which made her stepson also halt. "I guess I would just have to love him—fur, fangs, howling at the moon and all."

Nap studied her thoughtfully. There appeared to be more than met the eye with his stepmother. She genuinely did seem to care for his father. "And if some of my brothers or sisters were full-bloods?"

Rae smiled, amused. She could just imagine the sight. She'd go running into the night howling if such an awful thing were true. Having one ankle-biter in the family was more than enough. Imagine, having a whole pack of them!

"I'd have to make sure they didn't track paw prints into the hall when the moon's full. I'd also invest in a few dozen pair of stout walking boots for around the castle," Rae confided. "Alden's teeth are sharp enough in *human* form."

Nap smiled. Then he thought about her words.

Rae sighed in relief. She thought she recognized the trees up ahead. As she caught sight of a tip of the castle tower in the moonlight, she smiled, laughing at herself. Yes, her stepson knew his way about the woods. It hadn't taken them long at all. Her own lack of direction was deplorable. She must have ridden around in circles for hours.

The full moon shone brightly from the velvety black sky. The rest of the ride was in silence, each rider lost in his or her own thoughts.

Wearily they reached the stables. Nap kept a close eye on Rae. She looked up at a sprinkling of stars as the stable master took the horses. The real test of fortitude and devotion was about to begin.

"I do so hope your father's returned," she said. But before Nap could reply, the doors of the castle entrance suddenly flew open.

Fen came rushing out the door and down the steps. He had returned home to find that his wife was missing, gone to town, and that his eldest had gone looking for her in the dead of night. He knew from experience how very dangerous the woods could be. He had just been about to start out looking for both of them when he caught sight of them riding toward the stables.

"My dear! You two had me frantic."

Rae smiled at the concern in his eyes and trudged through the snow toward him.

Merri and Shyla followed their father down the steps at a more sedate pace, while four pups with very sharp teeth came tearing out of the large door behind them. Fen winced. Well, the wolf was out of the bag now. He had hoped to tell his wife at supper and prepare her, but he had been detained. And now, the truth was playfully snapping at her heels.

"Down, Poppy," he said.

Flabbergasted, Rae turned to Nap in surprise.

"See? I told you so. Four of my siblings inherited my mother's full blood," Nap said smugly, just as the littlest wolf snatched the fold of Rae's cloak and began to yank with its sharp little teeth.

"They . . . they really are little beasts!" Rae gasped. Then the ground rushed to meet her as she fainted.

# CHAPTER THIRTY-EIGHT

Truths Are Always Inconvenient

Fen rushed to his wife.

"Papa, she fainted again," Merri grumbled, and several shrill little howls stretched into the night.

"Ernst, don't you dare do that. You cannot mark your stepmother as yours! Put down that leg!" Fen said sternly, scooping up his wife. She was very pale. "Stop biting at her cloak, Alden. Poppy, quit howling like that, she'll be fine in a few moments."

Rae only faintly heard them as the blessed darkness took her.

Inside his study, Fen gently deposited Rae onto the couch. He rubbed her hands as the children and wolf pups gathered around. He hoped the shock would not be too much for his new bride. He could kick himself for not telling her sooner. What she must be feeling, his poor love. Fen sighed.

A few minutes later, Rae awoke feeling slightly disoriented. A cold, raspy tongue licked her hand, and something tugged on her skirt. She opened her eyes to find her large, handsome husband staring down at her with a worried look on his face.

"Are you all right?"

Glancing around the room, she noted that the children

who were in human form were strangely silent, and the rest of the bunch were rather subdued for wolf pups. "Alden, quit pulling on my skirt, and Fen, help me up please."

He did so gently. "Are you certain you're all right? I know you've had a shock." He patted her hand, wanting to lessen the blow. She had come to mean a great deal to him, bringing lightness into the shadowy world of his pain. She was his little Rae of sunshine. And he hoped the truth would not take her away from them.

Cocking an eye at him, she stifled the sudden urge to laugh. "A shock? You could say that." One of the wolf cubs was stalking a shadow near the fireplace. "When did you plan to tell me this little secret?" she asked with a hint of asperity. Carefully, she studied her husband for signs of extra hairiness. She also checked out his teeth. Then she breathed a sigh of relief. He appeared his same, wonderful self.

Fen appeared embarrassed. "I don't know, but I *did* plan to tell you."

"Tonight's the full moon! Were you just planning on letting the children chase me around the house, growling?"

"Of course not, darling! I had decided that I would keep them out of your way this time. I wanted to make sure you were a bit more adjusted to our marriage before you discovered our family secret."

Rae shook her head. No longer had she to worry about the wolf at the door; they were already inside in the castle. And what a snapping, snarling pack they were! She studied her new family: Alden chewed on her cloak, Ernst lifted a leg at the piano, Quinn chased his shadow and Poppy licked her paw. Fen was patting Nap on the back, apparently proud of his son for bringing Rae home safely.

Rae turned to Merri, who was stuffing her cheeks with nuts as Shyla retied a ribbon on her smock. As perverse and frightening as the whole scene was, Rae saw them through a mother's eyes. She had already fallen in love with the little monsters, so what difference did it make if they spent half their time as wolves?

Fen took a deep breath and asked with a hint of trepidation, "Well?"

"Well . . . ?" She knew very well what he was asking, but she decided to let him bear his guilty conscience a trifle longer. What woman worth her weight in salt, or rather gold, wouldn't?

"She doesn't like us, Papa," Merri whined.

"I told you so," Shyla muttered.

Fixing a rather stern eye on her stepdaughter, Rae declared, "Of course I do! I happen to like all of you a great deal, though heavens know why. You're unruly, raucous, rowdy, and devious to the bone."

Shyla tugged on her father's jacket. "Papa, are any of those compliments?"

A bark of laughter escaped Fen. "Yes, my little one," he answered as he patted his daughter on her bright golden curls. "All of them. She finds us trying and terribly havy-cavy, but she accepts us. We've grown on her, I think."

Rae nodded her head. "Rather like mold."

Again Fen felt a tugging on his jacket. "Was that a compliment, too? Who wants to be like mold? It's all green."

Before Fen could answer, Rae replied laughingly, "I've always been fond of the color of mold. Such a bright, cheery green. In fact, I have some ribbons the exact same color. They're my favorites. I think"—Rae tapped her chin with her finger, looking at Merri—"that the color would look lovely in your hair. Shall I braid your hair for you tomorrow, and you can wear my green ribbons?"

Merri's grumpy expression changed to one of delight, and she nodded enthusiastically.

"What about me?" Shyla asked. "I want to wear mold ribbons. And what about Poppy? She'll want some ribbons, too."

Poppy barked in agreement. Rae reached over to pat her head fondly. "Indeed, she will. Perhaps I can tie a pink ribbon around her neck tonight. It will be lovely with her gold fur." Both Merri and Shyla laughed, while Nap managed a small smile, and Rae added, "And I have a pretty blue ribbon the color of a robin's egg that would look very pretty in your hair and match your eyes."

Shyla nodded, satisfied, and Rae next began to tell how brave Nap was after he rescued her from her own folly. She praised him for his tracking skills and said he had made her feel safe. Nap blushed and stood up a bit taller. His stepmother had passed his test. She knew, and she hadn't run screaming from the castle. Yes, Nap decided. They would keep her.

At the looks on his children's faces, Fen's own expression became a wide grin. He had found a good woman, and he had found her in the most unexpected of all places: in *Fürst* Gelb's golden salon, dancing to the tune of a cockroach. But then, nature's first hue was gold, the hardest hue to hold. And to hold on to his golden bride was just what Fen intended.

Rae smiled up at him, and the two shared a sacred moment between man and wife.

Leaning down to give his wife a tender kiss, Fen volunteered, "I'll take the children out for a run. Come along now." He knew his bride might want some time to digest the fact that half her stepchildren were werewolves.

The cubs leaped up and began to follow their father, with the exception of Alden, who was now worrying Rae's blue cloak between his teeth. Alden ignored his father, too entranced with the cloak.

"Alden, let's go."

"I'll watch him," Rae said, grinning.

Fen started to reach over and take the tattered cloak away, but Rae stopped him. "It's all right. It's already torn." Then she smiled impishly. "Which means you will need to buy me a new one."

He answered her smile with a wicked one of his own, his eyes twinkling devilishly. "My pleasure."

"No, but it will be," she replied saucily. "And I want one with an ermine collar."

"And a matching muff, of course."

"Of course."

He leaned down and kissed her head again, then headed for the door. His noisy, barking brood followed.

Rae called after him, "Hurry back. I'll wait with bated breath."

He gave her a naughty little wink that sent her heart pounding in her chest. "I've married a saucy wench."

"*Ja,*" she smiled.

From the doorway, Fen turned to gaze at Rae and his human children gathered about the roaring fire. He had a family at last. *"Zwei seelen und ein gedanke."*

Rae's brow wrinkled in confusion. "Two souls with heels?"

He threw back his head and laughed. "Oh, Rae, you are a constant delight." Shaking his head he explained proudly, love shining in his eyes, "Two souls with but a single thought."

His tender wooing captured her heart completely, and Rae felt blessed among women. She had never thought to find someone with the same thoughts as herself, or that she would want to share those of another. Against all odds—or rather, against her vanity—she had found a prince among frogs, wolves, and men.

Fen's eyes turned the color of smoke, and he fought to control the overwhelming urge to throw his wife over his shoulder and carry her off to bed. There he would ravish her all night long. Instead, the sounds of his wolf pack caused him to turn and slip out into the night.

Rae smiled. It sounded as if the hounds of hell were at his heels. Or leading him.

# Epilogue

Rae and Fen finally had their true wedding night, and it had them believing that they would live happily ever after. Well, maybe not always happily, but then Rae had discovered she liked life with a bite or two thrown in for good measure. Greta escaped the clutches of the corpse-stealing vampire without a scar to show but a very juicy story, which of course sent her brothers into raptures.

At Greta and Rolpe's wedding, Greta's mother gloated happily. She had two daughters now married very well: a princess and a baroness. Let her sister put that in her snuff box and sniff it. At the wedding, Aunt Vivian scowled and drank a toast to the happy couple. Bitter dregs indeed. And as the children increased, Aunt Vivian became a sour old woman, lamenting her sister's good fortune. She became so deranged she went to live in a house that looked like a shoe. On nights of the full moon, all her great-nephews and nieces went there to frolic and howl. And so life started out (and went on) very well in Prussia for the sisters Grimm.

Their brothers drank in their letters about everyday life in the Black Forest with insatiable delight because, of course, none of it was quite so everyday. A werewolf for a brother-in-law was almost more than the brothers Grimms' creative little hearts could bear. To be honest, from this ever-entertaining correspondence two literary giants were born, and the two men had fascinating romances of their own . . .

But, alas, that's another story—and between us, something of a fairy tale.

# The Druid Made Me Do It

## NATALE STENZEL

For centuries he's worked his magic, seducing and pleasuring women as befits his puca nature. But Kane made one big mistake—punishing his brother for a crime he did not commit.

Oh yeah, he also left Dr. Janelle Corrington after the most amazing night of her life.

She thought she'd made a once-in-a-lifetime soul connection, but he was simply having sex. Why else would he have disappeared without a word?

That's why the Druid Council's punishment for Kane's other crime is so delicious: for him to be Janelle's ward, to make amends to all he harmed, to take responsibility for his actions. Finally, Kane would have to take things seriously. And only true love would be rewarded.

**Sometimes, it's good to be guilty.**

ISBN 13: 978-0-505-52777-6

# Kathryne Kennedy

### Author of *Enchanting the Lady*

Lady Jasmina was in a world of trouble. A simple spell had gone disastrously haywire and now there was a woman running around London who looked exactly like her—a woman with no sense of propriety whatsoever. All Society was whispering, and a baronet she'd never met was suddenly acting like he knew her…in a most intimate way. To find her double and set things right, they'd have to work together—braving the fog-shrouded streets, a mysterious group called the Brotherhood, and a passion stronger than any magic.

# Double Enchantment

ISBN 13: 978-0-505-52763-9

**It's never a good day when an ancient demon shows up on your toilet.**

# ANGIE FOX

For Lizzie Brown, that's just the beginning. Soon her hyperactive terrier starts talking, and her long-lost biker-witch grandma is hurling Smucker's jars filled with magic. Just when she thinks she's seen it all, Lizzie learns she's a demon slayer—and all hell is after her.

# The Accidental Demon Slayer

That's not the only thing after her. Dimitri Kallinikos needs Lizzie to slay a demon of his own. But how do you talk a girl you've never met into going straight to the underworld? Lie. And if that doesn't work, how dangerous could a little seduction be...?

ISBN 13: 978-0-505-52769-1

---

# Sandra Schwab

## *Sweet passion...*

After a magical mishap that turned her uncle's house blue, Miss Amelia Bourne was stripped of her powers and sent to London in order to be introduced into polite society—and to find a suitable husband. Handsome, rakish Sebastian "Fox" Stapleton was all that and more. He was her true love. Wasn't he?

## *or the bitter taste of deceit?*

At Rawdon Park, the country estate of the Stapletons, Amy began to wonder. It seemed that one sip of punch had changed her life forever—that this love, this lust, was nothing but an illusion. She and Fox were pawns in some mysterious game, and black magic had followed them out of Town. Without her powers, would she be strong enough to battle those dark forces and win? And would she be able to claim her heart's true desire?

# Bewitched

ISBN 13: 978-0-505-52723-3

# ✂ ☐ **YES!**

Sign me up for the Love Spell Book Club and send my
FREE BOOKS! If I choose to stay in the club, I will pay only
$8.50* each month, a savings of $6.48!

NAME: _____

ADDRESS: _____

TELEPHONE: _____

EMAIL: _____

☐ I want to pay by credit card.

☐ **VISA**　　☐ **MasterCard**　　☐ **DISCOVER**

ACCOUNT #: _____

EXPIRATION DATE: _____

SIGNATURE: _____

Mail this page along with $2.00 shipping and handling to:
### Love Spell Book Club
### PO Box 6640
### Wayne, PA 19087
Or fax (must include credit card information) to:
### 610-995-9274

You can also sign up online at **www.dorchesterpub.com**.
*Plus $2.00 for shipping. Offer open to residents of the U.S. and Canada only. Canadian
residents please call 1-800-481-9191 for pricing information.
If under 18, a parent or guardian must sign. Terms, prices and conditions subject to
change. Subscription subject to acceptance. Dorchester Publishing reserves the right to
reject any order or cancel any subscription.